Dating Daisy

Daisy Mae

Published by Clink Street Publishing 2017

First edition.

ISBN:
978-1-911525-75-2 paperback
978-1-911525-76-9 ebook

Daisymae_224

The Daisy

There is a flower, a little flower.
With silver crest and golden eye.
That welcomes every changing hour.
And weathers every sky.
James Montgomery

Quotes Source: A Field Flower
www.worldofquotes.com

"A Breeze of Daisies" by Malcolm Thompson

This picture has hung very quietly, in my house for 30 years.

This book is dedicated to my parents, who sent me to boarding school, with the best of intentions.. Little did they know that I was up all night, writing all kinds of stories by torchlight, for the girls in my dormitory.

It somehow took me half a century to finally finish and submit this completed
manuscript - But in the end, some stories just need to be told. And I did have to have a little life experience first!

I hope they would have been as proud of me, as I was of them.

Daisy

Contents

Chapter One
(In which Daisy goes online)

Saturday April 6th 2014.

So, here I am. Dating Daisy.

And who is going to date Daisy? That is the question.

When I signed onto the first dating site, I had to think of an Internet Dating name. Into my head flew the name Daisy. It just matches my mood today.

Fresh as a Daisy.

Crazy Daisy.

Quick as a Daisy.

What a play on words!

And not just Daisy, I'm Daisymae.

In fact, I had to be Daisymae_224 as there must be a lot of other Daisymaes out there, something that doesn't bear thinking about.

Here's the thing. I'm 52. Some of you reading this will think, *"Well, she's only 52!"* Others will be thinking *"My God, she's so old!"* That's the thing about being on the net, so many people from all different walks of life will see my profile, and everyone will have something different to say about it. That's scary.

In fact, one of the people who sent me a message said my profile was scary. *Scary? Me?* If they think that they must by definition be spineless and thank goodness they haven't penned me a message. That's the sort of person I wouldn't want my profile to attract.

So I am writing this to get my head around the whole concept of Internet Dating, which it has to be said is an unpredictable lottery, a foolish journey with few rules and no guarantees, for which no there are no navigation aids, and for which you need oodles of patience, and tact, and a skin as hard as a rhinoceros.

In fact, I have to admit that I have done Internet Dating once before. It was such a brief experience I felt it didn't count. But that's the truth. Sadly it didn't work out long term with Jeremy, and we split after 18 months.

So now, I have decided it's time to get back on the net. Jeremy and I had found each other on that well-known dating site, buzz.com. Strangely, he was the very first person to contact me. We met, were instantly attracted to each other and we took ourselves off the dating site immediately, same day in fact. Retrospectively, how likely is it that the first person you meet after your divorce on a dating site will be 'the One'?! But anyway, you can always hope. However, it didn't last, and I now need to do it all over again. But the thing is, I just know I have to get it right this time.

When I signed up before, I was only on buzz.com for a miniscule two weeks. So I really had no experience at all! I never got to send anyone a wink or a smile, or got the relative thrill of receiving emails from new people, or the anticipation of phone calls or dates. I don't know – when I think about it – why I was so immediately taken with Jeremy. I guess I was so flattered Jeremy clicked on me, and then we liked each other at first sight when we met, that I didn't think too deeply in the heat of the moment, about what really matters in a sustainable relationship. He was a good kind man, nothing malicious, we were just very different, and it took time for that to become apparent.

Like most people out there, if I'm truthful, I didn't want to be Internet Dating. It was embarrassing to think the rest of the world could log on and see my picture and my profile. I was humiliated wondering what my friends and acquaintances in their comfortable marriages must think of me. I wanted to find someone and be off the internet lickety-split. So when Jeremy clicked on me, the very first day I appeared on the site, we just met and got on with it. Instant success, or so I hoped.

This time, on the net, I predict the whole dating experience will take a lot longer. In fact, I know it will. I will be much more cautious. I think about what I learned from that experience, and how to approach Internet Dating in the future. I don't want a string of relationships. I just want one, lifetime mate. Simple. End of.

I guess you could regard my experiences with Jeremy as Dating Daisy's first date. But I don't want to do that in this book. For the sake of this book, Dating Daisy is an Internet Virgin! Last time doesn't count, let's wipe the slate clean, and here goes, I'm starting again.

This time, I need to be choosy, and wary, and not do anything reckless. How can I conduct this Internet Dating thing with decorum and integrity? I have absolutely no idea, but in my situation, where I wouldn't meet any eligible men unless I did this, it seems the only realistic way of meeting people. So, it seems the only option. I just need to log on and get started.

It seems to me there should be a manual of some sort. A sort of learner driver's guide to Internet Dating. I have googled it, believe me, and it doesn't exist...

— *Yet?... because I'm writing it! I'm thinking if I publish this book, I can share my experiences. Yes, it all about Internet dating lessons! Keep reading and you will see!*

Daisy, be brave! – that's my mind by the way, that constantly sends me messages.

It's very fundamental this desire to find a mate. But I'm not alone. Seven million people in the UK are currently using 43 Internet Dating sites. Fifty percent of people over 50 are now divorced or widowed. Internet Dating is a fast-growing industry. And why is that? Let's get to the nitty gritty. Is it all about sex?

Strangely perhaps, that is generally **not** what it's all about. Human beings have very strong, and fierce, social characteristics. Lonely and isolated we cannot survive. And it's not all about procreation. Sex, pleasurable as it is, brings us a strong connection with another human being. This is the case, even when fertility is not on the cards. Not even hiding under the table! Through sex we experience a feeling of power and self-worth. Through sex we are connecting with the world around us.

So it's a mate I seek. To give me the social passport, the wholeness of being, to exorcise the loneliness. Myself, Daisy and six million, nine hundred and ninety-nine thousand, nine hundred and ninety-nine others.

This time round, I've chosen a different dating site. I have chosen the *Britain on Sunday* dating website. I ask myself why quite often, as I don't read *Britain on Sunday*, unless it's lying around free in a coffee shop when I can scan the headlines and look at the TV page! I think I chose it because I thought it might attract a slightly more educated person than traditional old buzz.com.

My father, who is ex-Army, has read the *Britain on Sunday* cover to cover all his life. He is an amazing man, with great wisdom. Perhaps being a *Britain on Sunday* reader is measure of the soul? I don't know, but looking at the sorts of men on there, they tended to have university degrees, and take trouble over their profiles.

You see I haven't written a lot about myself yet, but the thing everyone knows about me is I absolutely live and die for words. I love reading, I love writing, I love talking, I love communicating and conversing and the forgotten art of conversation. The typical way people write their text messages really annoys me. Is it just me or perhaps you agree?

It's a whole new language!

Did you know that '459' means 'I love you'?

'F**K U' means F**k you!

And '531' means ... SEX!

I learnt that, Internet Dating and doing research for this book! But, when people use text speak for every day communication, like emails, I find it incredibly irritating. Give me lovely page of prose any day! But I'm probably showing my age now!

So much to articulate and so little time and people don't get it. They sway to and fro on the tube or the bus blinded to the world by their iPods, and they go home and sit in a trance in front of their mindless X-Boxes, like a load of space-age robots.

I need a man who can talk to me, who loves words like I do, who won't want to shut me up, but will want to interject and make me laugh and be on my wavelength. Someone who loves stories, and storytelling. I am a good listener, as well as a great raconteur, so don't get me wrong. But any man who can't write me some entertaining messages and maintain a great dialogue, will not pass GO. I hoped that the *Britain on Sunday* readers might be like that. Maybe more so than the buzz.com brigade, who just want your phone number, and a leg over. Job done. Not for me. So, I went for the *Britain on Sunday* site, logged in as Daisymae_224, and got started.

Daisymae_224, your first hurdle, is the profile.

When you actually come to do it – that is write about yourself for the world to see, how do you decide what to write? Suddenly caught like a rabbit in the headlights I challenged my brain to let me know what it was thinking exactly. In typical Daisy fashion, it gave me chapter and verse.

"Look!" it said, *"If you are going to do this, at least do it properly. If you want to meet the perfect man, he will need to know about you and like what he sees. No point hiding your light under a bushel. No point being brief or evasive, tell it as it is, but not with knobs on. Just be yourself, but don't write anything that's identifiable, or crass, or bawdy."* These adjectives could go on and on ... *"Fair enough, try and look fun and friendly,"* it said, *"but don't look domineering, ruthless, desperate or downright gagging for it!*

Be natural, be dazzling, be beautiful, be smart, be alluring.

Don't be cheap, flippant, annoying or downright square."

"Ok, Ok," I said, *"Let me start typing"*. And this is what I typed.

When you start to create your internet profile, it's actually quite daunting.

The first box asks for your Internet Dating name. Only this name is visible to anyone looking. So you can choose, and use your real name here if you want to, or a made-up name. Your real name is only known at Trust HQ! It's top secret, like MI5. It does give you some comfort knowing that actually. Most people do use a made-up name, no doubt to keep their true identity hidden until they choose to reveal it. If you look on dating sites you will be am amazed by the different variety of names. There are a lot of people out there with imagination it seems. (If only their profiles matched the ingenuity of their names! And – if only when you met them they lived up to their profiles! Read on! ...) If and when you get a hit and you start messaging, it's up to you if or when you reveal your real name.

So ... I thought about it for a moment and decided to use the name Daisy. I didn't know why at the time, but I got a clue about that as I was writing this book. Just keep reading and you will find out! But 223 Daisys had got there before me! So here I am on the net – Daisymae_224. My name does feature heavily in this book.

Then you have to write a little one-line ditty that appears underneath your name. Ah – what to write? I had a look at what some other people had written and this is what I came up with:

Daisymae_224

"Lively, out-going, fun-loving character seeks soul-mate for real-life adventures."

Now you have to understand the computer is trying to be your friend. It's in the spirit of friendship that it then asks you one hell of lot of questions. These are a few that I picked out to show you, so read on. Remember – "*natural, dazzling, beautiful, smart, and alluring"*. That's the plan.

Why should people get to know you? The computer asks? (They said this bit should be at least 20 words long.)

How long have you got? I am unique, creative, full of ideas and inspiration, generous and thoughtful. I love living life to the full but prefer someone special to share it with. I love walking, going to the beach, having fun days out, cooking and entertaining, watching great movies, sitting by the fire, being close and intimate. I hate awful TV programmes, staring at the wallpaper, greasy food, lobsters and tattoos. I am ambitious, positive and see the best in people. I am a loyal friend, kind-hearted and enjoy most doing things with and for other people. In fact, I'm not good with my own company.

I work in a busy hospital. I love my job which is interesting and which I am passionate about. I get a wonderful insight into the ups and downs of peoples' lives, and always have a few stories to tell. Confidentiality maintained of course! I am hugely enthusiastic

about my work, which my friends and family admire in me.

I firmly believe life needs to be grabbed by the horns.

Last year, although it was totally new to me, I went jet skiing in France for the first time. It was completely exhilarating and I loved it.

I then went flotilla sailing in Croatia. I am open to new challenges.

I have been ballroom dancing for a number of years, although no "Strictly" potential!

One of the best things about meeting new people is discovering what makes them tick. If you are reading this, what could I share in your life, as I am keen to consider any suggestions?!

PS. It occurred to me in the car just now. I like nice teeth!

I thought perhaps I should write about why I chose that list of dislikes.

Surely I don't have to explain what it is I hate about lobsters … they have spidery legs, look positively prehistoric, and they are just incredibly ugly. They also move in a silent and creepy fashion. I just shudder when I see one. That's it. If you yourself have a pet hate – it's usually spiders or snakes – you'll probably identify with this – and I pretty much dislike these too I'm afraid. (There is more in this book about lobsters later.)

As for tattoos, and there may be a lot of you reading this who have tattoos – what I don't like about them is that they are permanent. That's precisely what a lot of people do like about tattoos, but I used to work in a clinic that did tattoo removal, by laser. I saw numerous sad people who felt they couldn't get a job because their tattoos stigmatised them. Whether this is true or not, I witnessed their discomfort, and decided a nice necklace or a bracelet would just have to do it for me!

And the Morris dancers – sorry if you are reading this and you are a Morris dancer. In truth I love all types of dancing. So it's not the actual dancing I dislike, it's the frilly costumes and the jingly bells. It reminds me too much of *Bill and Ben, The Flowerpot Men*, which a few of you reading this may remember from children's BBC – about half a century ago!

Anyway ... I digress ...

Describe your ideal match, asks my friend the computer, next.

(This bit they said should also be at least 20 words long.) Again, I searched my soul for an appropriate response. What I came up with I hoped was heartfelt, but not too sickly sweet. To be frank, if you did cut the crap and write on your site, that only George Clooney's need apply, I'm sorry, but you just won't get any hits. (George himself as you know, is already spoken for! – Actually I'm more into Chris Martin, keep reading).

Well ... and this is from the heart ... my ideal match would be taller than me (I'm 5ft81/2), he would be generous (cuddly?) build (did I write that?) strong warm arms, big smile and genuine interest in people/relationships. Personality and making me laugh is everything.

I want to be happy, and make the best of every day. I love stories, reading, creative writing, and have great empathy, so someone who shares my love of reading would be ideal.

I need someone who understands my work–life balance, and what makes me tick, who can be reasonably supportive, in return for the same type of involvement.

Sharing and caring are the things that make life complete. I think empathy, and kindness are very important, and these are two of my greatest qualities.

I am sentimental, romantic, and imaginative, so if you are dull, single-minded and introspective, probably best you click on another profile. Or perhaps I can tempt you out of your comfort zone!!

But it's not over yet. Then there's the photo. That old hot potato. OMG. I don't know how other people approach this, but I have never liked having my photo taken. Not ever. Not even when I was at nursery school, or on my wedding day, or graduation day or any other day you care to mention. I don't know what that says about me. That I live in a dream world where I can go about my daily life kidding myself I am more gorgeous than Kylie Minogue or Cheryl Cole or anyone else too totally gorgeous to mention?

I do know that, I mean we all know that don't we, but we have to believe that today is not the day for the photo, it's a bad hair day, and tomorrow will definitely be better. Only thing is – it never is! If I can just eat a bit less today and breathe in tomorrow, maybe I will be able to confront my photograph – but it's all a pipedream! By the vagaries of imagination, maybe, just maybe, tomorrow I will wake up looking like a supermodel.

It does happen the other way. There was a photo of Britney Spears in the paper some time ago now, and she was unrecognisable. Baggy sweat shirt, dark glasses, matted hair, double chin, hands slouched in pockets, a baseball hat, and yes – you have to believe this – a cigarette in her hand. I had always admired her, when she did her first hit, *Baby, Baby, How was I Supposed to Know,* dressed as a raunchy schoolgirl. The archetypal sexy schoolgirl. But there she was, looking like me, well worse than me actually, on a bad day! And I would never have a cigarette anywhere near me by the way. Daisymae_224 is not and never has been a smoker. That is written very clearly on my profile!

Now, do not get the wrong impression. But what I mean is, we can all, including Britney, just have a bad day. If they can glam Britney up, then they can glam me up! – Bring it on! – I shoot upstairs, two at a time now, on a mission. Will Daisy pull it off? Can Daisy do a Britney – or a Kylie or a Cheryl? Watch this space.

In my wardrobe hang a load of useless dresses. Most women probably have the same. A few super-expensive evening dresses that have hardly ever been worn. (We women shop in the dream world we wish we were in, and ignore the real world we're really in, where the chance of going to that sort of a do is like the chance of life on Mars, totally unfathomable!).

Then there are some dresses I bought to diet into (never have), to wear to a fancy-dress party (did I really have the nerve?), because my friend said it suited me (and I secretly knew it never did but couldn't hurt her feelings!). There's a dress there HE (VOLDEMORT – by the way just read on – all will become clear) made me buy and I stupidly bought it to please him, but it's that drop down cleavage bit where everything is revealed I can't stand (when will men realise all that is best left to the imagination?) and there are sequins – sorry girls – I have to admit it – yes, sequins sewed around the tops of the little lace cap sleeves.

Why, oh why! And OMG this one, it has a drop waist. Drop waists are ok if you have a drop waist, but if it sits on your hips, which are always bigger than your waist, it looks like a concertina sitting on a space ball, the space ball being the fleshy hips that bulge out in a sort of a curvy lump, under the 'drop' waist band. Dearie me. What on earth will Dating Daisy do for the *Britain on Sunday* Dating Daisy Display!

So I settle for a red silk dress. It is a nice dress that I have actually never worn, mostly because I bought it reduced in a sale, and have never found an occasion to put it on. It is slightly off the shoulder, with bare shoulders and arms. I love the colour. Red and hot. Like I would like to be when I find my perfect match.

I look at it and realise that if I'm going to do this, I first need to wash my hair! My hair is one of my biggest concerns. It is blonde, but limp as a whistle. It used to be long, below my shoulders, but a few weeks back I realised how split and thin it had become. I had literally cried the life out of myself and my hair was a living reminder that I was dried out to a cinder. So, my kindly hairdresser suggested giving it a good cut *to do it the world of good.* So I let her, didn't have much choice. But now, I can't put my hair up, I scratch my neck with the brush, and I'm not sure it's growing again yet. It's sort of gone on strike. But the least I can do is wash it and make sure it looks its best. And makeup, I better put on a bit of makeup.

Scurrying is the word. I scurried and scurried. A squirrel couldn't have done a better job. In and out of the shower, whizz whizz with the hairdryer, splish splosh with the war paint, squirt squirt with the perfume. The camera can't smell it (can it, cameras are very clever these days?) but I can. I need to try and feel sexy when I take the selfie.

I need to remember my profile, what did I say *dazzling, beautiful, smart and alluring.*

Daisy, that's it! That's you! I look in the mirror.

The woman that looks back is quite striking. She has clear green eyes and corn-coloured hair that is shiny and hangs quite stylishly along the jawbone. She has flat cheekbones, not high or arching but flattened across the cheeks, which gives her face a smooth, almond sort of shape. She has a strong nose and a pretty mouth, with moist lips, and white teeth. Teeth have always been important to me, it says so on my profile. And the skin you can see, the bits not covered by the red silk dress, looks young and supple, surprising really that Daisy (me!) is 52! If I turn slightly to the camera it will pick up the natural tilt of my head and the slight hollow of my cheek. I click the button on the camera.

Don't blink, don't smirk, look ahead, look down, look serious, look as if you have just found something really funny, look horrified, blow a kiss! Daisy is obedient, the deed is done.

At 8.30 am Dating Daisy is dressed to kill, but sadly, ready to change for a day at work. In a jiffy the dress is back in the cupboard, the jewellery back in its box, the camera stares back at me. Simple really. Just import and go. Dating Daisy is going worldwide on the web. OMG. It's real, really real, and there's no going back

That night, I paid the money. I have had to draw my horns in since Voldemort left, and spending money on this type of thing is gut wrenching.

But what's the alternative? Life. On my own. On the planet.

Here's the thing, I really believe this scientific opinion about humans, sociability and loneliness. When God created me, he meant me to have a mate. I feel that within every atom of my body. If I was chimp in the zoo, and they put me in cage, on my own, without a cute male chimp to hold my hand and snuggle down beside me, I would just die of loneliness. I wasn't made to be on the planet by myself.

End of. It's a genetic fact. It's in my DNA.

This Internet Dating is just a survival skill. Ok, so I'm not in the Amazonian jungle, but it's a close shave – it's downtown Brighton. And there is a hell of a lot of Virginia creeper hanging around, my house is covered in it, and for me, the adrenaline and the survival instinct is no different. I need to find that other Homo sapiens who will fill this empty void that stands next to me all day every day. It's the space Jeremy filled for 18 months. He was good at that. He had warm hands and wide arms and a wonderful strong embrace. He was just one enormous teddy bear. Now he is gone there is a space next to me and another inside me that yawns vacuously. That's all I can say about that, for now.

I paid the money. Dating Daisy has now gone live, and the search has begun.

I went to bed in fevered anticipation, wondering fervently what tomorrow would bring.

Tomorrow would be the first day of the rest of my life.

Chapter Two (In which Daisy starts her Internet Dating adventure)

Sunday April 7th 2014

Couldn't sleep, the dating bug is well into my system. My bed was empty without teddy Jeremy. I hate the empty slot he has left behind. I put a pillow in it, with one of his T shirts over it. But it didn't fool me. I wondered, as I sort of slept, which ~~sleazy~~, ~~hopeful~~, ~~peculiar~~ Romeo would have contacted me overnight. After all, it was a momentous day for mankind yesterday. Daisy went online! Surely there should be half a dozen emails from possible suitors.

It's already nearly six am. The birds are singing! The sun is shining! Daisymae_224 is online.

Quick, boil the kettle and log on.

This is the first day of the rest of my life.

So I logged on, full of expectation. Last time I went Internet Dating I found Jeremy instantly. Where is his replacement? Surely any minute he will pop up in front of me and I will know. Know my fate. Know who I will be spending the rest of my life with. I press the cursors, the space bar, I watch the Google icons, I put in my daisymae_224 and the password, and ping – sigh!

There's nothing there.

My profile sits on the site obediently, like a chicken on an egg. But not a sausage has taken place.

Not one wink, smile, email or anything else. I am deflated.

Oh, wait a minute, 37 men have viewed me and one has listed me as a favourite.

One! Out of 37! How can I be so unattractive!

Didn't I say rhinoceros earlier? Time to think of ugly mammals. Hopefully not because I'm one of them!, but because I have to behave like one. The thicker the skin the better. Didn't the elephant get his saggy baggy skin by scratching it in the Limpopo River? I need to scratch mine somewhere. It's getting very itchy.

"What's wrong with me," my brain asks Daisy. *"Am I so ugly no one wants to speak to me?"*

"Now come on," says the brain, *"there are lots of reasons nothing has happened – yet. And it is early.*

"You only loaded your profile less than 24 hours ago. It has to be checked by Trust HQ!

"And anyway, remember men are like ostriches, they see a beautiful woman, they stick their head in the sand. You, Daisy, need to lead the way.

"Think about the men on BritainonSunday.com. The Britain on Sunday *readers of the UK have just risen early, downed a cooked breakfast and boarded the 6.48 to Clapham Junction. They are probably only now unfurling the daily newspaper, and may not even yet have reached the dating section.*

"And how many will be actually online-now? In the rush hour? Don't be ridiculous!

"And those who do like you, may be shy, they may be poleaxed, frozen with desire, helplessly in love with the tantalising image in the red dress, but uncertain how to make the first move.

"Daisy, you will just have to make the first move yourself. Now what did I say?

"Dazzling, beautiful, smart and alluring.

"Be brave! The world CAN be your oyster."

I press search. Hmm. I will search 20 miles from Brighton. I don't want to have to waste too much petrol seeing my date.

Maybe aged 50 to 60, I don't want a toy boy or a pensioner.

A non-smoker of course. What else narrows the field?

Better not put too much or there will be no one out there. Two eyes, two ears, a nose and a mouth would be nice.

I wonder whether to ask about who has a university degree, and who likes ballroom dancing, and who likes marmite and hates lobsters, tattoos and Morris dancers, but that might narrow the search a bit too much, so I leave all that out and press SEARCH.

Seconds pass. My fate is in the ether. Like a *beam-me-up* from the Starship Enterprise. I can't wait for my suitable matches to vaporise in front of me.

It is really only seconds, but to me an eternity. I need, just need, to find that special person. And I've done what they asked, written the profile, uploaded the photo, paid the hard-earned cash. Now it will all be alright.

The computer winks back and I stare in horror.

What! Three matches within 20 miles of Brighton! Three! Only three!

There must be a mistake. I was promised enough loaves and fishes to feed the five thousand!

I try again. I change the setting, 30 miles of Brighton, 50 miles of Brighton. About 12 profiles now. I am dismayed but this will have to do.

I look at the 12. Like 12 disciples they stare back.

Let me say that about one third of these hopefuls had no photo on their profile. Now I see why the photo is so important. I just can't get started without it.

If I read the profile without the photo, I tend to assume they do look like George Clooney. If they then email me a photo, which invariably makes them look like a cross between King Kong and the Incredible Hulk, and that's why they sensibly hadn't put it on there in the first place, let's be honest, the initial banal conversation was all in vain! So I soon gave up on those profiles without photos.

From the remaining hopefuls, I selected a few.

DDP1 (Daisy's Dating Possibility number 1)

Lexicon of Love
"Charm, passion and vitality"
54, divorced, Brighton
80% match (apparently)
You have 15 things in common
Last login today

Lexicon of Love. (Could I date a man who calls himself 'Lexicon of Love'? I park that for a moment. He does have two eyes, two ears, a nose and a mouth.)
I Google it, and guess what?

Wikipedia: *Lexicon,* formally, in *linguistics,* a **lexicon** is a language's inventory of *lexemes.* The word "lexicon" derives from the *Greek* λεξικόν (*lexicon*), neuter of λεξικός (*lexikos*) meaning "of or for words". – He loves words and I love words. This just might not be such a hard search after all. I rush on reading the profile.

Let me describe the photo of my possible future mate. He looks tall, 6ft according to his profile, and he has a squarish head with thick hair that grows in tufts like marsh grass around his temples and round his ears. Next good point, he is not bald. Voldemort was bald, and I now need hair. He has a wide mouth that is open and laughing. I like a nice mouth and good teeth, and good humour, so all bodes well. Could it be this easy?

I read on, and various words jump out of the narrative towards me, "a tall professional gentleman"... "athletic"... "eats five a day"... "needs someone to love and adore". Well, could it be me? (Shall we cut the emails and the phone calls and just get married straightaway?)

He loves everything I love, "outdoors, nature, singing" (singing? I just sing very badly to Coldplay in the car, so does that count?), cooking (I'm up for that), and here's the best bit: "reading, writing and poetry". OMG, I think this is it! Could he be my soulmate?

I knew the internet was downright marvellous.

Now I'm certain that that £20 first instalment was most definitely worth it.

A man that loves reading and writing and poetry!

I'll email him.

Now!

Hmm ... What should I say?

This is what I wrote:

Hi Lexicon of Love,

Just wanted to say that I like the effort you put into your profile, and I share a lot of your sentiments. Thought I would just say that.

Night, night.

Daisy x

Have I mentioned that Chris Martin is my hero? Now Chris Martin was most definitely married when I started writing this book – it's 2014. Married he may be, but he can still be my inspiration.

I've never asked myself why I'm so mad about Chris Martin.

I guess I didn't need to? ... But now? What is it that gives him this great attraction?

It's not just that I think he is the greatest rock musician that ever lived. Although that may be a large part of it. But he is tall, has bright eyes and long limbs and is brim full of energy. He has an infectious personality. A fabulous sense of humour. Every time I see him interviewed he has something to say that makes me laugh. If you haven't done it, you must Google Chris Martin on Carpool Karaoke. Then I think you will immediately get what I mean.

But now I'm thinking, he's my hero because? Because?

Because he's bright, articulate, passionate, creative and full of ideas. That's what I need from my ideal mate! Exactly that!

So I thought about it and this is what I came up with ...

If I could *Talk* to Chris Martin, I would no doubt have A *Sudden*

Rush of Blood to the Head. I'm sure he would fill my *Head Full of Dreams.* I am after all, *The Scientist,* at the moment I am completely *Lost,* and what I need is some *X&Y.* No doubt Chris could *Fix Me,* and show me *Life in Technicolor.* So I'm doing the dating now, at *The Speed of Sound,* the *Clocks* are ticking and if you read on, at the end, you will even find a *Ghost Story*!

For now, I have a picture of Chris, who unfortunately doesn't seem to be Internet Dating at the moment, and I've stuck it to my wardrobe door. He has blue eyes, and a big smile. It's a great big colour poster. He's playing the piano … to me!

So when I wake up, he's the first thing I see in the morning. And he's a great friend and confidante, as I've discovered lately.

Tonight, he's telling me *Every Tear's a Waterfall.* Daisy! No more tears!"

And if Chris says it, that's just how it has to be.

No more tears, ever.

Chapter Three (Daisy and the doctor)

Monday April 8th 2014

In the morning, before I went to work – in fact *before* I boiled the kettle but don't tell anyone – I checked for a reply. This is what it said:

Hi Daisymae,
Do you think we've got enough in common?
You are attractive and I'd like to get to know you better.
Philip x

The reply was not very dynamic. I tried not to be disappointed. But it was reply, let's face it. And a quick reply, and it said I was attractive. I reread the profile. Certain other things jumped out. "Horse riding ... cycling ... doing wood work ..." (Well, my garden gates needs attention.)

Then I spotted under *Occupation* – "*medical/ dental/ veterinary.*" Suddenly I wondered. OMG. Could he be a doctor? The thing is, I haven't written this yet, but I'm a doctor too. Now I didn't set out to find myself a doctor. You know that from what I have written.

But.

And it's a big but.

The advantage if he is a doctor, is that we have the same background, from the caring profession, and can really understand where each other is coming from. It's a great starting point. And suddenly I need to know.

Hi Philip,

Thanks for your message.

One thing we may have in common is our profession? What is yours? I don't know whether to tell you mine as it may be a conversation stopper... But I noticed your profile said "medical/dental/veterinary."

I am a doctor working in Sexual Health. I am not looking necessarily for another doctor, but, it is true that those of us who have done the training do understand best what the lifestyle is like and the difficulty of being committed to a job that is not 9–5.

Anyhow, you did ask what we had in common!

Daisy xx

I drank my tea, showered, dressed for work, got my work bag ready.

Oh, I just had a quick look at the screen last thing before I left the house – and guess what?

Instantly there was his reply. (Retrospectively, this was a bit weird in itself, as it was only about 7.45 am. Was he up watching the dating site at the crack of dawn, like sad old me?)

My goodness me Daisy, how spooky

I am Philip Braithwaite.

I am a GP

XX

I could hardly believe what I had just read. Of all the faces on the internet, well the 12 that were presented to me anyway, here was another doctor looking for love.

My brain started taking to me sternly at this point. It said,

"Daisy, Daisy, take a deep breath. A degree in medicine is not necessarily a guarantee to happiness. There are whole host of other things you need to find out. What are the chances that the first man you click on will be Mr Perfect? Remember Jeremy. Eighteen months, and he promised you everything, then deserted you over a power boat? Finding a perfect partner is going to take time, so deep breath and be a bit more discerning. There's an awful lot you don't know."

But my poor heart was hammering. We had a lot in common, more than we had realised. And hey he lives here, in Brighton. Very convenient for work. Maybe he has a big old house on the South Downs. He likes riding, maybe he has horses. Jeremy was not well off. He had no pension, and planned to work 'til he dropped. I would have had to support us. But Philip will have a good pension. We can have a good life together with our dual income. My mind was helter-skeltering along, out of control. But I had to go to work.

I don't remember that workday. Much like any other I suspect. But I know as I did the STI tests, signed the microbiology request forms and handed out the doxycyline, I was walking on air that day. I think I told Pinky at lunch time, I couldn't keep it in, and she said *"That's the spirit,"* and *"Good on you girl,"* and *"Go, go, go!"*. I suppose that was Pinky-speak for "how bloody marvellous".

Pinky is my best friend at work. It's important to have someone you work with on a daily basis who makes you laugh. We are so busy seeing the patients there's very little time to chat. Honestly, we hardly ever have time to stop for a millisecond or even have a cup of tea.

Anyway, Pinky and I worked together in another hospital 20 years ago – so long ago I can hardly believe I have just written that – 20 years ago. Such a lot has happened since. I moved here to Silver Mills Hospital around ten years ago, and got a surprise very soon after I started, as we had another new member of staff. What do you know! Quite by chance, of all the places in the south of England, Pinky had come to work here too!

Pinky is called Pinky because she has bright pink hair. It's short and spiky and she looks like a middle-aged punk rocker. She is about 100 years younger than me. She goes to Glastonbury, and wears safety pins in her ears, and she calls her husband Pork Chop. She's also – sorry Pinky – extremely large. Dawn French large – sorry Dawn, and doesn't care a hoot. Pork chop is actually rather thin, like a flimsy French fry. They make a smashing couple. She is the kindest of kind friends and has done so much for me.

"Heh Dais!," she whispered conspiratorially to me today, in between seeing the patients. "Look at this!"

She showed me a news article she had opened up on her mobile phone.

'**Ovipositor, New Egg-Laying Craze for Women**' read the headline.

Underneath it was a long, pale blue tube, in the mouth of which sat a large, rubber egg, perhaps the size of a hen's egg.

"What on earth? ... I was intrigued to read more. We giggled together as Pinky read it out loud.

The Ovipositor is a sensational new device for women's pleasure. Many have reported an amazing experience from inserting the device – which can only be described as a large dildo – into their vagina. The plastic "penis" is impregnated with gelatine eggs, which are then ejected into any orifice. The manufacturer has reported that since a video of the device was put on YouTube, the Ovipositor has been in high demand.

"OMG," I said! "Who would want to do that!" The things people think up never cease to amaze me. "I wonder how you get them out. No doubt we'll have a few of them in here!"

Pinky is always good for a laugh, and full of useless information!

The end of the day couldn't come quickly enough. I rushed in and logged on, breathless with anticipation. Would my Chris Martin have emailed me?

Yes! His email was there in the box.

07574 332456 phone me, Philip x

My heart did a back flip. When should I phone him? After supper? When is supper? What time do most people eat supper? Does it mean today or tomorrow or when?

Should I phone, should I not phone at all?

I had a brief vision of the lonely chimp in the zoo.

I reached for the phone. Our conversation went something like this:

"Philip?"

"Daisy?"

I felt very awkward, tongue-tied even, most unusual for me. After a very pregnant pause I was able to continue.

"Well hi. How are you?"

"I'm fine, and you? Thanks for phoning."

"No worries, all the messaging gets a bit tedious after a while."

I noticed his voice was quite high-pitched, and, well, effeminate. Maybe it's just me being critical, or a bad connection. Can you really judge a person, by their voice, over the telephone?

"Agree. Agree. Can you believe we are both doctors? Can't be that many on the website?" he replied, with a tone of disbelief.

"It's not just because you're a doctor – " I said. It really wasn't that at all, it was merely a coincidence and had struck me as common ground to get started.

"I didn't think – " he interjected.

I continued,

"It's just that when I look at the faces, at least I know you and I have had some sort of common past. You know. And we are both in a caring profession. So I thought it must say something about you." I was pleased I had managed to say that.

"Sure you're right," Philip said.

There was short silence.

Then we both started to talk at once.

Then stopped. So I continued.

"After you ..."

"No after you, sorry..."

This was all embarrassingly ridiculous. I had forgotten just how hard the telephone interview could be.

"Tell me about yourself then. Where do you work? Big practice, small practice?" I asked. I needed to know a bit about his medical background.

"There's a story there," he said. He sounded resigned.

"I love stories," I said. (I do, as you know.) And what a story I was about to hear.

Then, as Philip starts to talk, it all comes out in a rush, and as I listen, my dreams of Philip and I ebb away through the plug hole. I did listen, I didn't interrupt.

"I was working in this really busy practice in South London. I was married, my wife was a practice nurse and we have two children. Well, we're going back five or six years ago, you know, everything was ok, but then she had an affair.

"Well it was a nightmare, trying to work things out in the practice, especially as the guy she was seeing was another GP in the practice, and they basically wanted me out.

"So they started a witch-hunt, and they started making claims about my clinical practice, which weren't true of course. But it's like kicking a man when he's down.

"I was so distressed by what was happening, I wasn't sleeping, I was exhausted. So they reported me to the GMC and I had to be investigated. They came out with this list of things I was supposed to have done."

I was listening intently. This wasn't at all good.

"Like failing to keep a proper register for controlled drugs. Like breaking confidentiality which was a downright lie. Like refusing to visit an old man who was confused, (I had visited him the day before and all was in hand) – and so on.

"But I had to go to the GMC hearing and they found me guilty. On 11 counts of poor practice. You can look this all up yourself on the internet so I may as well tell you myself."

He hesitated.

"Oh dear," I said, encouragingly.

"So, I was forced to leave. To be honest I was so unwell by then I had to have some time off." There was a silent pause.

"So I actually had two years off sick. But that's behind me now, I've got a GP trainer who is overseeing my work and I've been working here for six months and really enjoying it."

He stopped abruptly as if he had said too much.

"How about you?"

I was stumped. I wasn't ready to do my bit I was thinking about what I had just heard.

"Oh I'm so sorry to hear about all that. Sounds like you had an awful time. (Am I talking to another Harold Shipman?) ... So are you full time?"

"Well, actually I don't like to tell you this, but I just failed my 'back to practice' exam, so I have to retake it in the autumn. It's pretty hard to study and pass exams at our age! ... Anyway, enough about me. Tell me about you?"

"Back to practice exam?" I heard myself repeating what he had just said. "Well how can you work as a GP if you haven't passed your exams?"

"I did say," he sounded irritated with me, "this GP tutor is helping me. I'll pass it next time. If I don't, I'll have to look for something outside medicine. Now come on, what about you?"

I think he wanted to hear some terrible secrets about my medical career. I had nothing to say, certainly nothing on that scale.

So I ignored this question. "So where are you living now?" I asked.

"In a room. I rent a room in shared house. It's in Marina Parade, on the seafront. It's quite nice actually, quite cosy!"

"Oh." (My dreams are fading fast. No manor house for me!)

"And you, are you full time?" he asked.

"Full time. five long days a week. I didn't want to be but I am."

"And where is it you work?"

My head was now reeling with what he had just told me.

He was a doctor in difficulty, a doctor who had got into trouble and was nearly about to lose his livelihood.

Yet he was cheerful about it.

"Umm, Oh yes, I live locally. I work at Silver Mills." I didn't want to say exactly where I lived, for obvious reasons. Everyone round here knows Silver Mills. There's been a hospital there since for more than a century. (It's named after the medieval silver mining industry in the South Downs.)

We talked on for a while but I must say I felt dispirited. There are so many people on the internet with baggage. I guess that is pretty obvious, that's one of the reasons they are on the internet.

I have personally had enough stress in my medical career to sink a battleship. Enough stress to break my 26-year marriage, and do you know what, I don't need anybody else's. I managed to finish the conversation, and then I will have to think about it all. I need to sleep on it.

But Philip, sadly, I suddenly doubted he was the one for me.

So I consoled myself, that DDP1 was not Mr Perfect. First line crossed through on what would probably be a very long list.

Back at home, I was not to be undeterred however, and guess what?

I went straight back online.

And guess again.

Someone had sent me an email.

It was from Frankie10.

But hang on, before I show you that email, a little more about me.

I live in a large, Victorian house in Hove, near Brighton. It's a great big house, on three floors, with six bedrooms. A pretty house, which we bought soon after we got married. When we divorced several years ago, somehow I managed to hang onto it. My friends thought it was strange that I didn't want a fresh start. *Too many memories* they said. But actually I found it comforting, that, although the marriage had been obliterated, the bricks and mortar had not.

The house, number 6, resides in a leafy road, a few blocks back from the sea front. It sits at right angles to the road, and has a portico round the front door with a little turret on top. There is a surprisingly large garden for a town house in a residential area. The gardens on either side has been sold off for new builds, but the land in front – and especially behind – the house, is quite considerable.

There are character features, such as a big square front hall, a beautiful staircase, stained-glass windows throughout and a gorgeous window seat in the dining room that I fell in love with the moment I set my foot through the door.

But, and there is a BUT. My house, my beautiful house, is a state.

There's only one person to blame, Voldemort. Read on and you will understand why.

But anyway, everything that could be wrong with a house is wrong with this one.

It's damp. The roof leaks. The boiler is 20 years old and unreliable. We don't always have hot water. The window frames are original, and a lot of them are rotten and need replacing, so the house is draughty, and cold. The whole house needs redecorating. The house needs a new kitchen and new bathrooms. The carpets are threadbare. The garden is overgrown like Sleeping Beauty's castle. I think the only thing it doesn't appear to have ... well so far anyway ... is subsidence! Well – bully for that.

Unfortunately, when we divorced, we were in the usual predicament. Most of our money was in the property, so we were advised by our solicitors, that the house should be sold. Neither of us wanted to try to find large sums of money at that stage in the relationship, to sink into a house we would not be able to share in the future.

I felt with every bone in my body that I should hang onto the house if it was at all possible. I just didn't know how. Anyway, after a year on the market, and no buyer, the asking price had fallen by £100,000. Eventually, I spoke to the bank, and it wasn't difficult to persuade them to let me increase my mortgage, actually by far more than I felt comfortable.

So in the end, I bought Voldemort out, and my daughter Imogen and I were able to stay there. Thank goodness, we did not have to face clearing out and moving out, on top of our inevitable emotional distress.

But, this left me, paying a huge mortgage, worried about money, and with little or no capital for any repairs. Imogen and I just put one foot in front of the other. I knew the day would come when we would have to sell the house, but for now, we were creaking along. We have become quite adept at putting buckets under the leaks and kicking the boiler from time to time in order to have a bath. If I could just manage to keep us there until Imogen left college I thought. She's 17, and she's had such a hard time. This would be one less trauma for her. And for me.

I love the house. I know all the little sighs and moans it gives off during the day. It's got high ceilings and wooden floors, and marble fire places. It's like a faded stately home.

And it's mine.

And I love it.

Chapter Four (In which Daisy meets Frankie10 and gets a proposition. Plus Introducing 'Plonkers')

Monday April 8th 2014

Frankie 10

DDP2

Frankie10

"Need warmth, love and communication? Please say Hi!"
50, divorced, Rottingdean
88.7% match (apparently)
You have 14 things in common

Heh babe,

Send a message. Welcome!

Frankie10 xx

I like it, I like it a lot. He chose me. He clicked on me!

I look at the photo. I see a guy who looks younger than 50.

Here's the thing, everyone lies on these sites, so be suspicious!

He is smiling, rather lopsidedly it has to be said, at the camera. He has a nice face, all there, the two eyes, nose and mouth, can only see one ear but assume he has a second one, as he is slightly at an angle to the camera. He is wearing a very pleasant green and blue check shirt.

Approve. Shame wherever he is sitting, there is something shiny behind him a silver colour, that looks as if it is growing out of his left ear.

Looking at him though, I am reminded of the Wasgij. You know those jigsaws where you see the picture, but the jigsaw itself is what they were looking at. I look at Frankie with his mouth slightly agape and I wonder where he is and what he is looking at. (Astute of me actually, as he turns out to be a Casanova!)

I type back:

Frankie hello!

You look like a veteran. Any tips?

Daisy x

(I hope that doesn't sound like he's undateable, as he's been on the site such a long time!)

I read his profile. The first bit is good:

"Friendly… relaxed … warm," he writes.

Yes, all good. But here's where it all goes wrong …

"Sporty type, loves cycling, running, weights and the gym. Fitness is so important to me. I seem to have the knack with just about any sport you offer me!"

And then it gets even worse.

"My ideal match will be a sportaholic too. She will enjoy and share all my sporting activities as I will share hers."

Pardon me. I am feeling dispirited.

Another thing I haven't spelled out yet in this story is that I am not sporty. Not sporty probably with a capital N. Now, in truth I am not badly coordinated and was in a few teams at school for netball and tennis, and I was a good gymnast. I could still do the splits until about ten years ago. I am energetic and active. Have been on walking holidays and walked twenty miles in a day. I can ballroom dance 'til I drop. I like to swim. I can ride a bike, although I prefer a leisurely pace to a tea shop, not a sprint uphill for 60 miles, which was Voldemort's pleasure. I hate the gym. Absolutely hate the smell of old sweaty bodies and the sound of the panting as several geriatric Lycra-clad individuals pump themselves up and down on the treadmill. What could be worse? So if Frankie wants a sports partner, it just won't be me. I need to be clear about this. I write:

Heh Frankie,

Thanks. Look, reading your profile, I think you want someone sporty. I have to say I am not a couch potato, but I am hardly sporty. So I don't think this would work.

I'm so sorry,

Daisy xx

(Daisy! How could you?)

He writes straight back:

Daisy,

Thanks for being straight with me. Good luck in your search.

Frankie x

And that's that. DDP2, discarded.

So I have another look around the site. There a couple of hot guys there actually. Really, quite suave. I can travel. I can hop on a train. If this is for keeps it's worth being a bit adventurous. I click on a couple, just say a quick *Hi,* and scarper. I am suddenly consumed again by the thought these guys may not like me and I may have made a fool of myself. Then I think a bit more rationally.

The thing is, you have to commit to three months' membership to be on here. So even if you have met someone and are having a relationship, your face will still show up until the three months is over, and, it has to be said, until you have remembered to cancel your subscription! (If you are reading this don't forget that bit, some people continue their subscriptions quite unwittingly for many months, not realising you must proactively contact the site and shut your account down.)

So if they don't reply it might just mean they have met someone else. *Someone who got there before me.* And that's unavoidable. So there's no point being upset about it.

And the world is full of all sorts. Some men like brunettes, I am blonde.

Some like long hair, mine is shoulder length.

Some want small women, I am tall.

Some want thin women, I am ... actually I'm not writing that! ... I am not fat. But I do hate the whole subject of size and weight.

Shall I write about it now and get it over with?

If you are thinking of embarking on Internet Dating you need to know there is a breed of men out there that are obsessed with thin women. They are a different ethnic group. I call then the plonkers. You can spot a plonker instantly, as it will say, often in capital letters on his site,

DO NOT CONTACT ME UNLESS YOU ARE NATURALLY SLIM.

Yes, a complete plonker. Now I'll tell you why I think this. Because, yes of course slimmer people are more attractive, I don't disagree. However, if it were as simple as just finding someone beautiful, it's not hard to buy yourself a new painting. And if you want sex, which by the way is probably all at least 50% of them are after, then you can buy that in King's Cross.

But if you want a long lasting meaningful relationship with a true soulmate, you need a combination of the two. And, knowing life is the way it is, rough around the edges, you may have to compromise to find that perfect person. If being thin is so important, what a miserable outlook on life for the pair of you.

Lucky if you are naturally thin, but many thin women live on laxatives and mineral water, smoke (Ugh!) and are as much fun on a night out as the proverbial wet blanket.

I can't believe that men really think that unless a woman is a size 10, they are unable to have a relationship with them. It's also arrogant, as many of these men are significantly overweight themselves.

Case in point my Jeremy. But you know, I loved him being cuddly. Voldemort was an old anorexic, nothing to hang on to but bone and sinew which makes for a bumpy ride. But Jeremy was soft and warm, and I loved his weight next to me and on top of me, and I wouldn't rule out a boyfriend ever just because he was a bit on the generous side.

Plonkers are plonkers because they have this thin women divining stick, a bit like a stick that tells you when you've found water, and they follow the twitches towards emaciation.

So I will never date a Plonker. That's one of Daisy's dating principles. Watch this space!

If I'm not a Plonker ... which as you can see I am not ... what can I call myself? Ok, not difficult – I'm a MAWD, just a middle-aged woman on a dating site! And just one of many thousands of other MAWDs out there!

So I go to bed that night and I can't sleep. Dating Daisy has been on the net for two days and hasn't got a date. This is not good. The bed is still empty beside me where Jeremy used to lay. I would stroke his hair on the pillow. He had loads of it, and big blue eyes. I get choked when I think about him.

The day after I met him he sent me a text early in the morning. It said "Kylie Minogue song, twenty-one letters beginning with C."

When I read it, an electricity bolt shot though my system. My spine and my legs were fizzing. I was on fire. It was like lighting a touch paper and standing back to watch the explosion.

It was a game we played. I replied, probably without even leaving a decent pause

"Celine Dion, fourteen letters beginning with F."

These are the memories that I wish I didn't have. He said he loved me, but I doubt he ever did. What is real love anyway? All I can say is that real love is fragile and precious. I never took his love for granted. But he took mine. I don't think he ever valued me. Not the way I want to feel valued anyway. So one day, when I opened the front door, that love – if that's what it was – jumped up, packed its bags and slipped away.

There is a pain inside me, which I can't explain to you, but it's such a monotonous, aching feeling and there is no antidote. At least if it was a headache I could take a paracetamol. But there is no remedy for this pain.

Was it love, or wasn't it? Just two traumatised people looking for something, probably, or should I say, possibly unattainable. In my heart I know, the only way to ease the pain is to find someone new. A new teddy with strong arms.

Some people would say it's too soon, and I should wait.

But I can't.

If you remember what I wrote right at the beginning, it's in my DNA.

If I don't have a soulmate soon, I will be like the solitary chimp in the zoo.

I got into bed. Chris was still there, hanging around, tinkling the ivories.

"Night , night," he said.

"I love a day out at the Zoo!"

Chapter Five (In which Daisy goes on her first date)

Tuesday April 9th 2014

It's work again today.

We had a bad night last night, as there was no hot water. Again. Imogen couldn't have her bath, and I had to wash this morning with a kettle of hot water. I forget how many times we've had the plumber out this year already. He told me last time that if the boiler broke down again, because it's so old, they might not be able to get spare parts for it. I just pray this isn't the case. I've left a message with the plumber and I'm hoping somehow he can go round today. Maggie will let him in for me I'm sure.

On the news, there's a missing plane, a Malaysian Airlines flight, en route between Beijing and Kuala Lumpur, just disappeared off the radar. I guess it's crashed somehow. Imagine the terror of being in a plane crash! Poor people and poor families. Better drive carefully to work I guess. Car accidents are more common than plane crashes as we know. And people drive round here like nincompoops. Believe me. (How did I get that dent in my front bumper?)

Anyhow, actually more important to me even than hot water! I wish I had something to come home to. I wish I had someone to text me, or to send a text to, just to say have a good day at work.

Jeremy and I always texted when we got to work. Just to say we'd got there safely. I always looked for a message on my phone around lunchtime. I always spoke to him when I left the clinic and walked to the car. I find myself fingering my phone.

We haven't spoken since the day we argued and he put down his key. He told me he was looking for me for three years before he found me. And I bet it won't take him long to be back on buzz.com. No grieving. Just instantly over it.

And I feel consumed with tears when I think about him with anyone else. I need to stay focussed. I need to move on. There are lots of reasons why Jeremy was never going to be a great lifetime partner, and I chose to just put those out of my mind.

"Onwards Daisy, come on!" says my indefatigable brain.

So I thought it might be amusing for you the reader, to have a fly on the wall view of life in Sexual Health. Here's the thing, although I've been doing this for 30 years, some things never fail to surprise me. Read on and see what happened to me today.

Imagine the scenario.

The patient says "Can I ask you something doctor?"

"Of course," I say. "What can I do to help?"

She is woman in her 50s with a large scruffy holdall balanced on her lap. A Mary Poppins carpet bag, I think fleetingly. (If she suddenly delves in there, she might just pull out a hat stand.)

"The thing is, "she says, and her face has turned a vivid shade of scarlet, "How can I say this ... It's not about me. It's about my partner."

"Um hmm," say I, encouragingly. (What else was in that iconic Mary Poppins holdall ... it's bugging me now ... must be in the old memory recesses somewhere ... two turtle doves and a partridge in a pear tree?... a hat stand. All I seem to recall is a hat stand.)

"Well," she says, "the thing is ... Oh I'm just going to have to say this as it is. You must get this all the time."

"It's no problem, you can tell me anything."

"Well, my partner ... you know when we're doing it ... you know... having sex. He can only last ten minutes. Is that normal?"

I need a bit more explanation here.

"So do you mean start to finish is ten minutes ... from ..."

"Oh no, I mean the bit you know, where he goes inside me ... to the bit where he actually comes. That bit. It's ten minutes."

"Ten minutes?"

"Yes ten minutes, we timed it. Is that normal? Only he's worried he isn't able to keep going you see, and he thinks he's got that what do you call it – premature ejaculation?"

I couldn't help suppress a giggle. I hope the amusement didn't show on my face. We are trained to be non-judgemental so I need to get a grip.

"Listen," I said, "ten minutes at that stage of proceedings is pretty good going!"

"Is it?"

"Absolutely! Most men can't manage that bit for than thirty seconds believe me.!"

"Really?"

"Yes! And what's more, ten minutes is a long time! After ten minutes ... most women would be lying there composing a shopping list!"

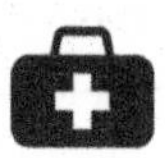

So I'm home. Guess what! The plumber's been and the heating's on. There seems to be hot water. And yes of course, he's left me a bill. I don't want to look. How long until the next time, but for now, thank goodness, it's warm.

Imogen has gone to the cinema with her friend Izzy. She didn't want to tell me what she was going to see. Probably something terribly unsuitable, like *Fifty Shades of Grey.* Is that really what a seventeen-year-old should be watching? I did read the first book. Behind my parasol. In Tenerife. But nobody saw me. Perhaps I'm secretly jealous!

I've made tea. There's nothing on the telly. Only *Eastenders* or *Emmerdale* or that programme about doing up houses, *Impressive Creations* I think they call it. Everyone's been talking about this as they do these amazing house transformations in a remarkably short space of time – if you like grass on your roof and space age minimalism that is. How can people live with so little furniture? Where is all the clutter? It isn't real. It can't be. Although I'm biased as I had to live with Voldemort the hoarder. Read on.)

So, I'm back in front of my trusty friend the computer. Now I'm logging onto BritainonSunday.com dating site.

Now I've had 147 hits.

Three people have added me to their favourites.

There is an email from Philip.

I feel a sense of trepidation.

Dear Daisy,

It was so good talking to you on the phone the other night. It seems too amazing to be true we found each other on this site. I really want to meet up with you. I will phone you later. Please let's make a date.

Philip x

PS Are you really called Daisy?

Here's the thing. I have had a lot of very difficult things happen to me in the NHS. If anyone knows how stress at work can kill a relationship, it's me. Am I being unkind, by not at least meeting this guy and giving him some support.

That's another thing you don't know about me. I am extraordinarily kind, and you will see that time and time again in this book. I like to be needed and wanted, and I love doing things for other people. I just knew I would have to meet Philip and give it my best shot.

Here's what I thought. If he is actually drop dead gorgeous and we have some chemistry, maybe I can help him. I can encourage him to study, we could do some past papers together, maybe give him some feedback and so on, and maybe he can support me, and just maybe it will all work out tickety-boo.

So I said yes, which was not a good idea as you will see and we had a coffee date.

And it was. An unmitigated disaster.

Daisy's First date

So we arranged to meet at Costa Coffee in the Reception at Eastbourne Hospital, as I was working near there that day and it seemed a reasonable sort of halfway point for us both.

I'd been working in the morning, so I wore work a black work dress, unremarkable but smart, sleeveless, A-lined, and will always do for a number of different situations.

I had made sure I looked well groomed. Clean hair, nice light make-up, cleaned my teeth in the toilets just before we met and reapplied a little lipstick. Minimal jewellery. Plenty of perfume.

I was good to go.

Fifty-two, but looking 42, as sure as eggs are eggs.

So I arrived in the foyer and swept the reception area at a glance, looking for a tall, 6ft man with marsh-grass hair and a huge smile. No one anywhere matching that description?

Perhaps he wouldn't turn up.

Perhaps I was being stood up?

Perhaps he was late. I hate people who are late. I am always early.

But hang on, someone stood up and started pumping my hand up and down. It was a short man. I am 5ft8½ and he was shorter than me. And he had a grey crew-cut, worn out jeans and a grungy anorak.

And looking more closely I could see he wore a cheesecloth shirt that is missing a couple of buttons, and had a large gap between his front teeth (Those photos were definitely taken at an angle for a reason!), and he had a wobbly head.

In medicine we call it *titubation*, and it's a manifestation of extreme anxiety.

And I find he is kissing me on the cheek!

It must be *him*, but as far as I am concerned, it's an imposter.

Anxiety? ... Well it's me that's filled with anxiety!

This is not what it said on the tin! I haven't much choice but to allow my hand to be shaken by his, which is limp and slightly sweaty. (No doubt his penis would be exactly the same. Daisy, how uncharitable, banish such thoughts from your mind.) It's only coffee.

Baptism by cappuccino.

Or cremation perhaps, over a latte?

(How did we get to funerals already? There's more on that in just a minute!)

So we sat down. Well actually first we queued up for drinks. The conversation in the coffee queue was stilted. When we sat down, I tried to make the best of a difficult situation, as I saw it.

I just knew, from the instant I set eyes on Philip, that there was no way I could fall in love with him. And I am sorry about this because believe me, as Dating Daisy, I am very anxious to get off the site, very anxious indeed. And I believe what I said about paintings and sex and King's Cross, and plonkers. (Philip is not a plonker by the way, that's one good thing in his favour.) But, I also believe in pheromones.

So it was time for a trip to see my two Amigos. They live in the big swanky house with the swimming pool in the best position on the street. They are a retired couple who have been my best friends for as long as I have lived in my house. Maggie has been almost a surrogate mother to me since my mother died, and Malcolm is *in loco parentis* when my father is not paying one of his frequent visits.

I rang the bell, Malcolm, Amigo 1, as always, answered the door. He was adjusting his two hearing aids as he let me in, preparing for a good natter. Maggie, Amigo 2, always calls me 'gorgeous' and makes me copious pots of tea. We sat on the sofa, an upmarket scene from

The Royle Family, but never with the TV blaring. (And Malcolm has never been heard to say "My arse!")

Maggie is small, slim and very energetic. She's always cooking. Cooking for everyone. Cooking for England. The first time I met her, she rang the bell with a huge chocolate cake for my daughter's birthday. She had heard of this new family that had moved into the street, and that there was a child's birthday today. So she had baked a cake. It was a stupendous cake, on a silver cake board, covered in chocolate buttons, hundreds and thousands, and she had even added some candles. "I wasn't sure how old she was," she said apologetically, "so I'm sorry I had to guess, but she is called Imogen isn't she? I got the name right?" I stood looking in wonder at this petite angel, to whom I had never previously been introduced. It was incredible that such an amazing person could just flutter in to our lives. I was and still am dumbfounded by her kindness to myself and my family.

Yes, she had the Imogen's name right. It was so kind. And so much appreciated as I am pretty useless when it comes to making party cakes and it saved me a trip to Marks & Spencer! And Maggie has been in our lives, making cakes, and doing all sorts of things for us ever since.

What can I say about Malcolm? He always reminds me of Geoffrey Palmer. If you don't know this, he played the dentist husband in *Butterflies,* and I mention this series again later in this book. Shades of my youth! He has a strikingly serious air about him, but he's actually hilarious. His sense of humour is second to none. He can take a difficult problem and turn it into a mere trifle with his dry wit and his 'deputy dawg' attitude to life.

So I sat on the sofa, in between the two of them, my two Amigos.

So you want to know why they're *Amigos*?

It's the name we three have for our special friendship club. When my marriage was in trouble, I got into the habit of paying them a visit most evenings. We all became very close. I don't think I ever meant to burden them with the marriage issues, but inevitably they affected every day. Lots of problems, and decisions to be made for myself and Imogen. Then, when my mother died, and as my father lived so far away, they just sort of adopted me. I hope it was actually a two-way friendship, not me in need of free psychotherapy! They have reassured me many times this is not the case and I think I know that, but I also feel indebted to them for helping me through the biggest crisis of my life. They helped me to live. Quite literally. I will always love them very much.

So ...

"Dating news!" I began.

"Come on then, what's the latest?" replied Amigo number 1 (Malcolm)

Maggie, number two Amigo, poured the tea. They listened intently to the story about Philip. They agreed I didn't need all that stress to add to my own. When I got to the undertaker bit they were shocked.

"Cold hands can be quite sexy," said Amigo 1.

"Not where I'm standing," said Amigo 2, and this is what happened next ...

"You always have cold hands and you put them on me as soon as we get into bed every night."

"What rubbish, it's you who puts his cold feet on me."

"No I don't, because you don't even come to bed at the same time as me."

"Not true, I come to bed with you. I just get up if I can't sleep."

"Well then you never sleep because whenever I wake up, you're never there."

"But you never do wake up so you don't know I'm not there."

"Yes I do, like the night before last."

"That was different as I was shooting squirrels."

"Yes, shooting squirrels, and half naked! Do you know what Daisy, I found him pacing the floor with an airgun rifle at three in the morning, wrapped only in a loin cloth! Actually, when I got a good look at him I burst out laughing. It was so funny!"

"Well I only do it because you don't like squirrels."

"I do like squirrels. It's just the ones in our front garden eat all the birds' nuts."

"How do you know it isn't a squirrel from the back garden that comes round the front to eat the birds' nuts?"

"Well I don't."

"So you see, killing a squirrel has to be good."

"Well I just don't like killing things."

I had been looking left, right, left, right, like a ping pong ball.

"Stop!" I said. "Let's call it '40 love' and change the subject!"

They are such a comic act. That's what you get after 40 years of marriage.

So I trudge back up the hill to my weary old house. I love the Virginia creeper. It comes out in May and the house looks romantic somehow. It's in October when I have to clear up all the fallen leaves that I change my mind!

*Remember that 'Oviposter' Pinky told me about? The fake penis that lays eggs in the vagina? Well, Pinky just texted me and it says, "Have a look at 'Plop Egg Painting' online?"

When I've turned the key in the lock, I log on and look immediately. Now I see there's a woman who does a show, in which she pushes paint coloured eggs out of her vagina, and makes paintings out of this! How even more extraordinary is that!

Vaginal art? Whatever next?

Chapter Seven (In which Daisy becomes creative on the internet)

Wednesday April 10th 2014

Not a work day today, but I couldn't stay in bed. The internet is like a magnet. The minute I opened my eyes I felt this sort of electronic beam reeling me in.

On the news, it all about Ebola, this horrific West-African virus that is some sort of haemorrhagic fever. You bleed internally to death. Its incurable and highly infectious. Even the gravediggers won't bury the bodies for fear of getting the infection. I read up on it a bit, and was horrified to learn that live virus can be extracted from body fluids like semen some months after death. I don't think most people would know that Ebola could be thought of as a Sexually Transmitted Disease. I must tell Pinky. She'll love to hear about that.

I've been thinking about love and life and physical attraction. Have you ever seen *Phantom of the Opera*? If not, you absolutely have to go. In my real life, when I'm not being Daisy, I have a *Phantom* fix at least once a year. My friend and I have a day out in London and drool over Raoul.

You see, we don't drool over Phantom, isn't that strange, but we do love him. He is so tragic with his hideous face. But it's the romance that draws us in, and never ceases to leave me weeping at various stages in the evening. My absolute favourite part is when the Phantom appears to Christine when she is in her dressing room. He beckons her towards him, and somehow, mesmerised, she falls into a trance and helplessly walks towards him. This next bit is absolutely true. He physically reaches out, *through the mirror,* and takes her hand. She then steps *through* the mirror. Yes, you did read those bits correctly – *through the mirror. You then* see her in the labyrinth, finding her way along the twisted walkways with a lantern. She enters the crypts, the thick mist rising around her, and a little boat – magically it's a gondola – then appears to take them through the underground waterways. It's just too romantic for words! But anyway, the reason for writing this is, that if you needed proof that the physical side just has to be right, this is a fabulous example.

Christine just couldn't fall in love with Phantom, or fall in love with him *enough.* Not even when he taught her to sing like the Angel of Music. He brought her fame, stardom, and worshipped her so adoringly.

However, she couldn't love him because – and let's just be brutal here – he was downright ugly!

So ugly he had to cover half his face with a plastic mask in fact.

So here's the thing, as Daisy, I need a man with two eyes, a nose, two ears and a mouth, and preferably one who hasn't had his face indescribably disfigured by elephantiasis.

Let's hope the internet doesn't disappoint.

I made tea, poured some cereal into a bowl, flipped the switch on the dishwasher. There's so much domestic trivia that needs doing but Daisy is on a mission. Maybe today might be the day.

Click, click. Infuriating pause and Da Na Na Na. Hey presto! Back online.

BritainonSunday.com, where life was as dull as a graveyard.

Not a sausage.

No one had emailed me.

Oh, now 217 guys had viewed by profile – probably all the PLONKERS from the dating site archives.

Hang on. Someone else has listed me as a favourite!

I pulled up the photo.

His dating name is Cool Jaguar. (I wonder where that name came from?)

I opened the photo page.

Hmm.

A man, with a dark grey suit, a dark tie with a paisley print, and a distinguished head of greying hair looks back.

Yup, it's all there, the two eyes, two ears, the nose and the mouth. And what's more they seem to be fitting together like a jigsaw. He's quite dishy ('dishy?'... Daisy, where did that come from?) Dishy is what my mother would say when I was a teenager and I had a date. "Was he dishy?" I need a reprimand for that one.

I'm wiser now. I read the profile. More critically.

This is what it said:

Cool Jaguar

"Dance to the music of time"

DDP3?

Why should people get to know you?

(This should be at least 20 words long.)

Am a business man working with local enterprise. Enjoy travelling, new cultures and photography. Like eating out, cinema. Musical tastes are varied my favourite being classical. Love cooking. Like leisurely cycling and golf. Whilst not desperate would be great to get off this site once and for all!

He describes his ideal match thus:

(This should also be at least 20 words long.)

Somebody who is caring, passionate, self-motivated, has ideas of her own of places to see and things to do together. And wants to spend time exploring life, the world and its pleasures. And is as open to the idea of relocating as I am. – And that's all he put! – although it is more than 20 words! – it's pretty concise if you ask me!

This always makes me laugh as how could anyone possible say who they were looking for in under 20 words! It doesn't sound like some people are very fussy. His 'ideal match' description was so brief – blink and you would miss it!

So, am I being too critical here as maybe Cool Jaguar is just very open to suggestion? Just a nice open-minded guy who is so amiable he befriends most people? I think not.

Even as an elementary internet dater I can spot desperation when I see it. Some men just can't be bothered to even put pen to paper. They just want to snap their fingers and have women come running.

Well? Can I be honest? He talks in abbreviations. There's just a collection of nouns and verbs. Why can't anyone use the Queens' English? So that rather put me off. Plus where is the spark, the vitality? The profile is as flat as a bottle of flat lemonade. A businessman! Too much minding your own business! If you want a date you have to be interested in other people's business. And I think he's only interested in himself.

"Leisurely cycling?" What's that? A tricycle? An electric bike? An exercise bike? A rickshaw perhaps?

Wonder what he cooks? Ah, I know – marmite sandwiches?

And he's not desperate, but in his next breath he's very willing to relocate! And to look anywhere in the world! My father warned me about men like that. They're called 'spongers'! And look at who he's looking for, basically anyone, anytime any place. It's sad really.

Can you see that I am learning already? I don't really believe a word he has put on the site! I have decided to believe he may be a businessman, as he has written as a businessman would do business. Guess he can't disguise that. But even that could be untrue. He could be pushing trolleys in Tesco's. Or working as an embalmer, maybe? Anything was possible.

I felt in a flippant mood, so I decided to make his day, and send him an email.

Hi Cool Jaguar,

Daisymae! I like cooking and cycling. Tell me about your day?

Message me?

Daisy xx

Well why not? Maybe he's rich and will fall madly in love with me and take me away from all this!? Who knows God's master plan? I press send and slope off to wash up.

I made more tea. I drummed my fingers on the computer table. I looked out the window at the ivy and the clematis from next door's garden. That plant just climbed over the wall. Without permission, it just stuck out its tiny tendrils and crept into the bosom of my garden. It was an outsider than muscled its' way in and now I love it being there. Will the internet produce a boyfriend for me in a similar way?

The house is quiet today. It seems forlorn. There was water on the floor in the porch when I went to get the post. It tends to seep in under the front door when it's been raining. It's such a nuisance as the letters are all sodden wet. I have to dry them out on the radiators before I can open them. Plus I get wet feet.

Back on the screen, OMG a message. It's a message from Philip. I really don't want to read it, but common decency says I have to. Click.

Dearest Daisy,

My goodness I'm in love with you already. You are quite the most lovely lady I have ever met. Thanks for coffee today. I can't wait to see you again. How about Saturday?

Lots of love

Philip xx

PS I got the embalming job, so lunch is on me!

I read this with horror. This is not good. I didn't want to add to his unhappiness. He was already recovering from a lot of difficulty and sadness in his life and I have just made it 100 times worse. The thing is, you just don't know when you start out on these things, how they will end up.

What's the saying, "Better to have lived and loved, than never to have loved at all?"

I didn't want to hurt him, but I just could **not** go out with an undertaker. (Sorry if you are an undertaker reading this by the way. Someone has to do it. We are very grateful.)

I ignored the email for a while, and had a think about how best to reply.

The problem with Internet Dating is that it takes over your life. You feel this narcotic pull to sit in front of the screen. And yet most of the time, things only happen slowly. It was a nasty shock that after signing up, there were so few men who matched my profile within a commutable distance. At that stage of my life, I was looking for something unique, and the chance of finding it in the next street in Brighton was probably remote. I guess I had to accept casting the net wide, and be prepared to travel to find the right person. And instead of worrying about that, just trust that in these days of mobile phones, *Skype*, email (it won't be long before teleporting is fully operational), we could somehow make it work.

I searched again and widen the area to 80 miles from home.

Ah, here was a nice profile. 'Love Bug'. Love Bug – I ask you! A handsome face came into view. Dark hair, quite a lot of it (so many middle-aged men are bald). Dark brown twinkly eyes. (Teddy bear eyes?)

He was laughing. Laughing is good!

He had the required facial anatomy.

I scanned the profile, 6ft1. Great, I love tall men. Apart from Chris, my other pinup is Aiden from *Sex in the City* and he is 6ft4. I like men taller than me as they make me feel small, as I am 5ft8½, and although not fat, I am not a small person.

This was looking possible. I read on, and then I spotted it ... it says: "medical/nursing/veterinary".

Could it be possible? Another doctor? Maybe a doctor who hasn't recently been almost struck off?!

As I read on through his narrative, I spied something that makes me very happy.

A poem! He has written a limerick on the site and it says:

In the middle of a dark stormy night,
I signed on to this dating site

If you like what you read,
Have the credentials I need,
Get in touch for the ride of your life!
It's irresistible. I start typing.

A young lady from Brighton indeed
Saw a man on the net, a good steed
She messaged him then,
As it was half past ten,
And she thought he deserved a good read!
Message me?
Daisy x
DDP 4?

So what else is new? It's still raining. They haven't found the missing Malaysian jet. The Ebola crisis continues and there may now be a case in the UK. We've all had Major Incident Training at work. George Clooney is engaged. It's official. So the world keeps turning, and Daisy keeps dating.

Who knows how this story will end?

Great news! Coldplay have got their new album out now. It's called *Ghost Stories*, and I love it.

Although, at the same time, the saddest thing is that Chris and Gwyneth are splitting up. 'Conscious uncoupling' they call it. Celebrity marriages must be especially tough. Maybe Chris will appear on *Britain on Sunday* Dating, after all?

"Still believe in magic?" Chris said last night when I was getting ready for bed.

"Of course I do, Chris. I have to. It's only magic – I guess – that's going to get me off this dating site, forever."

Chapter Eight
(Daisy and the limericks)

Thursday April 11th 2014

Do you know what's the worst thing? Today is my birthday. And I miss Jeremy like crazy. I miss his warm hands and his warm arms around me. There is an empty space where he used to lay his head on the pillow. I can reach out and stroke the place where he used to be. But it's the bits I can't touch that bit that ache inside my heart and which are causing me the most trouble.

When Voldemort left, it was the same pain, although that was a pain so gargantuan it was like a bolt of lightning, again and again and again ripping through the core of me. And I wept. When Jeremy left, the lightning bolts started again. Although in truth, it was different because I had been there before. I anticipated their arrival, and I knew they would diminish with time. No human has the right to short circuit your heartstrings for a lifetime. You just have to ride the shock waves until the tornado has passed.

My lovely daughter didn't forget me. My friends texted and reminded me we are celebrating on Sunday. They have arranged a surprise day for me. Where did I ever such an amazing daughter and such lovely friends?

My daughter Imogen is 17. A difficult age, is how people regard it, and roll their eyes to heaven. She's not doing A levels. She – and I too it seems – are doing a catering course. Well, after a fashion. She spends all her time on Facebook, taking photos of what she made for breakfast, lunch and dinner. and posting it on her webpage. And of course anything and everything else in her life goes on the web page too. Her friends know what's happening in our lives before I do! I've told her to be careful, but she just doesn't care. Maybe all young people are truly addicted to Facebook.

I'm similarly obsessed with NOT being on Facebook!

Anyhow, more about Imogen later.

My father phoned.

"You're elusive," he said. "What the Dickens is going on?" He has a deep military voice. He loves me to pieces and thinks I am about four years old.

"Well Dad, I've started Internet Dating."

"Daisy! No! You don't need to be doing that." He's always got an authoritative tone. It does rile me.

"Dad, Dad, it's ok, it's–"

"– No darling. You mustn't be doing that. You can meet awful people." I can hear him tutting.

"Dad!"

"It's not safe is it? These people who do that are peculiar. You hear about it, rapists and murderers and people who just want your money. You have so much going for you–"

"Well they're not peculiar Dad, because I'm one of them!" Do I think I'm peculiar, well perhaps just a fraction ... but that's me, not the Internet Dating.

"You don't need to do that, you -"

"Dad, I'm 53. Today! Where else am I going to meet anyone if I don't do this? My friends are all married or hitched. I work with lots of middle-aged women. I'm certainly not going out with any of my patients!" This is most definitely true.

"It's not safe!"

"Dad, it's perfectly safe. We just email. I have a code name. They don't have my home address or my mobile number or anything!

Don't worry!" The things is, unless people have tried Internet Dating they don't know how it works.

"I just wish you wouldn't do this. I'd like to pay for you to go one of these upmarket London singles clubs. Much better."

"Dad, I'm grown up! I'm doing it. Don't worry!"

"Well. Happy Birthday!"

"Thanks Dad." Somehow that conversation was not very helpful.

My father lives in Norfolk. He loves the flat, country terrain. He plays golf, and walks on the beaches. He retired there to a little village called Holme-next-the-Sea after my mother died five years ago. I really thought it was a mistake for him to do this, after they had lived together in their home in North London for 37 years. But he was adamant that he wanted to spend what was left of his life in the country. And off he went. And ... he's happy and making a success of it. It's just a jolly long drive whenever we want to see each other.

One day, perhaps I'll get Dad to do some online dating? Now there's an idea...

I don't like birthdays. I log on.

Cool Jaguar has sent me a message!

Hi Daisy,

I spent today with my finance director as we are starting a new company. We spent a lot of time going over the business plan and then putting together ideas for the website. We had lunch, and it's been a cold day here. I have two daughters I see regularly and they come most weekends for Sunday lunch.

Look forward to hearing from you

Cool Jag xx

Hmm. Think I might shake him up a little.

Hi Cool Jag,

Did you ever watch Dallas? Business is something I know nothing about, but you remind me of JR Ewing? Do you have a big leather desk and a pot plant? How is the oil business these days?

Love from Sue Ellen

- oops- Daisy!

Philip has sent another message.

Daisy,

Please contact me. We could have so much fun together. I need to see you.

Philip x

I'm going to have to email something soon. It's not fair to him, but what to say?

I have a look around the site. Lots of plonkers.

One profile says *do not reply unless you have naturally slim hips.* I ask you.

Another one says *I don't know why but I am only attracted to women 7–10 years younger than me.*

Extraordinary. Men who think they are so handsome that women ten years younger will fall at their feet.

Some people write, *do not be offended if I don't reply, but I know what I am looking for.*

Again, oil paintings and King's Cross come to mind.

Ah a reply from Love Bug. This is what he said.

Fresh as a Daisy that's who you are,
Me thinks you live a bit too far,

Southampton to Brighton is quite a way,
We couldn't do that every day,
But yes I think you're very pretty,
And I hope you like this little ditty!
Love Bug x

I am enchanted!

In these days of internet heaven,
We can converse 24/7,
We skype and text,
Whatever next,
Don't disregard, don't laugh and snort
As soon, no doubt we"ll teleport!
Daisy xx

And I pressed SEND.

Do you know what suddenly occurred to me, how will I know when I've met the right person? I thought Jeremy was the right person and it took 18 months to find out he wasn't.

I haven't got 18 months to wait, or to waste. I'm 53, my youth is ebbing down the plug hole.

So much wasted time. I just need loving it's a simple as that.

So I thought about it. It's not as simple as clicking on a nice face. It's not as simple as checking you have shared interests. It's not as simple as finding someone who makes you laugh. It's not as simple as shutting your eyes and thinking of England. Somehow there is a magic formula for that perfect someone. If knew what it was, or how to calculate it, I would be the richest person on the planet.

But what I do know, is that when it is right I will know. So what I've done is written a poem, and it's in my handbag. When I meet that person and I'm sure it's him, I will give that person, and only that person, my poem. I don't know if it will be on a first date, or a lot further into the relationship, but I will do it when I feel the time is right. And this is what I have written:

Finding True Love

When I find true love I will know,
By the way you carry your head,
And how your eyes light up to see me enter a room.
Needles of sunlight will grace my path to you,
The breeze will cool my beating heart,
An electric current will course through my limbs.
I will fall into a love with you like falling into quicksand,
Helpless, with no chance of rescue.
I will savour the sensations I feel, like raindrops
Do you feel them too?
For we can create true love only if you drown beside me.
I will breathe your breath,
Inhale you within me,
Grasp your warm hand in mine,
Delight as your strong arms embrace me,
And slip into a delirious heaven.
Come, will you join me?
Daisy xx

Chapter Nine (In which Daisy revisits the Amigos)

Friday April 12th 2014

It's after work and I went to visit the Amigos.

I rang the bell. Amigo 1, answered the door. He was adjusting his hearing aids as he let me in, in preparation for a good natter.

Amigo 2 said "Hello gorgeous," and made the tea.

We sat on the sofa, like three ducks in a row, as was our custom.

"Dating news!" I was desperate to tell them.

"Come on then, what's the latest?" said Amigo 1, intrigued. They were both so curious to hear all about it. I heard myself saying,

"I've met a man who talks in limericks, and a guy who's just like JR Ewing."

"Ah limericks – listen to this! – A wonderful bird is the pelican. His bill can hold more than his belican. He can take in his beak. Food enough for a week. But I'm damned if I see how the helican. What d'you think?" My Amigo always had an answer for anything. Just like that!

He slapped his left knee.

"Ha Ha!" I said. "How can you just come out with that?"

"Oh, there's more where that came from, how about – There was a young girl from Madras (say Madr-arse with the accent on 'ar'). Who had the most beautiful arse. Not rounded and pink. As you probably think. But gray, with long ears and ate grass." He chuckled to himself and again I marvelled at how he can just pull it out of the hat.

"Ok, I get it Ha ha! But are you listening? I have news?" I was impatient to get to the details.

"News of Southfork? We used to watch *Dallas* all those years ago. I think the whole country did! – Who did shoot JR?" said Amigo 1.

To which I replied, "He's an arse – emphasis on arr-se."

"Why, what happened?" asked Amigo 1.

"He messaged me to say *I interest him*, and he has appointments next Wednesday at the Regent's Hotel in the town centre, and he could fit me in between 2 and 3 pm!" I said. I said it rather scathingly.

Maggie, handed me a mug of tea at that point. She always gives me tea in my very own Daisy mug, with daisies on it. "Here's your tea."

Amigo 1 continued, "Doesn't sound good."

"No. I sent back a funny message. I said 'Sue Ellen would like to thank you for the invitation to the Oil Baron's Ball. However, she is uncertain whether to accept!' Ha Ha!"

They laughed, then they started all over again ...

"Well, are you going or aren't you?" asked Amigo 1

"She hasn't decided, that's what she's saying," replied Amigo 2.

"Well she needs to decide, she can't keep him hanging around."

"She won't, will you? She just isn't sure."

"That's not what she said."

"It is what she said."

"No it isn't."

"Yes it is."

"No it isn't."

"Yes it is."

"Come on you two! Well I haven't decided, that's the thing," I interjected.

"You said you had and you weren't going."

"No she didn't."

"Yes she did."

"No she didn't."

"Yes she did."

"Come on you two, I'm thinking about it," I said.

"Don't think too long. He's JR Ewing. You don't know what he might get up to."

"What's happened to the undertaker?" asked Amigo 2.

"I'm getting forlorn messages."

"You heartbreaker!" said Amigo 1.

"I couldn't, I just couldn't."

"But he did have two eyes, a nose and a mouth," she said, laughing.

"Yes and ice-cold hands. Mortuary hands! Oh my God!"

"Narrow escape!"

"Yes, Daisy. Thank goodness he was honest with you. What if you had only found out down the line."

"Imagine, I would have smelt the formaldehyde!

I would have started wondering if he was an axe murderer, dismembering bodies!"

"Can't you find somebody normal on there?" they asked.

It seemed a simple request. Why was it so damned difficult?

I went home and made myself a sandwich. I thought about the internet and how it functions like a great big accordion. You switch it on and fire it up, and there are so many buttons to press, so many choices to be made. If you press the right ones, you make wonderful music.

If you don't know what you're doing, all you get is drivel! You need the skill. You need another accordion player to show you how to hold the damn thing, and how to make it make sweet music.

So I do really need more lessons please!

Internet Dating Lessons.

But they don't exist. I had just better get on and finish this book!

So I went up to the bedroom, and Chris was there, hanging out on the wardrobe.

He's still sat at that piano. Tonight he's practising 'Violet Hill'. As I sink onto the end of my bed, I can hear him singing that if you love someone, you have to tell them! Don't be shy! Come on out with it!

Do you know Chris Martin had singing lessons? It was in the paper. (So it must be true!) But he said he wanted to have singing lessons, "to bring out the best in me".

He is a singer. I'm a writer. Even Chris Martin has had lessons. Everybody – no matter how big and how famous – needs a little help sometimes.

"It's ok," says Chris. "Daisy, just keeeep writing! Your *Paradise* dreams will come true – if you let them. Now go to sleep."

So I tried to do just that. I really, really did.

Chapter Ten (In which Daisy ties up some loose ends)

Friday April 12th 2014

Now it's a Friday, so I log on. I find the weekends are peak times for the lonely hearts. The weekend beckons and the loneliness sets in. I feel it myself now I haven't got Jeremy. He was always here on a Friday.

His motto was "Feed me, and love me, in that order," and for 18 months, that's what I did. I used to always ask him what he would like for supper, at the weekends when he was here, and cook him his favourites. They say food is a way to a man's heart. He took the food and then he stopped loving me. I don't know why, but I need to learn from this, as Dating Daisy.

It's fine to be nice and thoughtful, but it's not fine to become a slave to the other person. That's where I went wrong, and in doing all those things I did because I thought that I loved him. Too much it seems. I lost myself.

Next time, if there is a next time, I need to be more reserved. The thing is, it's just my nature.

Have I told you about the prairie vole? This might be a good time to mention it. The prairie vole is the most monogamous species on the planet. It mates for life, and if it's partner dies, and you put a nice, young, pretty prairie vole in with it, it will eat it.

I think I am a prairie vole.

I guess I have to take steps not to eat my perfect partner, when, if ever, I know who he is.

You know I read something inspirational on the internet today. A lovely boy called Stephen Sutton died recently of bowel cancer aged 19. (Google this yourself?) He was diagnosed when he was 15. How unbelievable is that? And he devoted his life to raising money for the Youth Cancer Trust. He set out to raise £10,000, but he actually raised £5 million! What an inspirational boy. He also managed to achieve a lot of things on his bucket list, like going skydiving, and playing the drums in front of 90,000 people at Wembley. After he died, his mother collected an MBE on his behalf. I just can't stop thinking about this. This is really sad, the saddest thing, worse than any of my problems. And what a fantastic young man. To turn that terrible situation into something so positive. I feel his mother's pain, I really do. I have huge empathy.

I think it's important to take inspiration from the world around you. My mother had bowel cancer but she was in her 70s. She had at least lived a good life. But true stories like Stephen Sutton's just focus the mind. We need to get on and live. Who knows what's round the corner? I want to make sure something purposeful comes from my existence. Maybe an *Internet Dating Manual* is a start? It's helping to spread a little happiness after all!

What I have is hope. Hope that everything will somehow be alright. More than alright. Amazing even. Here's the thing, I read the following quote the other day:

"Hope is not a lottery ticket you can sit on the sofa and clutch, feeling lucky. It is an axe you break down doors with in an emergency."

This is from a novel *Hope in the Dark* by Rebecca Solnit. I think it's a fabulous statement. In this phrase, Rebecca has captured the fact that we are all masters of own destiny. Wishful thinking is impotent. Creativity is the tool to the future.

My 'axe of hope' – in fact it's a large machete – is hacking me through this Internet Dating experience. If I didn't have hope, there's no way

I could continue. So I need to click the cursor, summon fortitude and imagination, and remain very definitely, proactive. It's occurred to me, since reading that, that for me, my life situation at present IS an emergency situation. This 'axe of hope' is my tool to the future.

I'll stay hopeful, don't worry. No hopelessness ... at least not yet.

Guess what – Cool Jaguar has emailed me. What a surprise! Look what he said:

Hi Daisy,

The thing is, I have lots of friends, and business colleagues and associates. I don't need any more of those. What I need is a lover?

Hope you can make the meeting at the Regent's Hotel at 3pm?

Cool Jag (CJ) x

PS: Would love to see more photos. Please send.

I replied:

Dear CJ,

Here's the thing. If you want an oil painting, you can buy one anywhere. And if you want sex, you can buy that in King's Cross. But if you want something out of this world, a soulmate and a truly magical experience, you need a combination of the two, with some personality rolled in for good measure.

I think if we met for coffee, I wouldn't meet your expectations.

I 'm sorry, and wish you well in your search,

Daisy xx

I wanted to put PS: are you a plonker? – but he wouldn't understand.!

Who else is on line? I better reply to Philip

Dear Philip,

I'm so sorry to be writing this to you. You have had an awful time and been through such a lot. But here's the thing. So have I. And I really can't take any more stress at the moment. You seem a very nice guy, but I just can't have a relationship with you. I'm so sorry. I'm happy to send you an email sometimes and see how you are. Please understand, and good luck in your search.

Daisy xx

I pressed SEND. There was – I'm sorry to say – a feeling of instant relief.

I'm sure there is someone for everybody.

He just wasn't for me.

So, I was busy with my emails when I heard the front door slam, and Imogen stomped on in. She came – surprisingly as she usually avoids me – into my little study and threw herself down on the sofa by my desk. She's tall and blonde like me, and just a bit plump, although she wouldn't want me to say so. Its pleasing to me that she doesn't look anything like Voldemort. At least when I look at her, there are no instant reminders.

As she sat down, she must have glimpsed the line-up of internet hopefuls,

"Oh God Mum, you're not Internet Dating are you?!

"Well actually, if you must know, I am."

"Oh my God. It's like – so embarrassing!"

"Well I don't' see why. It's nothing to do with you anyway."

Imogen is doing a catering course, at Brighton College. She says she wants to be a chef. She loves to watch *Saturday Morning Kitchen*, and then to try and copy the recipes.

"Jasmine's father is Internet Dating. What if you went out with him. God, how embarrassing."

"Well I don't know who Jasmine's father is. And it's most unlikely we would both be on the same site so I wouldn't worry about that one."

"I've got to make 24 identical parmesan and prosciutto puffs by Friday," she said looking gloomy. "They have to be all *exactly* the same. That's the thing. It's the stupid piping bag."

"Well I'll help, and we'll practise," I said, I must say with a sinking heart, visions of *x*-dozen batches of parmesan and prosciutto puffs floating in front of me.

"Mine were the worst in the class today. Look I've got a photo." She pulled out her mobile phone.

There was a bedraggled array of various lumps of choux pastry.

"That's great!" I said, as Mum's do. "It'll be fine – just a bit of practice that's all."

I patted her on the knee.

"I don't want you to do this dating" she said suddenly. "What if you find someone. And get married. And they live here. Or we have to move house. What about me?"

"Im!" I said, "Really you don't need to think about that! It's very hard finding someone nice enough to spend the rest of your life with. And it will probably never happen! And if it ever did happen, you would of course be involved and have a say. For goodness sake. Some people internet date for years and never find anyone!"

"Guess it depends if you're too fussy! You won't find Chris Martin on there you know!"

"Sadly I have come to accept that fact! I said. "And what about that boy, Luke? The one who came round last Saturday? Do I need to be worried about him?"

"Mum"" she replied, "He's just a mate. We're not together or anything."

"Oh, ok, is that why his trainers were still in the hall when I came down for breakfast on Sunday morning?" I do worry, like mothers do.

"It's not what you think," she replied defensively. "Don't pry!"

"Well you don't pry either!" I saw my chance.

"Now come on, let's go to shopping. We have some parmesan puffs to make I believe."

I suppose Internet Dating is not just hard for those dating. It affects all those around you. Notably the children.

Chapter Eleven (In which Daisy introduces Jeannie)

Saturday April 13th 2014

It was another night of misery for me. Insomniacs anonymous. Perhaps there is such a website.

Here's the thing, I have tried everything. I go to bed late, well after midnight, tired, usually after several hours of writing Dating Daisy, actually! I don't drink caffeine after about 6 pm. I often have a bath or a hot shower to relax me. I write a list of all the things I have to remember and put it by the bed. I snuggle down. I love clean sheets and a pillow to cuddle. My room is quiet and pitch black, up in the attic. So I lie there waiting for sleep to come. And I wait, and I wait. I turn from my left onto my right side. I try to think of happy things.

I think the problem is that lying in the dark I have a carte blanche to remember Voldemort, and Jeremy. And it doesn't matter which side I lie on, even on my back or my front, those thoughts come trooping in on hobnail boots.

I won't cry. I've done all that, dried myself to a crisp. It's useless. I still have the pain afterwards, except now I also have blotchy face, swollen face and headache. And then I feel even worse.

So I force Voldemort and Jeremy into a box and tie it with string.

Interesting as until I wrote that I hadn't thought of putting them in the same box, but why not. it's a box for wasters. A box for men who don't keep their promises, and let you down. I just hope there won't be many more to go into the very same box.

A Waster's Box

A Waste Box.

Only one place for that.

The Nuffield Household Recycling Centre.

But it's certainly NOT for section signposted Recycling.

Sometimes, after a couple of hours, I get up and go downstairs. The computer is like a magnet and it reels me in, but there isn't anyone online (or at least that I want to talk to) at 4 am!

I make tea, I read my emails, I have a look at the news, the weather forecast, I search for jobs. I write some more of Dating Daisy. Eventually cold and fed up, I go back to bed. My stupid body then has the audacity to let me sleep, wretchedly, in the early hours, such that I am jolted awake by the alarm.

Can it be morning already? I drag myself through the morning ritual of shower, tea, teeth and clothing. Some mornings I don't even get that far and I am wide awake before the alarm goes off. There seems no point lying there just to wait for that annoying tune, so after a while I get up, switch it off and come back downstairs to see what's happened, if anything, in the murky world of Internet Dating.

Now, as I write this, I am beginning to wonder if the dating sites have taken over my mind. Have they caused my common sense to fly out of the window? Maybe it's *because Daisy is dating* – she can't sleep!

If that is true, is the dating really necessary?

Should she take a break?

And now we're back to prairie voles. I know Daisy doesn't have a choice.

It's in the DNA.

So, it's early Saturday morning,

3.37 am to be precise.

Today I have something on, and I'm going to tell you about it.

When my father was in the army, he had a very close relationship with his brigadier, whose name was Lionel.

Lionel was married to Jeanie, and I heard a lot about Lionel and Jeanie, all my life. They were a devoted couple, who sadly never had any children, and I think regarded my father, nearly 20 years younger than Lionel, as the son they never had. They were, so I am told, the first people to see me after I was born. They appeared over the years at my graduation party, and I remember they bought me my first stethoscope. They were at my wedding, and at many family events over the years, notably my father's surprise 70th party, and my parents Golden Wedding celebrations. Now I am all grown up and have children of my own, I can get a sense of what they must have felt, to see my parents enjoying their offspring, when they themselves could not conceive.

Anyway, the story continues. I was very surprised to answer the telephone one day, probably a couple of years ago now, to Jeanie. She and I were not in the habit of chatting. However, she had heard from Dad about the terrible upheaval of my divorce from Voldemort, and she wanted to be supportive.

I must say I wondered how this little old lady, lovely and kind as she was, could possibly understand the pain of divorce after 26 years, when she and Lionel must have been together at least a couple of centuries. So you could have knocked me down with a feather when she said, towards the end of the conversation, "I do know how you feel dear. Lionel, after all, was my second husband."

"You were divorced," I said incredulously.

"Oh yes, "she replied. "I don't talk about it often. My first marriage was a disaster."

"Oh my goodness," I said, voicing my shock out loud.

"We were too young when we married. I was only 19. He was very nice looking, used to take me to all the dances. My father cried the night before my wedding. He knew I was making the biggest mistake of my life but he couldn't make me see that. He was a womaniser, you see."

"Jeanie, I'm so sorry."

"Oh my dear, it's in the past. I never think of it. But when I heard about you I wanted you to know I do have some understanding. You see I moved on. I had to. I met Lionel and we had 62 very happy years, such happy years."

"That's so good to hear."

"Yes, I wouldn't change it for the world. But now he's gone and left me. I say to him every day, why did you have to die and leave me a sad old woman, here all alone. I'm 97 you know. Surely there's no more use for me on the planet."

"Jeanie, don't be silly. Here you are being such a friend to me. Don't say things like that!"

"Well it's the truth, Daisy. And there you are. But nothing I can do about it."

"Jeanie!"

"Now – no more tears! You know I was the first person, after your parents of course, to see you after you were born!"

"I know, you have told me!"

"Have I? Well that makes you special to me."

"And you to me, Jeanie."

"No more tears. Men are not worth it. You will find true love. It will be just round the corner. I did! The rest is history!"

"Jeanie, thank you for ringing me."

"Right-oh dear. I'm always here if you need me. Not much to do now I'm 97!"

So here I am Saturday April 13th 2014. A couple of years have rolled by, and today is the day I am going to meet up with Jeanie. I have been in touch with my dad. A lot. Every day, since this awful business began. And he has been the most amazing father, even though he still thinks I am about four years old. And thinks I am about to be raped and murdered by someone I've met on the internet. (But more about that later.)

Anyhow, Dad said he was going to visit Jeanie in the Sunshine Retirement home where she lives. And wait for this – Jeanie has asked to see me. But, it's so sad.

The reason she he wants to see me, is just the saddest thing. She wants me to read the eulogy at her funeral, as she hasn't got anyone else to ask! Well, of course I will, I said, but I would like to see her alive first! So we're going to see her. The Sunshine Retirement Home is in Dorking so it's quite a drive from here, but Jeanie is special, and 97 now, and lonely, and she's my friend, so of course I am going, but Dad will be there too.

I set off. Today is etched in my mind, as it was this date, last year, that Jeremy dropped his bombshell. We had booked and paid for a holiday, but he suddenly announced he wouldn't be coming on the holiday. He was going power boat racing instead. Actually that's not completely the truth of the matter. We had discussed and agreed the holiday, well in advance, but as usual, it was me who had booked and paid for it, and me who stood to lose about £2000. I have to say, that Jeremy wasn't ungenerous at all. He just didn't have a lot of money, and I wasn't bothered about paying for things like holidays. I think holidays are what we go to work for. But I hadn't realised when we agreed it, that he would ever change his mind and I would lose £2000, and also lose the relationship. It was a sad fact that when push came to shove, he chose a power boat over me.

I could be tearful, but I won't be. (Chris told me not to.) The sat nav does its business and here I am, driving up a sweeping driveway to a beautiful old Georgian manor house. It's now inhabited by 57 elderly residents. Dad is already there. I ring the bell and a member of staff guides me through the corridors to Jeanie's little flatlet. She may be elderly, but she is still basically self-caring. Amazing for 97.

Jeanie is only about 4ft7 in height. And now that nature has taken its toll, she is slightly stooped, and uses a stick for balance. She opens the door to the flat to me in, and I see her peering up at me over the rim of her glasses. She has beautiful white hair in a bun on the back of her neck. She looks so elegant and smart. There is a whiff of camphor and polish as I bend to kiss her.

I give her the flowers I brought, and she seems so pleased. Now I just wish I had spent a bit more money, and bought some that were a bit nicer. Maybe M&S, and not Tesco. But there you are. I don't know how to mention the funeral so think I'd better not. Guess she will raise the subject in good time.

After we have taken Jeanie to the pub for lunch, and after she has told me certain stories ten times over and I have tried to look interested, ten times over, and the rest of the pub has also heard the stories at least ten times as she is also very deaf and tends to shout, we go back to her flat for coffee. She is such a sweetie. She clutches my hand and tells Dad and I, in no uncertain terms, that life is unpredictable, and that she is sure I will find true love round the corner, as she did.

In the flat she makes us tea. She does it all supremely well, but slowly, and properly as older folk do. A tray, a cloth for the tray, the best silver teapot, a water jug, sugar cubes with tongs. We sit to drink tea out of proper bone china cups and saucers. The sofa is made of old brown corduroy, and the cushions are a faded floral with rather grotesque fringing. Guess at 97, you don't think it's worth replacing your cushions.

As she passes the rattling cups I am anxious they will spill. But the moment passes. Now Jeanie has heaved herself to her feet and has pattered off with her stick, telling us she needs to find something important. We drink up obediently and don't ask any questions. Maybe this is going to be about the eulogy. I am a little nervous as it's not an easy conversation to have, especially with someone who is 97.

When Jeanie reappears, she is carrying a small, pale green box.

"This is something I wanted to give you, Daisy," she says. "I wanted your mother to have it, but as she's not with us any longer, I thought I would give it to you." She hands me the box.

I feel instantly embarrassed. I'm not good at receiving presents at the best of times. I am acutely aware of how much this little green box means to her, and how emotional she feels to be parting with it. If I refuse it, I will cause more upset, so I know, however painful, I have to take it. It's the right thing, however hard.

As I open the box, she is telling me about the contents.

"Lionel gave that to me 60 years ago. It's a watch. He wanted me to have a pretty watch to wear with cocktail dresses. He said he had picked it out especially for me. It has two little diamonds on the strap see, and it's very delicate. I have always loved it."

"Jeannie! How can I take this? It's meant so much to you, I feel, very uncomfortable."

"Don't be ridiculous! I never had any children you know. Who else am I going to leave my treasures too? I would very much like you to have it."

In the box is small, elegant, antique silver watch. It has an oval-shaped face, tiny, with little black hands. The strap is made of a black fabric in two woven bands, gathered at various points to give a slightly ruched effect. Adjacent to the watch face are a pair of small diamonds. The watch is held in the case at each end of the strap, by a small pin. It would be tricky to remove it and get it out of the box, so I decide not to do that. I stroke it gently. Jeanie seems pleased with my reaction, which is gentle and respectful.

"I will treasure it, Please know that," I say, looking up at her.

"I know you will," she says.

I don't know whether to close the box, or try to take the watch out of the box, or what to do, and I stand there, I suddenly realise Jeanie is crying. Real tears.

Oh my God. "Jeanie," I put my spare arm around her and I look at Dad helplessly. "Please. Don't cry."

I don't think she can even hear me. "It's all so stupid," she says, loudly, with a sob that tears at my heartstrings.

"He went and left me. A poor old woman. No use to anyone, and just waiting to die."

"Come on Jeanie," says Dad kindly. "Come on."

"I'm ready to go," she says. "I am. I pray every night I just won't wake up in the morning. But he's just not listening!"

I fetch tissues. I try to get her to sit on the sofa but she is glued to the spot. It's horrible seeing an old lady cry, and crying for this reason. Because she wants to die. And what can I say to calm her. I have my arm round her and I am holding quite firmly to her shoulder.

"You can't go anywhere yet," I say, loudly, so she has to hear me. "I need you. And you can't pop off until Dating Daisy finds the right date! Ok?!"

She smiles at me through her tears. I know she will help me if she can.

And 97 years is one hell of a lot of experience.

Chapter Twelve (In which Daisy gets more than she bargained for)

Sunday April 14th 2014

I'm so fed up with my kitchen. I'm going to describe it to you as you wouldn't believe it. This is not in any particular order of annoyance, as it's all annoying. But, here goes ...

Someone painted the units, years ago, with pale green paint, and it's worn off gradually, so the old teak is showing through.

All the cupboard doors are hanging off. Quite literally. With a few of them, I open the door and whole door comes off in my hand. Usually it falls on the work top, or the floor, or my toes. I have learnt when this happens, to step quickly out of the way.

The work tops have been tiled and all the tiles are cracked, the grouting is filthy and much as I have tried to bleach it, it has crumbled and come away.

The oven door is broken and the oven door has to be propped shut with a broom handle.

There is a tiny three-foot high fridge under one of the units, not big enough for one week's shopping.

There is a small circular kitchen sink, that isn't big enough to even wash up a roasting tin.

The ceiling spotlights don't work. One by one they went out. I climbed up to replace them, precariously, but the new bulbs won't work either. I think the fittings must be burnt out? What would I know about electricity?

I always imagined that when we bought this house 20 years ago, at some point we would have a new kitchen. But Voldemort being Voldemort would not spend one penny on the kitchen. He said it was a perfectly good kitchen as it was, and then one day grudgingly, perhaps that I just needed a new oven. It never arrived. One day, I saw red and went to a kitchen shop, agreed a new kitchen plan etc. and paid a £500 deposit. He screamed and shouted, and took me back to the kitchen shop, and stood over me while the poor shop assistant put the money back in our account, and the proposed new kitchen was cancelled. No new kitchen I'm afraid. It has to be said, a Victorian mansion it might be, but we at present, we live in squalor.

It's very difficult to explain to someone, why for example, having a new kitchen makes life just so much more pleasant, but it just does. Oh to have a drawer that doesn't stick, a tap that doesn't drip and an extractor fan that does what it's supposed to. And quietly. If only I could pop down to the local B&Q and order a lovely new kitchen.

But for now,, I have to dream on.

Come on Daisy, it's only a kitchen, says the brain.

So, who's in the Muppet factory today? ... Let's see ...

DDP5

Wackee-J

"Old sea dog seeks mermaid for maritime adventures"

57, divorced, Falmer

82% match (apparently)

You have 16 things in common

Last login today

Here's the thing. He hasn't got a photo!

Now when I started on all this, and that was more than 18 months ago, the first time round, when I met Jeremy, I didn't have a photo on my site either. I felt too embarrassed and self-conscious to do that. I think lots of people feel like that. But read on!

I clicked on someone, a guy who looked nice, and he immediately sent me a message saying "Send photo".

I was a bit annoyed. So I sent a message back saying – which I probably shouldn't have but I did – "You guys are all the same. You are obsessed with body image." and pressed SEND.

He replied "Well, would you have sent me a message, if you hadn't seen my photo?"

And I guess the answer was "touché!"

He is actually absolutely right – I wouldn't.

I know I am drop dead gorgeous – Dating Daisy – practically perfect in every way, but they don't know that! They can't know that!

So, the photo is vital.

And I learned that the hard way. Hence the ordeal right at the beginning putting my photo on the site.

And Mr Wackee-J has committed the sin. No photo! Hmmm!

Mustn't frighten him off. Something gentle?

Dear Mr Wackee-J,

Wacky Daisy-Mae here! Are you really an old sea dog? I have always liked dogs. Oh, and the sea.

Message me?

Daisy xx

PS If you want to chat, I'm sorry, but please can I see your photo?

SEND

Do you know, he messaged me immediately? Like greased lightning! The fastest message service on the net!

Hello Daisy-Mae,

Yes I am a man of the sea. I can't really speak about dogs as I don't have one, but get the joke. Ha Ha!

If you send me your email address, I will email you a picture, off this site?

Wacky-J

Well there you are! So I sent the email address and went to make a cup of tea. As the kettle boils, I am thinking, it's Sunday. I wonder what Dad is doing, and Jeannie, and the Amigos. All of us, getting up to start a new day.

Dad will be plugged into this tranny. He is addicted to Radio 4. Jeannie will be having a word with Lionel. The Amigos will be arguing about whose turn it is to butter the toast, or something equally silly. Malcolm may be stalking round his house with his airgun rifle shooting squirrels, possibly naked.

I won't think about Jeremy. We used to have lie-ins on Sundays. Well, actually, as he used to get up at 5.30 am in the week, he found it quite hard to lie in, but I made him! And if you are thinking, were they *that* sort of lie-ins, well. No they weren't. He wasn't an "early morning sort of person" he told me, so a nice cuddle, head on his shoulder and arm across his chest, was my lot. And then I would actually sleep if you can believe that. Yes really!

I made him breakfast in bed every morning he was with me for 18 months. So I would trot downstairs, fry the bacon, turn the eggs, make toast, and scurry upstairs with it before it got cold. Then, when he had finished eating it, sitting up in bed, I would remove the tray and snuggle into prairie vole position, for maybe an hour or so while we snoozed and before we got up for the day.

When I look at what I have written, I was a bit of a sap wasn't I? I looked after him, and I did it too well. But now, I would love to be making his breakfast and taking it up to him. My friends say it was too one-sided, and that he took me for granted. But I loved having him to look after, and you know what, I was content with that. I was.

I texted Pinky this morning actually, I saw this article on the internet I thought she would find fascinating. "*Man in Middlesborough who had his penis chopped off!*" I read more about this, and in fact, I don't think anyone was charged with the crime. The feeling is, he did it to himself, by what's called autoerotic asphyxiation. Something to do with tying your penis up to increase your sexual pleasure, then letting it go just at the critical moment. Although it sounds like he didn't manage to let his go. The noose round the penis tightened, and the penis ... was amputated! The chap was found wandering up an A-road, somewhere up north, confused and bleeding extensively. He had to be sedated in ITU.

Pinky was shocked, I could tell. But she still managed a joke.

"What's the most insensitive part of the penis?" she texted.

Answer ... "the man!"

Anyway, my tea is made. Time to confront Mr Wacky-J.

I log on to my emails, and there it is, his photo attachment. In fact, there were two photographs, to be completely honest.

I hesitate before I click on the first one. Will I see the man of my dreams? Maybe an Aiden lookalike (from *Sex in the City*) will be looking back at me?

I don't think that when I pressed the button to look at that photo, I realised that I had any expectation as to what it would be. After all, when I look at the men on the site, I call them the muppets, the undateables, they are almost all a load of weirdos, so why should this one I have singled out, be any different?

I guess I had a thought that perhaps he hadn't put a photo of himself on the site, because he was very attractive, and perhaps (Ha Ha!) he wanted someone to get to know him for his amazing personality before they were bamboozled with his charm.

Anyhow, I clicked on the photo and this is what I saw.

Have you ever seen *Crime Watch*, when they show you pictures of wanted paedophiles?

Well this was it. A man in late middle age, thick grey beard covering at least two thirds of the face, round, metal framed glasses perched on his nose, hairy eyebrows, thick hair brushed down over the forehead, flattened against the scalp. He was hunched in front of his computer, non-smiling. His eyes were like two electric drill bits boring into the lens. Presumably a selfie, as it was such a close up.

I shivered, literally. I can only have looked at it for what, a fraction of a second before I shut the attachment as if touching red hot coals. I stared at my computer, as if it had just physically dealt me a punch. That's how it felt.

I really felt unhappy about that picture for some reason. Looking at it made my hair stand on end. But, being the positive 'MAWD' I am, I did open the second picture.

OMG now what did I see.

Even as a Sexual Health guru I am shocked and embarrassed to tell you but here goes.

It was a penis. Large, erect, and through the end of it what I think they call a Prince Albert Ring. He was holding it between finger and thumb, as if trying to restrain it from jumping down the camera. Or perhaps ... well I don't want to think about perhaps – as this I found quite shocking ... it's called *sexting* isn't it!

And sorry guys – but it doesn't do it for me!

Old fashioned may be but I do at least need to know your name.

Talk about decisive.

Then I sprang up, found my handbag and coat, and went for a walk. You just don't know who you will meet when you open yourself to the kamikaze world of Internet Dating.

I walked quickly up the road. Being a Sunday morning, everything was quiet and still. Most people enjoying their lie-ins, the one I just can't have. It gives me no pleasure to be in the bed without Jeremy. When I'm awake, I have to get on asap and get out of it. It's lonelier lying there on my own than getting up.

At least the computer is my friend, although it did just punch me! I guess it would make me a cup of tea if it could. And say sorry.

Most men can't say sorry. Certainly not Voldemort and very rare for Jeremy. I say sorry all the time, probably not because I think I'm wrong, but because I hate to think anything I did or said had caused pain to someone else. Men don't get that. They have to be right on all counts, maybe it's to do with fact they don't have much empathy. I ooze empathy, that's what makes me such a crap doctor as I frequently cry with the patients. But Voldemort and Jeremy, funny how they have become a couple in my mind, they are like blocks of stone.

And there, like a beatific apparition in front of me, is my Amigo. Maggie!

"Heh! Daisy!" said my Amigo. She was genuinely pleased to see me. I felt her arms round me and a great big hug. From nowhere a tear erupted and slid down my cheek. What was I doing with this internet stuff, exposing myself to the paedophiles of society? Was I totally bonkers?

She had been gardening, and she stood in front of me in gum boots and Barbour jacket. Before I knew it, she had taken me inside, and the kettle was on. Amigo 1 is still asleep. It was cosy in the kitchen. I wasn't really crying. It was just water running down my face.

She wanted to know what was wrong. It was hard to explain when I didn't even know myself, but I did know, if I'm honest. I just hated being in this situation.

Whatever did I do that drove Voldemort to do what he did, and then for Jeremy to leave me? That's a question I ask myself over and over again. No answers. I am said to be pretty, witty, amusing, loving and kind. I am generous, thoughtful, creative, hardworking and fun. I get things done. I am a party planner. We had a lovely social life, great holidays, lovely friends, amazing children. I wasn't a gambler, a drug addict, an alcoholic. I wasn't unfaithful. I was the greatest wife and Mum and daughter and friend and lover I could be.

But it wasn't enough.

Voldemort ran off with a simple woman with bulbous eyes and fluffy hair. I always knew Voldemort had no taste. He thought it was funny to play in the local football team in white shorts (tennis), green knee length socks (rugby), an old saggy grey, forlorn, torn and totally disgusting old-as-the-hills-tee-shirt with 'Not Old, Just Antiquated' plastered across the front, an orange quilted body warmer (charity shop methinks) and a knitted balaclava. And he thought he looked presentable. What a complete and utter idiot.

I don't like to hate anyone, but I hate him for the pain he has caused me, my daughter and my friends and family. People say with time that pain will go away but no sign of that so far. I am just very good at keeping the Waste Box tied up in the back of my head. Because of what he did to me, I am now Dating Daisy, but I never wanted to be in this situation. Inside me I am still kicking and screaming. I do know though, that **I have** to do it. I have no choice. It's in the genes.

But I think this Internet Dating thing, brings out all your insecurities. After a divorce, your self-esteem is low, and some aspects of Internet Dating feed on that. If you click on someone who doesn't reply, you feel a pang and you think, what's wrong with me, and it's a negative emotion. And if you inadvertently stumble on a paedophile, that's not very nice either. Apparently 10% of men on dating sites are sex criminals of some sort. It's important for any prospective dater to remember that.

My Amigo poured the tea and passed the tissues.

"Long ago," she told me, "I was like you. We didn't have dating sites then of course, the internet hadn't been invented!"

Believe it or not, at 53, I am old enough to remember that too, although now it seems totally incomprehensible!

"My first husband was womaniser. Oh, and he was so controlling. He wanted me straight home from work."

I sipped my tea and listened hard. There's a lot of good advice out there, if you choose to listen to it.

"If we had an argument, he wouldn't speak to me for two weeks. He would literally pass me on the stairs, blank me if I asked anything, sleep in the spare room. It was awful. I used to cry and cry, but he didn't care. Any tears were wasted on him."

"So what did you argue about?" I asked.

"Well he was very controlling. He wanted me to come straight home from work. We lived in London then and after work I used to want to go and look round the shops, you know, and if I was late, especially if I bought something, like a new dress, he would be so angry." She seemed sad remembering it.

"Why? You were earning, weren't you?" I continued. I knew she had a job, for a handbag company.

"Yes, but he tried to make out I was dressing up for other people. He said awful things to me, like I was a slut, and a whore. Once he slapped me across the face."

"My God!" I was shocked.

"I knew I shouldn't have married him, but I didn't know what to do."

"What did you do?"

"In the end, when he went to work one day, I packed my things, I left a note, and I moved back home with my mum and dad. They were relieved to see me. They knew I was unhappy. In fact, my father couldn't wait to say I told you so!"

"And then you met Malcolm." I knew that part of the story.

"And then I met Malcolm, but I had to live apart from my husband for two years to get a divorce. It wasn't like it is now, and it was very difficult for Malcolm and I. Once we met we just wanted to be together. But you see, I do remember the pain I felt, that I couldn't be good enough for him, in his eyes. That's what I mean."

"Why do women always adopt that position? They say I wasn't good enough, or what did I do wrong? Is it a female thing? Because it's quite possible we did nothing wrong. It's the men who can have the position of not being good enough. We are good, they just don't deserve us." I hate the fact that somehow it's always our fault... when it's very often – not."

"Now you're getting the spirit," she said smiling and pouring me more tea. "The thing is Daisy, you are gorgeous. Quite simply ... you are! And you have so much going for you, your medicine, your writing, your fabulous family, your friends, your ballroom dancing. You're beautiful, bright, creative, funny, generous! Honestly, what more could a man want!" My Amigo is always very complimentary about me. She's so kind. (And she needs new glasses!)

I couldn't meet her gaze. I find it so hard to accept compliments. I hope she's right. *"Listen,"* says the brain, *"listen and start believing."*

"And if you see a 'paedophile' on the internet, just delete him. It's one flick of a button. You just don't have to have anything more to do with him!" She banged her fist on the table when she said this.

"Now tell me, Dating Daisy! What's the latest? What else has been happening?"

I love this bit. The banter with my Amigo about the guys on the site and the happenings.

After a while she fetches her laptop and we log on. She looks at Lexicon of Love, and Cool Jaguar, and Love Bug and Frankie10 and Wacky-J. We giggle about them as they are all very comical in their own ways. There's the undertaker, JR Ewing, Mr Limericks, Mr-I-do-do-casual relationships, and now the paedophile!

Funny it may be, but will Dating Daisy ever find true love?

Perhaps you'd better read on and see...?

Chapter Thirteen (In which Daisy speaks to Lovebug)

Sunday April 14th 2014

It's still Sunday and the day yawns in front of me. The news is, that David Cameron, just back from Brussels, has announced we are to have an EU Referendum. The date will be the 23rd June 2016. He's got plenty of time to prepare for it then! He is backing the 'Remain' campaign, and says he will resign if he loses the vote. The country is in uproar as everyone has to make a decision which way they will vote – remain or leave. That is the big question. This political issue is huge for Britain and will dominate the news indefinitely no doubt. I would hate to be the prime minister. Some decisions are so big, and the repercussions of those decisions so enormous, they are unfathomable. In fact, that is the reason some people believe a decision like this should not be made by giving a vote to the electorate, most of whom do not know enough about the subject to make a proper informed decision.

I think we all feel like tiny cogs in a much bigger wheel, but all utterly useless. What will happen now? Well, we've got two years and a whole lot of hot air to get through before we know the answer to this one.

My referendum is simple, to internet date, or not internet date, that is the question. Remain or leave? I think for now, I choose to remain, Even though it's far from plain sailing.

Back at home, and logged on. Here's a reply from Love Bug

Daisy Daisy,
You drive me crazy,
I'm feeling quite lonely,
Please get on and phone me,
05671234888
I will be waiting,
Don't make it too late!
Love Bug xx
I phone. And this is what he says

"My God it's Daisy!"

"My God, it's the Love Bug!"

"Come on, are you really called Daisy?"

"Are you really called Love Bug?"

"No, it's Jonathon. But Love Bug sounded so much more romantic! And Daisy? Daisymae in fact?"

"Of course. Fresh as a daisy Daisy! Don't you know!"

"So what are you up to, Fresh as Daisy, Daisy?"

"Um, well I just got back from my friend's house. She's called Maggie, although we call each other the Amigos."

"Amigos?"

"Don't ask. It's complicated! How about you?"

"Well, I'm just off to the pub after speaking to you. To meet some mates."

"Is that code for I have a hot date tonight?"

"No, sadly not. I have had a lot of hits though. Women seem to like limericks, strangely enough."

"Did you like mine?"

"Loved them! I have to say Brighton to Southampton is a long way away!"

"Well I have a broomstick and its pretty good at finding its way!"

"What on earth is a gorgeous woman like you doing on the internet?"

"Flattery will get you everywhere! Ok, I'll show me mine if you show me yours! What is a gorgeous man like you doing on the internet?"

"Ok, ok. It's a sad story but are you up for it?"

"Of course, fire away. If you're ok about it. You don't have to tell me anything you don't want to!"

"It's fine, of course I'll tell you. Well I was married for ten years and that fell apart many years ago, so we got divorced and that bit is history. No children thankfully. We were just too young and grew apart. Usual story."

"Hmm Hmm..."

"So then I met and married again, and I was with my second wife for five years. The problem was, she was a lovely lady, but she was an alcoholic. It didn't matter what we said, or what help we got, she just couldn't stop drinking. And when she was drunk, which was pretty much all the time, she was violent and she used to hit me. Anyhow, eventually I moved out. I didn't want to leave her as I thought she would kill herself, but I couldn't take it anymore."

"This is terrible. I'm so sorry."

"So, we divorced, painful as it was, and a few years went by. I work in a hospital, I'm a physiotherapist, and one day, there was a medical admission where I was working that day. It was my second wife, and she had cancer. Bowel cancer. I was so shocked to see her there so ill, and on my ward!

"So I cared for her personally, while she was on the ward, and I felt just so sorry for her. She was on her own, as she had never had much family, and she was suffering. I realised I needed to be with her to the end.

"And then for sort of bureaucratic reasons, because I wasn't her next of kin so I couldn't be really involved in decision making etc., we decided to remarry. So we got married again! On the ward. It was all very sweet and touching.

"The thing is I wanted to take her home to die, but in the end she became so ill she never made it home. But at least she died with me back in her life and holding her hand, and it comforts me. So now you know."

I am feeling very humble at this point. This guy sounds amazing. What a heart-rending experience.

"I don't know what to say," I say. "What an amazing, amazing man you are."

"Oh no, it was her who was amazing. She never complained. She never felt sorry for herself. She was so positive and so dignified. It was a privilege to be able to help her, really."

"Well, how are you now?"

"Fine. I mean as fine as you can be. I miss her, but it was four years ago, and I need to move on. Hence the Internet Dating."

"And how's that going?"

"Yes, I have lots of hits, and it's all been a bit of a blast I guess, but no one special yet. And you?"

"Just a load of idiots really. I can tell you a few stories!"

"Tell me why you're on the internet?"

So I fill him in on Voldemort and Jeremy, but briefly, and as uncompassionately as I can. Being Dating Daisy this probably doesn't come across as brief and uncompassionate but the effort is there. Really. I just have to move on.

"So, you've had a tough time."

"Guess so, but you know what? What doesn't kill you makes you stronger!"

"The thing is Daisy, I think you sound fabulous, but, and here's the but, I just don't think I can do a long-distance relationship. Maybe I should have said that at the beginning, but the thing is I'm always up for chatting and not being rude, and I've enjoyed our chat, really, but broomsticks or not, the distance is a killer. I did try it once before and it just didn't work."

I have to admit I felt a bit despondent at this point. He sounded such a decent guy. The best so far by a long chalk. And what did I say about casting the net wide and Mr Perfect not necessarily being on the doorstep.

Anyhow, I am new to all this, and this may just be a brush off as he doesn't like me. I don't want to beg!

"Well I say, you're obviously far more experienced than me at all this, so if that's what you think, that's what you think. I'm sorry, as you seem so nice!"

"And so do you. You've got a great profile and you're very pretty Daisy! I'm sure you will be falling over yourself with suitors! Just wish I lived nearer!"

And so, after a few pleasantries, we finished the call.

I reflected on it.

It's bedtime and I'm getting ready for another night wrestling with whoever or whatever is up there and stopping me sleeping. It's relentless. And exhausting.

See You Soon. Chris is singing to me. It's a song about long-distance relationships, so he's been there himself. It's very consoling.

"Night, Night Chris."

"Nighty Night, Daisy."

Chapter Fourteen (In which Dr Daisy reflects on her life working a specialist in contraception)

Here's the thing. Many people ask me how, after I qualified in medicine, I chose to become a Contraception Specialist. After all, there are so many varied speciality areas in Medicine. Why didn't I end up as a GP, or a cardiologist, or a cancer specialist? Why did I end up in the niche area that is Contraception and Reproductive Health? In fact, this speciality has only fairly recently become recognised as a specialty, and is still viewed even in the medical profession as a 'Cinderella' specialty.

Here's the thing, many moons ago, about 30 years to be exact, I found myself in a very strange position. On a Monday morning I was doing an infertility clinic and seeing large numbers of women who for a variety of reasons could not get pregnant, or if they did get pregnant, suffered recurrent miscarriages or had obstetric complications, that meant they remained childless. For these patients, this is incredibly painful, and highly emotional, a situation that is really only fully understood by the women themselves going through it. The urge to have children is very strong, and for many women the inability to have children is impossible to bear.

On a Friday, however, I was doing a clinic for women with unplanned pregnancies and requesting an abortion. For these women, the terror of parenthood, at this stage of their lives – being frequently too young, having financial difficulties, being unable to support or nurture a child at this stage of their lives – was immense. Anti-abortion protesters have their own views and I respect that, but, at the end of the day, a lot of women are anti-abortion, until it happens to them. The only person who knows how it really feels is the person standing in those shoes. Not me, not you. It is a personal decision for that woman to make.

So there I was, seeing the infertility patients at one end of the week, and the women requesting abortion at the other. What a strange dichotomy.

And the more of their anguish I experienced, and I was frequently in tears with the patients, the more and more a certain conviction grew inside me.

This is my working motto and I think it in each and every consultation.

'Every Child, a Wanted Child.'

A simple code of practice that would revolutionise the world. Think about the effect that one member of the human species has on our planet. Each individual will both consume the planet's resources, and at the same time, add their share of pollution. We live, we breed, and we die. We make some contribution to society. We pay tax. We claim welfare. Each and every human being on the planet should be here because they have a right to be here, conceived and born into a world as a wanted child. How much less suffering would there be across the globe, if we could just achieve that.

And so ... there are two choices.

Stop having sex ... well who is going to agree to that?

Or, use effective contraception.

Now isn't that a better solution?

So, I vowed to be the best contraception specialist I could be. I accept this all comes down to personal choice, but I believe a lot of women don't really know the facts about all the 15 types of contraception – yes, 15! – so they are slightly suspicious and a little bit afraid. In absolute truth, there is no need for this to be the case. The benefits of using all forms of contraception almost always outweigh any risk of using them. There is a plethora of research to substantiate this. Knowledge is power. Once fully aware of the facts, women can make informed choices. And many women once they have proactively made a good contraceptive choice, will wonder why on earth they didn't do this years earlier. I've seen it many times.

In fact, I believe that if doctors, nurses and health care managers in other branches of medicine took more interest in contraception, there would be innumerable benefits across the board. When there are budget cuts to be made, it's always the local contraceptive services who are top of the list. It's precisely because many health professionals do not give Contraception the priority it deserves, there are so many negative consequences, the most startling obvious and painful of these, is a job lot of unnecessary unplanned pregnancies, and a splurge of sexually transmitted infections.

It's a lottery you see. Imagine yourself, as a woman of reproductive age (the oldest natural pregnancy in the UK is aged 56, so this does equate to about half the female population.) As there is nothing else commercially available for men, apart from condoms or vasectomy, I'm afraid for we women, the action planning most often falls to us!

By the time you realise that you:

- might have,
- OMG have had,
- OMG will be having more,

... sex – with this guy, it's often too late.

The first time we see women in the clinic, is often for emergency appointments. They need to be seen asap for 'emergency contraception', commonly known as the 'morning after pill.' Yes – it's true – many couples use condoms, BUT, this is fraught with problems. Case in point, who saw *Bridget Jones's Baby* recently, where Bridget Jones, and this was *live* on the big cinema screen, used an *out-of-date, eco-dolphin-friendly condom, at 43,* and got pregnant!

The condom does need to be

- **fit for purpose**
- **in-date**
- **applied correctly**
- **removed correctly**

and if all this has taken place, please God it won't burst. In reality however for many women, something goes wrong somewhere along this conveyor belt of activity ...

According to Sexual Health patients, burst condoms are a frequent occurrence. That's despite all the condom training in the world – and believe me our department is full to bursting (no pun intended!) with plastic penile condom demonstrator models. You can't visit our department for an appointment and escape the ten-point condom teach. Teenagers are also taught this in schools, and in Youth Clubs – in fact at every opportunity. But this hasn't changed the fact that condoms seem to burst with alarming frequency. I have removed fragments of burst condom with long handled forceps, from women's vaginas on many occasions, while doing a vaginal examination. Most of the time the women were completely aghast when I held the offending piece of latex in front of them! They had no idea this had happened.

In one survey about one-third of men said they would never disclose a burst condom to their female partner – for fear of upsetting them! This makes the whole situation even more unsettling!

At Silver Mills, we run training courses for GPs and practice nurses in Sexual Health, and at these events, we regularly blow into condoms to inflate them to the size of a small balloon, and then apply a few drops of baby oil.

Guess what! They explode **Wow, Ping, Kboom**!

Yes, you could try this at home!

Why is this happening? It's because you shouldn't use condoms with *oil-based* lubricants. And that's exactly what's taking place out there in your bedrooms! A whole host of baby oil massages, Vaseline-type lubricants, and Yes ... lipstick! (Use your imagination here.) Please note, and this is extremely important, **I am not writing this to discourage couples from using condoms.** I am simply pointing out why a condom won't always prevent a pregnancy, or for that matter an STI ...

... And, that there are more reliable, more effective, much more convenient methods of contraception you could use. So please if you are reading this, and it has made you think, do make an appointment and go and get some good advice. We are keen to encourage women to use Long Acting Reversible Contraception in the UK – so called LARC methods. These are intrauterine devices ('coils'), implants and injections. These are safe to use for the vast majority of women, and have numerous health benefits.

So, the condom burst? – and it wasn't even an *out-of-date, eco-dolphin-friendly condom* – Let's go back to emergency contraception. Thank goodness we have this as an option. This is a pill you can take after unprotected sex that has a pretty good chance of preventing a pregnancy. But – there are rules for prescribing it, there are time limits for taking it – after which it is ineffective – and there is a failure rate (i.e. a pregnancy rate) that no one has really been able to quantify – but could be as high as 2–5%. A better option would always be an emergency copper coil – the intrauterine device or IUD. Any contraception clinic worth its salt will give you the lowdown on this.

Surely it would be better if you weren't in this scary situation in the first place! Easy in hindsight, I guess, But the message is, think ahead because now ...

Imagine this happening to you. You are busy, working, and OMG this sex thing has just happened. Like a lightning bolt. Motherhood could be beckoning. And it most certainly is not on the agenda. What do you have to do now?

You have to google local contraception clinics in your lunch hour, hang on in the never-ending telephone queue at the clinic/GP surgery to try and get that almost impossible, quick appointment. Then you have to get there, perhaps by bus, or get a lift or there's nowhere to park. There's a huge queue in the clinic/surgery so you may have to wait. Sometimes the wait at Silver Mills has been over two hours. Then you may/may not, depending where you go, be seen by someone who is trained in contraception. Extraordinary as it seems, Contraception and Sexual Health is not a mandatory part of GP training in England. A GP chooses to get this training after their generalist training if they want to do so. I find this totally extraordinary.

But going back to the you and your burst condom. It's a fact that many women don't get pregnant from the sex they came to see you about from last night. It's the sex they have tonight or tomorrow night that is the problem. So it's vital that whoever sees you for today's prescription for emergency contraception, discusses the options for longer-term contraception with you, there and then, and gets something started straight away! This is called Quick Start Contraception.

So now, hopefully you've been seen, and you've taken the emergency pill. It's just a question of having to wait two weeks to do a pregnancy test to make sure it's worked! Yes – two weeks! It takes two weeks for a pregnancy test to become positive. Some people find that difficult to understand but it's true. It takes 14 days for the hormones produced in pregnancy by a developing foetus to be detectable in the urine. It's a physiological fact of nature. So … it's a long two weeks!

Going back to the beginning of all this – what did I write earlier about discussing LARC with your local clinic/doctor? Surely this would be far more preferable?

I recall one emergency contraception story. A 50-year-old man brought his 20-year-old girlfriend to the contraception clinic as she needed emergency contraception. They had had sex the night before and the condom split. However, they did say they did want her to become pregnant, but they felt at 50, his sperm was too old, so they wanted to wait until they knew she wasn't pregnant this month, and then his son was going to have sex with her to father the pregnancy. There's something ethically very debatable in that I thought, but not for me to display any emotion. My working role is to be non-judgemental at all times.

So in my long career in Contraception there are many stories I could tell. The subject covers a wide area, from young people/children to the elderly. I've seen young women worried about their periods, too heavy, too painful, too infrequent, too irregular or simply never had any. I've seen women (erroneously) still having 'periods' in their 60s and 70s (really not necessary to have periods in your 60's and 70's on HRT- you should be on a no-bleed regime!). A lot of the time I am seeing women who are using a particular contraceptive method and having problems with it. For example, having abnormal bleeding on the pill, or PMT-type symptoms, or headaches. There is usually a solution for everybody. They just need to come and talk about it.

Sometimes I see women, who want a coil inserted. Sometimes it's women who want their coil removed. The coil as you may know is a device which sits in the womb (known as 'the uterus') and has one or two threads that dangle out of the neck of the womb, ('the cervix'). When a woman wants her coil removed we grab these threads, give them a quick pull, and the coil comes out in the blink of an eye. However women are often referred to the contraception clinic, if for some strange reason the coil threads have got lost, and this makes removal difficult. Lost threads are an uncommon occurrence, but from time to time and for unknown reasons, the threads can migrate up into the cervical canal. With the right experience and the right instruments, we usually manage however to remove these coils in the clinic, without the need for a general anaesthetic. But women are often very scared and may have had a few failed attempts at removal before they get to our clinic.

Going back to the fitting process, when the coil is inserted, it has very long threads that protrude through the cervix and actually right out through the vaginal opening. They need to be cut, usually 2–4 cm, from the cervix, to finish the procedure. Patients are encouraged to come back to clinic after six weeks to have a six week check at which time the threads are checked. I remember seeing one patient many years ago, who came back for a six-week check, and the coil threads were full length and dangling out right through the vagina. She had been scared to touch them. Whoever fitted the coil obviously completely forgot to cut the threads at all, before they let her go home!

I also do implant insertion and removals, especially deep removals, which can again be difficult unless you've had the relevant training and experience.

Here's the thing. If you are fit and healthy, it is most unlikely any contraceptive method will harm you. But if you have any medical conditions, contraception has to be prescribed with care. So a lot of patients referred to our clinic are in this category. Perhaps they have a blood clotting disorder, or a heart condition, or epilepsy and so they need specialist help and guidance.

I love my job and see it as very worthwhile. I guess as we face retirement, it's natural to wonder if we've made some sort of contribution. In the 30 years I've been qualified, I wonder how many unplanned pregnancies I have helped prevent? The answer to this is of course unknown, but when you think about it, I guesstimate I've seen more than 100,000 patients in my lifetime for contraceptive advice and help. So this must add up to a pretty incredible number, during which I have accumulated huge amount of experience.

Every Child a Wanted Child.

I recall a phone call some years ago from a local GP.

"Which coil," she asked me, exasperatedly, "has four threads?"

"There isn't one," I replied.

"Well my patient has a coil in and it has four threads."

"Well, your patient has two coils," I replied.

"She can't have."

"She can! If she wants it removed just pull on all 4, you'll see."

I was right.

The reason for this was that this lady had become pregnant with a coil *in situ*. (The coil is extremely effective but no method is 100% effective and any method can fail occasionally, that has to be remembered.) She had continued with the pregnancy and given birth, but the coil was never retrieved at the delivery. The coil was assumed lost along with the membranes and the placenta. The patient then opted for another coil as a method of contraception. When she came to have this removed to have baby number two, the threads from both coils were now visible! Amazing but true! The message is to always retrieve the coil if this happens at the delivery. (A forgotten coil has been found before, on scanning the uterus when investigating women for infertility purposes, clearly the patient having forgotten they ever had one fitted in the first place!)

Coils are actually pretty marvellous. Did you know there is an interesting history to the development of the coil? Some say that the idea came from Bedouin tribes who inserted stones into a camel's uterus to stop them getting pregnant when they were crossing the desert! In 1909 there followed something called Richter's Ring, which was two loops of silkworm gut sewn onto an aluminium and bronze wire inserted into the womb. In the 1920s, this idea was further developed into the Gräfenberg ring, a ring of silver wire again inserted into the uterus. But I digress ... there is so much I could write here ... suffice it to say that over the past hundred years, technology has led to better, improved devices, that fit more snugly in the uterine cavity, are easier to place and remove and have much less in the way of unacceptable side effects, for example less in the way of painful periods and less irregular bleeding.

The 'Mirena IUS' is a superb device that is impregnated with a small amount of hormone, such that once its inserted, a women's periods usually disappear, or virtually disappear. Please just take it from me, you don't need to have periods to be healthy. This is quite safe. Once the IUS is removed your periods will quickly return. Who wants to bleed once a month when they don't have to?! And yes, it's highly effective, and is actually less likely to fail, than female sterilisation! Yes, you did read that correctly!

I have no idea how many coils I have fitted in my contraceptive lifetime. Literally thousands. I can't recall any where there were serious complications. That's an amazing thing to be able to write, but it's true.

The coil fitting procedure can be an interesting experience. Women are usually nervous, which is quite understandable, as they need to have a vaginal examination, then a speculum inserted (the metal thing like a duck's beak), then a degree of discomfort while the cervix is stretched open a little, or "dilated" in order to get the coil through the cervical canal and on up into the womb cavity itself. Pretty intimate and invasive. So, we do try to be as helpful and supportive and understanding to the patient during the procedure as we can be.

I recall one youngish woman who wanted her copper IUD exchanged for a Mirena IUS. She was probably about 18. She asked if her boyfriend could stay in the room while it was done. Foolishly I agreed to this.

Anyhow, the patient undressed and lay on the couch. I did what I needed to do, and the boyfriend stayed at the top end of the bed. After a few moments I became aware they were kissing. Kissing very noisily, with a lot of wet lip smacking and murmuring going on. It seemed very inappropriate, but I decided, if she was suitably distracted and it wasn't harmful, let them carry on.

The situation did change suddenly however, when he glanced up at me, to see what was going on, just as I held up some long-handled forceps on which there was a blood stained ball of cotton wool.

He promptly fainted. The nurse ran over, as he had bashed his head on the floor rather heavily, still breathing of course!, while I completed the procedure as quickly as I could!

Both of them were fine 20 minutes later. He just had a large lump on the back of his head. But it did put me off having any relatives/ partner in the room, when I'm doing a coil fitting!

Another coil fitting that I recall, was a black African lady called Glory. I had a trainee with me at the time. Now, very rarely patients can collapse at coil fitting with a condition known as cervical shock. It's not a fatal condition, but what we think happens is that tugging on the cervix somehow stimulates the vagus nerve and causes the heart to beat more slowly. As a result, the patient's blood pressure can fall, and they can may pass out, temporarily. It can be very unpleasant and quite nerve-wracking for all concerned, especially the doctor who is in charge of the whole caboodle!

So, I had fitted this coil, no problems at all. I had had a trainee with me observing. The patient was lying on the couch flat for a few minutes recovering. I was called to the room next door to help a nurse colleague in the room next door, with a different patient.

I remember the trainee knocking on the door and saying quietly to me, and in a very unhurried manner I might add, "Excuse me doctor, but can I give your patient some atropine?"

"Atropine!" I was on my feet and back in the original consulting room in a flash. This is an emergency drug we only use extremely rarely in the worst cases of cervical shock.

My patient had suddenly had a vasovagal reaction, and was blue and unconscious!

Now, the first rule of resuscitation – 'ABC, Airway, Breathing Circulation' – is to try to rouse the patient,

So, as I had been trained to do, I grabbed her by the shoulders and shook her, looking into her face for a response – and intermittently glancing up to heaven – which was completely ironic – as I was shouting her name:

"Glory, Glory, Glory!"

It struck me afterwards, when she was sitting up and having a cup of tea, that that in itself, was highly amusing! She was fine by the way. It was however, one of the rare occasions in my working lifetime where I have had to administer the atropine.

More about coils? I had read in medical textbooks that a patient can have their first ever epileptic fit at coil fitting. I didn't believe it, as in my whole contraception career I had never seen it. Until it happened to one of my patients. She had had a history of a *funny turn* with a previous coil, which had been put down to a vasovagal attack (as above.) But with this lady, I inserted the speculum, and as soon as I touched the cervix with the local anaesthetic, she went rigid, and blue around the mouth, then started convulsing. The rigidity is the tonic phase of the fit, when the whole body goes into a tight spasm, teeth clenched, not breathing. She was so rigid it was hard to even get the speculum out of the vagina, which I had to do immediately to be able to turn her on her side. She was fine by the way, but had to have some rectal diazepam and a trip to A&E. She won't be having a coil again in the future.

I also remember a patient who suffered with terrible migraines. She had been to the London Migraine clinic and been recommended a Mirena IUS. So she arrived for a coil fitting appointment, but actually in the throes of a terrible migraine. She was clutching a vomit bowl, and in a lot of pain, but insistent that I fit the coil today, now. It was especially hard for me as when someone has a bad migraine attack they often can't stand the light. They have to lie in a darkened room. So, my mission was to fit the coil – in the dark! I did have a lamp at the vaginal end of the bed, we just had to have the ceiling lights off for the procedure!

On another occasion I was doing a training clinic with a GP in a small coastal seaside town that shall remain nameless. The trainee was doing her best, but the coil just wouldn't pass up through the cervix. The patient was in pain and all was very tense. I was just about to take over the procedure myself when there was a loud knocking on the door. "It's the police," they shouted. "We need you to move your car immediately. You're about to be given a parking ticket!" They obviously didn't know what we were doing as they were rattling on the door handle and quite aggressive. That didn't help me much, as I donned the gloves and finished off quite a tricky procedure. By the way, in the end, we all escaped without any parking tickets!

Implant stories abound as well. The implant is an excellent little device, the size of a matchstick, which you can have inserted just under the skin of the upper arm. It releases a hormone that stops you producing eggs, and is a fabulous contraceptive. It is very simple to insert. And very simple to remove, if it's been inserted properly. If it's been inserted too deeply, it's a whole different ball park. I would recommend you make sure your implant is inserted by someone who has been properly trained and does it regularly. I do see a flow of women who have lost implants. Being a specialist clinic, this is where they are referred, if there is a problem, so to some extent we expect to see them from time to time. In general, you need to be able to feel the implant in the arm to be able to remove it easily. The implant should be just under the skin surface. If they are really 'lost', the next step is an ultrasound to locate the device in the arm, and then remove it, preferably at the same procedure, using a specific technique. If the scan fails to reveal the implant, the patient may well require a CT scan of the arm, and/or a blood test to measure the amount of hormone in the blood. If the blood test is negative, then we know for sure there is no implant present. But this is an expensive test, and the blood is taken by courier to Belgium! So this is only reserved for the trickiest cases!

I just want to take the opportunity to write down the funniest ever contraception story.

I was working in a busy, inner city community contraception clinic, perhaps ten years ago. Certainly at a time when it wasn't at all easy to find an interpreter in an NHS setting. It was a hot summer evening, and the patients were queuing down the road to come in.

I had a trainee with me. I was exhausted and worried about how on earth we were going to get through the clinic or ever get home that night.

It was also a time when because we were cash-strapped, we had a waiting list for coils and implants. We were only allowed to fit so many of these devices a month. It was about three months to wait if you wanted one of these, and we would contact you when your name came to the top of the list. I'm happy to say this is absolutely no longer the case.

Anyhow, a young Chinese woman came into the clinic, and stood in front of me.

She held up her left hand and index finger and said "Wait, wait".

We waited. She then held up a sign that said "I speak mandarin".

This was a nightmare.

"We don't have interpreters here!" I said. "No interpreters. Sorry."

Now what could we do? There was a brief pause.

"Wait, wait" she said, fishing in her bag for her mobile phone. She dialled some numbers, made a call, and when the person on the other end answered, she spoke, presumably in Mandarin, to whoever it was. Then she handed me the phone.

"Hello!" I said, unsure what was going on.

In my ear the person, it was a man's voice, said "I will be interpreter." He had a heavy Chinese accent.

"Oh," I said, "you must be a friend".

"Yes," he said.

"Ok," I continued, "please ask her what she's come to the clinic for today?"

I handed the phone back to the patient.

She listened, then spoke into the phone, and again handed it back to me. I could see this was going to be a very lengthy consultation.

In my ear the other person said, "She would like a contraceptive implant."

My heart sank. How could I explain about the three month waiting list? If we sent her a letter in three months' time to say her name was at the top of the list, she wouldn't even be able to understand it. Plus, I would not only have to do a full medical history, explain all about the implant, all very time consuming, but also try and start some other form of contraception in the clinic today, so that she had contraceptive cover straight away. This would also take a long time. For example, teaching her how to take the contraceptive pill over the phone, by handing the phone backwards and forwards to this friend, it was going to take forever. I was feeling pretty desperate about how long this was going to take and what on earth I could do to sort this out.

I decided I had better just get on with it as fast as I could. So, I said into the phone to the friend who was acting as interpreter, "Please ask her when was the first day of her last period?"

I handed the phone back to her, and she spoke to her friend, again presumably in mandarin. The phone was handed back to me. I put it to my ear, expecting to hear the date of the last period. Imagine my surprise when I heard,

"Two spring rolls and one egg fried rice."

"Pardon," I said, confused.

"Please be quiet," said the voice. "Two spring rolls and one fried rice. I'm taking this order." Then I got it! Something clicked! Our interpreter was working in a Chinese takeaway!

So I had to wait, while he took the order, and eventually came back to the phone to answer my questions.

I was amused to think what the customers in the Chinese Takeaway thought when they were in the shop and listening to the details of my patients' periods!

When commissioning NHS services, these sorts of events are not anticipated by NHS managers! – by the way!

So, what happened next? Well, I knew we had one spare implant that someone hadn't come in to have fitted. Sometimes a woman would put her name on the list for an implant, but by the time we contacted her, she had either moved away, or got one somewhere else, or let's face it, got pregnant! So sometimes we would have a spare implant, and this is what happened. I found one, and after a great, long 'Chinese Takeway' consultation, I fitted the implant.

Eventually the patient left the consulting room. The trainee and I exchanged huge sighs of relief, and I have to say, giggles. We were just writing the notes when there was tap on the door. The Chinese girl had come back into the room, and once again, she had to phone the Chinese takeaway. The phone was handed to me. This is what had happened.

She had come to the clinic with a girlfriend. The friend had seen one of my nursing colleagues, who had put her on the three month waiting list for an implant. In the meantime, after a proper consultation of course, the friend had been given a contraceptive injection that lasts for 12 weeks, to give her contraception until her implant was available. This friend wanted to know how my patient had got an implant while she was being told to wait for three months. – So – I had to explain all about the waiting list and why we had one spare implant available etc … and wait until all this was translated, and then, they finally left.

That one consultation took one hour and a half. Almost the supposed entire length of the clinic!

Chapter Fifteen (All about Daisy and Henry)

Monday April 15th 2014

This was the day I felt despondent. I have to drive to Crawley, near Gatwick Airport on Mondays, as I am training to be able to do ultrasound scanning in early pregnancy, and believe it or not, seemingly the only place in the world I could get this opportunity, was Crawley. So, to get there on time and beat the traffic I get up at 5.30 am, leave the house at 6.15 am and then if I get there early, I get a good space in the car park, wind down the seat, and have a snooze for half an hour. Such is my determination. But I am tired and irritable today, with so little sleep, and no teddy bear to fill the vacancy.

All I can hear on the news today is Brexit, Brexit, Brexit. Already I wish we could listen to something else. Brexit or no Brexit, I've got to find a soulmate.

Learning to scan is a strange experience. There's so much to learn. First you have to know how to switch on and enter all the patient details, as after the scan you have to write a report. It stands to reason then you need to see the patient and understand why they are being scanned. Then you have to able to do it, hold the probe and keep it the right way up!, manage not to squirt the gloopy gel all over your own knees and all over the floor, and then position the probe usually in the vagina so you can actually see an image. It does take a lot of practice to get your eye in. For a long time, I was squinting at the snow storm in front of me and bemused, but now I can pick out the images, or at least after a fashion. What bothers me most now is knowing which buttons to press to measure all the things you can see, namely gestation sacs, and foetal poles and ovaries, for example. It's quite a magical experience peering inside the secret world of the uterus. All is dark and quiet. A little jelly bean lurks there, that has quirky little limb buds and hiccups. Just so incredible. The miracle of human life.

Getting home I start to feel sad, so I ring my friend Wendy.

Wendy by the way is well known for being very up front. No flannel. She tells it how it is. She made me laugh because when she was in hospital for a few nights, not long ago, she phoned her partner George and asked him to bring in her vibrator. She said she was in a four-bedded bay, and all the other women had theirs, and she felt left out!

So Wendy, is completely right on!

She listens.

"Here's the thing, I say, I've paid the money now. I need to find someone on this site."

"No you don't," she says, as always she is much more experienced than me. "You just need to go on a different site."

"Another site! But I've paid BritainonSunday.com for three months."

"Yes but what's it all about Daisy? If you want to meet someone, and you definitely do, what's the issue? You can afford it. Go back on buzz.com. It's where you found Jeremy. It's where I found my George. It's the biggest site."

"Well, I s'pose ..."

"Of course I'm right. Just do it. I'll even pay your first month subscription as a birthday present, how about it?!"

So, I gave in, and I signed in again, to buzz.com

I decided Wendy was right. In for a penny, in for a pound. My mission was clear, and I couldn't afford to fail. The chimps and the prairie voles needed me to succeed. Dating Daisy was too much for the solemn, newspaper reading, grandfatherly, BritainonSunday dating scene. She needed a new outlook. Yes, I was happy with that, and so that is what I did.

I have to say I'm a bit blasé this time. I feel like an old hat at this. I quickly fill in the profile thing, upload the same photo, tick the boxes for what I want from my date.

I press SEND, and I'm on. Now I can search, and what a sea of faces. They come up in front of me like rows and rows of stamps in a stamp album.

You'd think that would be good wouldn't you, and at first glance it seems very hopeful. But when I have adjusted my glasses on my nose, and focussed, and refined my search to within 30 miles of Brighton, what do I see, about another 12 faces.

OMG, what's going on. The muppets, the undateables, they have taken over the planet. Hang on, there's Dumbledore, just a thatch of shoulder-length thick matted hair and beard, the spitting image. Spitting image, I wondered when we'd get to that, as they do resemble a load of 'spitting image puppets'! And hang on, there's even a woman on here. A woman? I assume she's trying to look like a man, but is a lesbian. Maybe not. All a bit baffling really.

There's so many weird photos. Pictures of men cuddling dogs, and holding babies, and swilling pints of beer. And men covered in tattoos, my pet hate, some naked torsos, and most that would look better covered up. One man even has a can of beer in one hand and the other arm around the shoulders of what looks like a female Thai sex worker. Does he think that makes him attractive to most of the women on this site? Some of these photos are in black and white. Probably taken yonks ago, more of that later. Are there any decent men out there? I feel very despondent.

Suddenly I feel a punch in the solar plexus. Jeremy's face flashes up on the site in front of me. It's the very same photo he used to lure me 18 months ago! He hasn't even bothered to change it, especially as he now weighs three stone more!

I see some of the write-up ... "Kids have grown up and moved on now, live by myself now, empty nest and all that" ... Isn't that exactly what he put on the site last time! In fact, heh! It is *exactly the same profile*!

He hasn't bothered to update it at all! The wording is identical. The photograph is identical. Taken of course about ten years earlier. Too lazy to make the changes? Or no imagination to update or describe things differently. Who knows. But actually, as usual, it's not honest.

And it's not true. His younger son lives with him and his older son practically lives there as he's always over for supper, or needing something. I know that those two boys sponge off their father. In fact, one of the reasons we split was because one his sons felt he was spending too much time with me, and not enough time with them! It makes me think again how so many people are just not truthful.

I was told to be wary on the net as people lie. They may lie about small things, and they may lie about big things, but as someone looking for a perfect partner, even a small lie can lead to a big disappointment. Anyhow, I shrug. He is gone. He took the love I had to offer, and he wasted it. It was precious and fragile, now it is wilted and on the breeze. I mustn't be morbid, I have a job to do.

And suddenly, there is Henry.

I see a face that is quite smiley. It is rounded in shape, and the eyes are bright. He is almost bald, but I have to get my head around the fact many middle-aged men are in that category. He is wearing a pink jumper. I have always loved pink, and it's not common for a man to wear a pink jumper.

So I hesitate. I read the profile. He's divorced, no children. He's 6ft tall! All good. He loves cooking, and travelling.

Hang on, it says nursing and medical again – not another medic. Bound to be a disappointment.

And where does he live? In Hastings. Not so far. It's hardly Edinburgh!

I email, and what happens next is a story.

DDP6

Henry is a character who's larger than life. He gets on the phone and I can't get a word in edgeways. He talks, and I listen. I have met my match. It's quite endearing really. I can't work out if he's trying to please me, or whether he is really always like this.

"The thing is, the thing is Daisy, there's someone out there for everybody, right?" He has a Scottish accent which somehow absolutely sends me, although I've never experienced this before.

"Right–"

"So, when you meet the right person, you'll just know. That person will be so special, you'll just click, they'll be so into you. Like, let's think, what would you do for a favourite Saturday night with a date?"

"Um–"

"Go on, tell me!"

"Well, it depends–" It's impossible to get a word in edgeways with Henry.

"I'll tell you. If you were here right now, I'd be cooking you one of my amazing – as I am amazing at it – Italian meals! You would have nice glass of wine, we'd have some music on, we could dance."

"Dance?"

"Dance between courses, you know, a bit of smoozling.

Smoozling?" – Never heard of smoozling but it sounds good.

"Yes, bodies pressed together, that sort of thing. You like that Daisy?"

"Sort of–"

"It's great, just to be that close, just the two of you and no one else, and you can say anything, anything at all and that person won't tell you to shut up, or change the record because he will really understand where you're coming from. Do you like stars Daisy?"

"Yes–"

"I would take you out to look at the stars. I would tell you about the stars, Daisy."

"I don't know much about stars."

"We can learn together. So romantic don't you think?"

"Er, Henry–

"Yes, do you think we should ask each other a few basic questions before we get to – um – smoozling – and stars?"

"Daisy, do you have to be so damn practical?"

"I don't even know what you do for a living."

"I'm a theatre technician. I work in a spinal unit. Now stars. Moon and stars. The moon, that's something else–"

Henry was on the hook, for a few days he was emailing and texting me round the clock. In the end I knew everything from his shoe size to his drug allergies. I had heard chapter and verse about how he and Veronica had gone their separate ways five years earlier, and she had taken him to the cleaners. I knew about his love of Classic FM in the morning and Radio 2 on the way home. I knew he loved DIY and had painted every room in his house himself, even painting the hall stairs and landing where he had hand painted a mural of a Chinese dragon. He loved motor bikes, and Alice Cooper and scrumpy cider, and hated thunderstorms, crap television and football. Yes, crap television, and football. This rang loud bells with me after Jeremy who liked nothing better than to surf the million and one TV channels and find something mindless like crocodile wrestling to watch, or Voldemort who listened to football nonstop either on the TV or the radio. Not with Henry. I had hope.

We texted quite a lot. The texts went something like this:

Ping: Daisy: I have an unexpected teddy bear vacancy, can you apply?

Ping: Henry: I need to read the advert very carefully.

Ping: Daisy: It goes like this. Unexpected teddy bear vacancy has arisen. Must have big, warm embrace and soft paws. Long hours, overtime anticipated, no remuneration but many additional perks. Could you be my teddy bear?

Ping: Henry: Is there a tick box application form? I could tick all those boxes!

My mind was in a whirl. Well a sort of whirl. You see, I liked the image of Henry, as a pink-jumpered, teddy bear substitute, who could cook me amazing Italian food, and smoozle me under the stars. And very knowledgeably by all accounts. And a working in hospital theatres is a very honourable profession. I was impressed by that.

One night he kept me awake nearly all night, my arm ached from holding the phone to my ear and I think I may have dropped off for a bit, while he was talking. He was convinced, we were soulmates. Convinced I would be the love of his life. He had no ties in Hastings he told me, no ties at all, and would happily move to Brighton if that was needed.

This was all moving a bit quickly for me.

Moving in, when we hadn't even met. Wasn't this all moving a tad too fast?

So, we had to do it, meet and make or break. It was as simple as that.

So we agreed the meeting would be half way, in Eastbourne. I would drive, he would go by train, and I would meet him from the station. I recall the fevered anticipation on that day, as I drove to meet him.

I had texted him in the morning

Ping!: Daisy: Henry, top tips for success: no earrings, no tattoos, no designer stubble, no white socks, no trainers, no graffiti and definitely no Morris Dancing!

Ping!: Henry: Understood! I've just selected a shirt I just know you'll love, and I think I look pretty cool. How about you? What are wearing?

Ping!: Daisy: Little black dress. Always a safe bet. But you'll recognise me as I'll be wearing my red coat. A bright red coat.

Ping!: Henry: I'm so excited I can hardly wait. This may be the day I meet the person who will make my life complete! It can't come soon enough. I can't wait to meet you xx

As I drove I couldn't help but think of my first date with Jeremy. Much closer to home and so easy and uncomplicated. I saw his big, blue eyes and the Cupid's arrow was fired. And then I thought about the lies, and the let downs and I tried to think differently about him. He took all my love and he threw it away. I should hate him, but I can't. Hate is a terrifying emotion undeniably reserved for Voldemort.

I suddenly remembered the weekend Jeremy and I had a surprise weekend away - for his birthday – a lobster pot birthday. Because he loved lobsters, and he let it slip he had a secret desire to throw the lobster pots off a real fishing boat and then help haul them back in again, I arranged it, but it was all a big secret.

We travelled down to Padstow together, and stayed at great expense but what the hell, in Rick Stein's at The St Petroc's Hotel. We had supper in Rick Stein's seafood restaurant. Jeremy of course had lobster thermidor. I wore a new red dress, and had my hair up. We walked a little after dinner on the sea front, and he, my gorgeous teddy bear, he cuddled me and told me he loved me. We went back to the hotel. No sex that night as Jeremy had a headache, if I recall correctly. Isn't that usually the woman's prerogative?

Sadly, but in a way fortuitously for me, we had a message to say the lobster fishing scheduled for early Sunday morning was called off due to bad weather. So I didn't miss the luxurious lie-in after all. And a proper breakfast of fresh orange juice, and organic sausages and mushrooms, and homemade bread for the toast.

And then, giggling, we popped over the road to Rick Stein's fish stall, and bought three live lobsters to take home. They were huge. At least 20 inches long, with their spiky antennae waving about. Goodness me are they ugly. And we brought them home in an icebox, for Jeremy's mother, who cooked them for herself and Jeremy for supper that night. Not for me, I hate shellfish of any sort. But I just wanted Jeremy to have something he loved, on his birthday.

Anyhow, I was now driving to meet Henry, this talkative, charming, perfect soulmate who wanted to be my teddy bear, and today Dating Daisy had a date. Nothing was going to get in the way. Jeremy took my love and threw it away. Jeremy is history.

I arrived at the station. The train was due in 20 minutes but it seemed the longest 20 minutes in history. He had texted that he was in the front of the train. I waited in the waiting room as it was very cold that day. I popped in to the ladies to brush my hair and apply a bit more lipstick. What would he think of me, this 53-year-old, Dating Daisy? I was aware that I had my love poem, *Finding True Love,* folded in a an envelope in my hand bag.

Would I, oh would I, in my wildest dreams, be able to give this to Henry?

The train slowed, a whistle blew, the doors opened. A lot of people were moving about, getting on and off the train. I scanned the front of the train for a tall, balding man with a smiley face.

But what was this. A carriage door opened and a man was smiling and walking towards me. But it wasn't, it couldn't be, Henry? I guessed it must be as he was hugging me and grasping my hand. I looked over his left shoulder as he enveloped me on that station platform. I am 5ft8½, and he is shorter than me.

First lie.

Second lie. He didn't look anything like his photo. The picture I had seen must have been a picture of someone else.

This man had had seriously bad acne, and had a very scarred face. Deep craters peppered his rough complexion. In addition, his cheeks had caved in, rather like an old person who has taken out their false teeth. I knew he didn't have any hair, so that was not a surprise, but he was very, very bald. And you know what else? He was wearing a purple and green striped shirt over a pair of tatty jeans, and what had I said? No Morris dancers!

So I stared over his left shoulder as this unknown man was clasping me to him and rubbing his hands up and down my back. I had to come to my senses.

Not here Henry, let's find that pub. I managed to shake him off as we walked towards the car, and I realised I couldn't just drive off, I would have to sit through this lunch that's been arranged, even though I knew instantly, when he stepped off the train, there would never be any spark, at least not on my side.

The lunch for me progressed agonisingly slowly. I had a Caesar salad, and I forgot to ask them not to put anchovies in it. So, of course, it was inedible and I pushed it round the plate. Henry ordered a lasagne and chips, and talked expansively, often with his mouth full, without pausing for breath. I was fairly quiet, not sure how to cope with the disappointment, and the awful drive home. How could I have got this so wrong.

After about an hour, the game was up, all of a sudden. Henry said to me:

"So Daisy, what do you think then? How about it?"

I didn't know what to say.

I decided honesty was the best policy. I looked at this little, scrawny, man, dressed as a Morris Dancer, and I said

"Sorry Henry, I have to be honest. But I'm so sorry. This just isn't doing it for me."

"It's not?!" (Incredulous!)

"No–"

"Wait, listen–"

"Henry, I..."

"Now listen, we're in this together, surely..."

"Henry. Please don't make this any more difficult than it really is."

"But there's nothing wrong with me!"

"There's nothing wrong with you Henry, it's just..."

"No there's really nothing wrong with me."

"No there's nothing wrong with you, it's just, well I'm afraid I don't have the spark!"

We left the restaurant. I paid. The drive back to the station was very awkward, and in the end he said he needed to get some money from the cashpoint so I dropped him off before we actually got there. I suspect he just wanted to get out of the car! And you know what, I really missed Jeremy then, and I drove home, all the way to Brighton, in floods of tears.

After Henry.

I needed some time to lick my wounds. I think it's important to try and learn from my Internet Dating mistakes. And my poem had remained resolutely still, in my handbag. It hadn't moved a muscle.

Internet Dating Lesson

So, here's the thing, I was so hung up on finding someone with a big personality, I had told myself looks were relatively unimportant. But actually, that's not true. For a possible match, they do need to have both, a physical attraction, plus a vibrant personality. I had looked at Henry's photo, you know, the one in the pink jumper, and thought he had a nice face. He wasn't Aiden, or George, or Chris, but he looked ... ok. But when I met him in the flesh ... Same old thing. Again. It was Henry this time, who had posted a dishonest picture of himself on the site.

I need to be more suspicious, less trusting. There are lies everywhere and I open myself to miserable let downs. And I'm not snobbish, or class conscious, but I said my date needs to be educated, be able to converse. Henry was indeed educated, but thinking about it – he did talk, but he talked a lot of bullshit. It was my fault, I should never have let it get that far.

Chapter Sixteen (More tea with the Amigos)

Still Sunday April 15th

The house is freezing again today. I had to call the plumber. Yes, on a Sunday. In fact he can't come until tomorrow anyway so we will have a cold night again, and another night with no hot water. This is beyond a joke.

That night I went to the Amigos. I needed warming up after all! Malcolm let me in, adjusting his hearing aid. Maggie made the tea. We sat on the sofa like three ducks in a row. It was unseasonably cold and Maggie put a rug over my knees. She has always been very motherly to me. She was apologetic as they were having some work done in their kitchen and things were in a bit of a mess.

I told them about the disappointing date with Henry.

"Put it down to experience. You win a few, you lose a few," said wise Amigo 1.

"But why did he pretend he was so tall?" asked Amigo 2.

I replied "Who knows?"

"And the photo? Do you think it was a photo of someone else?" asked Amigo 2.

"I don't know, but it's possible. It was probably just taken a hell of a long time ago," I said.

Amigo 1 looked concerned. He had his hand on his chin. Maggie passed me a plate of biscuits. I took one, absentmindedly as I knew I shouldn't be eating biscuits.

"What I'm thinking is, when you have your next date, quiz them about the photo? It's obviously very important!"

"So sorry Daisy," consoled Amigo 2.

They are such lovely Amigos to me.

"It's ok," I replied." It's just that I'm realising this Internet Dating isn't a quick fix after all. When I met Jeremy, he was the first person I met and we took ourselves off the site the same day, I guess I thought the same thing would happen again. Now I know it isn't going to be like that. It's scary really."

"Listen, the thing is, about Jeremy. You were so low and so vulnerable at the end of your marriage, you probably weren't being choosy. You just thought here's a nice man, I'll just go for it! Now, you are stronger, and you know more what you're looking for!" said Amigo 1.

"Guess that's right. What did I say, no earrings, no tattoos, no designer stubble, no white socks, no trainers, no graffiti and definitely no Morris dancing!"

"It's more than that though isn't it?!" said Amigo 2.

I knew it was definitely about more than that.

"I know, I was being facetious. I want someone who is what Jeremy wasn't. If that's making any sense. He had some lovely qualities, but, he was very steady, not prone to highs and lows of emotion. And he didn't like conversation that was about anything meaningful. If there was anything difficult, he would just say Let's not talk about it as it probably isn't going to happen. Let's watch the TV, and before I knew it he would be entranced by crocodile wrestling. Again!"

"That's it, you see. You love words, you love conversation and communication, and reading, and storytelling. Jeremy, nice man that he was, he didn't bring out your creativity at all. You can do so much better," said wise Amigo 1.

It's funny because I kept thinking how good it was to have a man who liked to talk. With Henry, we had a lot of laughs, like the teddy bear vacancy for example (and I told them that story) but here's the thing. "Your mind can convince you, you like someone very much, when you haven't even met them!" I said.

"That's what's dangerous about the internet, you can't see who you're talking to, and when you are writing you get sort of disinhibited, or at least that's what I would think. I haven't actually done it of course," said Amigo 1.

"I should think not! – but come to think of it Daisy, how would I go about logging on? ... Ha Ha!" That was Amigo 2

"It's not quite like that," I said. "You *can* see their picture – unless they don't put one up of course. And some people don't. It seems silly to me, but some people are so touchy about who sees their face!"

(Maggie! Internet dating?... Watch out!)

So I said, "People of all ages are Internet Dating. I actually had a look for Dad the other night. I put in that I was 70-year-old man looking for women between the ages of 70 and 80. Dad was so embarrassed! But I showed him it was completely anonymous, and the thing is, there were some lovely ladies. Ladies with their own homes. Probably widowed and not badly off. Very smart. They liked gardening and cooking. I said *Dad, Dad look at this one*! But he walked away. Says it's not his scene. But it shows, anyone can do it!"

Back at home there's a smell, oh dear, of burning cakes. OMG! Had I left something on the hob? I flew into the kitchen to see a guilty faced Imogen, and a blackened baking tray, on which sat an array of what appeared to be – lumps of charcoal. The kitchen seemed to be full of smoke.

"Oh Imogen!" I said irritatedly, before I could stop myself.

"Go on, have a go at me," she retorted. "I said I couldn't do it."

"It's not that you couldn't do it," I replied, "It's only a question of using the timer!"

I grabbed the oven gloves and catapulted the whole lot into the kitchen sink. Then I opened the kitchen window. I was trying to collect myself, and not lose my temper

"What happened? Did you forget what was in the oven?"

"No, I was just ..."

"On Facebook! – Probably . . and not concentrating, I know!" It wasn't hard to guess.

"Sit down," I said to her. "I'll make you a nice cup of tea."

"Miss Cunningham will be so cross with me. She doesn't like me any way. I have to take them in, in the morning."

"Well," I said, a lot more brightly than I was feeling, "Come on, we'll just have to make another batch won't we! Come on, where's the recipe?"

After Imogen had stropped off upstairs a few times and been called back down, and after she had completely made me lose my rag as she refused point blank to put her glasses on (hence there was no way she could even read the list of ingredients! Let alone set the timer...), and after I had asked her repeatedly to put down, no, to switch off her bloody mobile phone, and after I had greased the tins, and reset the oven, grated the cheese myself, and stood over her while she tried an innumerable number of times to separate the eggs, and so on ... we finally had a tray of parmesan and prosciutto puffs fit for Miss Cunningham. Imogen of course, took a photo and posted it online straight away.

It became a bit of a late night.

But when I finally limped my way up to my attic bedroom, there was a knock on my door. Imogen.

"Just wanted to say thanks Mum," she said. "You're the best."

"And you know what I said about the dating? I thought about it and do want you to do it. You don't deserve to be lonely. And Dad was a shit to you."

Then she was gone.

No hug, but at least a few kind words.

Chris of course, gave me a wink. He's a parent too.

Chapter Seventeen (In which Daisy gives advice to other internet daters about the art of kissing)

So in this Internet Dating manual … it occurred to me that few practical lessons might be necessary, or amusing, or both. So I wrote these Kissing Tips one night, and made myself laugh. So here they are … take heed! If I ever meet anyone, I might just be able to put this is into practice!

Daisy's Dating Kissing Tips

Now we all know the mesmerising, ephemeral, supercalifragilisticexpialidocious feeling of an amazing kiss.

And kisses just have to **be**.

They do.

The world would be a far worse place without them.

Kisses are recorded in Greek mythology, so they have been around since civilisation began. The world is full of famous kisses. Screen kisses, paintings of kisses, and sculptures of kisses. One kiss uses 146 muscles. You wouldn't think that, would you? That's an awful lot of nerve impulses and muscle fibres contracting just for my mouth to suck yours.

Here's the thing, if you had to describe to an alien what a kiss is, they would probably think you were mad. To fasten your lips on another persons', let's face it, so it's hard to breathe, and then insert your salivary tongue into their oral cavity and wipe it all around theirs, while they do the same to you, is actually pretty disgusting.

And what about the noses? The robotic noses would clink and clunk and fall off. Humans' of course are more malleable, but do get squashed, it has to be said. But kissing really, when you think about it is – disgusting.

Especially, and let's be honest again here, if they've been eating anchovies!

Please no anchovies, any of you out there planning a kiss for dating Daisy?!

So, it's not just the muscles and the saliva then. So, what's in a kiss?

If we put two robot's mouths together, and mechanically put their electronic tongues inside each other's mouths, there would be no physical or emotional reaction, no sensation. So that tells us it's something about the psyche that makes a kiss special. It's about feeling the other person. I suppose the mouth is an intimate place, situated inside the body, and to invite another tongue into your mouth, is only slightly less intrusive than allowing a penis into your vagina.

So, I could go up to any man in the high street and say "S'cuse me sir," grab him firmly and snog the pants off him. Would he like that? He may not resist, as I'm not that bad looking! But the experience will not be a patch on those deep and intimate kisses that I will exchange with my new-found lover (if I find him, ever, somewhere, on the planet?).

How can we guarantee a mind-blowing kissing experience? Come on Daisy, you are the oracle on kissing. You always were, and always have been. Although in your marriage to Voldemort, when the 'kissing nonsense' stopped, remember, love flew out of the window.

You see, in love, we need to kiss as we need to breathe. If we don't kiss, we lose our way. It's simple. So when I find this Mr Perfect I think I might kiss him forever.

But let's get practical. **Dating Daisy's Kissing Tips** ... hmm ...

1. Make sure you love this person, even just a little bit. If you kiss without love it is just a wet fish, flat fish affair.
2. Find somewhere private. Privacy is essential. No one can perform well in the department store window. I like behind the beach huts, don't you? Oh, and there are seven miles of beach huts on Bournemouth seafront.
3. Music is good, very good. Not heavy metal, please, women do prefer romance, so something soothing and melodic. Not "Talk Sport," either, ok?!
4. A little alcoholic refreshment always goes down well, especially mouth to mouth, but that's Advanced Kissing, part 2, so please don't jump the gun!
5. I prefer sitting or lying, to standing, for a kissing session, and my preferred choice is lying on the bed, head on the pillow, totally relaxed, with my fellow kisser stretched out right next to me. (Standing up, you do risk accidentally setting off the fire extinguisher as a member of staff recently discovered in our hospital.)
6. Remember when you are pressed up closely, face to face, you have to have room to manoeuvre! If you rush in and crush your kisser with a ferocious smackeroony, your face ground into hers, noses colliding as they do, she won't be able to move her tongue against yours, and in shock, she may well not be able to breathe, and she will then push you away for air! You of course will assume she is just not that into you, and storm across the floor to grab your coat, go out and slam the door. What was all that about? Incompatibility? – No, it was just about breathing! What a strange turn of events.
7. Be prepared. I love clean men, with clean teeth, and soft, warm lips, and sensuous aftershave. Use all the senses, smell, visual, touch, taste.
8. Breathe the other person in. Let the pheromones do their magic. Drown your body, saturate every last nerve synapse with hormones. This ensures your body is warm, relaxed and sensitive to all your cues.

9. Don't hurry. The best kisses are slow and sensuous.
10. Don't talk. Bobbing up to ask if you can check your lottery numbers halfway through rather spoils the moment. The lottery can wait, these kisses just can't. Even if you won the lottery, all the money in the world could not guarantee an experience like this. Sex, I agree, can come cheap. But sensuous, meaningful love and closeness, cannot be bought for all the tea in China.
11. Hold the other person close to you. Hold them by encircling your arms around them, encircled in love like a warm cocoon. I sometimes like to hold the other person's face towards me, my two hands gently pressing against each cheekbone. It's really quite sensual, I find. But don't dig your nails in, ok? In this way, I can get the mouth to mouth angle, about 62 degrees should do it, just perfectly, and judge the manoeuvring distances better. I think I copied this technique from an old black and white movie I saw in childhood. I watched the screen stars kiss for about 30 seconds ... and then I said to my mother "When I'm all growed up, I want to be a kisser." So here I am. All *growed up,* and very definitely a kisser. Just a mere mortal fulfilling a lifetime ambition, if anyone is listening up there?!
12. Feel their body pressed to yours. Feel the length of the body, including the knobbly bits. It's ok to do this, really. There's nothing perverted in that. Believe me, the erection is the biggest compliment.
13. Close your eyes. You can't kiss seductively with eyes wide open. It's a biological impossibility, so just don't, ok? If the Tsunami arrives, eyes open or eyes closed, you've had it, so just fall into the delicious darkness of the soul.
14. Run your tongue over their teeth, explore their mouth. Kiss the lips, the jaw, the tongue and everything on the homunculus. Allow the joy of sensation to quiver through your limbs and down the length of your spine. It's a bit like going up in an elevator but leaving your stomach on the ground floor.

15. Come up for air every now and then, but not for too long, the longest, closest, sexiest kisses are continuous, not interspersed with "Do you fancy another half of cider?" or "Anyone got any pork scratchings?"
16. Tell your kissing mate what you feel. Now don't be shy. You can say "You're an AMAZING kisser," and they will be flattered and kiss on and on. People need positive feedback. It's a fact.
17. If it's not a good kiss, ask yourself why not...
    - *Is it the yellow sheep's teeth, or the cardigan that's the problem? If you can, tell them to visit the dentist, or advise a bit of wardrobe refurbishment, believe me, they will thank you in the future.*
    - *Is it because you should never have kissed them in the first place, because, you just didn't love them? Probably this is the mistake most people make. If you can't even say I love you a little, you really shouldn't be kissing at this stage. It's bound to fail.*
    - *Or is that silent killer, the pheromones. These, as I have mentioned, are something we can do nothing about. Invisible chemicals we all exude naturally, but ate totally unaware of.*
18. Don't slobber. Just don't. Swallow the saliva, ok? Watching a kisser wipe their mouth on the back of the hand or the jumper is revolting and such a turn off.
19. Breathe, breathe heavily, Pant if you need to, but listen here, **not** so much you need to re-breathe in a paper bag! It may depend on how long you have waited for this kiss. The more anticipation, the greater the anxiety. Will it be good, will it be ok, will it be heaven, will it be hell, will he go off me after, will she go off me after, what happens next, kiss, kiss, kiss ... then sex, sex, sex ... so kisses can be scary! Don't let them be. You can set the rules beforehand: Look whatsit, whatever the name is, I really like you and I will kiss you, BUT, and here's the but, I'm not ready to have sex with you. So it doesn't matter about your knobbly bits, I'm just not doing that tonight. Ok? They will be surprised you are so up front, and may then seem a little timid, but with complete abandon, you now have permission to snog them for England! Oh joy!

20. So, I've reached point 20. I didn't know when I started putting this on paper, that could be 20 points about kissing but there are. This last point is so vital I'm ashamed I have to write it, but I do. So listen, this is the bottom line, and it doesn't get more important than this. Listen guys. Tell the girl you love her. She needs to hear it. If you love her, just do it, Ok. End of. There are too many mixed messages and misunderstandings, rejoice in it, and then you can kiss some more. No I Love You's? – And you, mate, are missing out on one hell of an opportunity!

Chapter Eighteen (In which Dating Daisy has some blueskythinking)

Tuesday April 17th 2014

Today is a work day. Life in the clinic is so unpredictable and some of the stories so funny. I thought I would tell you a story and here it goes:

So here we go. Another day. Another dollar.

This made me laugh.

A 45-year-old lady came to see me asking for a hormone coil to be fitted. This coil –the previously mentioned Mirena IUS – is a brilliant way of controlling heavy menstrual bleeding, as well as providing fabulous contraception. They are very popular just now. (Go and discuss it with your doctor when you've finished reading this book!)

Anyhow, my patient spoke good English but had a foreign accent, I think she was Polish, and did seem a little peculiar. (Not because she was Polish! Just because she was peculiar!) Later I wondered if she was, or had been, a drug addict. Anyhow my job was to assess her period problems and fit this hormone coil for her. The coil by the way, has to be inserted right up through the vagina and on up into pelvis, to a final resting place up inside the womb itself.

So I explained that in view of her bleeding pattern she should have an ultrasound scan first, to check for any abnormalities and look for example at the thickness of the womb lining etc. We agreed I would see her again after the scan, to discuss the scan findings and if all was well, I would then fit the coil.

Anyhow, about two weeks later, this same lady came to the clinic again. She seemed a bit vague, and hadn't been for her scan as she lost the appointment details and forgot. She assured me everything would be fine, she didn't care about the scan, she just wanted to have the coil fitted today, and be on her way.

Exasperated, as doctors often find themselves, I explained that we get much better pictures of the womb and the lining of the womb when a coil is *not* present. Ideally the scan should come **before** the coil is fitted. However, there was obviously a degree of urgency about this for her, and she did also need contraception. In the end we agreed I would fit the coil that day, but she would definitely have the scan in the next couple of weeks, after today's fitting.

I did say to her clearly "I will have to do an internal examination before I fit the coil. That means me putting two fingers into the vagina and feeling around your pelvis to assess the size and position of your womb."

She nodded.

"And if I find anything that means I can't go ahead and fit the coil today, please bear with me. If I do find anything I'm not happy about, we won't be able to do this for you today."

I had a trainee with me in the clinic, who was watching on in amused silence.

So the patient undressed and lay on the examination couch. We also had a Health Care Assistant (HCA) with us in the room.

I washed my hands, put on some examination gloves, obtained consent and then performed my pelvic examination.

Oh No! ... Now I've done a lorry load of pelvic examinations in my lifetime ... and Something was clearly not right here? ... I felt something hard and rubbery on my fingertips ... what on earth was this?

"There's something in here!" I said ... bemused.

"Really?" she said. "What do you mean?"

"There's something in there!"

"What do you mean? ..."

I fiddled and twiddled and pulled. Suddenly, into my gloved hand, out popped, what I immediately recognised to be, a cervical cap. It was covered with old menstrual blood.

"What's this?" I said, holding it up in front of her.

"Oh my God!" she said "It's my old cap. I put it in there two weeks ago to help control my bleeding, and I forgot it was in there! I should have told you! I'm so sorry, I just forgot!"

"No problem" I said, as the HCA stepped forward with a sterile dish.

"We'll clean this up and give it back to you." This was indeed a moment of utter professionalism because a two-week-old cap filled with stale blood is a pretty revolting sight and accompanied by a very revolting aroma. The trainee quietly moved to one side and opened the window.

"Well," I said "It's not a big problem, it's just that I can't fit your coil today, as the vagina is full of old blood. There 's too high a risk of infection."

"Oh dear. So do I need antibiotics?"

"No" I replied, "You just need a bath." (Then I wondered if that had sounded a bit rude.)

So the patient got dressed and went home, and I chuckled to myself, as that was all totally unexpected and quite extraordinary really. Who could forget they had a cap in for two weeks? Very strange.

So ... the story progressed, as about two weeks later this lady came back again to clinic.

This time she was extremely insistent that she wanted the coil fitting done that day. She had still not had the scan, as she hadn't got round to going for the appointment. I was exasperated.

So we had the same conversation and I tried to get her to understand that the scan was important. There are lots of causes of heavy menstrual bleeding, mostly not serious and usually treatable, but it was important for her to have the test.

She agreed she would definitely have it done, but please, please would I fit the coil today.

I reluctantly agreed, but as before I did say to her clearly "I will have to do an internal examination before I fit the coil. That means me putting two fingers into the vagina and feeling around your pelvis to assess the size and position of your womb.

And she nodded.

"And if I find anything that means I can't go ahead and fit the coil today, please bear with me. If I do find anything I'm not happy about, we won't be able to do this today"

Again, I had a trainee with me that day, (a different one) who was watching on in an amused silence.

So the patient undressed and lay on the examination couch. We also had the same HCA with us that day, as at the previous visit.

I washed my hands, put on some examination gloves, obtained consent and performed my pelvic examination.

Oh no!... Now I've done a wagon load of pelvic examinations in my lifetime ... and something was clearly not right here? ... this time, I felt something hard and strangely metallic on my fingertips ... What on earth was this?

"There's something in here!" I said ... bemused.

"Really?" she said. "What do you mean there's something in there?!"

"What do you mean? ..."

I fiddled and twiddled and pulled. Suddenly, into my gloved hand, out popped, a round silver ring, a bit like an oversized nut for a bolt. It was covered with old menstrual blood.

"What's this?" I said, holding it up in front of her.

"Oh my God!" she said "It's the ring from my shower head. How could I have gotten that up there? Oh, how embarrassing!

"No problem" I said, as the HCA stepped forward with a sterile dish.

"We had better clean this up and get it back to you, or you will need to buy a new shower head!"

The mind boggled at the thought of what she must have been doing, as the washer is from the handle end of the shower head, not the actual shower head itself. I had never imagined anyone using a shower nozzle, upside down, as a type of vibrator. (Was this what she kept so closely guarded in the Mary Poppin's carpet bag!)

I have to say it's very rare in medicine to find any untoward objects in a woman's vagina.

I once pulled out a chocolate condom, intact! And we've all dealt with forgotten tampons (once smelt, never forgotten! But to find two forgotten objects in anyone's vagina, and in quick succession, is something I have never heard of in any medical circles!

So it's been a hell of a day. The house is cold as usual. I give the boiler a good kick. I am delighted to throw off my shoes, make a large mug of tea and log on. I had a feeling of trepidation as I felt I hadn't heard the last of Henry.

And I hadn't. Henry has emailed.

Dear Daisy,

I am so wounded by your rejection. I don't know what to say. So much of what we said before we met made perfect sense. I was ready for anything, would have even moved to Bournemouth for you. You really know how to make a guy feel bad about himself don't you. Anyhow, whoever gets you is a lucky man, and all I can say is sorry it didn't work out. I really am.

Love from

Henry (who wanted the teddy bear vacancy very badly). xx

Later I wrote back.

Dear Henry,

What can I say. The meeting was a gamble and sadly it didn't pay off. I am really sorry. We did get on every well I agree, but when we met, for whatever reason I'm so sorry, but I just knew it wasn't to be. I do wish you success in your search of course, and am so sorry it can't be any different.

Daisy x

SEND

I tried not to think about Henry, as I searched online. What was happening on the dating scene today?

On the BritainonSunday site, the muppets were sleeping. No messages, no new fans and nothing to report. The homepage stared back at me. I did the quick search and there was nothing there to interest me. Time to look at buzz.com.

Now here's a guy that looks promising. **Blueskythinking**, that's his name? I like the name. It's dreamy, like me! The photo is always what first attracts you to the person. It just is. I've written about that already. No photo, no messaging. It's one of my rules. And after all I've had to put my photo on there, why shouldn't they?

This is a photo of a man who looks tall, but is squatting down on his haunches, hands resting across his thighs and clasped in the middle. He is laughing. I always wonder who took the picture, where and why. He has dark hair, quite presentable really, perhaps a little thin on top but still, more hair than many middle-aged men. It's all there, the two eyes, two ears a nose and a mouth, and no obvious Daisy dislikes. He looks fun, someone I could talk to.

There are two other photos. In one he is sporting a backpack, and walking along what looks like a mountain track. It's a sideways shot taken to show the steep drop behind him and the long way he has climbed. Was it taken in the UK, or abroad? I wonder if he likes foreign travel. The next is a picture taken along the side of a yacht. The yacht must be in full sail and is leaning to the port side, the shot being on the starboard side, and there is spray as the contours of the boat cut through the water. He is not in this picture, but I guess he put it in to show he loves sailing. And the third shot is of a black Labrador, sprawled on all fours in front of a log fire.

I read on ... divorced ... 6ft ... professional career... a son and a daughter... likes sailing, walking and ballroom dancing.

Dancing!

Hmm – someone who likes ballroom dancing. I don't believe it ...

DDP7

Now one thing I haven't written much about so far is dancing. Voldemort and I did ballroom dancing for seven years. We loved it. We started on a dance holiday for beginners, where, as the teacher put it, we assumed no one had ever danced a step. In five days we learnt the basic steps to six dances.

One of the cleverest things the dance teacher taught us, was how to recognise which tune is which. For example, you are sitting round the dance floor, and the music starts, and you grab your partner and rush onto the floor to do a nice little quickstep – only it's not a quickstep – it's a waltz.

So you quickstep – trying to keep to time to the wrong dance which makes you both look even more like the funky chicken you are doing already, and dance right into the waltzing couple dancing next to you.

"So sorry!" you shout over the music as the startled couple brush themselves off and get back into hold, visibly irritated. And with a nod and a count, you both career off in quickstep. Unwittingly to do the same again.

Kamikaze dancers!

So you see, you do have to be able to name that tune!

So, if you count along to the music, slow, slow, quick, quick, slow, you will see you can recognise the difference between a quickstep and a waltz, which of course, is 1,2,3 – 1,2,3.

And the cha cha cha folks is 1, 2, cha, cha, cha, 3, 4, cha,cha,cha. If you are dancer you will know this.

When Voldemort and I finished (and what a relief it was the day he finally packed a bag and left the house), amongst everything else I lost that day, I lost my dance partner.

And here, is a man, who dances. This is a good omen, perhaps? A very good omen. He might be a very good dancer, better than Voldemort who was frankly conceited and had ideas above his station. (He never could remember the 'run round the corner' and let me down every time). It would be so lovely to find someone who dances. Is it possible?

I send an email:

Dear Blueskythinking,

Is your blue sky like my blue sky? A great blue sky day for growing daisies? Message me?

Daisy xx

SEND

And I sit back and wait. It doesn't take long. But the time I have boiled the kettle and gone for a pee he has answered. He's on the hook.

Hi Daisy

I hope your blue sky is my blue sky too! Thanks for contacting me. I'm not great at email so can we speak on the phone? Send me your mobile number?

Robert

Robert. Nice name. Not particularly original or inventive but nice. Famous Robert's flash before me. Robert Redford? Robert (Robbie) Williams? Robert Pattinson?

I could go for Robert.

I make more tea and force myself not to ping back an instant reply. That looks too keen. Make them wait. – Oh, at least ten minutes!

And then I ping back the number, and as if by magic my mobile phone is trilling seconds later. Isn't the internet marvellous. It's just a "Dial-a boyfriend" service really.

Hello I say, in my most beguiling voice

"Daisy?"

"Robert?"

"... Call me Rob."

"Ok ... Rob." Giggle.

"... Thanks for your email."

"... and thanks for yours."

Stilted silence and then.

We both talk at once.

We both stop at once.

We both say "after you".

We both giggle.

"I'll go first," I say. "So, tell me a bit about yourself."

"Not a lot to tell if you saw my profile? I work for a brewery, and I travel around the south of England selling contracts to pubs and clubs."

"Um..."

"And I'm divorced, about six years ago. After 22 years. Just one of those things. I have two children as you saw, they live with their mum but I see a lot of them. They're just down the road."

"Looks like you sail?"

"Yup, I have a little sailing boat. Down in the Marina. I race at weekends when I can get crew that is. Had quite a good year this year. Do you sail?"

(Here's the thing, Jeremy and I went to Croatia flotilla sailing last year and I loved it. He can sail, not me, but as I was the only crew, I just had to get on and do what I was told. Should I mention that? I decide I will.) So I tell him. He sounds impressed.

"So, I can get you down here on a Saturday to crew for me, can I?"

"Maybe, you just never know."

(In fact, crewing in England, in the winter is not something I would remotely entertain but I'm not saying that now!)

"Tell me about you."

"Well, you've read my profile? I'm a doctor, that's the thing. Not that it matters, but yes I am, and I work in a Sexual Health department..." So I go through the usual patter. Here's the thing, they love it.

For some reason when they hear I'm a doctor it's a turn on, no idea why. Perhaps they have a fantasy of passionate sex with a woman in a white coat, a stethoscope dangling round her neck, and high heeled shoes. Now I'm not a prude, but if you are reading this, sorry to disappoint you, but that is not my style.

"Sounds really interesting. Why on earth is someone like you Internet Dating? Oh, and is your name really Daisy by the way?"

"Long story. My ex-husband ran off with someone else. Not an original story. Anyhow, I'm as over it. And yes of course, I'm Daisy. Fresh as a daisy, Daisy! "

"Look, I'd really like to meet you. I just know that, and I've got to go to work now! It is only eight o'clock in the morning! "

"Oops! I don't sleep. I do my best Internet Dating searches in the early hours of the morning!"

"Can we meet for a drink tonight? What time? Where?"

So we fixed it. Eight pm at the Ladybird pub.

Just like that.

Another hot date for Dating Daisy.

Chapter Nineteen (In which Dating Daisy reflects on being FREE)

Tuesday April 17th 2014

After that I got to thinking, about what I said earlier. About the enormous, unbelievable, intense feeling of relief, when Voldemort finally left.

The night he left, we had spent several hours, him in the conservatory and myself in the lounge. If I tried to go and speak to Voldemort myself, I just burst into uncontrollable tears. I was also so lost, and so angry, I then found myself hitting him with my fists, beating him on the chest, (me – Daisy!, who can't kill a wasp! – and hasn't got an aggressive bone in her body!), for doing all this to me and to Imogen.

I didn't know then about the affair, you see. He hotly denied there was anybody else, and I just couldn't understand what was happening. We had been married 26 years, and I had always trusted him, and, stupidly I suppose, it never occurred to me he might be lying about this. I was confronted with this man I didn't recognise, behaving incomprehensibly, and was completely unable to get a handle on why all this was happening. It didn't make sense. I had always been a brilliant, hardworking, loyal wife and mother, and nothing had changed, so why? I was completely bewildered by these events.

But that night we kept coming back to the fact that we could not resolve this. And if we couldn't resolve it, and we had tried for a year, wasn't it time he moved out. We –Imogen and I – needed space. It wasn't fair on any of us, a decision just had to be made. The atmosphere in the house was like a poisonous gas cloud before a major volcanic eruption. Totally unbearable for us all. Something had to change or we would have ended up killing each other, quite literally.

In the end, just before midnight and several hours after this particular scene had erupted, Voldemort finally went and found a blow-up mattress from the hall cupboard, a duvet and pillow, and then he walked out of the house, with a hastily packed suitcase. I screamed, I screamed and I screamed. Imogen got into bed with me and hugged me tightly as I cried and cried and cried.

We both slept in the end, and when I woke up, although the tears started again the very moment I opened my eyes, a little blossom of a comforting thought fluttered into my mind and settled there, right where I couldn't fail to see it.

I knew then, that that was the first day of the rest of my Voldemort free life. A better life, free of the stultifying, angry, irritable person that had tainted our lives for so long. No more Voldemort, and a new life where I could unfurl my wings and one day learn to fly again.

So, in the days that followed I began to compile a list of benefits of life without Voldemort. And here they are, in no uncertain order, but as they occurred to me today. I'm writing them in this book, as I now see these as very funny! I thought you the reader, might find them amusing.

I stood in front of his wine collection that day. As you can imagine, as someone who wouldn't pay £2.50 for a cup of tea, Voldemort was hardly a person who would invest expensively in vintage wine.

But we had had our fair share of cases of wine from grateful clients, and the odd nice bottle of something usually at a Christmas or as an anniversary present. I spotted a few bottles such as Veuve Clicquot, Moët and Chandon, and a couple of bottles of good Barolo for example. All thick with dust of course.

I'll drink those I thought.

And over the following months…

I did.

One of the things that happens when you live with someone for nearly 30 years is that you get used to their annoying little habits. Or do you? There are a lot of things I could write here, but one of the most irritating things about life with Voldemort was this. Every morning he would stand looking out of the bedroom window after his shower, wrapped in a towel, and clean his ears out with two small pieces of cotton wool. He would screw them up and use his little finger to revolve around the inner part of each ear. When he was finished, he would deposit these two little bits of ear-stained cotton-wool on my chest of drawers. Then get dressed and go to work. Seemingly, it was beneath him to ever physically put these in the bin. I rejoiced in the fact that never again would I have to clean up after Voldemorts' dirty ears.

Result!

He also had this addiction to a Radio Sports Programme called *Live Sport.* This is one of those programmes that can only be described as a drone. On and on in a relentless monotone it was hard to tell if the commentary had changed from football to horse racing. I'm not tolerant about sports commentaries at the best of times. You have to see it to believe it. But the fact this was 24/7 was so annoying. I would switch the radio off at the slightest opportunity. Then he would switch it on again, and this time even louder. It was like living with some form of torture. From now on, we could have peace and quiet, or Chris Martin. Again, result!

And do you know, standing there that morning, looking down the garden, I realised that I would now have a second set of chest of drawers and another half a wardrobe, all to myself. He would take his revolting out of date, charity shop, antique and falling apart clothing away, very soon if I had anything to do about it, and I would be able to use all that space for me. So you see, whoopee, separation and divorce have their finer points to be sure!

This brings me to the next thing on my list. Voldemort was always sneering and rude if I bought my own clothes anywhere other than a charity shop. So I had relatively few nice things. Now, I could shop as I wished, with no one to ridicule me. So I went on to do just that. Soon after he moved out, I quite literally took ALL my clothes TO the charity shop, and deposited them there. Then, I took a large suitcase to John Lewis and bought myself a whole new wardrobe. It was marvellous. And that was before the divorce settlement was finalised, so guess who was still paying!

It was also a great opportunity for me, at last, to *throw away his rubbish.* The stained tee shirts, the odd socks, one orange and one green football sock come to mind. (Yes, he used to wear them together thinking it was all very funny.) His slippers, each full of holes, in fact all the crap that he just wouldn't throw away.

Voldemort, you see, is a hoarder, just like the weirdos you see on TV who live in houses full of piles of newspapers and rat poo. He won't throw anything away so we accumulated clutter, and more clutter for 26 years, which I did my best to manage (newspapers maybe, but I assure you no rat poo here!). Thank God! Now I can actually get on and declutter. At last!

There's something else that has just sprung to mind too. No Tour de France hysteria. Zippee. Every summer the world would stop turning as he rushed in from work, where the kids were happily ensconced in front of the TV, and without a by your leave, he would instantly switch the TV to the Tour de France. There would be a lot of loud protestation and shouting. (Good grief would he let them do that to him? I think not!) But he would be hysterical, fanatical about it, breathless, squatting on the edge of the sofa, talking loudly to anyone but no one is listening, and talking of course over the commentator so he was actually not listening to the programme either, clutching the remote to his chest, seemingly obsessed by this imperative need to watch every minute of the Tour de France TV coverage, or maybe the world will stop turning. It's the hysterical attitude about that that really irritated me. He could after all, have recorded it and watched it later, without kids and without interruption, if he wanted to see the whole thing so desperately minute for minute, but no, it had to be World War Three.

All this, very definitely something I don't miss one little bit.

I have also suddenly realised, I can have coffee in Costa, without having to face the music afterwards. As I've already said in this book, for my entire married life, he would never allow me to go and have a coffee/tea, in a coffee shop. He said he wasn't paying anyone £2.50 for a cup of hot water and a tea bag.

If I insisted, which I occasionally did, for example at the airport waiting for a flight, he would either refuse to come in and stand with his arms crossed outside the coffee shop, arms crossed, scowling, smoke rising out of his ears, or, he would stand by the till shouting "How much! How much!" to the poor cashier, who of course had nothing to do with pricing of cups of tea, and was just doing her job, and was trying hard to ignore him in front of a queue of surprised customers.

There was a real similarity between Voldemort and Basil Fawlty, when I think about it! Except that Basil Fawlty was funny. Voldemort was just rather pitiful, and after a while nobody took any notice.

You know what? I've realised something else.

I can throw mouldy fruit in the dustbin. Voldemort was fixated on the fact that we throw away too much food, and that sell-by dates can be ignored. Now, I do partly agree with this point of view, BUT, as usual he took it the whole hog.

Here's the thing. You know when an orange has sat in the fruit bowl for that little bit too long, and it becomes marbleised, like a cricket ball? Well, when it got to this stage and I put the cricket balls outside in the black wheelie bin, on more than one occasion, he found them in the bin.

He came storming into the house holding the mouldy fossilised orange, manky and extra smelly, from its overnight spell in the black bin and shook it in my face.

"How could you," he snarled. "How could you? Throw away a perfectly good orange?"

He then took a sharp knife from the kitchen drawer and proceeded to peel the orange and eat it in front of me, although I had to suppress a smirk because even with a very sharp knife, peeling and eating a fossilised cricket ball is not easy. He probably needed a Black & Decker drill, but he wasn't going to be defeated, and so, sweating and grim faced, he proved his point, chiselling away interminably, painful to watch, and quite disgusting, trying not be sweating and swearing over the task in hand that wasn't quite as easy as he thought.

No wonder for the most part of the last years of the marriage, I never wanted to kiss him!

This brings me on to the fact that he never visited the dental hygienist, as he thought it was just a waste of money. And you know how important teeth are to me! How can anyone want to kiss anyone with rollmop herring stuck in their teeth?

More reasons to celebrate! These reasons are coming thick and fast now.

I no longer have to buy economy peas. Here's the thing, Imogen won't eat economy peas. They are scraped into the bin. This has been a fact for more than 20 years of family life. But if I buy petits pois, which cost a few pence more, she will eat them no problem. However, Voldemort thinks petits pois are extravagant, and if, as usually happened, I shopped, and he was in the kitchen when I was putting the shopping away, I would dread the moment he found the petit pois as the row would erupt all over again!

Mind you, the peas are a good example but he would berate me about most things. Why did I buy *Dove* deodorant and not *Tesco* own-brand which is cheaper? Surely I know that economy toilet rolls are three for two so why did I buy the quilted stuff? Why buy ice cubes for god's sake, let's just make our own! – I'd heard it all before.

And no bloody rollmop herrings. Not only do these look like jars of pathology specimens when I open the fridge, they make his breath smell like dog food. Ok maybe cat food. But pet food. No wonder the 'kissing nonsense' flew out of the window.

And there's more, I can now have a reliable car!

Voldemort spent the 26 years of our marriage gnashing and wailing about cars. He doesn't know anything about cars and refuses either to listen to anyone else, or to pay the money for a decent car. So I had years of driving clapped out old cars that broke down and broke down and broke down.

So when I could afford it, I bought us a new, people mover. I wanted the children to be safe and comfortable on our journeys to Europe for holidays etc. All Voldemort had to do was drive it.

But he moaned and carried on. It was a stupid crap car, and not worth the bloody money. He would kick the hubcaps. And, in the summer, during the heat waves, he refused let me put the air conditioning on in the summer as he said it used too much petrol, I ask you! If I put it on, and then got absorbed in a book, I would look up to see he had surreptitiously switched it off. I got so angry. I would switch it on again and he would switch it off.

One day I was so angry, we were in France and the car thermometer read 50 degrees, and the same was happening. I was so hot, I thought I was on the verge of committing a serious crime.

So many stories about this very issue, it would be a book in itself. But the main point is that now, I can go to the garage, choose a pretty, reliable, comfortable, top of the range car, covered with a seven-year warranty, pay for it an affordable amount from my salary, and know I can rely on getting myself around, for the first time in my life, AND not be shouted at! AND put the air conditioning on whenever I want without contemplating murder! Bliss!

And! Now he's left – I can go boating! Voldemort was seasick on a lilo! The day or two before going on the cross channel ferry he would start hopping up and down at the thought of it, hyperventilating and popping ginger tablets. Pathetic. It's all in the mind. So there was no chance boating or sailing would ever be on the family agenda. So Jeremy and I went sailing, and it was liberating and totally amazing. No clutching the sides of the seat, eyes rolling and drama. Just wide open sea, and wind, and fun, fun, fun!

So you see, when the husband moves out, there are endless opportunities. Peace and tranquillity set in! There are oodles of reasons why life is so much better without a miserable husband.

Why not pick up a pen and compose your own list? It's a great list. I found compiling this list very therapeutic.

If there's an Internet Dating lesson in there, it's out with the old and on with the new! For certain!

Why I didn't throw him out years ago, when I read what I have just written.

Chapter Twenty (In which Daisy copes with disappointment)

Tuesday April 17th 2014

I got ready for my date that night with Dating Daisy precision. I had a little black dress on that ticked all the boxes. It was quite snug on me, and showed off my curves. It had a wide neck, and short capped sleeves. It was just above the knee, and my legs are one of my best features. I like wearing black which looks good with my blonde hair. My poem of course sat quietly in my handbag, awaiting its fate.

I jumped into the car and buzzed off up the Ladybird pub. My timing was impeccable, I am never late, and I pulled into the car park at one minute to eight. Robert was already there. I could see a man sitting in his car looking expectantly at the comings and goings and I knew it was him. Would he take over where Jeremy left off? Could this be the end of my journey?

Robert. I reminded myself. It's Robert, not Jeremy. Daisy get the name right. And remember *dazzling, beautiful, smart and alluring.* You have to really "be" your profile.

Ok, so I am trying to be fair when I write this. Credit me at least with that. I liked the fact he was tall. As he swung out of the car and walked towards me I was pleased with his larger frame and height. He was smiling. He wore a black sort of donkey jacket over jeans and a nice check shirt, open at the collar. (No white socks, no trainers.)

But here's the thing. Screamingly, obviously, unarguably, in-your-face and indisputably, *he looked absolutely nothing like the man on the internet photo.* The man with the dark hair, the two eyes a nose and a mouth.

Instead, here was a man, pretty much bald, save for a few sprouty hairs at the vertex of the skull, and a lined collapsible forehead that sagged over his eyebrows and was in desperate need of fortification. He looked very much older, and I was reminded of how many people lie on the internet, as I felt his arm on my shoulder and myself being propelled into the pub. I had no choice but to endure the next couple of hours, but I knew instantly, the minute I knew this was him, that there could never be a love interest here for me.

He looked at least 70.

I'm not going to write much more about this date. Robert was a nice man. He seemed decent and kind and everything else. But, there was just, and I feel sorry writing it as it seems so unkind, but there was just no physical attraction, at least on my part. Just no chemistry. Absent pheromones. I nodded and smiled and made all the right noises as told me all about the beer industry, then all about his divorce and his two children. But I couldn't tell you one detail of what he said. I am, when all is said and done, polite, so of course I didn't jump up and run away. But inside – I was screaming.

Here's the thing. Why do they do it? It's the photo thing again. They either don't have a photo, won't show a photo, show a crap photo (Wacky-J), or show a photo of themselves that was taken 20 years ago! It's frankly dishonest, and no way to start a relationship by pretending you are someone you are not.

I do honestly think personality is more important than looks, as I have said many times before, but the looks have to be right too. They just do. It's like getting someone to do something under false pretences. Or extracting money with menaces perhaps. It's getting your own way with disregard for the other person. I suppose they think if they show a real photo of themselves they won't get any hits. But this just won't be the case. There is someone there for everyone and, thank goodness, we are all different and have diverse views on what we consider attractive. Plenty of men have clicked on my profile and seen my picture and not contacted me. But I am fine with that. I am only interested in the people who have clicked on it and liked it, and come back for more.

I escaped after about an hour and half with an excuse about the children. I think he was surprised I left so early, and as I had several emails and texts afterwards asking me for a dinner date, I realised that he was keen. Painful, to have to tell someone you just don't feel a spark towards them, but somehow it just has to be.

As for my poem, it slumbered on in my handbag, not even a flicker of possible activity there. The envelope was getting crumpled.

Internet Dating Lesson

I've said enough about lies and photos. But this underlines it, again. Perhaps the secret is to get your prospective date to take a selfie and email it to you before you actually meet?

But the other take home point from this meeting, is the complete absence of any spark of attraction. There is probably another way of saying, there just weren't any pheromones. These are explained in more detail in "All You Ever Wanted to Know about Pheromones but Were Afraid to Ask" – see Chapter 32.

Chapter Twenty-One (In which Dating Daisy takes a break, and undergoes a period of reflection)

Wednesday April 18th 2014

It's a work day. I'm 'back at the orifice'.

I love my drive to work as I go through the country lanes. Often I have to stop to let a huge herd of dairy cows cross in front of me. I must be passing by early in the morning, at milking time.

It's a Wednesday and it's always busy on Wednesdays as we have a drop-in clinic and we see however many patients choose to attend. It turned out to be very busy indeed, and I worked on frantically. Not on my way home until 7 pm.

In fact, on my way home in the car and reflecting, I thought I might tell you a story about one patient I saw today:

So it was a busy clinic. The patients were knee-deep in the waiting room and there was at least a two hour wait. My colleagues and I were sprinting around the department, reminiscent in fact of our very own Usain Bolt.

I saw a 30-something-year-old chap, a routine consultation, who was seen yesterday in the Walk-in Centre. They told him he had genital herpes and that he should come to the Sexual Health Clinic. We see lots of patients in this type of scenario, so I am well used to dealing with it.

I took a full sexual history, and then explained I would have to examine him. Any patient with symptoms would have a full STI screen. Unfortunately, STIs travel in twos and threes, and it's not uncommon for patients to have more than one infection at any one time, so they are always offered and encouraged to have the full battery of tests.

It's also strangely true that most STIs do not cause symptoms, so most people who have them, do not know they have them. That is why STIs are successful infections, because if you knew you had one, you would get treated! (To be a successful STI you have to remain hidden!)

As is our protocol I asked if he would like me to find a chaperone for the genital examination, or if he was happy for me to examine him by myself.

Most men don't want a chaperone – they want as few people in the room as possible as they find it all so embarrassing. So, as is usually the case, he said 'No' to the offer of a chaperone, and we went into the examination room.

He lowered his boxer shorts to the tops of his thighs and climbed on the examination couch. I seem to recall he fixed his gaze on the ceiling and apparently taking no notice at all of what was doing.

I washed my hands and put on my examination gloves.

I started the examination by picking up the penis for a split second, and checking the urethra, the tube that runs down the inside of the penis to the bladder. A common finding for men is infection in the urethra, known by its proper name as 'urethritis'. (Men who have urethritis frequently complain of an unpleasant penile discharge. This discharge can be clear, or coloured, and if they have gonorrhoea, may run down to the knees and stain the underpants.)

"Oh good!" I said as I dropped the offending organ immediately. "You **haven't** got a discharge." I said this out loud, as the urethra was dry.

I then swivelled on the spot about 90 degrees momentarily, to pick up the herpes swab from the medical examination trolley parked next to the bed.

When I looked back at penis, literally a microsecond later, I heard myself say, "Oh my goodness!"

And then ... "You **have** got a discharge!

"... Oh, goodness..."

Because as I stood there ... what I had initially thought was a penile discharge... was really – semen.

This man was ejaculating all over the couch.

I have never had this happen to me ever before. Visions of court cases and being accused of inappropriate examination swam before my eyes. I hadn't touched him, other than for the briefest of moments to do my job. I was horrified, terrified and actually for once – considering I do this job every day of my life and I thought I had seen it all before – I was embarrassed!

"You'd better clear that up," I said. "Then go and do me a urine sample." I handed him a urine pot and hastily left the room.

Next, I fled down the corridor to tell my manager what had happened, and to declare my innocence.

Do you know what? He just laughed. He said it had happened in other departments before. It's just very severe premature ejaculation!

Very severe if you ask me!

In fact, when I told this story to one of my nursing colleagues she said to me "I had a female patient once. She was on the couch being examined, her feet up in the stirrups. You know. I was doing the swabs and she said to me

'Can you tell me how long this is going to last?'

"Not long" I said. "Just take some deep breaths... "

"Only that speculum you just put in..." she continued, "It's giving me an orgasm!"

If only all women were so easily pleased

So when I arrived home that night, I looked at the computer, and the computer looked back at me, and do you know what? For the first time, I took breath and decided, I needed a rest. I turned around and left the computer sitting coldly alone.

A night off.

So it's official. Dating Daisy is having a rest. It's hard to resist the pull of the internet but life does go on, away from the screen.

There are a lot of domestic things to do. The washing machine seems to have leaked all over the utility room floor. So I need to clear all that up. Do I need to call the plumber again? There seems to be a damp patch on the ceiling in the downstairs toilet. This is underneath the upstairs bathroom, maybe something is leaking. Yes, OMG, it is time to ring the plumber, again.

But it's always the Internet Dating that seems to have a magnetic pull.

When I thought back over the past 12 days I realised so much had happened. Not just taking the plunge in signing up in the first place, but the emails, the phone calls and the dates. Ok, so they weren't successful. Ok so I'm still in the same boat. But, I've proved there are men out there interested in me, and who knows in another 12 days, or 120 maybe, but I don't want to think about that, there will no doubt be countless more.

Here's the thing. What's going to happen when, if, I meet Mr Perfect, and we have a kiss, and a fumble, and …?

My mind sort of stops there. Let's be honest, I'm actually quite shy. And to get to the nitty gritty, there's a lot to be embarrassed about. I am 53, and I have had three children and, Ok, I'm being totally honest now, I am carrying a few spare pounds. I can't, just can't, stand on the scales. But I know when I look down or have to breathe in to do up my waistband on my jeans, that there a few inches that just shouldn't be there.

So come on Daisy, *beautiful, dazzling, smart and alluring.*

Time for complete honesty. You need to lose some weight. And fast!

So today is the day. There is one comforting factor in my Dating Daisy weight loss programme, I have stopped eating. Since Jeremy put down his key, and I can't remember when that was exactly, I have hardly eaten. I've just been too busy doing other things and I haven't felt hungry, or interested in food. Imogen can sort of cater for herself. She is pretty grown up really, so that leaves me free to ignore my dietary needs for the moment. Some days I have just had a yoghurt and a banana, or a bowl or two of Special K with skimmed milk. I find it's been easy just to skip meals. Instead of thinking what will I have for supper, I think, I won't bother with any supper at all. And I haven't dropped dead yet. And I'm getting thinner.

So, tonight is the night. Dating Daisy hits the swimming pool.

I drive to Rosemount Pool. It's only a five-minute drive. Just long enough for one round of U2's 'Bad'.

No I don't want an *Everyone Rosemount Active Card.*

I may never come back again.

I change, and slide into the water hoping I'm invisible.

I sink under the water, feel it rush above my head, feel the weightlessness.

Breathe.

I swim up and down a bit.

Like a fish.

I have always loved being in the water.

I can float too and stare at the ceiling.

Blue sky today. I need blue sky thinking. And so I think. Over the years so many people have advised me that exercise is good for stress – and distress? – and perhaps it's time I listened. Fitter, slimmer and physically tired, maybe? I will then actually be able to sleep. A decision is taking shape in my head. I strike out in front crawl, powering through the water, breathing hard. I reach the deep end, I turn and swim back to the shallow end. To and fro I go. Thirty lengths in about 30 minutes.

While I swim I am creative. I think of Daisy, and what happens next.

I think maybe she will never find that perfect someone. Maybe she is destined to be alone. And what is so bad with being alone? That list of benefits of being without Voldemort resounds in my head.

But not all men are like Voldemort. He turned out to be particularly loathsome to live with.

But Jeremy wasn't loathsome to live with. He didn't snore, he was clean, he hated fish soup, he liked going out for coffee. The Jeremy thing wasn't about domestic trivia, it was about the personality issue. He couldn't, just didn't have the ability, to think about things deeply, or communicate his thoughts to me. In fact, he was quite simple, at his happiest clutching the TV remote and surfing the crap TV channels, *Alligator Wrestling* and *Storage Wars.*

I need, and this is me, Daisy and I metamorphosised into one now, to find someone with a tick in all the boxes ... Which boxes?

Look at the excel spreadsheet that lists all the requirements.

The boxes are headed:

Looks, Personality, Educated, Solvent, Local.

Not necessarily in that order but to be a successful dating solution, Daisy needs to find someone with a tick in each box. Five essential characteristics. Like a five-pointed star. (Although Amigo two would add another box that says, "No Pixie ears" but more of that later.) Who will be my star? Who will allow me to join up the dots, and follow the stairway to heaven? I am naturally impatient, and just want to skip to the end of the puzzle. But the sensible Daisy says to enjoy the journey. You can't hurry love. It takes time to make a selection, to decide someone has the potential, and to allow those feelings to grow.

So, this was the first day of the Dating Daisy Fitness Campaign. My swim became integral to the dating success. The more I swam, the better I felt and the fitter I became. And what's more, as I swam, ideas came to me, about Daisy and the dating and the book.

And now, as I write this some months later, I know during the time Daisy was dating, she actually lost about three stone.

Maybe another benefit of life without Voldemort?

One person who wasn't happy just now, was Imogen. When I arrived home from the swimming pool, there was very loud music emanating from her bedroom. I went up the stairs immediately and knocked on her door – not that she would have heard me.

She was lying on her bed, propped up with pillows, her laptop on her knees. She seemed surprised to see me.

"Please," I said. "Turn that down. The police will be round if you're not careful."

"It's not loud," she grumbled, reaching for the volume button.

Then I could hear myself think.

I don't go into her room very often these days. It's part of my plan to help her grow up – to let her live in her own squalor. I regularly ask if she has changed her sheets this, week, if she needs clean towels, if she has hoovered etc. ... but she looks at me like I am Neanderthal man and completely ignores me. Today I am struck by the pigsty. There are dirty plates with tomato sauce dried on the surface, crisp and chocolate wrappers, old cans of Coke, all lying on the floor and the tops of the dressing table and chest of drawers. There are discarded clothes everywhere. Shoes, tights, sock, and underwear as far as the eye can see.

"This room!" I can't help it, I think I'm going to explode. "How can you live with this?"

She sneered at me, and that was the last straw. I was across the floor in about three strides.

"Right, up!" I heard myself shouting, "Turn that thing off. Now!"

"Mum!"

"Come on, I've had enough. This is my house and I can't stand to see it in such a state any more. We've got some sorting out to do!" I reached over and pulled out the electric cable from the side of the laptop.

"Up!" I repeated loudly. "You can start by taking all those filthy plates downstairs and putting them in the dishwasher."

"Mum, I'm tired. I don't want to do this now." She was scowling at me. "Anyway, I've got an essay to write. It's got to be handed in tomorrow"

I sank onto the end of her bed.

"Imogen, you have to grow up. You need to organise yourself a bit better than this." I gesticulated around the room at the carnage.

"Have you heard the phrase, tidy home, tidy mind? It means if you're clean and sorted in your home life, your mind will be straight too. You can't keep saying I'll do it tomorrow – tomorrow never comes! You need to put things away, clear up after yourself, think ahead, make sure you've done your washing and ironing in advance. All that sort of thing. There are no magic fairies just waiting to come and help you out! And I won't be around forever!"

Imogen, who had heard all this before was fiddling sulkily with her nails.

"We'll think of something about the essay."

"It's got to be in tomorrow."

"Have you started it yet"

She shook her head.

"What's it on?"

"Three thousand words on "My Perfect Menu, for a Perfect Balanced Diet."

Inwardly I was seething. But that was just maturity talking. Hadn't we all been there before when we were young?

"Look, this is the deal. You help me sort out this bedroom, and I'll help you with your essay. If I ask Miss Cunningham, perhaps she can give you a few days' extension. You have had an awful cold and we can say you haven't been well."

"I hate this course," she said bitterly. "Why did you make me do it?"

"I didn't make you do it!" I retorted. "You wanted to do it! I told you it would be hard but you were determined to do it. Don't give me that!"

Then I said more calmly, "All things that are worth having, are hard work. It's the sense of achievement you get from doing what the course required, meeting the standards, and then getting a qualification not many other people have. Everyone who has a skill for a particular job has worked hard to achieve that skill. You can't just get a skill my magic! You have to work at it, like everyone else! It will all be OK, just hang in there!" and I put my arm round her shoulders.

Later, after we had filled numerous black bin bags, sorted out the clothes and the washing, changed the sheets, hoovered and dusted, sprayed the room with air freshener etc. it looked like a different room altogether.

Then we made tea, switched on the computer and started on the essay. It was already late by this point, so we were only able to make a start. I sent an email to Miss Cunningham.

"And there's something else," said Imogen as she went upstairs to bed.

"By Friday I have to have made *Confit of duck with pea and parsnip puree.*"

I groaned.

The perils of motherhood.

It didn't sound like there would be much time for Internet Dating over the next few days anyway.

Chapter Twenty-Two (In which Daisy is reinvigorated)

Saturday April 21st 2014

So I can't resist it. I log on. This is the third day since I last looked on the site. The weekends are always the worst times to be on your own, and I find that's when you get the most hits. I haven't been on here for several days now. BritainonSunday, 371 hits, 12 favourites, two emails. Not doing so well. How can 359 men not like me? I won't dwell on that! buzz.com – two emails.

Onceuponatime has written:

Cool Daisy.

What's a great gal like you doin in a place like this?

Fancy a chat?

I look at the picture on his profile. A bald-headed man with a squished face, a protuberant chin and an earring is looking back at me. Not for me thanks. Here's the thing, I will not be interested in anyone who can't write a proper sentence. But, I guess it's rude not to reply.

So I write:

Hi Onceuponatime,

Thanks for your email. Sorry but I am actually seeing someone at the moment.

Daisy

SEND

It's a white lie but well meant.

Razzledazzle has written:

Heh Daisy,

I can razzle dazzle you, if you can razzle-dazzle me!

Shall we chat?

RD x

I look at his profile. He looks passable, two eyes, nose and a mouth but here's the thing. He is small. Five foot seven. I just can't have a boyfriend shorter than me. It's a Daisy rule.

Dear RD,

Thanks for your email. You look very nice but I'm so sorry. I can't date someone shorter than me. Apologies

Daisy

SEND.

So I look around the two sites. The muppets are there, all staring back at me with their unattractive faces. They look such a motley crew. I am struck by the unattractive nature of the species. Ageing is not a pleasant business. Some of these guys don't help themselves either. I can see men holding small children, or dogs, or cradling cans of beer and cigarettes. Some are apparently naked, at least from the waist up. There is just no one I want to click on. I feel a sense of urgency about this suddenly. It may only be about two weeks, but where is everybody? Is the world really just full of undateables.

Wendy rings. She is the Internet Dating oracle. She found her George on buzz.com and is always full of advice.

"What no one?" she says disbelievingly. "No one at all on buzz.com? You're not trying hard enough! Have another look."

"No one," I say gloomily. "Well no one with two eyes, a nose and a mouth"

"Sorry?" she says.

"Don't ask," I say. Too much to explain.

"Daisy, you have to be realistic," she continues. "I know you love Aiden from *Sex in the City*, but he doesn't do Internet Dating!"

"I know, I know, it's just..."

"You have to be a bit less fussy. At our age, most men are not oil paintings. Most women too actually, present company accepted. Go on, go and have another look."

So I scurry off and start my hunt for an Aiden look alike.

It just looks bleak. On buzz.com I decide to search differently. Maybe just simply click on who is on line right now. I click and up come the postage stamp faces.

No, no, no, no, OMG ... no ... no. This is soul destroying. I continue.

Eventually I see a pleasant face smiling up at me. And yes, two eyes, a nose and a mouth. And his name is **ChocolateLover**.

Chocolate! – Lover! – Lover of chocolate? ... perhaps love or loving – with chocolate? How fun is that?!

That's what I need, fun. Oh ... and chocolate too.

The profile is short. But heh, you know what, I am feeling charitable. There's nothing in there that's off-putting, and today that's good enough for me. Here's the thing – he is local. He lives in Preston, which is a suburb quite near here, and he has nice eyes, really nice eyes. He reminds me of someone, but I can't think who.

Deep breath and I type:

Boo!

Did that get your attention?!

I like your profile

Please message me?

Daisy xx

DDP8

SEND

Now hang one, there's another guy there who looks quite nice. He's squatting down as he obviously very tall. I read the profile. He's a university lecturer, and a ballroom dancer! He's called **Supernova100**. What's a *supernova,* isn't it something to do with stars and galaxies?

Here's the thing, I like tall men. I just do. Because I'm tall and, weight loss excepted, I am not small boned. I think it's because when I stretch up to kiss them I need to feel myself stretched out, like a piece of elastic. As I stretch up, my stomach flattens, my ribs expand and my hip bones lift out of my pelvis. It's a much more sexy position, than say wrapped around someone short, where my bosoms are somewhere around his ear lobes and my mouth is in line with the forehead.

I send another email:

Hi Supernova100

I loved your profile. Here's the thing, I am a ballroom dancer too! Message me!

Daisy xx

SEND

DDP 9?

Now I'm tapping my nails on the keyboard.

Moments passed.

Then, in an instant I did something rash.

Very rash, but very necessary.

You see, I had made a serious commitment to Internet Dating, and so I decided if I was serious, really deadly serious about finding someone to share my life with, which of course I certainly was, I should leave no stone unturned to find my Prince Charming. And there it was, staring me in the face. The possibilities on these two sites just weren't enough. The dating options were limited, stagnant, unprepossessing. What I needed now, were new sites and new challenges.

I signed up to two new sites that day. To skyfullofstars.com and coulditbemagic.co.uk – Dating Daisy goes quadrivalent!

It's time-consuming signing up for two new dating sites. More info required. Everything from hair colour to shoe size. Favourite book, favourite films, favourite holiday destinations, I answered them all. On skyfullofstars.com I can't tell you how many questions I had to answer. Interminable. I almost lost the will to live. Then of course came the moment to upload the photos, more agony, but I swallowed and did it. In my short dating lifetime I had learnt the photos were actually vital to success. Little did I know how much that would ring true in the future. But for now, I was doing what was required. Dating Daisy, fully wired and ready to go.

*

In the evening, the phone rang.

It was Jeanie phoning if from Sunshine city. "Daisy, how are you my dear?"

"I'm good, and you Jeanie, how are you?" I replied

"Well it's all the same at 97 my dear. You get used to feeling the bits of your body that are protesting as it were. Hips and knees today. Hard to get up out of my chair today but there you are." This was pretty much power for the course for her these days.

I do feel very sorry for her. "I am sorry, perhaps–"

"Did I ever tell you I was the first person to see you apart from your parents of course, after you had been born?"

"Yes I think you did–"

"You see, Lionel was in command, and he and your father were away on exercise. Like they do. You know. And you weren't supposed to be there for another six weeks! You decided to come out far too early! So anyway, I was the Brigadier's wife and in our house we had two telephones. An ordinary every day telephone, black I think, but another telephone, bright red. This was the 'war telephone' and Lionel told me over and over again never to use the war telephone as it was his personal phone, and must be left unoccupied 24 hours a day in case of emergency. Well ... when you were born, and it wasn't what it is now dear, we didn't have mobile telephones or computers or anything like that you know – I didn't know what to do. So I took a deep breath, and I phoned Lionel on the red telephone! Yes dear, your birth was announced on the war telephone! Fancy that!"

I had in fact heard this story several times before.

"Now I need an update dear. What's happening to dating Daisy?" she asked.

"Not a lot," I hated to admit. Success at the moment seemed very elusive.

"Not a lot, that's not what your father says! He's very worried about you."

I was well aware of my fathers' suspicions. "Oh I know. He thinks I'm going to be raped and murdered! I can't convince him otherwise."

Jeanie took a deep in-take of breath, on off she went ...

"Always meet them in a public place. Never give out your address and phone number."

"Right–"

"Carry a pair of nail scissors in your pocket–"

"Right–"

"My father always said to me, use them if you need to. Hold the point of the scissors between the first and second fingers of your right hand, and then thrust it. Into the front of their trousers preferably."

"Ok, I'll remember–"

"– or the eyeballs, that's a good place too."

"– Oh–"

"A pair of matchsticks in the eyeballs, that's a good one too. Just leave one in each coat pocket in case."

: "– um–"

"You can't be too careful. I once went to one of those self-defence classes. They showed you how to bring your knee up, hard, you know, and knee them in the groin. That works too you know."

"Yes well ..."

"There are a few special types of arm lock you can use too. I can't say I ever really got the hang of those but I believe they are very effective."

"– uh uh."

"The other thing is the pepper spray."

"Pepper spray?"

"It isn't real pepper. It's a chemical that stings their eyes. Buy it in *Boots*."

"Do I use the pepper spray before or after the scissors?"

"I didn't hear that dear, pardon."

"–Do I–"

"–They like underwear too. Some of them strangle women with it. Don't show them your underwear or remove it."

"Ok."

"I think you can buy a rape alarm. It's a loud buzzer type of thing, and you push the button, hard, when you need to. It's very loud. The police come running."

"Jeanie, I really don't think I'm going to be raped or murdered."

"You can't be too careful. There's a lady here, called Doris. She's only 88. She says before she came in here the man who brought the meals on wheels made advances."

"– Oh really–"

"Every day, he used to put the meal down, just where she couldn't reach it. Then he would say, lift up your blouse or I won't give you your dinner."

"No ..."

"–and she had to do it. And undo her brassiere. Then he would squeeze her um – lady parts – you know – her *breasts*. And when she told the care lady, but no one believed her. And the whole sordid business continued. Well, one day, when he came in and he told her to show him her breasts, this was the last time. I don't know how she did this, but its true! Are you listening? ... She always had a box *of* Newberry Fruits on the bedside table. So she gave him a Newberry Fruit. *'Don't mind if I do,'* he said. He ate it, left the room and dropped dead. Just outside ... In the corridor. She heard him gasping his last breaths, and I think she took a little while longer than she needed to ... to ring the bell!"

"My goodness–"(I wondered if Jeanie was a little mad?) "– killed by Newberry fruit!

"How can that be? – My mother loved Newberry Fruits." I said, wistfully.

"Poison!" said Jeanie conspiratorially. "But they could ever prove it."

"What a story!"

"Yes dear, we all have to look after ourselves. That's why I do carry a Stanley knife in *my* handbag. One can never be too careful. Night, night dear."

And she was gone.

So I thought about Internet Dating rules, as decreed from The Sunshine Nursing Home in Dorking. Jeanie, at 97, certainly had plenty of advice!

Chapter Twenty-Three (In which Daisy meets a couple of hopefuls on line and the Amigos take a turn for the worst)

Sunday April 22nd 2014

I log back on

On BritainonSunday.com, an email to delete (sadly) from Philip. A hello from Frankie10 (predictably suggestive). On buzz.com, um... here's a message from Supanova100:

Dear Daisy,

Thanks for your message. I am away visiting some friends in the Lake District , so I can't get to the computer easily. I would love to know more about you. I will email properly later in the week. Meanwhile ... keep dancing!

David xx

DDP9

Well, what do you think of that? This internet really is a dial-a-boyfriend service! He sounds friendly, normal and nice. I will look forward to hearing from him later on. I'm back to imagining going dancing again. Here's the thing. Jeremy had not one dance molecule in his body. When the music started, he would run in the opposite direction, literally. If I got him to stay put and tried to gee him up a bit, he would stand stock still, like he had developed roots and embedded himself into the floor. He would remain absolutely motionless with a look of abject terror on his face until he was allowed to run back to the safety of the bar! Here I find a dancer, a real live potential dance partner. Maybe I can slip back into glittery frocks and sparkly shoes and we can tango into the night.

So, and what about my new sites?

Nervously, I log on to coulditbemagic.co.uk and instantly the muppets are in front of me. Now if you are or have been on coulditbemagic.co.uk you may feel insulted by this and I'm sorry, but I have vowed to be nothing but truthful writing this manuscript.

You would expect to find on an Internet Dating site, a variety of eligible, well presented, clean(!), smiling, engaging looking men, wouldn't you think? Then why in god's name did they createcoulditbemagic.co.uk?

I can honestly say as I clicked through the sea of hopefuls, I could hardly reject them fast enough. These people need a face transplant. Honestly, who would pay money to be on a site and look like this? I'm sure you have seen the TV programme *Crimewatch* at the end of which they put up a chequerboard of wanted criminals, and then invite the audience to phone in if they know their whereabouts? Well I've realised now, that all the *Crimewatch* team need to do to find the most wanted, is to log on to coulditbemagic.co.uk. That's where they are all hiding. Perhaps the websites are coterminous? Perhaps one is an undercover version of the other?

Click, click, delete, delete …

All of a sudden, there is face that looks backs at me and grabs me in the solar plexus.

A rather distinguished middle-aged man gazes out of the computer screen. I take him in. He has a pleasing face. It is lean and longish, and yes, there is the usual receding hairline so many older men have to contend with, but there is also fairly charming grin. He has bright, kind eyes and his head is tilted slightly to one side as if he is considering something. I imagine that whoever was taking the picture, was asking him a question, and I wonder just what question they were asking? I wonder if the picture is recent, or ten years old? I wonder if the picture is really him at all. I have become quite suspicious of anything I find on the internet.

I read the profile and this is what it says. Coulditbemagic.co.uk by the way, is a very 'up for it' website and all the profiles are sparse.

Asterix

Location: Tintagel, Cornwall
Age: 59
Height: 6ft1
Hair colour: grey
Eye colour: blue
Occupation: not specified
Income: not specified
Smoking: Never

Dating profile: Eligible older guy seeks damsel for fun and frivolity. I have a full and happy life, but would like to find someone to share it with. Someone who is fun, outgoing, and happy.

I have many interests, including horse racing and cricket. I love going to local and county cricket matches. I played a lot of cricket when I was younger, and I still play for my local cricket team. I also cycle and run I also love horses, and going to the races, something I have done since childhood.

DDP10?

Here's the thing. On coulditbemagic.co.uk, whenever you hover with the cursor, and stop to look at someone's profile, a little square flashes up on the screen to show you someone on the site is viewing *your* profile. You are then instantly presented with a little picture of this person who is viewing you, inside the box. So I guess that's what happened to Asterix. As I was looking at him, he was looking at me, although I didn't know it! But guess what happened next?

... I suddenly received a message. It said:

Hello Miss Perfect.

I laughed. How did he know! I am of course, perfect, by the way? That was just the right thing to say to me. Without any hesitation, I typed back:

Well Hello Mr Asterix. You are right about one thing, I am perfect! But I'm actually a Mrs – even though I'm divorced!

SEND

He replied immediately:

Well you look pretty perfect to me!

What is someone as gorgeous as you doing on a dating site?

Please tell me.

Oh, and is your name really Daisy?

Patrick

I loved it! It's true guys, the compliments and the flattery will get you anywhere. Instant reply:

Hi Patrick,

Flattery always works ! Is that your real name by the way?

Well come on, tell me a bit about you? Why Asterix for example?

I am 'fresh-as-a Daisy'- Daisy, 'Crazy Daisy'!

Daisy mae xx

PS: Of course it's my real name.

SEND

Hi Daisy,

Well, it's because my wife was French and she had a thing about Asterix. We always had the books in the house and read to my daughter, and when I had to choose an internet name, it just seems a good idea. I love the name Daisy by the way.

I'm a boring old solicitor by trade. How about you?

Patrick xx

I laughed. Books. Stories. France. All good. And a professional person, on coulditbemagic.co.uk, NOT a wanted criminal! This was a result. The internet is really a dial-a-boyfriend service.

Well Patrick,

I'm a doctor. My speciality is a real conversation killer, but I guess I have to be truthful. I work in a Sexual Health department seeing people who need testing and treating for sexually transmitted diseases. I'm full of funny stories, but all confidential of course!

I also love reading, writing, and words, and conversation. This internet messaging is right up my street!

Daisy xx

SEND

I waited a little while after that. I wondered if there had been a hidden disaster. A nuclear bomb in Tintagel, Cornwall, or something suitably mega to interrupt our messaging that had started out so well. In the end I made a cup of tea and had a quick look round the site. The most wanted were sulking in their internet prison cells. Eventually I saw the reply

Daisy,

You sound fascinating. I had no idea there were creatures like you to be found on the internet! But, I have to mow my lawn! So I will say cheerio for now and message you again later? Hope Ok

Patrick! X

I was enchanted. I giggled. Fine, I had jobs to do myself. I replied. Maybe I didn't strictly need to but I did.

Dear Patrick,

Thank you! Do you know, no one has ever referred to me as a fascinating creature before. But, you may just be right!? Enjoy the lawn mowing. I will be out for most of the day, but I hope we can chat a bit more later. I will look forward to it.

Daisymae xx

SEND

Then something pretty much like a nuclear bomb in Newton Abbott did happen. Maggie texted.

The text said:

Amigo. Your amigos are in hospital. Silver Mills Hospital. We had a car crash. Sorry to tell you and to tell you like this. I am fine but Malcolm has a cracked bone in his spine. Just thought you should know.

I was stunned. I grabbed my car keys and set right off for the hospital.

Sunday April 22nd 2014 (In which the Amigos have a great escape.)

I was able to piece together retrospectively what had happened. My Amigos had set off for a trip to London in the car, yesterday afternoon, Malcolm driving. Their sons had bought them tickets to see *Blood Brothers*, and they were all meeting for supper before the show. They had been looking forward to this for a long time.

It was a nice dry day, good driving conditions, traffic flowing without incident. There is a well-known piece of dual carriageway on the way out of Brighton, where there are a series of roundabouts.

As they approached one of these roundabouts, in the right-hand lane, Malcolm was slowing the car and indicating to turn right. This roundabout, was one of those roundabouts that is a bit like a flyover, and has another dual carriageway running perpendicular to it, underneath it. Maggie, in the front passenger seat, who was bending forward at the time to retrieve her mobile phone from her handbag, suddenly noticed the trees passing the front windscreen overhead, and felt the car lifting on its haunches, just like Chitty Chitty Bang Bang. In that split second, she realised the car was flying through the air and simultaneously, rolling over. She felt in no doubt, they were about to die.

So this roundabout, best described as similar to a giant polo mint, had a large hole in the middle of it. Consequently, the car, went hurtling through the air and literally jumped over the rim of the edge of the polo mint, and fell down through the well in the centre. It landed, absolutely incredibly, not on the road, but on the grass verge adjacent to the dual carriageway underneath, and facing in the direction of the oncoming traffic.

As the car smashed down on the grass verge, my Amigos were catapulted forward in their seats. Their seatbelts sprang into action, and the airbags shot out, filling the car with what Maggie thought was smoke. Unbeknown to her, one of them had burst.

But Maggie of course didn't know that, and assumed, with horror, that the car was on fire.

Terrified and coughing, she managed to undo her seat belt and lean over Malcolm.

He was still belted in and had streak of blood running down his right temple.

"My God," she said. "Are you alright? We have to get out of here." Coughing madly.

"My back" he said, groaning, "I've hurt my back."

"Oh God, Oh God," cried Maggie. "I'd better not move you. Or should I?"

She turned to try to open her side door, but it wouldn't budge. It seemed jammed, locked tight. She tried not to panic.

"I can't open the door!" she said. "I can't open the bloody door. What do I do. Oh my God!"

She was sure they would die. Any minute now the car would go up in flames.

Then suddenly, the door was wrenched open. Two men stood there.

"We'll get you out," they said. "Are you alright?"

She was so relieved she didn't know whether to laugh or cry. These two men were passing in a delivery van, and had witnessed the whole thing. They had stopped immediately and run up the hard shoulder to try and help with the rescue. They wrenched open the door and lifted Maggie to safety.

A soon as she was out of the car, she was sent limping, up the grass verge, to sit away from the mangled vehicle.

"I don't know about Malcolm," she said. "He's got pain in his back. You need to get him out, the car's full of smoke."

They had already phoned for an ambulance.

They reassured her it would be there any minute. And it was. Blue lights flashing.

The fireman arrived at the same time. The team set up cordons around the site and closed off the road.

The paramedics gave Malcolm a strong shot of morphine. Finally they managed to extricate him from the crumpled side of the car, and lie him flat on a firm stretcher. He was quiet after the morphine. Drowsy. He said nothing in the ambulance on the way to the hospital. It was Maggie who did all the talking.

The funniest thing, was that Maggie had made cakes for her sons, and these were tucked up safely in the boot. In the ambulance the team found it highly amusing, when she produced the tinfoil covered parcels and asked "Cake? Anyone?"

That's Maggie, for whom food is love.

At the hospital, they were both rushed into A&E. Malcolm was assessed in the ambulance by the Consultant on call. He was then sent immediately for a CT scan of his spine, and put on oxygen. A lovely little nurse called Emily stitched up the cut on his right forehead.

Maggie was given some ibuprofen, a small dose of diazepam, and was encouraged to rest. She was – they said – in shock. She could go home later, with one of her son's if he was there to look after her. She has a few small cuts and bruises only, but was quite shaky.

Malcolm it seemed, had fractured one vertebra. But the facture was stable, and in due course he could go home with a spinal brace. He was to stay in hospital overnight as he had obviously had a bang on the head.

The big question was, how did this happen? What on earth had gone wrong?

So, on arrival at the hospital, I went straight to the ward. My Amigo was looking a bit worse for wear. He had a nasty laceration across the bridge of his nose and a black eye. Across the back of his hands there were red welts. He sat gingerly on the bed, legs outstretched, his face pinched. But he was alert, and not confused and just glad to be alive.

"Oh my God, are you alright?" I asked.

"Fine. I'm fine," he said irritably.

"Well you don't look fine," I said. I kissed the top of his head gently, my hand on his shoulder. I sit on the bed. "What on earth happened?"

"I really don't know. One minute we were driving down the carriageway, the next we were spinning through the air. I just have *no idea* what happened."

Maggie is there too. I have kissed and hugged her, and she is now perched on the visitor's chair by the bed. She looked pale and had some scratches across one cheek, but otherwise seemed unscathed.

"You do know," she said. "You must have put your foot on the accelerator, instead of the brake. You must have done."

"Well why the hell would I do that?"

"I don't know, because your foot slipped, or you weren't concentrating?"

"That's rubbish, I've been driving for years and I've never ever, had an accident!"

"Well you have now, and you nearly killed us!"

"We've been through this Maggie. Do you really think I did it on purpose? Whatever happened, it was an accident. Just an accident."

"Well it was pretty bloody serious. What were you thinking of?"

"I told you, I don't know. I wasn't thinking anything. It just happened. I can't explain it. I keep getting flashbacks. I can feel the car spinning, and I can feel the thump as it landed on its wheels, and I can see the clouds of smoke in the car from when the airbags burst open."

"Look, whatever happened, we all know it wasn't done on purpose. Maybe you blacked out Malcolm, even momentarily and that was why your foot dropped onto the accelerator."

"It's a possibility. I did have a blackout once before didn't I Maggie, when I took too many blood pressure pills."

"Blackout? If he did blackout it wasn't for long as he was wide awake when the car thumped to the ground and then we realised we couldn't get out."

"I would know if I blacked out."

"No you wouldn't, that's the point."

"Yes I would, I'm sure I would."

"No you wouldn't, not if it was brief. You were sitting in a chair so you wouldn't fall over would you. It might be like one of those sort of sleepy seizures people get.

"Is it called *petit mal*?"

"Here you go again treating me like an imbecile."

"I'm not, I'm just saying–"

"Yes you are, you're accusing me–"

"No I'm not, I'm just saying you're 82 for god's sake. You could have had a mini-stroke or anything."

"So you're writing me off."

"I never said that."

"Look you two," I said, "It's nobody's fault. We'll probably never know what happened. Let's not go into whose fault it was, the point is you are both ok, and only one cracked vertebra. That's amazing."

But the argument rumbled on I'm afraid, and even in hospital, it was like sitting on the sofa with the pot of tea.

Deuce?

Chapter Twenty-Four (In which Daisy gets to know Patrick)

Monday 23rd April 2014

There was a little more messaging with Patrick that night.

Hi Crazy Daisy,

My lawn is now fit for a King! I have feasted tonight, on roast pheasant and quail of course, and indulged in a little champagne, ready for some jousting with you! I must be in bed by midnight as I have a busy work day tomorrow. We accountants are always so in demand you know!

I have two sons. One is 24 and lives locally. He's doing his accountancy training. My other son is 12 and lives with his mother in France. I do see him as much as I can, which is not as much as I would like, but it's the way it is. I have to admit to having had two wives, which I'm not very proud of, but there you are.

Are you bowling or batting? You can choose?

Patrick

Dear Patrick,

Sounds like a banquet. Were you serenaded by lutes and harps? Sounds like you live in a castle. There is a castle in Tintagel isn't there? Perhaps you live in it? Do let me know. Fancy someone so rich and famous being on *coulditbemagic.co.uk* (Dreadful site by the way, don't get me on the subject.) Pour me a glass of champagne and we can have a glass together? Ha Ha!

Don't worry about being married twice. It's just a fact like having no teeth, or a glass eye, none of which applies to you obviously. I am divorced after 26 years, but you know what, I have come to realise it is a happy release. I was married to Voldemort by the way, yes one and the same if you read Harry P.

I have one daughter aged 17 who lives with me. It's a happy, household, although chaotic at times.

This virtual cricket is all new to me. I fancy bowling, so off you go and fetch your cricket bat!

Daisy xx

*

Dear Daisy,

Do I need to go the whole hog and put on my cricket whites, or can we just pretend. You see I am nervous. You may be a hidden talent. A first class bowler and you don't even know it! So I am concerned I should at least wear my shin pads and my helmet with a visor. Especially as love have no wrath than a woman scorned. After your marriage break up, you may bowl like a Viking, and me a mere mortal!

Yes there is a castle in Tintagel, and it's very near here actually. Tourist attraction. Don't think I have ever actually been! Oh and by the way, if you must know – supper – it was beans on toast!

Now, what's a great woman like you doing on a dating site anyway? Why did you part from your husband? He must need a brain transplant! (Don't tell me if you don't want to.)

Me, my first marriage was a mistake, we were too young and had no idea what we were getting into. Divorced after five years. My second marriage lasted 20 years, but she was French, and decided she wanted to go back and live in France. I can't work in France as a solicitor, so what could I do? I miss them terribly, but now nearly ten years has gone by and I am used to keeping busy with the cricket and going to the horse races.

I'm not a Harry Potter fan, but I do believe in Fairy Tales, don't you!

Patrick Xx

Dear Patrick,

Well I have been told I have a mean right arm! I think you may need the visor as in truth, aiming things is not my forte! I once went ten pin bowling and scored less than a woman with a brain tumour! I kid you not. I would like to see you in your cricket whites. I bet you look handsome! (There are a lot of adjectives I could have put there, if you think about it, but handsome seemed to fit the bill!)

How is life in Tintagel castle? I bet it's your secret ancestral home and you are trying to be modest and throwing me off the scent! You did say in your profile you were looking for a "damsel", so I bet you do come from a real-life castle. I must be right!

Sorry to hear about your marriages. Bad luck. Bowled out twice! Never mind. Maybe better things to come?! I know only too well how painful marriage breakups can be. Voldemort was having an affair. He tried to keep it a secret from the outside world, but he shot himself in the foot when he made her pregnant. Such a silly, silly man. He got the worst punishment. Having to be a father again aged 58. I think I had

the last laugh actually. (There is a chapter in my book Dating Daisy listing all the reasons life is better without Voldemort. I will have to send it to you one day!)

Anyhow, you know what Patrick, it's nearly midnight! Will you turn into a pumpkin?

Daisy xx

Dear Daisy,

Can we have one over before bed time? If you bowl, I will try and bat, if I can touch the ball at all!

Marriages are definitely tricky. Some husbands definitely need to get real if they can lose someone like you! And I don't even know you – yet! That's the fun bit!

So tell me about what you have been doing today, being Monday? I have had a busy day at my office's seeing clients. I set up by myself after my divorce, and I run my own small business. It works well, but sometimes it grates on me. If I'm away on holiday, or off sick, nothing gets done. It's as simple as that. For example I'm going to the races on Wednesday, so the answer phone will be on and that's that! But at least I'm my own boss. Did I tell you I'm mad on horse racing?

On Wednesday there are six races, and I have looked at all the entries. One is a horse called Doctor Mystery. I wonder if that could be a good omen. Think I may place a bet!

Thanks for clicking on me today. I am loving the emails!

Patrick xx

PS Life at Tintagel castle is pretty top notch, if I say so myself!

Dear Patrick,

Now come on! That was an LBW! You weren't concentrating! That wasn't a very long match! I don't know a lot about cricket

but my mother was very into it and we used to have it on the TV a lot at home.

I am doing some extra training at work, all complicated as to why, so I did some ultrasounds scanning today. It's is a hard thing to learn, and I am plodding along. It's very interesting as you never know what you will find. It's early pregnancy scanning, mostly women having miscarriages, so it's sad sometimes. For me, it's hard being a student again at 53! But I am giving it my best shot.

A solicitor!! My brother is one of those! It must have advantages working for yourself. I could do with a good one, so watch this space!

Doctor Mystery sounds a dead cert to me. I know nothing about horse racing. Is it just phenomenally expensive and you never win anything, or is there more to it than meets the eye?

You know what, it is nearly midnight, and you will be turning into a pumpkin, so I think I'd better sign off. Time to go in the garden and look for that darned glass slipper! Chat more tomorrow?

Daisy xx

And so I started my correspondence with Patrick, alias Asterix, from Tintagel in Cornwall.

Chapter Twenty-Five (In which Daisy reflects on sexual health)

Tuesday 22nd April 2014

Guess what? Today I had a message from Supanova 100. I read it, early in the morning. I am up with the lark as usual. I am still coping with dreadful insomnia. Will someone please tell me a cure? It's very debilitating. I do everything I can. No caffeine, get physically tired, go to bed quite late, write lists for the morning, have a hot bath, drink milky drinks ... but nothing works. I just lie there, eyes shut praying for sleep to come and it rarely does. So quite often I come downstairs and write *Dating Daisy*. It's a good way to pass the time.

So here I am, just after 6 am and it says:

Dear Daisy,

Is that your real name by the way? I am now back from my weekend in the Lakes. I'm so pleased you contacted me. I am a University Lecturer in Southampton. I lecture on history, mainly about early 20th century. I do love all history of course.

In my spare time I like to do all sorts of things. I cycle, walk and play tennis, albeit rather badly. And dance! I have been going to a dance school for several years now, and love the Cha Cha Cha!

Today I have been walking in the woods near me, through the bluebells. All so pretty at this time of year. I live in Woodingdean by the way.

So how about you, do email me and tell me about yourself. Hoping to hear from you soon.

With love

David xx

I wish it said what time he sent that. Maybe he is a fellow insomniac. Maybe he is sitting as his computer just as I am sitting at mine, a mug of tea resting on a speaker. Maybe insomnia and dating are irrevocably linked.

I don't think I lie awake thinking about dating, or that dating keeps me awake, if those are different things. But I do feel a bit lost in the world, like I have lost my pecking order, and I do think if/when I find someone and settle down into a relationship, I will sleep better. That's all I can say about that one.

I type:

Dear David,

Thanks for your email. What an interesting profession you have. I guess the hours are more in the term time and you have good long holidays too. I'm not much of a history bod myself, although my mother was a history teacher, and regularly despaired of me! Perhaps I shouldn't write that!

I am so interested in your dancing. I have had private lessons for seven years, but prefer ballroom to Latin. I can do the Cha Cha Cha however, so it would be fun to dance with you sometime. Can you do a foxtrot or a quickstep?

Bluebells are pretty I agree. They are only out for such a short time, so it is nice to enjoy them. I love daffodils which are always out for my birthday in April.

Did I tell you I am a Sexual Health doctor, usually a conversation stopper but there you are. I spend my life seeing people who need testing and treatment for sexually transmitted diseases. It's quite fun actually, and I have lots of funny stories to tell, although confidentiality maintained of course!

Daisy xx

PS Yes, Daisy is of course my real name. Why shouldn't it be?

SEND

I have a quick look around my sites. A few dating possibilities have come my way but I click, OPEN, DELETE. Click, OPEN, DELETE in multiple quick succession. – No way!

I look at who is online now, but precious few so early in the morning. There is an email for me from someone in Paris! Extraordinary! Plus someone in the Isle of Wight, twenty years younger than me, has sent a message saying Hello Gorgeous. DELETE. It only takes a split second. Why on earth would a man nearly half my age, be interested in me? Or a man in Paris? Weird or what!

Time to shower and get ready for work. And from today, here's another story.

Today was the day I learnt a bit about what goes on in sleepy old Silver Mills. It may be a cathedral city, beautiful countryside with undulating meadows, and cows and sheep for far as the eye can see. But … there seems to be plenty of sex going on in them there hills!

So a couple came to the clinic today who reminded me of Jack and Vera Duckworth, from *Coronation Street.* Some of you reading this are probably too young to remember Jack and Vera but they were a memorable couple, always at each other's throats, but in reality completely devoted. Jack was a gambler, a drunk and a womaniser, while Vera, only ever filmed it seemed, in her curlers and headscarf, worked in the local knicker factory, and had the sharpest of sharp Mancunian tongues.

Jack and Vera, fifty-plus, but looking even older, stinking of cigarettes and unwashed clothes, sat before me. Vera, a peroxide blonde with strikingly dark roots, and Jack, just wispy on top. They sat looking defiant.

"What can I do for you?" I asked.

"We've been down the swingers' club," said Vera.

I had no idea there was a swingers' club in Silver Mills, until now.

"Yeah," said Jack.

"They're ever so clean in there or we wouldn' go. Would we Jack?" said Vera.

"Na'ah," said Jack

There's a lot of guys. But they always use condoms. So I shouldn' 'ave anythin'. But they say you should be checked sometimes, just to be sure – y'know."

"Ok." I said." Well done for coming. Let's see how we can help."

Vera reached into her bag for a handkerchief, and she sat plucking at it, like a harp string.

"You can sign up you see," she said, "Online. You put down what ages you want, not over a certain age that sort of thing, or just from abroad, he likes just Asian, just black … y' know … y' can 'ave as many as you like, it's only thir 'een quid to get in."

I nodded.

"And you can say if you want a condom, or not. Or just for the mouth or down there, up the arse, it's up to you."

"I see."

"I mean, we're not gettin' any younger. And my friend does it, and she said you might as well 'ave a go. So we did."

"How long have you been going?"

"About three months, isn't it Jack?"

"Yeah"

"We 'aven't got no symptoms. There's nothing wrong. They just said we should … you know … get checked."

"So how often to do you go to this place?" I continued.

"Once a week, it's every Saturday you see. And they bus in a load of people from London who do all this a lot and know what they're doing.

"– D 'you get it? Know what I mean?"

"And how many partners would you have on a typical Saturday night?"

"Oh, I've never counted."

"Well – a rough guess"

"Ummm, maybe 30? Somethin' like that."

I did a bit of mental arithmetic; 30 partners for 12 weeks meant exposure to 360 people, not counting these people's partners (another 360?) and their partners and so on. This was high-risk sex. A lot of the people in these types of places are sex workers, not mere members of the public and they are being paid handsomely to do this.

"I'm sure I haven't got anythin'" she repeated," but I said I'd come and get it done 'cos they told us to, right Jack?"

People generally have no idea the risk they are exposing themselves to. Or the consequences of these. Most people have heard of chlamydia and gonorrhoea which can be treated with antibiotics (although antibiotic resistance is a big problem and there is a real issue with this for some types of gonorrhoea). Some STIs are also incurable, and can cause cancer, such as some strains of the human papillomavirus (HPV). Hepatitis B causes liver disease, including liver cancer. HIV infection can be controlled, but the treatments are unpleasant to take, have side effects, need to be taken lifelong etc. Surely far better never to get these infections in the first place.

I looked at Jack and Vera and wondered if anything I said would make them change their lifestyle. I doubted it.

So I did the examinations for them both. One of the things we do in the clinic is take a tiny drop of vaginal and cervical secretions, and place this on a glass slide. Then we stain it up with various colour dyes and have a look under the microscope to see what organisms are alive and well in the genital tract. It's very interesting as it's a curious world down there, and fascinating to look.

So, I put Vera's slides under the microscope. My colleague Frieda was at the sink staining her own slides, as I was doing this. Vera and Jack were still sitting in the consulting room right down the corridor and out of earshot.

I twiddled the dials and brought my first slide into focus. Instantly I made an exclamation – as right in front of me was a little bug we hardly ever see. It's called trichomonas vaginalis. It is a tiny amoebic sort of organism, slightly pear-shaped, that has a long tail. It swims, a jerky breaststroke, through vaginal secretions, in a breathless fashion, who knows where it thinks it's going.

"It's TV!" I said, to myself really, but Frieda heard and put her own slide down immediately, rushing over to have a look.

"You're joking" she said. "We haven't had one of those for as long as I can remember!"

"It is!" I said, moving the slide around the carousel to check for more organisms. "They're actually so pretty! You can't help admire how hard they try to swim!"

I moved over and Frieda bent over to have a look. "Better call the others," she said, as when we have something interesting everyone has a look, as it's a teaching opportunity.

The she said "How old is the patient?"

"About 60!" I said, "She's been to the Silver Mills Swingers' Club! I didn't even know there was one!"

"Oh yes," said Frieda, "Everyone knows about Banana Bill's. It's in Fotherington Place, you know, by the old corn market."

"Banana Bills!" I burst out laughing! "Is that really what it's called?"

"Oh it's well-known," replied Frieda, "They bus sex workers in there from London and Manchester. They have a website. You can…"

"… I know what you can do on the website!" I finished the sentence for her.

The next step was to explain to Vera that she had a sexually transmitted infection and that she needed treatment. As did Jack, and all of her partners in the past three months…"

"… But what is it?" she kept saying. "I don't have any symptoms. Why does it matter if I have it? What if I don't get treatment? Why would it do me any harm anyway?"

I tried to explain that other viruses and bacteria can hop on the back of the TV and hitch a lift higher up into the pelvis where she could develop an infection in her fallopian tubes. I tried to explain that most STIs are successful infections precisely because patients don't have symptoms. Also that even if she doesn't have symptoms today, that might change and it could be very unpleasant.

She said she couldn't pass it anyway, on as she always uses a condom. I tried to explain something most people don't seem to able to understand. Even using a condom every time you have sex does not guarantee you won't get an infection. It will reduce the risk, but it won't take the risk away completely. Condoms are better at preventing the spread of bacterial infections like chlamydia and gonorrhoea than they are at preventing the spread of viruses for example Herpes, HPV and HIV. This is because the condom only covers the end of the penis, not all the genital area, and because most people only put the condom on after a considerable amount of foreplay and petting, and once you have mixed any genital secretions, it's too late.

In fact Vera argued with me until I was rather fed up. I have the patience of a saint. I also explained that some tests, like the chlamydia and gonorrhoea tests, take about a week to come back. So we don't know yet if she might have other infections. It would make sense to get on and treat what we had diagnosed today, the TV, and then treat anything else as soon as possible if any of the other tests were positive, rather than to just leave it.

Also, some tests, like the HIV test, take three months to become positive. If today's HIV result is negative, it only means she didn't have HIV three months ago. To know she doesn't have it today, we need to retest in three months' time. During that time, it would be advisable not to have sex, and if she can't do that, to use a condom carefully, as she is at risk of passing this to any new partners.

Vera wasn't having any of it. She regarded me with a very hostile stare, grabbed Jack and left the clinic, seemingly aghast and having had a consultation with the worst doctor in the world. Here's the thing, it's very hard to give any one news they don't want to hear. I would love to have told her I hadn't found anything and everything looked healthy, but it didn't. I saw my little friend TV doing backstroke up the M1! I had to be honest, and she didn't like it.

The message is, steer clear of Banana Bill's as at the last count approximately half the population of Silver Mills was at risk of being infected.

*

Between patients Pinky grabs me. She is such a kind, supportive friend, and she thinks I look tired. She is in the process of typing a consultation into the computer, and I am on my way to collect a new patient from the waiting room, so we only have a few minutes.

"How's Dating Daisy?" she asked, with a smile.

"Don't ask?" I replied.

"Why, has something happened?" she continued, looking concerned.

"No, not at all. I have met someone nice though–" I said. Of course I was thinking of Patrick.

"Is this the doctor guy?" she asked.

"No, No. He was a disaster. It's another guy. He's a solicitor, called Patrick, and he lives in a castle."

"Castle?"

"It's a joke. He lives near Tintagel Castle and I've been teasing him."

"Yes, oh I see." (It's funny that when you are even a little in love, everything seems funny, but not necessarily to everyone else, have you noticed?)

"Well," I continued, "he's just funny. We had a sort of online cricket match. He's into cricket big time. It was just so funny. Anyhow, he lives so far away I very much doubt it will ever come to anything. But you know, who's to say my perfect partner will live in the next road to me! To find them, whoever they turn out to be, I've accepted, I'll have to cast the net wide."

"You're probably right I guess," said Pinky. She had luckily never had to do any Internet Dating.

"It's just so hard. If it's a non-starter, because of the distance, why put all the effort in, only to be disappointed? But then you don't know at the beginning, what you know at the end and it's all a journey. I guess a sort of virtual journey if you like, with a lot of pit-stops along the way! I like that – a virtual journey! Poetic don't you think?"

"Be careful, I don't want you getting hurt," Pinky replied.

Everyone says this, but how do you put this into practice, I asked myself?

"Thanks. I will. But I think there'll always be heartache. It's inevitable. Probably impossible to choose the right person first off, and for them to choose you. And for it all to be plain sailing. It's just the way it is!"

We had to get on then, and do the clinic but I did appreciate her concern for me. How did I feel at this point in time? Answer?: Probably – Tense? ... On a knife-edge?... Expectant?... And watchful?

"No wonder you can't sleep," said Pinky kindly, patting my shoulder.

One of the greatest things Pinky and ever did together, was to go to special birthday party. It wasn't for a friend, or a child, or a relative, or anything like that. It was a celebration with a difference. And I want to tell you about this for a reason, so keep reading.

This was a birthday party to celebrate a monumental event in history. An event comparable to the development of penicillin, to Neil Armstrong taking his first steps on the moon, or to the arrival of Facebook!

It was a party to celebrate none other than 50 years since *the birth* of the combined contraceptive pill!

I'm deadly serious. We went to the Pill's 50th birthday party.

You can imagine the marketing opportunity for the pharmaceutical companies! The first contraceptive pill – Conovid-E – was made available in the UK on December 1st 1961. So in Spring 2012, off we went, not business class of course, but very comfortably thank you, to the Hague.

Remind me never to go away with Pinky again.

We met me at the airport. "OMG," I exclaimed, as I took in the magnitude of her suitcase.

"I didn't know what to wear – so I brought everything!" she replied, with a smiley shrug.

We set off to find the flight check-in, where as usual the horrendous queue snaked around and around for at least a few kilometres.

"We should have checked in online," I said miserably, as we took our place at the tail end.

"You're only allowed 20 kg," I said doubtfully. My bag sat next to Pinky's looking very compact and humble. We were only going for two nights.

"Well it won't weight much. It's only clothes. It's just a big bag!" she said joyfully. "It's ever so light when you pick it up – really!"

Not so joyful when we reached the check-in desk.

"You're 7 kg over the baggage allowance," announced the po-faced check-in lady. "That'll be £140." (If you recall Mrs Danvers, the creepy housekeeper in *Rebecca,* she was the very reincarnation!)

"£140!" retorted Pinky. "That's ridiculous. It's only a few clothes. OMG!"

"It's the rules I'm afraid. It's all on the website. The cost is £20 per kg over the agreed amount," trotted out humourless Mrs D.

"I can't do that!" said Pinky, aghast. "OMG! What can I do?"

"How much is my bag?" I asked.

She weighed it.

"Seventeen kilograms."

"So, she can put 3 kg in my bag. That'll help."

"Indeed."

The people in the queue behind, who inevitably were watching and witnessing this whole spectacle, were not amused. There was an audible degree of sighing and tutting, and a defiant folding of arms.

"And then you can just wear some of it!" I said. "Come on!"

So, in front of the million-mile queue of impatient – but let's face it curious – passengers, we bent down and opened the cases. I can't tell you all the clobber Pinky had in there. A leather jacket, a dressing gown, two long dresses, full length leather boots, three handbags, three pairs of stiletto shoes, two baby-doll nighties, peephole bra's, suspender belts and stockings, a variety of coloured thongs, hair straighteners, curlers, hair spray, a photo album, magazines, two bottles of champagne, Pringles, two bars Cadburys Dairy Milk, a bag of pistachio nuts ... do I need to go on? ...

"Pinky!" I was flummoxed! What kind of two nights away did she have in mind! "Put some of this on," I said. I was being a bit authoritative, but we just needed to get on and out of there.

"Now!?"

"Now!"

So we scrabbled and scrabbled while the queue watched on, as Pinky zipped herself into her boots, and put on some T-shirts, jumpers and the leather jacket, underneath her coat. I threw on a couple of jumpers. We wedged some of her belongings into my case. A lot stuff of course tipped out on the floor, including a large pink vibrator complete with charger, which was hugely embarrassing. Eventually, red-faced, and togged out like two fat penguins, we handed over the suitcases. This time, she only had to pay grumpy Mrs D £20. Result!

So we two penguins then waddled over to the bag check-in area. There of course we then had to strip off the numerous layers of clothes. In the midst of this, the security guard took us to one side and exasperatedly removed from Pinky's handbag, a canister of body spray, a pair of nail scissors, a glass bottle of passion fruit J2O, a bottle of mouthwash and a cigarette lighter. She was clearly not a seasoned traveller.

So we robed up again, and waddled, in penguin fashion, to Costa.

And the holiday hadn't even begun!

What else do I recall about this conference trip with Pinky? She kept disappearing on me, obsessed it seems with buying presents to take home for the kids and for Pork Chop. Three cuddly gorillas and two bottles of duty-free whisky were stuffed into her overhead locker on the plane.

You may never have been to a medical conference? It's a bit like being invited to tea at Buckingham Palace, but not with quite so much aplomb. There is a dress code, smart casual usually, although the conference dinner may involve cocktail dress/smart suit. No jeans, no trainers! You have to sign in and out on a register, to prove you were there. You are given a Conference Pack, which contains a programme for the conference, and a lot of printed material, usually a book of abstracts, which is a little resume of each presentation. Also, information from drug companies about their newest products etc. You are given a badge to hand round your neck that says who you are, which I personally detest, but it's also for security.

In the main communal areas there are lot of different stands. It's a bit like going to the Ideal Home Exhibition of the Boat Show, you are propelled around and grabbed by a variety of sales reps to hear all about their products.

Contraception and Sexual Health lends itself to this as there are always a variety of gadgets on display, some of which, are pretty hilarious! Over the years I recall the 'glow in the dark' condom, designed to be able to applied at night without switching on the bedside lamp! A 'flat-packed' condom called 'Ezon', that looked like a rosette, and the beauty of this was it didn't matter which way round you applied it to the erect and offending member, you could just line it up, and 'ease it on!' And a whole host of other implements and devices like "C" film, a type of contraceptive cling film, use your imagination here, no it's not a murder weapon! And the Femidom, the female condom, which does have a lot of positive advantages, but in the full flagrante of proper use is apparently as noisy as having sex with a crisp packet!

And there are intrauterine devices i.e. coils, both copper coils and hormone coils. The manufacturers have tried hard to design inserter devices that are easy for doctors and nurses to use and less traumatic for the patient.

Just in case you don't know what an inserter device is, the inserter is a plastic tube a little wider than a drinking straw, which you 'load' the coil into. Then, with the coil tucked up inside it, you pass the inserter device up through the vagina and on through the cervix into the womb cavity. Then when this is correctly placed, you remove the inserter device by simply, withdrawing it, and leave the coil behind in situ. The coil can stay there for anything from three to five years or longer, depending on which coil is used. Isn't that amazing!

Anyhow, this means there are often stands at conferences where there are plastic female pelvises on display (torso to thigh only!), and where we are encouraged to have a go! We insert a plastic speculum into the plastic vagina, take a placebo inserter device, and fit the device using the inserted tube, into the model pelvis! Anyone looking in through the window, who didn't know what we were doing would think we were a crowd of perverts! By the way, the plastic pelvis has a name, it's called 'Zoe', no idea why, and yes there is a male equivalent. He is called 'Percy the Penis', and comes with a jar of artificial semen!

So we sat in the lectures and heard what was new in contraception. At this particular conference, set up specially to celebrate 50 years of the pill, there were a lot lectures about the Pill, the development of the Pill, the different types of Pill now available, all the evidence of the benefits and risks of taking the Pill ... no stone left unturned. It has been a truly incredible development in science and I have absolutely loved working with it.

Young people today don't appreciate what the Pill has achieved. At the turn of the century, women regularly had 12 or 13 children. They were always pregnant or breast feeding, and could never go to work, they were tied to the home. When the Pill arrived, women could make a choice. They could control their fertility, and balance life so they could finish their education and work if they chose to do so. The socioeconomic aspects of the development of the pill are astounding. The Pill remains an excellent choice of contraception for many woman today.

Now that night, Pinky and I went to the much-anticipated birthday party for the Pill – the Conference Dinner. The drug company had hired a huge aircraft hangar for the event, which had been decked out with opulent glitter and sparkle. There were an ocean of round tables each seating ten, and a guest list of over 1000 people!. There were also some prestigious speakers there that night, such as the CEO of the drug company sponsoring the event, a speaker from the World Health Organisation, some well-known revered professors and faculty representatives, who were all excellent raconteurs and gave some witty and memorable speeches.

We were lavishly entertained with a five-course banquet, flowing champagne and expensive fine wines. The evening progressed with great success. Pinky and I were happy, chatting to the other conference delegates.

Out of the blue, and very suddenly, the background music was silenced. We then heard several very loud bangs. The hubbub settled to a perceptible hush. Pinky and I looked at each other. What on earth was going on? The bangs were loud and imperious, and staccato.

Amazed, we turned our heads to see what the commotion was about.

To my absolute incredulity, coming down the central aisle towards the stage area, was none other than Queen Elizabeth I*!* Her carrot red hair was piled high on her head, and her face deathly white. She wore a magnificent mosaic-type ruff that framed her neck and shoulders. The dress was black, but deeply embroidered with coloured motifs of fruits. There was a deep square neckline and her waist had been laced tightly to emphasise the hourglass figure. She was heavily bedecked in gold jewellery with heavy gold and pearls around her throat and wrists. Head high, and crimson lipped she sailed majestically down the aisle, followed by a few ladies in waiting. A very regal scene indeed.

I couldn't quite believe what I was seeing. However, pinch myself as I did, the spectacle continued. She stood on the stage, in full costume.

"Citizens of England!" began Queen Elizabeth *I,* in a very loud and commanding tone. And there followed a speech in which the Queen scolded the public for the debauchery in 16th century England, and the scourge of syphilis that was sweeping the nation! (She of course was 'The Virgin Queen' so quite a hilarious choice for the Pill's birthday!)

Elizabeth then proceeded to give a talk about items from the Museum of Contraception, such as 'linen sheaths', sheaths made from animal intestines, pessaries made from dung pellets, and ending with a demonstration of a real antique chastity belt!

Having relayed her displeasure at the depravity of her subjects, Queen Elizabeth *I* thumped her sceptre several times on the stage again, to obtain order, and then swept in the regal procession off the stage and back down the aisle, to a brief of musical accompaniment.

Pinky and I have never forgotten it! You can Google this for your next corporate function by the way. Queen Elizabeth *I* is contactable, believe it or not, on the net!

On the way home I asked Pinky if she had had a good time.

"Yes, it was great," she replied. "I was just disappointed about one thing."

"What was that?" I asked.

"All those displays they had there, the weird condoms, the gadgets, the coils, the Pills – but you know what? ... No Anne Summers!"

"Anne Summers?" This was funny.

"Well it's a family planning conference. I was sure there would be stand from Anne Summers! I had a good look round but they weren't there. Nothing in the Conference handbook either."

"Pinky!" I replied. "It was a contraception conference! We're trying to stop unplanned pregnancies, not the other way round!"

"Well, Pork will be disappointed as I promised to bring home a surprise! Anyhow ... I'm just I'm glad I took my own vibrator along," she said. "That's all I'm saying!"

She always makes me laugh!

I started thinking about sex and the internet on my way home.

They say men are programmed differently to women. That they think about sex every 15 seconds. Could this be true? They can't ever think about much else then! Women, do not think about sex every fifteen seconds, not even every fifteen minutes. No wonder – *Men are From Mars and Women are From Venus.* This is a great book I highly recommend by the way.

Here's the thing – and these facts are true. The male brain is like the reptile brain. It sees things as very much black and white. The male brain has its origins in caveman times, when all a man had to do was be the hunter/gatherer.

Women however, have a brain that sees things in shades of grey. This is because women have always been multi-taskers, gathering the fruit and berries, tending the fire, minding the children, pleasing the husbands.

That is why, even today, women think differently to men. Men have the one objective, sexual gratification, whereas for women, the sexual encounter is an emotional and touchy feely experience. A woman will think around an issue and see things from other perspectives – the *what ifs* and *maybes.*

So, there it is. A grave genetic difference in what makes men and women tick.

I need to remember that on the internet. Finding a man that thinks in shades of grey, is probably as impossible as purchasing a ticket to the moon.

So, here's the Dating Daisy question. Just when is it appropriate to have sex with someone you meet on the internet? Many would say not on the first date and probably not on the second. They would argue a slow build up is preferable and more likely to be the start of something long lasting. But here's the thing. Like me at 53, I have certain advantages.

Firstly, two partners in 28 years, is hardly promiscuous. Secondly, at my age, I am hardly likely to get pregnant, although women over 50 do need to use contraception until menopause. I'm sorted as I've got a coil. Many men over 50 have had a vasectomy, so that might be the solution if you're lucky. But look at Voldemort! He got caught out good and proper! His girlfriend is no spring chicken, she's in her 40s!

In addition, I feel at my age I can make a mature decision. I'm not 16 and worried about losing my virginity. If I want sex, I can have sex, but equally if I don't want it, I can say No to it. No hang ups. I don't care if I am said to be 'easy' or 'frigid' It's entirely up to me what I feel comfortable with.

When I was at boarding school, if I had told my dormitory that I'd gone *all the way*, they would have had their eyes popping out of their heads (of course I hadn't at that age!). All young and innocent and full of wonderment as young girls are. But now, if I told my friends we had got on and done it, they would probably not bat an eyelid and just flick the switch on the kettle for another cup of tea.

But here's the thing, I don't want to get it wrong. I don't want to build up a shopping list of sexual partners, or risk the embarrassment of a sexually transmitted disease.

So how can I guard against all this?

Wendy, who is the oracle on Internet Dating says you should wait at least six dates. For some that may sound like nothing much. For others, it may seem an eternity. She says that the key thing to remember here is that men love the thrill of the chase. If you give in too soon, you just never hear from them again! I think there's probably a lot in that.

And I one thing I do know, now I am strong and not putting up with Voldemort or making do with Jeremy is that I really am a prize. I shall continue to value myself. I can't say if it will be sex on the first date of the twenty-first, it will be when I feel ready emotionally and when my body tells me. It will give me a signal. I don't know what it will be, but when the signal comes, I will be ready for it.

At my post, a signal-man, or should I say signal-woman, in a signal box.

Keeping my eyes out for a hidden signal. That nobody knows, but me.

Chris was hanging around as usual when I went up to bed.

"What do you think?" I asked him. "My mind's in a whirl. I need some encouragement here!"

But he just carried on smiling. No messages tonight.

"It's all in the past. I'm moving on now. It just takes a bit of time, OK?" I said to him.

And I tried to sleep. No success really, but I tried.

Chapter Twenty-Six (In which Daisy sets her sights on a space mission.)

Tuesday 24th April 2014

It's a work day today.

And Imogen has overslept. Methinks she may have done it on purpose, I thought, when I had finally extracted her from between the sheets, supervised her washing and dressing ritual, and dropped her at the bus stop. She was rather dishevelled and still eating toast sat in the passenger seat of my car. She had then told me she had another essay to do she hadn't finished – 'The Practice and Importance of Food Hygiene in the Kitchen'.

"I'll help you when I get home tonight, "I reassured her. How many parents get embroiled in the essays of their teenage children? I couldn't be the only one.

My day was busy as ever. I had a variety of different patients today but as usual I will just write about one. Which story shall I choose today?

OK, so today I saw a youngish woman who travels the world selling perfume. She makes her own at home, and sells it abroad at exotic locations. She was probably in her late twenties, with long blonde hair and an engaging smile. Nice teeth!

She came to the clinic to tell me what had happened in the Red Sea.

She had been staying a hotel in Sharm el Sheikh. After breakfast, she went to the beach for a swim. She left her deckchair, and wandered into the water in her bikini. There were a lot of other people all doing the same thing, as it was hot, and the water was quite crowded.

All of a sudden, waist height in the water, she was aware of someone tugging at her bikini bottoms. Caught unawares and frightened, she turned round abruptly, only to realise a bearded man stood close behind her, one arm flung casually around her neck, the other thrusting his penis into her vagina, under the water. This was a total stranger. She was terrified and froze on the spot, as is common in sexual assault, while he completed his task. Within moments it was over and he had floated away, leaving her disbelieving of what had happened. She had never met this man before and he had raped her under the water.

The microscopy of her vaginal secretions revealed a whole host of strange organisms. Whether this was due to the Red Sea, or the stranger rape, I have no idea. I treated this as a stranger rape, and she was given three different lots of antibiotics.

She wasn't able to press charges. The Red Sea very efficiently removed any traces of DNA.

Now I'm home. I've made the tea, and logged on. Guess what?

I saw this. It was just there on the website, I read it and I had to have a sharp intake of breath. Read it, and see if you experienced the same thrill as me. Here's the thing. A man with an imagination, wow what an imagination, and with a brain.

Unheard of, but there it was.

This was all he put on his profile.

Spacetime3000

I'm going on a voyage into outer space. This is a mission few men have attempted before. The going is unpredictable, the terrain largely unknown, the challenges are huge. Here is a list of essential items for my journey:

- ***A space map. Where we're going "In a Sky Full of Stars, I Thought I Saw You...?"***
- ***Oxygen, lots of it, one lung at a time.***
- ***A face mask – most becoming. Mine's a George Clooney look-a-like. Will this do it for you?***
- ***Water, pure and so essential. It's also the elixir of youth. Although I prefer champagne.***
- ***A thermometer of love, for our blood will surely boil.***
- ***Heaven scent. Let's utilise all of the senses, in fact I have a sixth sense about you.***
- ***Intergalactic magnetism. Our attraction will be instantaneous and nothing will keep us apart.***
- ***Centripetal forces. You WILL be swept into my circle.***
- ***A space suit. But mine does have buttons and a zip. Does yours?***
- ***An iron will. When I find you, this WILL be literally, a cast iron relationship.***
- ***A Geiger counter. Are your alpha particles colliding with mine?***
- ***Bags of cosmic radiation. The cosmic heart radiates 24/7, believe me.***
- ***Factor nine. Warp speed Mr Spock.***
- ***Antioxidants and vitamins. My stamina must never falter. What travels in space, stays in space. Well does it? Let's see.***
- ***An emotional telescope, for interpersonal scrutiny.***
- ***Nitrous oxide, so we don't get too serious.***
- ***A moon landing pod. Am I landing on yours, or are you***

landing on mine?

- ***David Bowie. Ground control to Major Tom.***
- ***So, what can I ask you to bring on this space mission? I am fuelled and ready. Let's start the countdown?...***

I loved it. I absolutely loved it. I was seized with immediate desire to put pen to paper. Or maybe finger to computer. So that's what I did. Here was a man with a mind. Just what I had been looking for. A person who could think and dream ... just like me!

DDP11?

A little voice in my head whispered a few warning points to me just then. I glanced back at the profile.

I looked through it. I saw he said he was 6ft1, I saw he lived in Manchester. Not a million miles away, but very nearly.

And I registered that there was no photo on his site.

In fact I will write that again, just here.

There was no photo on his site.

No matter. With a profile like that he must be attractive, he just has to be, I thought. A host of images of handsome men floated through my mind and floated out again, leaving a blank page. But that's the thing. A blank page, not a page tainted with undateables. Somehow my brain had already started believing this man had to be attractive. He just had to be. I had to get on and compose a list.

Forget about Dating Daisy's philosophy on Internet Dating and photography. It's a lot of old baloney. The person is so much more important than the photo, I just know that now. And excitedly -

This is what I wrote:

Dear Spacetime3000,

Please invite me on your intergalactic mission. I have always been a *Star Trek* fan. I can always pretend to be Lieutenant Uhuru. (Yes, that is how you spell it!)

For the space journey I would bring

- **A set of spark plugs, as one set would not last a lifetime.**

- **A virtual space sat- nav. If you know your stars, you can find your heart's desire.**
- **My very own, bright pink, designer spacesuit (see www.spacesuitsfor romance.com.)**
- **Moon boots. These boots are made for Moon walking.**
- **My Frank Sinatra CD. Does this require explanation?**
- **A large bar of Galaxy, as no journey is complete without it.**
- **Vintage champagne. Bubbles are like laughter. (What does happen to champagne bubbles in space?)**
- **Peanut butter, as we would both be nutty about each other.**
- **A pack of cards, as you may have just found yourself a diamond.**
- **Fireworks as these there will surely be.**

Now message me!

Daisymae xxx

Is it surprising after that I had a rubbish day? I think I thought he, whoever "he" was, he would message me back by return of computer post, the minute he read my witty reply.

I wasn't fazed by the competition.

It didn't occur to me how many other dating women would turn their hand to a space inventory.

You see, if you really want a fulfilling relationship with someone, you just have to start with the mind.

You just do.

Anyhow the day passed and I rushed home from work this evening as I had arranged a phone call with someone called Raging Bull!

What do you think? The name conjured up images of a raven-haired, Italian stallion!

In fact ... his name is Steve!

But before you lose interest, he looked very hot in his kite surfing gear! Here's someone not afraid to use a photographic opportunity!

What a man!

What a fabulous hobby!

I studied his picture with care. He stood in the foreground, in a black harness, obviously waiting to be hitched to his kite. He had lovely blond hair, a big smile, and behind him numerous different coloured kites, like enormous silk handkerchiefs, were bobbing over an emerald sea. He said the pictures were taken in Turkey. It was hard to tell because of all the gear, and the way the photo was taken, how tall he was, or even whether he was fat or thin, but he looked refreshingly – normal! – and I liked him. Instantly.

So Raging Bull – Steve – had arranged to phone me tonight. At 8pm. I wanted to be cool, calm and collected. Well *dazzling, beautiful, bright and alluring* actually. Over the phone. If I can! We had been emailing and he suggested coming to meet me. But he lives in London actually, so it's quite a trek. It seemed much more sensible to at least have a chat on the phone first.

You'd be surprised how nerve wracking even a phone call can be. Is it because you are so keen for success and nervous about (another) resounding failure. These internet dates usually are, as you have seen in this book. It's only a phone call. But it doesn't feel like that as you wait for the phone to ring.

I read on the internet the other night, that for the greatest chance of success, you should prepare for a telephone interview as you would for a face to face interview. It said that feeling smart, sophisticated and in control, would in some way emanate into the phone conversation. Can this be true? I suppose feet up with my slippers on and a half-eaten tub of Haagen Daas isn't quite the same. I know they can't see me ... but I suppose just as I have to imagine what they are wearing, where they are sitting, what they have been/are doing, when they ring me. It's the same in reverse.

These days with Skype, Facetime and the nosy webcam, anything is possible. That's scary too. I would like to take this one step at a time. A phone call to start with will do just fine.

So, I've washed my hair, done the makeup thing, put a sexy dress on, and some heels actually, and I'm on the sofa, curled up with a glass of Sauvignon Blanc. My heart is doing little back flips and I've got sweaty palms. Is it because I like him and I really want this to go well? Or is this power for the Internet Dating course?

I don't like clock watching but I can't help it. The minutes are interminable. I had the TV on and the remote in my hand. As soon as he rings I would click off. They were talking about holidays. Things that go wrong. One poor family were unable to get a visa to go to Turkey for their eight-year-old son. They had no idea why. Every time they tried to apply for it online the visa was declined. Eventually, having contacted the BBC, they found the reason was that someone with the same name and date of birth had been refused entry there in the past! The poor family couldn't go on their holiday and weren't entitled to a refund as their insurance didn't cover that! What bad luck was that?! In another scenario, having boarded the aircraft, a father and son were escorted off the plane, as their visas had just been refused for entry to the USA. And they don't know why to this day. There was nothing in their details that would suggest they could be related to terrorists in any way. They again were unable to go on their holiday, for reasons beyond their control, and were also unable to claim on the insurance.

It made me think about holidays as it's so long since I had one. Now it's hard as I just don't want to go on holiday by myself. I haven't the nerve to do a singles holiday. If I have time off work, I stay at home and get some jobs done. It's cheaper! But very unexciting. Another really good reason for looking for a mate!

Holidays with Voldemort were always a barrel of laughs. Here's the thing, a person who won't buy you a cup of tea is let's face it, most unlikely to fork out for anything decent on holiday. And our holidays were pretty dire and unmemorable. In my new life, holidays will be everything. And with luck, not on my own. The sky's the limit. Now let me see …

So I was lost in a reverie about future holidays, when the phone sprang into life. Raging Bull!

Bright, smart, dazzling and alluring.

Even if it is just on the telephone, Daisy!

"Hi," I said. "Steve?"

"Daisy!" he replied. By the way is your name really Daisy?"

"Why shouldn't it be?"

"I don't know, I just love it by the way!" I heard a chuckle. Then the scrape of a chair. He must be settling down to talk to me!

"Well you're not really Raging Bull are you? But you are Steve?"

"I don't know why I chose the name. If you've seen the film, he's not a very nice character."

"He's a boxer isn't he?"

"Yup, and he destroys everyone around him. I saw it years ago. I don't think I was thinking about the film when I chose the name. I think it kind of flashed into my mind as a sort of Red Indian name."

"Well, it caught my attention! But I'll stick to calling you Steve!"

"OK!"

"So, what do you usually do on a Wednesday evening?"

"It's my chick night!"

"Oh right! Tell me more!"

"Yup, every Wednesday I get a list of phone number and ring a list of hot chicks!"

"Is that supposed to be a compliment?"

"Sure is! … actually, that was a joke. You are the first person I've rung who I've met on the internet!"

"Am I! Well I'm flattered!" (He had got me wondering).

"So I'm not yours?"

"My what?"

"First person you've spoken to on the internet?"

"Er, no. I've spoken to a few, met a few." I had to be honest.

"It didn't work obviously?"

"Well its early days. You have to see someone a few times I guess before you know it's going anywhere. But no, I'm not seeing anyone regularly if that's what you mean."

"So, tell me a bit about you?"

"You must have read my profile?"

"Yes of course, but I'd like you to tell me a bit about you." I liked this as I do want to find a guy that likes me for me, and if they don't have any interest in me as a person, I can tell straight away it won't work. So this was good.

I won't write what I said about me, as you know all that. But he did listen and seemed to have really read my profile and taken an interest. I will write however what he told me about him. And this wasn't on the internet.

Here's the thing. I said something to him like:

"A lot people on the internet have been divorced, it's so common, isn't it?"

And he said "Actually, I have to tell you I've been married twice. I'm not very proud of it but there you are. It's a fact."

I have to say I didn't like that much but if it was a fact, it was a fact.

"The thing is," he continued, "I didn't divorce my first wife. She died."

"Oh, I'm so sorry," I said. I must say it hadn't occurred to me that some people on these sites might be widowed. But why not? It happens.

"She had breast cancer," he said. "She was only 43 when she died. She found the lump, and was dead within 18 months. It was terribly quick."

I didn't know what to say.

"But the thing is," he went on, "The next part of the story is even worse! My daughters were only twelve, ten and seven, when their mother died. So as time went by they kept telling me I was too good to be on my own, and that I must meet someone else and so on. I didn't want to hear it, but I guess I did miss a woman's company and all that. So ... it happened."

I was listening intently.

"I went on a holiday. I went on a cruise round the Med. I had never been on a cruise before but a lot of my friends have raved about them. So I tried it. And I met this woman. She was about ten years younger than me, and I suppose I was flattered by all the attention. We fell in love. It was all very romantic. She was Russian, divorced many years earlier, no children. So, cutting a long story short I couldn't wait to introduce her to my daughters. We were married within a year. I decided I didn't want to live with her where I had lived with my wife so I bought us a new house, not far from the old one, and I completely refurbished it with new furniture and everything. It's not about the money, I chose to do it, but just so you know, I paid for everything. She didn't have any money.

"Now I told you I work away a lot, on the oil rigs? I'm a diver and an engineer, and I'm sometimes away a month at a time. As far as I knew, everything was fine.

"But one day – I don't know why I'm telling you all this but I just am–"

"Its fine, tell me if you want to tell me..."

"– One day, I came home from being away in the North Sea for four weeks. I opened the front door, and there was nothing there. The house was empty. All the furniture gone. I thought maybe I had gone to the wrong house? But No. It was my house. But everything was gone! I rang the police and they came straight away. I thought we'd been burgled. But the police said there was no sign of forced entry. They said whoever did it, had a key. Meanwhile I was ringing and ringing Valentina but she wasn't answering her mobile. I couldn't make out what was happening. A few days later, there was a knock on the door and a recorded delivery, a letter saying she was starting divorce proceedings. Basically, she had planned the whole thing, and I was a complete mug."

I couldn't believe what he had told me. How could anyone be so calculating? And preying on someone who has been so horribly bereaved. I was very moved by the story.

"I don't know what to say," I said. "You poor thing. You've had a terrible time. I didn't know anyone could behave like that!

"I must have 'mug' written on my forehead," he replied.

"I guess it must make you very nervous about trusting anyone else."

"Yes and no. I can't believe lightning will strike twice. Otherwise I wouldn't have been persuaded to try this Internet Dating."

"Well, I'm very honest. Trust me on that one. And I'm not looking for marriage, or money. I just want a person to share things with. A best friend I guess. And because I'm not a lesbian, it has to be a man!"

"Daisy, you're a good listener."

"I'm pleased you said that. We do learn about listening at medical school. You might not believe it, but it's a clinical skill."

"I hadn't thought of it like that."

"If you listen to patients, you most often get the diagnosis from what they say. Not, as people often think, from the examination."

"Maybe you've listened to the history, and it's now time for my examination," he replied!

I was very shocked by what he had told me. Guess I'm Little Miss Innocent, but how could anyone plan to do such a thing?! And take advantage of someone in that situation. I was completely astounded. I suppose there's a dating lesson in there somewhere too, although these two had not met on the internet.

Have a healthy degree of suspicion.

Take is slowly.

Watch your back.

I came off the phone and I felt really sad for Steve. There is so much emotional pain in the world, and it comes in different guises. Who could have dreamt up a plan like that? What kind of devious woman could or would do that? I suppose men can do it too, to women, what's the difference.

And as I was pulled again, by this extra-terrestrial magnetic force, to the computer, and logged on, I heard the front door slam.

Imogen was home.

She flounced into the study and flung herself on the sofa. I always wonder why they wear these jeans ripped at the knees, and clompy trainers, and a tee shirt that read:

"Old Enough to do Better, but Young Enough Not to do It."

How appropriate I thought.

"I need to talk to you," she said crossly.

"More duck confit? Another essay? What can I do for you?" I asked.

"It's not about that," she said, "although I might need some help later."

"Oh?" What was she going to hit me with this time?

"This guy came round the house on Friday, you were at work. I answered the door bell."

"Who was it?"

"Mum! It was an estate agent! Weren't you going to tell me we're selling the house?" and she burst into tears.

I left the computer and moved to sit next to her on the sofa, my arm round her shoulders.

"Im, you always knew we can't stay here forever. Now Dad and I are divorced, this house is too big for just you and me. We need something small, cosy and cost effective! I know it's sad, but we just have to do it."

"But we love this house. We've been here 20 years. I can't remember living anywhere else. I don't want someone else in my bedroom. It just doesn't seem right. It freaks me out."

I had been meaning to have this conversation with Imogen, and putting it off it has to be said. I didn't want to move either, but I knew we had no choice. It's only bricks and cement, I told myself, and there are some awful memories here as well as the good ones, that it will be good to leave behind. He wasn't often physically violent, but for example, one time he pushed me roughly, where I was standing by the front door in the hall, and I fell and hit my head on the tongue-and-groove panelling under the stairs. Ever since, I have had a flashback of that moment, every time I went in and out of the front door, which of course, was pretty often.

"Imogen," I said, " it's just a house. A pile of bricks. It's a lego house. There are houses everywhere. We'll find another one, you'll see. Nicer than this house. Smaller no doubt, cosy. You'll have a really nice bedroom I promise. You know it's very hard for me too."

"You don't want to move, do you?" she sniffed.

"Of course not. But things are different now, we don't need six bedrooms. We rattle around in here, and it's very expensive to keep it all going. We have to be sensible about money."

"I thought you and Dad were well off." The misgivings of youth.

"Not really! We earn good money, but still have a huge mortgage, a lot of outgoings, not many savings. If we sell the house I can raise some capital as I really need that. For all sorts of things. Your college fees, holidays, cars etc. ... there's always so much to pay for."

"But the house, we love the neighbours, my friends all live round the corner, it's in the perfect location. Where will we find another one that ticks all those boxes?"

I had had all the same thoughts of course. But I had to believe there would be something out there for us. There just had to be.

"Look Imogen, I know this is very hard for you. But I've thought about it and talked it over with my solicitor. The house has to be sold. We have to be brave, and unsentimental about it. It's time to move on and start a new chapter in our lives. You can help. You can come with me and help us choose a nice new home for both of us. Try and think of it as exciting. This house needs a new family in it now. Its empty and lonely. We'll be fine, honestly. It will help us move on, you'll see."

We sat for some time curled on the sofa, and talking over the pros and cons. Imogen it seemed, remained convinced that we should not move, we should find a way to stay there at any cost. So I explained the finances to her, and the costs. The possible costs of all the renovation and refurbishment that would be necessary and the lack of funds to do them. I explained everything to her in quite a lot of detail and she listened carefully. It is emotional selling a family home after 20 years, of course it is, but I was already resigned to having to do it

Imogen was defiant. "We're not selling!" she said again and again. "I'm going to find a way!"

"Flying pigs perhaps?" I said. "Unless we win the lottery Imogen, we don't have a choice."

"I'll think of a way," she said. "You just watch me."

Chapter Twenty-Seven (In which Daisy starts to get confused.)

Wednesday April 23rd 2014

It's David. I'm actually just off to work and I've checked my emails before I ran out of the door.

Dear Daisy,

Well if it is real, it's a lovely name. Not such a lovely profession, but worthwhile I should think. And varied.

You will have to tell me more.

Today I had a class of 14-year olds. They were more interested in making paper planes than listening to me. One of them had to go to see the school nurse with an asthma attack. I could have done with you!

How is your Internet Dating going? I have met quite a few people on here. I have a date tonight actually. This site is quite busy.

I have danced for about ten years. Salsa is really my thing although I can do a quickstep. Maybe we should go one day. I

have to admit I'm taking a girl to a dance at the weekend. So we'll see how it goes.

Nice chatting to you,

Regards,

David x

Ps Can I have your mobile number? It might be easier to chat or text?

I thought about what I had just read. That's the thing about Internet Dating.

Note I said *Internet Dating*, not, *internet mating*!

When you are looking for a mate, you date. But once you are mating, I would say the dating ought to stop. I wondered if David was really just meeting and greeting, and then seducing, all his conquests. Or if it was just, a date, or a dance? And if I asked him, would he tell me the truth? And if I met him, would I be next on the list.

I decided to go to work and brood on it. And for now, hold onto to my mobile number.

So it was a Wednesday. A day of patients and swabs as usual. A day, as I poetically put it "at the orifice".

There is an enormous variety of normal in my job. I spend all day sitting in chair looking at women's nether regions. It's my job. I have been doing it 30 years.

Many people say *Oh I couldn't do your job*, or *How on earth do you do your job?*

Well the truth is it's like being a factory hen. The vaginas and vulva's pass before me like a conveyor belt of chickens to be plucked. From the 13/14 year olds, just starting out, whose tail ends are small and its often painful for them to allow me to proceed, to the post-menopausal women, who having had numerous babies, are often left with quite prolific vaginal wall prolapse. In addition, women vary considerably according to their body habitus. For example, last week I fitted a coil in a woman with a BMI of 59! (In case you didn't know this, BMI stands for Body Mass Index: it's the relationship between your height and your weight. A normal adult female BMI should be 21-25.) Suffice it to say I needed a step ladder and had to almost climb in!

I get a lot of ideas for my work environment. I love Murder Mysteries, do you? Have you ever played one of those boxed sets, where you all get dressed up in fancy dress, and spend an evening over dinner trying to guess the murderer? It's great fun!

But, take heed, when you open the box, there will be a little booklet, one for each character in the game. You put one of these at each place setting round the table. When your guests arrive and they are all seated round the table, you each open your own booklets at the same time. BUT, one of the booklets will say very boldly on the first page "You are the murderer!". Now what you must absolutely NOT do is say out loud "OMG, I'm the murderer" because if you do, the game is over." Even before it started!! – So just take that bit of advice from me!

Anyhow, I wrote a Murder Mystery once. It was a Medical Murder Mystery, set in a fictitious hospital, where the obsessed Chief Executive – Mr Iwan Twa'Knighthood, went to any lengths to balance the hospital budget. The story began, with an important meeting in the Executive board room to hear the results of the prestigious Golden Nugget Hospital awards. The meeting however, was sadly interrupted when the dead body of Dr Donowrong, the well-known and much loved, handsome cardiologist, was discovered in the toilets. There were plenty of characters under suspicion. Mr Rock Steady the Cardiac surgeon, Miss Sterility Matters the Female Registrar, and Auntie Septic, the theatre orderly, who read everybody's tea leaves in between cases. The plot in fact was all about organ trafficking, and my idea was to have little boxes of "organs" in the box as part of the game ... shame I never got round to finishing it really. Perhaps that's a project for me when I've finished this book!

A patient made me laugh today.

She said, "Can I ask you something doctor?"

"Of course," I said.

"The thing is, I keep getting this pain in my vagina."

"Ok. Pain in the vagina?"

"Yes, I get it whenever I use two vibrators at once. Have you heard of that before?"

I considered this.

"Well, have you tried only using one vibrator at a time?" I said.

"Now there's an idea," she replied.

People can be very strange!

Pinky came to find me.

"Well – Patrick?" she said. "How's it going?"

"Not sure. We are having some very funny emails!"

"Yes, tell me more!"

"It's email cricket! Have you heard about that before! I never knew I had such talent in internet bowling!! But he seems to manage to score a hell of a lot of runs!"

"Are you going to meet him? Should you?"

"Well, we do have a lot of fun with the emails, but he lives so far away."

"If it's meant to be you can work round the distance?"

"I'm not sure I can. I know myself. I need a boyfriend I can see. If not every day, several times a week. But anyhow, I do realise my perfect partner isn't likely to be living in the next road along to me in Brighton. And I will have to compromise. So we shall see."

"I think if he's so funny and you like him, you should meet halfway, say for dinner? You need to know if there's a spark there, or not? Surely?"

"I guess. But maybe I should let him suggest it?"

"I don't see why. It's 2014. Women can take the lead! Anything goes! He will probably be pleased you suggested it."

I thought about this on the way home. She was right of course. I loved the emails, couldn't get home fast enough to read them, but if we weren't compatible, shouldn't we stop this in its tracks before it got too painful. It probably would be good to meet.

I logged on, and Patrick hadn't disappointed me.

Daisy,

I am off work with a fever and a sore throat. Have been in bed all day with Lemsip and TV. And laptop. And waiting for you to get home and email me! I have attached a photo to show you me on my sick bed. If you look carefully you will see I have written a list of likes and dislikes ... and you feature heavily ... in the "likes" of course!

I can't wait for you to mail me.

Yours, a feverish,

Patrick xxx

I clicked on the photo.

Chapter Twenty-Eight (In which Daisy and Patrick play 20 questions.)

Thursday April 24th

Here's the thing. However you try to convince yourself otherwise, the photo is very, very important.

The photo had been taken presumably in Patrick's kitchen. Red gingham curtains hung in the background, and I could see the corner of a walnut-coloured unit. Propped on the work top was a small blackboard. A man, presumably Patrick, was sideways on to the camera, and pointing at the blackboard, on which there were two lists, headed 'Likes' and 'Dislikes'.

Under 'Likes' the first word, was Daisy, and next to it, a big tick!

Underneath this was written:

- *laughter,*
- *magic,*
- *dreams,*
- *and love.*

Under 'Dislikes', was written,

- *rain,*
- *winter,*

- *more rain,*
- *lonely Sunday afternoons,*
- *and marmite.*

I had to laugh. It was funny. But there was something in the picture I didn't like. Something that stood out immediately and gave me a worrying jolt in the pit of my stomach. Patrick's face. It just wasn't the same as the face on the website, when we had first got talking.

This face was rounder, and red cheeked. He was ill, and had taken the photograph with a temperature, so I had to be a bit forgiving. And I knew he was bald, so why was this a surprise. I don't think it was, it's just that in the photo, he was SO bald. And the face was not the face had first associated with him. I was so used to being cheated on the internet it didn't surprise me, but I did feel unsettled. Was I in for more disappointment?

I messaged back:

Hi Patrick,

Tee Hee! I did laugh! How funny! So sorry you are ill.

Nice to have a day off work. Love the Likes and Dislikes and glad I feature in the Likes.

I have an idea, let's play 20 questions. I will send you 20 questions and you can reply, then send me 20 of your own. OK?

So here goes...

Love from Daisy xx

PS: Is that really you in the photo?

20 Questions for Patrick

1. **Why did you go on the internet?**
2. **Have you had any dates so far?**
3. **Where were you born?**
4. **Where did you go to school?**
5. **Why did you become a solicitor?**
6. **What is your biggest achievement?**
7. **What is your favourite song?**

8. **What is your favourite food?**
9. **Do you like teddy bears (important)?**
10. **Do you like kissing?**
11. **Do you have big feet?**
12. **Do you have a warm heart?**
13. **What's your favourite book?**
14. **Would you like to kiss me?**
15. **Would you like to read Dating Daisy's kissing tips?**
16. **What would you do if we were together on a rainy Sunday afternoon?**
17. **If you named a racehorse after me what would it be?**
18. **Some people say Internet Dating is dangerous, do you agree?**
19. **Do you snore? – Please elaborate.**
20. **Would you like to meet me?**

I pressed SEND

I got a reply instantaneously.

Daisy, of course it's me. Why wouldn't it be! I have an idea. Tell me what you want me to hold in my hand and I will do a selfie and email it you straight away! And yes, let's do 20 questions but it may take a little while for me to reply!

So, tell me about the photo!

Love from,

Patrick xx

I laughed.

Ok, I replied, I want you to hold a bottle of good quality champagne in one hand and a corkscrew in the other! – and woe betide you if you haven't got a bottle of good quality champagne in the house!! Ha Ha!

Lots of love

Daisy xx

I'm on it, came the reply, give me a little while but I'm on the case! P xx

At this point I flew round to the Amigos. They were there as usual and we sat on the sofa and opened the laptop, the three of us sat in a row. I breathlessly explained what was happening and they laughed. It seemed such a funny idea. The computer stayed mysteriously quiet. Maggie made tea. Patrick was taking his time.

It's just that the photo is so important, I tried to explain. "I can't go all the way to Cornwall – for someone who is a Quasimodo equivalent!"

We sat, waiting. Waiting for an image of a bald middle-aged man holding a bottle of champagne in one hand and a corkscrew in the other.

And that's why… when it finally came… we all had such a shock.

When the email arrived, my finger hovered over the cursor.

"Ready?" I asked, "Are we ready?"

… But imagine the shock, as what flashed up in front of us what was not at all what we were expecting.

Instead of a bald, middle-aged man, there looking back at us, was none other than … Scooby Doo!

Yes, the real Scooby Doo. A complete Scooby Doo in full cinematic costume.

And yes, he had a bottle of champagne in one hand.

The message attached said:

Daisy, forgive me, but it's actually impossible to take a photo of yourself with something in both hands, so there's no corkscrew! And, if you were wondering why it's Scooby Doo … I will explain … but you'll have to wait until tomorrow.

Oh, and now I will embark on answering the 20 hilarious questions … for you for tomorrow.

Over and out,

Patrick xx

I laughed and laughed, as did my Amigos. This guy had style, and a fantastic sense of humour. Whether he was better looking than Scooby Doo was still unknown, but he certainly was entertaining. And I was so intrigued. How could he suddenly happen to have a Scooby Doo costume to hand? And why did he choose to jump into it for the photograph? And I had to wait until tomorrow to find out! I was dying of curiosity!

I went home, feeling warm and happier than I had for a long time. There were men out there with brains and originality, you just had to find them. Could this be the beginning of something big? I didn't know, but so far the signs were good. The email cricket and the photo episode was hilarious and I found I was enjoying the escapades, and looking forward to the next one.

I sat at my computer quite late that night, hoping I suppose that Patrick would put me out of my misery and email me early.

He would know I was – on the hook – waiting … but he was enjoying the wait too. And it gave me some satisfaction to think of him creating some fascinating answers to my questions. I wasn't too proud of my questions come to think of it, but if we were ever going to have a relationship we needed to start finding out a bit about each other, and tedious as it seems all those questions would give me a bit of an insight into this creative person who had wowed me with his imagination.

Then there was another message. ChocolateLover, I had completely forgotten about him.

Heh Daisy!

You scared me! Boo this is me booing you back again!

I'm not great at all the emails and would prefer to chat. If you send me your phone number, I'll call you. It will have to be in the evening as I'm at work in the day time.

Love from Jack.

It pleased me that he had seen my profile, my photo and my message and responded so positively. I had another look at his photo. He had white hair but a young face, seemed to have gone white prematurely, but it was distinguished. He had blue eyes, and I decided he was a bit of a Robert Redford lookalike.

I didn't reply straight away. Better tactic to let them wait a bit, so I did a cautious nothing and carried on searching. I also don't like giving my phone number to strangers, it's not recommended, and in terms of Internet Dating lessons, a No No until you know something about them, and feel fairly comfortable. We had only exchanged one email each. I hadn't even spoken to Patrick yet, and despite this we were so the same wavelength.

Then I thought about this some more and has another look around my sites. Still nothing from Spacetime 3000. This was hard to believe as my reply had been so clever and witty I couldn't believe he could ignore me. I was still bowled over with his imaginative space journey and desperate to know more.

On a whim, I typed an email.

Dear Spacetime 3000,

Why, oh why, haven't you messaged me!

Love Daisy

And pressed SEND

Time for bed. I was getting dangerous. And tomorrow the secret of Scooby Doo would be revealed!

Chapter Twenty-Nine

(In which Daisy learns about Scooby Doo.)

Friday April 25th 2014

Daisy,

Here is the story behind my spectacular starring role, as Scooby Doo! You will think I'm crazy, and I think I must be, but there we are.

As a teenager I was mad about Scooby Doo – The cartoon series?

I watched it over and over again and found it totally hilarious.

So I promised myself one day, I would be Scooby Doo!

Well here's the thing. I'm 60 this year, in August. So I decided I would have a big party, and invite all the people who mean something to me and who I have to say thank you to. All the people who helped me when my marriage broke up and I got divorced.

I would have this amazing party, with a succession of different sorts of entertainment, a band, a magician etc. ... anyhow it's all organised. I've done it. For the 2nd August.

But the surprise is, towards the end of the evening I am going to appear on the stage, as Scooby Doo! I'm going to come up in front of everyone, thank them for coming etc. ... then Scooby out into the audience – as it were – to shake hands with everyone! Don't you think that's funny?!!

I'm a little anxious in case it's a terrible flop, but I don't think it will be.

I saw this Scooby Doo costume on eBay the other day, so I thought I'd buy it, ready for August. When it came I left the box in the lounge and I keep peeking in there and giggling.

When we came up with the photo idea, I couldn't resist putting it on!! And there you are!...

And now two things...

1. I'm going to answer your questions
2. What are you doing on August 2nd?

Lots of love,

Patrick – totally crazy in every way! Xx

Daisy,

20 questions – Answers from Patrick:

Why did you go on the internet? *Looking to see who was out there. Wanted some love and companionship.*

Have you had any dates so far? *Two. Both a disaster. One was a woman who said she was 50 but looked at least 80. The other wasn't much better but she drank a lot of very expensive wine at lunch time and proceeded to tell the whole restaurant very loudly, the details of her recent hysterectomy. Actually I was just going to give up – then I saw YOU!*

Where were you born? *Birmingham. Can't remember it! I was a breech delivery, which is my mother always said I live my life upside down.*

Where did you go to school? *Birmingham. Grammar school. I loved school as I was sport mad and in all the teams going. It was where I started my life's addiction to the fascinating world of cricket.*

Why did you become a solicitor? *I really don't know! It's nothing to do with liking the law! I don't! It just seemed a good idea at the time. I always wanted to work for myself, and it gave the chance to do that.*

What is your biggest achievement? *Hitting a six at the Caribbean Premier International last summer!*

What is your favourite song? *You'll have to wait and find out!*

What is your favourite food? *Love hot food, chillies, chillies and more chillies!*

Do you like teddy bears (important)? *Who doesn't? (Tell me and I'll black their eye!)*

Do you like kissing?... *who doesn't ... but it does depend who you are kissing! I love Scooby Doo but I wouldn't go for tongues ... put it that way!*

Do you have big feet? *Size 11. Is that big? – That may not be what you're asking. I'm not known for tact or diplomacy I'm afraid.*

Do you have a warm heart? *Very, and cold hands ... that need warming up!*

What's your favourite book? *So many I can't choose! I loved childrens' books both for myself when I was little and reading them to my children later in life. I read sports biographies of course. I like a good thriller, enjoyed* The Girl with the Dragon Tattoo, *recently for example.*

Would you like to kiss me? – *Bearing in mind we've never met, IF you don't look 80, and IF you aren't drunk and post-operative, and IF you have nice clean teeth – you betcha!*

Would you like to read Dating Daisy's kissing tips?

Wow! Would I! Send immediately!

What would you do if we were together on a rainy Sunday afternoon? *Well, bearing in mind we've never met... and assuming the* *chemistry is fizzling...I see no reason to get out of bed!. You never know, we can listen to music, cuddle, chat and @@@? Don't let me start thinking about that!*

If you named a racehorse after me what would it be?

Dr Daisy, what else.

Some people say Internet Dating is dangerous, do you agree? *It's a wilderness territory and you never know what you're going to meet out there. You need hob nail boots, mosquito netting and a rifle. You don't want to surprise an unsuspecting wilderbeast!*

Do you snore? – *Please elaborate. I've never heard myself snore, but I've slept alone for eight years, so you'll have to ask Mrs Nobody.*

Would you like to meet me? *The more I think about that one, the more the resounding answer is – Yes!*

So now you know all about me!! Here are 20 questions for you Dating Daisy...

Questions for Daisy

Is Daisy your real name?

Why are you talking to me on the internet?

What made you want to be a doctor?

What's the best diagnosis you've ever made?

How do you deal with a) work stress b) Internet Dating stress?

Have you had any other Internet Dates?

Give me three top tips for Internet Dating.

What would you do on a rainy Sunday afternoon?

And what next...? Ha Ha

Do you like teddy bears (still important)

What is your favourite colour?

What is your favourite pastime?

How far is it from Brighton to Tintagel?

Tell me a few things about your children?

How would you spend a day out in London?

Give me three pet hates.

Do you have any pets?

Do you like being petted? ... oops did I write that?

Do you like Scooby Doo?

Can you make July 15th?

Over and out,

Loads of love

Pxx

I was enthralled by his answers. And by his questions too actually. I typed back straight away

Questions for Daisy

Is Daisy your real name? ***Of course.***

Why are you talking to me on the internet? ***I guess I like talking to you.***

What made you want to be a doctor? ***I never wanted to be anything else. Cliché perhaps but I am very kind and I love showing kindness to other people.***

What's the best diagnosis you've ever made? ***I can't answer that. I've been seeing patients for 30 years and there are just too many to choose from.***

How do you deal with

a) Work stress

b) Internet dating stress?

a) ***I use the drive to work, about an hour, and the drive home to mentally switch in and out of work mode. I am determined not to let work stress affect my home life. It contributed to my marriage breakdown, so I will not let that happen again.***

b) Internet Dating stress is a difficult one to answer. I've been doing it long enough to know there's a load of timewasters out there. I try to treat it as some sort of a game. If you start thinking every time you meet anyone they will be the love of your life, you are in for a hell of a lot of disappointment. Some people have been doing this for years. So my advice is be patient, be open minded and don't be too serious about it. It's just a lottery and if you hit the jackpot you are incredibly lucky. It's more likely you will buy a lot of tickets and never win a bean!

Have you had any other internet dates? ***Yes, several, but disaster with a capital D. For example one turned out to be an embalmer!***

Another a Rumpelstiltskin look alike!

Give me three top tips for Internet Dating.

Tell the truth about yourself. How can you expect others to the same if you are not honest yourself?

If you want to find a partner, get busy. I am on four sites as I am serious about finding someone to share my life with, and I am online every day. New people sign on all the time and I don't want to miss out!

Make yourself interesting. Most people want physical attraction of course, but also good company. So, make your profile upbeat. It shows a lot about you. I won't click on or reply to anyone who has a blank profile or who can't write some decent paragraphs.

What would you do on a rainy Sunday afternoon? *Cuddle up to you of course ... IF we are attracted to each other and IF you have clean teeth of course.*

And what next..? Ha Ha! ... *if we @@@ and you are up to it, more @@@?...*

Do you like teddy bears (still important.) *I love my teddy bear who is called Teddy Robinson. I am arranging a Teddy Bear's Picnic shortly. Don't ask. More later.*

What is your favourite colour? *Red. Bright scarlet red.*

What is your favourite pastime? *Ballroom dancing. Shall we dance? Slow, quick, quick, slow.*

How far is it from Brighton to Tintagel? *234.9 miles.*

Tell me a few things about your children? I just have one daughter, Imogen, who is 17. She lives here. She's at college studying catering. She's a lovely girl but she does drive me mad sometimes, don't they all!

How would you spend a day out in London? *Ah. Well I'm not a big city person and don't go very often so if did I would plan it. Stay in a really nice hotel. Walk by the river, visit some art galleries, do lunch, shop a little (I'm not madly into shopping and if I go I prefer to go alone), go to the Real Greek for dinner my absolute favourite restaurant in London, and do a show. Probably* Phantom *as I love it and go every year!*

Give me three pet hates. *Shellfish, smoking and Morris dancing.*

Do you have any pets? *No. We had three guinea pigs but they died.*

They did live seven years which is a really long time for a guinea pig!

Do you like being petted?... Oops did I write that? ***Yes please.***

Do you like Scooby Doo? ***Not until yesterday when I saw a special one online.***

Can you make August 2nd? ***I'm checking my diary.***

Chapter Thirty (In which Daisy meets the notch bedpost gatherer)

Saturday April 26th 2014

It's about 3 am and as usual I am as wide awake as wide can be, left side, right side, wriggle about, up and down, off to the toilet, radio on and then off, and I'm exhausted. Soon the birds will be singing. And I'm so tired.

Patrick's emails have made me smile. Our correspondence has given me something to smile about. He has a nice way with words. He's amusing, seems genuine, has good ideas. I feel drawn to the computer like a magnet to see if there something there from him. After yesterday's 20 questions we did it.

We spoke on the phone.

It was scary waiting for the phone to ring. He rang the minute I typed in my number. I can't write out the phone call as I strangely can't quite remember who said what and when.

He speaks nicely. I hate slang. He has permanent laughter in his voice. Talking to him is like being entertained on a comedy show. Is he really that funny or am I seeing him through rosy coloured spectacles? I am attracted to him because of his infectious personality. I'm still unsure about the – Scooby Doo – good looks.

But anyway, the die is cast. We're meeting up. Next Saturday. Half way between here and Tintagel, near Yeovil, for dinner. I plan to drive there and back afterwards so I won't be drinking.

He chose the venue, it's a pub with a restaurant called The Goldfinch, where he's been before to meet some clients. We agreed 7.30 pm. I tried to sound nonchalant about it, but when I put down the phone, my hand was shaking. The biggest question of course – what on earth do I wear?! I've got six days to think about it. Refuse to panic. But OMG! I feel so nervous I wonder if I can do this.

In the end, I gave up. Kettle's boiled and I'm back in computer pose again. I'll be getting repetitive strain injury soon.

And guess what, an email from David, who I've started thinking of as "Mr Bluebells".

Hi Daisy,

Well the weekend beckons. I took this lady to a dance last weekend and it was a real flop. Firstly, she was at least ten years older than she had said on the profile. Secondly, she couldn't dance at all. Thirdly, her children kept phoning her all evening, I think they were checking up on her and in the end she said one of them was ill and she had to go home. I hadn't even got past first base!

Internet dating has its frustrations I'm sure you'd agree.

I just wondered if you fancied meeting for coffee?

Regards Miss Daisy!

David x

I chuckled to myself and replied:

Hi David,

What are you doing trying it on with the elderly?! Sounds pretty unpleasant to me!

Also – she couldn't even dance. The evening sounds a complete failure!

So if we meet for coffee, I guess it's just "coffee"" and not "a date". Is that right?

Regards

Dancing Daisy xx

Seeing as I sent this at about 4 am I was amazed at the speed of the reply! (I couldn't help wondering if Patrick too was awake or asleep – but ... I had no way of knowing, and anyway we hadn't met yet, and anyway there was no guarantee of any relationship).

Daisy

I'm not into long term relationships, I need to make that clear. I like playing the field. That's not to say I can't have a relationship at all, but it's most unlikely it would be for the long term. I just want to be honest. But I love your profile, your picture and your texts and it would be great to meet you.

How about coffee at *The Fig and Furkin* at 11am, tomorrow morning? No strings. Just coffee and chat. See what happens?

More regards Miss Daisy

David x

I read and mused over his email for a while. It didn't bother me he didn't want long term. At least he was honest, that's true. We hadn't even met! I am not prepared to be a notch on the bedpost of a notch bedpost gatherer. But, I have nothing on for the weekend, he is at least local, and he dances. It has to be worth a cup of coffee. I didn't owe anything to Patrick. Not yet.

So I emailed back,

David,

You're on! See you tomorrow,

Living dangerously,

Dangerous Daisy! X

PS. Now go to sleep!

I had another look around the site. The muppets were sleeping. As usual I was horrified by the hideous collection of hopefuls gazing up at me. I had the *Crimewatch* feeling again.

I read some more profiles. One guy had written "Is there anyone out there who can help me get off this site forever?"

I could identify with that right away. In his profile he said he was an ex-Olympic rower. Ummm, I looked at his photograph carefully. He didn't appear big and muscle, but if anything, quite short and small framed, but it's hard to tell from a photo. He had dark hair and the Daisy prerequisite of two eyes, two ears a nose and a mouth. So I sent him a message.

It was just a Hello, late night, liked your profile, can't sleep, agree about finding one person to get off this site. Nothing happened though. I seem to recall I got a polite email in reply a few days later saying thanks for making contact, but he was bit tied up with things just now and would get back to me in due course. He never did. Hard to accept but I guess I just wasn't his type.

Or maybe he had met someone else. It's a continuous ebb and flow Internet Dating, and at least he was polite and honest.

So it's coffee time at *The Fig and Furkin* with Mr Bluebells.

"Where are you going?" asked Imogen, looking me up and down.

"I'm going" I said, perhaps with a note of triumph in my voice, "to have coffee with Mr Bluebells. See you later!" and I grabbed my car keys and swept out of the door. Out of the door before she could collar me about any VRQ catering homework … again.

Here's the thing, I felt relaxed and up for some entertainment. My heart – if I can call it that – already felt a belonging to Patrick, and this was not even a real date. Just coffee.

I have new jeans. I've never been size 12 before and they fit perfectly. Swimming is such a great way to get into shape. It's also a great stress buster. (During the time period of writing this book I lost three stone!) I have a white crew necked sweater and black suede boots. My hair is clean and shiny although I wish there was more of it. It's blonde and healthy. I never wear much makeup – prefer to look *au naturel.* I walk into the pub with nothing to lose. My poem lurks in the hand bag 'off duty'... this isn't even a real date!

Mr Bluebells is already there. I see a very tall man standing by the bar, strategically placed to watch everyone coming and leaving. I like tall men so that's a good start. He has some hair. I like that too. So many middle-aged men are bald. He's wearing a blue checked shirt and jeans. So far impressions are good. When he shakes my hand and kisses my cheek I can tell he likes me.

"Daisy!"

"David!"

"– Even more beautiful than I imagined."

"Ha Ha!" – I am momentarily off my guard as I'm not used to compliments.

"– What can I get you?"

We sit on a sofa side by side. If I try to alter my position so I'm not at right angles to him we have to sort of brush knees. It's a bit awkward. Also this feels a bit too close. Afterwards I wondered if he has met women here before and used this very sofa for the same tactic. He does have some not very designer stubble, now I'm close up, that would be satisfying to remove.

"So Daisy – and is that your real name by the way?"

"Of course."

"How's the Internet Dating going?"

"So so ..."

"So so? Good so so, or bad so so?"

"Good I guess, and you?"

"Ah. Well I regard it as a hobby. A pleasant pastime, with infuriations and sometimes – only sometimes! – a hidden pleasure!"

"It's important not take it too seriously I agree. I find there are many disappointments."

"Such as?"

"Ok. So no one ever looks like they do in their photograph. They *always* put a picture there of themselves taken 20 years earlier. It's so stupid."

"Do I look like my photo then?"

I thought for a moment. "You were a long way from the camera in your picture and you were squatting down. And you didn't have your glasses on. But, apart from all that I guess I would say, yes. You are pretty much as I expected."

"And you are identical to your picture."

"Well thank God as it's me. No frills no fancies! Just plain ol' me!"

"Well you are super – gorgeous." And he squeezed my knee.

I moved away a bit abruptly. "I love swapping dating stories," I said.

"I can tell you a few stories." He chuckled." Where shall I start?"

So I listened to Mr Bluebells tell me a couple of hilarious stories.

"I met this woman on the internet. She seemed quite nice, chatty, presentable. She was working as a dietician in a London hospital. I won't say her name.

We were getting on fine, so we agreed to meet."

I was nodding. He was quite cute the way he kept shifting his glasses up his nose with the index finger of alternate hands. There was something school boyish about him.

"So we agreed Guildford as it seemed sort of half way. We then said for some reason, Let's meet at the service station on the motorway, leave our cars there and take the park and ride in. Then we can have an afternoon in Guildford, have dinner and not worry about the parking. So that's what we did."

I was sipping my coffee..."and.."

"Well, we met and she seemed very nice. She was quite smartly dressed, nicely spoken, we seemed to get on. We took the bus into Guildford and then walked around the city, went into the castle and had a look at the cathedral, that sort of thing. It was a sunny day, all very pleasant, and she was good company. I though all was well. I honestly didn't know there was a problem.

"... So what was the problem?" My female intuition knew the answer. (She didn't have the hots for him and didn't know what to do about it, with her car so remotely ensconced at the Guildford Services station.) But I stayed quiet and listened.

"Anyway, so we had dinner. At this little pub we found. Right in the centre. We couldn't drink much as we were both driving, but it was a terrific meal and we had one glass of Moet. I tried to be good company. Generous host etc.. Well after the dessert, I seem to remember it was a chocolate pear pudding as she told me she loved the combination of chocolate and pears, she said she needed a trip to the Ladies. So, off she went, and I poured myself a coffee, and another coffee.. and I waited.. and waited.. after about say 15 minutes I was getting a bit worried. I texted her a couple of times, but no reply. So I walked over to the Ladies and I asked a woman going in there if she would look for this lady for me. I said I was concerned she might be unwell. But the woman popped back out a few minutes later and said there was no one else in there. I was stunned. Are you sure? I asked. Yes, she said. So I called the waiter and explained. He shrugged his shoulders. He did look quite apologetically at me. I was saying I didn't know her well, and this was our first visit to Guildford, and that maybe she had got lost, or collapsed somewhere, or been abducted.

The waiter raised an eyebrow. "Sorry to be blunt Sir," he said kindly., "but we do see this sort of thing from time to time."

"Do you" I said incredulously, "But why?"

"Maybe," said the waiter, "She just wasn't that into you."

And with that cutting home truth he trotted off to find the bill!

I just couldn't believe that. The fact she had found me so abhorrent she had escaped through the women's toilets. Like some monster, which I am not! So you know what I did next?

I shook my head.

I went to the Police. I told them the whole story. I just said I didn't want her to be reported missing and for me to get the blame. You read about this sort of thing sometimes. I was wondering about the cars, her car, my car, would she steal my car, was it a set up?

Anyhow the Police said a person isn't missing until they have been out of contact for 24 hours. They said it's not uncommon for one or other party on a "blind date" to jilt the other. They took all the details but said for now there was nothing I could do but I should go and retrieve my car. So I did. There on the windscreen was a note that just said "Sorry - just one of those things. Nice meeting you. J x"

I was – still am – flabbergasted that I was so awful she had to plan an escape from me. After all she only needed to go back to the car with me, the day was nearly over. And then she didn't need to see me again.

She could have made any excuse. It's a bit insulting she went to such lengths."

"Well" I said, unable to contain a large grin" after the dinner it's pay-back time and she didn't want what she feared might be on the cards! Why not, get a bloke to buy you a slap-up meal, then disappear before you have to give anything back. It may be a technique she's used many times before!"

"Well she didn't need to play that one on me! I was quite hurt by it really as I didn't think I was bad looking or that awful company."

"You're not. Forget it!"

"But she could have just said.. "

"...Said what?"

"... That it wasn't working, that she didn't fancy me . . whatever."

"She probably didn't know how to tell you that. It's quite hard to say to someone in those circumstances, sorry this isn't working for me – and then get up and go back to the car. There's the problem that after she's said it, you might insist on going back to the cars with her. Then she's got to go for quite a little journey in a bad atmosphere, and she couldn't bear that.

"I wouldn't bite her head off!"

"She knows that. But she probably also knew you were a bed post notch gatherer, and she wasn't prepared to become one. A notch!"

"Oh come on!"

"Oh come on what!"

"Well it's as plain as the nose on your face."

"I hadn't said anything honestly! I hadn't even decided I wanted to go there!"

"Well it's a great story. I guess you can learn from it. Make the first date somewhere local, where you can have a quick getaway!"

"I'm still brooding over it. You're not about to go to the Ladies are you?"

I laughed. "No, I'm rather enjoying this actually!"

"I've got another great story. Shall I tell you?"

"I'm all ears!" I was really intrigued by these internet dating stories.

"Well I met this woman I had been chatting to, in a pub in Brighton, for a drink. It was only a few months ago. She was called Tessa. I had always liked that name. She was younger than me and quite nice looking, blonde, quite slim, leather jacket, She told me she was into buying and doing up houses. I love that sort of thing. Do you watch that programme *Impressive Creations* on the BBC? I love it! So she was telling me about her current project which is a large house, seven bedrooms, not far from the pub. She'd just had some antique fireplaces put in and I was showing interest. We'd been chatting for a couple of hours. She suddenly said I'm going back there now actually. Why don't you come with me for coffee and you can have a look?

I considered this, wondering if I was being invited back for more than just coffee.

"So," she said, "are you parked out the back there? Tell you what I've got a white Ford Cabriolet. I'll drive it round the front and you can follow me? It's about 20 minutes from here. Is that too far?"

I said " No, not at all." I was quite intrigued. I wasn't sure if this was an invitation for anything more than coffee or fireplaces but I figured it was worth a trip. So we – well, I – paid for the drinks and went out the back and got my car. I drove round the front a few minutes later and I saw a white cabriolet in front of the pub straight away. I pulled in behind it and off we set. It was quite a journey, the roads are narrow and twisty and I didn't want to lose her so I had to keep close behind. It seemed more than 20 minutes but I wasn't timing it. I wasn't in a hurry, I had all day. Eventually we pulled into a gravel drive in front of a huge house a bit like a stately home. I was just thinking how well she had done for herself, and was undoing my seat belt when there was a violent rapping on the window. A different woman, someone I had never seen before, was yelling at me. Confused I wound down the window. Where was Tessa? Who was this woman? What was happening? And then I pieced it together! This was the wrong Ford cabriolet! I had been following the wrong car! The driver thought I was some sort of stalker . . . ! . . and was about to call the Police! I tried to explain but she was so hysterical. I tried to calm her but she was ranting and raving, calling me a pervert, and a stalker and saying all kinds of unspeakable things! I was still sitting in the car. I didn't know what to do. So after a few moments, I drove off. I left her screaming and shouting. I was quite shaken up myself!"

"What about the woman you were supposed to be meeting?"

"Well we hadn't exchanged mobile numbers. So all I could do was email her when I got home. I never heard from her again! Maybe she didn't believe me! It was all so weird and so unfortunate!"

I was laughing. That was such a funny story. I couldn't believe it! You couldn't make that sort of thing up!

So David and I had a fun time swapping Internet Dating Stories. I told him about the undertaker Philip, Frankie 10, Cool Jaguar and Love Bug. I have a good memory so the limericks were tripping off my tongue and David seemed highly amused!

He told me how he had bought a house a few years ago, brand new, and was proud of the way it had all turned out. The house was in the grounds of a private secondary school for boys and looked out over the cricket pitches at the front. "It's ideal," he said, "as I have worked there as a supply teacher. And anyway at weekends, as it's a boarding school, there are no pupils, so it's very quiet. Suit's me down to the ground."

"In fact," he said giving me an intense stare, "Why don't you come back for coffee? I'd love to show it to you.

A million alarm bells were ringing that I absolutely should not do this. A single middle-aged man I have only just met wants me to see his etchings. Everyone would say, Don't Do It! So ...to spite them all ...as I'm Dating Daisy and I do things differently now ...I said

"Yes."

I followed him there in my car.

I know you are probably having a fit now and waving this book in the air and shouting incredulously... she did what?!!

But yes, I did it ...read on ...

So we drove up a scrunchy gravel driveway in the dusk and parked parallel outside the house. It was pretty, rendered and white washed with a late roof and two dormer windows upstairs. I noted a host of climbing plants growing around what turned out to be the kitchen window. He opened the front door on a house that still smelt of fresh paint and putty.

He took my coat, and I watched carefully so I could retrieve it in a hurry if needed. I was driving anyway, so we agreed on more coffee, and I followed him into the lounge a few minutes later, as he carried the coffee tray. We sat side by side on the sofa.

I made some comments about the house. "Lovely house."

"Glad you like it."

"Very ...homely. Like the rug ..."

"Oh that ...it's a zebra skin from a zebra I shot in Kenya."

"What!"

"Oh I like shooting. I go clay pigeon shooting. And hunting in Scotland sometimes. Killed a few deer. And fishing. I love fishing."

I don't like killing things. End of

"Not my thing I'm afraid," I said after a long pause.

"Is that your parents?" I asked referring to a large framed photograph on the mantelpiece.

"Yes, you're right there. Thomas and Dorothy. And what a formidable pair they are. Father irons - yes irons - *Daily Britain* before he reads it every morning, I kid you not!

And mother is reminiscent of Hyacinth Bouquet!"

I found this very amusing.

"I've still got my Dad," I said wistfully, "but my mother died of cancer 3 years ago.

She was a bit of a force to be reckoned with. But she wasn't a Hyacinth. More like Margaret Thatcher!" I didn't really want to get into talking about my mother as I usually ended up in tears, so I changed the subject.

"How did you get into dancing?" I asked.

"I started as a child. My sister had dance lessons and I got fed up with going to see her and having to wait and watch. So in the end I did it too. But I was much too tall to ever have a career in dancing. So as I got taller, and in my teenage years it was a bit embarrassing. I stopped. Then a few years back it struck me, it might be a good place to meet women! So I started going to a salsa class. It was so much fun. So I asked around and started going to a Ballroom & Latin class once a week. The problem is I don't have a regular dance partner, so when I go I know I have to wait for someone to be free to dance with me, usually one of the teachers. And I hate that, so now I don't go very often. But I can do a mean Cha Cha Cha!"

"I used to dance with my ex-husband," I said "Only he didn't want to do the medals, and he wouldn't go to any dances, so we didn't make much progress. I do miss the dancing though. I know it's a problem not having a partner."

"I'll let you know then, " he said, "And maybe we could go to a dance sometime?"

"Maybe!" I said perhaps hesitantly. (After all today's meeting was only 'coffee' – not a date! Was he offering me something a bit different?)

There was a huge bookshelf, full of books, and I felt the urge to go and look at them. A person's books can tell quite a lot about their character.

"Tell me about your books" I said in the end, feeling a bit self conscious about standing up and parading across the room to the bookcase in my skinny jeans.

"I read a lot," he replied. "lots of stuff, from Dickens to John Le Carré. I like spy stores and adventure stories and travel and intrigue! How about you?"

" I love crime stories!" I said, "But I love the psychological thriller with a twist, not really the ones with a detective. Have you read Barbara Vine? She's Ruth Rendell but writing with a different name. They're fantastic."

"I didn't know that, I'll give that a try."

He was edging a bit closer to me on the sofa, or was I imagining it? I sipped my coffee.

"How's your book going?" he asked.

"Great! I said. "Watch out or you'll be in it!"

He was definitely closer to me now.

This time I felt his arm snaking round the back of the sofa and onto my shoulders. I froze.

I didn't exactly jump up that second. But it can't have been much longer.

"Sorry I have to go" I said, "I have an appointment early tomorrow morning. It's been nice to meet you."

I smiled politely, backed out the door and scurried to the kitchen to get my coat.

When I looked round he was standing in the door way, effectively blocking my escape route to the front door.

"Not so fast, young lady," he smiled down at me. "We were getting on famously." I felt his hands on my shoulders. "Come on, we both know where this is going to end."

"Is this what you said to Mrs-I'm-not-into-you in Guildford? If so, no wonder she ran away!"

I side stepped away from him.

"Look I told you, I'm not into bed posts and notches, and nice as you are, I really have to go home," I said firmly.

"I really like you Daisy. You're fresh and funny and I love the blonde hair. Can't I persuade you?"

He had moved again towards me and his arms round me in an embrace."I know you want to really. You're just a little tease."

"David, please," I said. "We've only just met. Please, I really just need to go home. It's as simple as that." And I wriggled out of his grasp, squeezed past him and headed for the front door.

He stood on the doorstep and waved at me, as I reversed my car rather badly out of his driveway. He wasn't a rapist but he was certainly a notch bedpost gatherer, and this definitely was not for me. (No use for my poem either, which was still sitting in my hand bag, that was very definite.)

Funny thing was he emailed me the next day with a flattering email. The man not interested in relationships. And daily for a few days after that. He even texted me in the middle of the night one night, about 2.00am, saying he was fantasising about kissing me and holding my naked body. I deleted it and blocked his number and email address.

Is there an internet dating lesson to be had here, I asked myself. Not really Daisy, it was coffee, not really a date.

Hmm ... any sort of meeting with a guy you meet on a dating site is probably a date really. And anyhow he was attractive and fun to talk to. But I knew he wasn't into relationships, he had made that quite clear. If I'm honest, I think I wanted to meet him as he is a dancer. I do miss my dancing. It's on my profile. Is there anyone out there who wants to learn to dance? Wouldn't that be just so amazing?

Perhaps you learn a little more about yourself when you go on each date? That's something I hadn't considered before.

Chapter Thirty-One

(In which Dating Daisy has a date with Patrick.)

Saturday 3rd May 2014

So was Saturday and I had to be dressed to kill. And *beautiful, dazzling, smart and alluring.* It was not going well, with a bad hair day, my skin looked a bit spotty and I just felt unconfident. I don't know why. I had washed my hair, dried it and washed it again! I had thrown on and off countless outfits. I looked in the mirror and I felt middle-aged and frumpy. And then I wonder what he was thinking as from my Scooby Doo memory, he was not Adonis either.

So I had on my beloved yellow daisy blouse. It's loose, but not baggy, feminine and floaty and fresh as Daisy ... me! – I had designer white jeans. They cost me a fortune and are quite tight and I hope quite flattering. If I breathe in and stand sideways to the mirror my stomach looks flat-ish (?). I had some black shoes with a bit of a heel, which I almost never wear! And I had black earrings and a necklace, which I chose after much deliberation. My hair is sadly thin and lank, but was shiny, and smelled good and swung nicely around my face at my shoulders. I wish I had more of it. I have always wanted to look like Daryl Hannah – the mermaid in *Splash*! Dream on!

I've never been one for makeup – just a bit.

It's ok close up – as I don't have too many wrinkles or lines, but I always wish I was twenty-one. However, I consoled myself, as you know what? He was probably wishing that he was twenty-one too.

As I had to drive nearly two hours to get there, I decided to stop and change into my designer jeans in a lay-by when I was nearly there, so they're not too creased.

Was that mad or what? So I got in the car in my old jeans, the new ones carefully folded beside me. I had the sat nav, and a print out from the AA auto-route and lots of CDs and some water and some fruit. It was a bit of an expedition. And I'm nervous. Nervous as hell.

The funny thing about Patrick is that he doesn't have a mobile phone. He's never had one and doesn't want one. So, on this journey, if I were to get lost or change my mind or have an accident, I can't let him know. Guess I would have to phone the pub. But I drove on there nervously, on my own.

I was driving wondering if this will be a wasted expedition. I was thinking of my previous dates that were all a disappointment. The trick had to be to regard this all as a great big game and try not to be too serious about it. If it ever, and I mean if it ever, produces a perfect partner, that would be a huge bonus. But it is a big 'if.'

The chance is that most of these dates will be a life experience and nothing more.

And if you can think that that, to save yourself a lot of let downs and disappointments.

What else would I be doing on a Saturday evening apart from sitting in, in front of the TV? I might as well see some countryside and allow a perfect stranger to buy me dinner?

I found the pub easily, as it was on the main road. So I drove on past it and found a lay-by, where I wriggled into my jeans and brushed my hair, applied more lipstick then wiped it off, squirted on a bit more perfume, checked my watch and then set the alarm for another 20 minutes as I was early. (It probably looks hilarious to any passer-by seeing someone change their trousers in the car, thinking no one knows or can see what they're doing, when of course they can!) I wound back my seat, put my head back and did some deep breathing. It seemed a very long 20 minutes. I kept checking the alarm to make sure there wasn't anything wrong with it. In the end, I switched it off, took a deep breath and switched on the ignition. Time to turn the car round and face the music.

My heart was hammering in my ribs as I nosed into the car park behind the pub. I wondered which was his car, the rather battered black Renault Clio, or the dark green Mercedes convertible. My car is a bright red Kia Sportage, and it's a great car, just right for me, but maybe not prestigious.

I wondered if he was watching out of the back window of the pub and felt ridiculously self-conscious. I tried to look calm as if I did this kind of thing all the time, as I flipped open the car door, grabbed my handbag and crunched across the gravel.

To enter the pub, meant walking round the front of the building and entering through the little covered portico at the front door. I walked towards it, feeling suddenly shy at going into a pub by myself, and telling myself not to be so silly.

Suddenly, and it was very sudden – I realised I was being attacked!

Someone sprang virtually on top of me, embracing me with long gangly arms and a wearing a purple floral shirt. It was such a kerfuffle. I didn't know whether I was supposed to be enjoying the moment or fighting for my life. I was momentarily confused. Was this what was supposed to happen or was I the victim of an unprovoked crime. I didn't know whether to fight my way out with a handbag, or find and shake a hand.

Gasping for breath I wriggled free to take stock.

A thin bald man wearing a purple lotus flower shirt, was grinning at me. He was shorter than me.

"Daisy!" he said, extending a bony wrist.

"Patrick!" I replied, perhaps less enthusiastically than I had meant to. I could see one thing immediately. He didn't look anything like his photo.

"I thought you were Jack the Ripper!" I said. Then as it sounded rude I said "Wow, what a welcome!"

"I've been waiting for you just in there," he replied, gesturing towards the little porch.

"I didn't want you to have to come into the pub on your own. So I thought I'd make sure I greeted you out here!" He was smiling and seemed very pleased with himself.

It was thoughtful, I registered that.

"What if it wasn't me!" I said. "You could have made big mistake and been had up for assault!"

"I saw you drive in, and I'd recognise that blonde hair anywhere! I was pretty sure! – You look great by the way!"

"And so do you!" I lied graciously. Wherever did he get that shirt?! I comforted myself that he needed a good woman to help him with his wardrobe.

So we went into the pub, together. He had booked a table, in the far corner of the room, right at the back, all very private, but, it meant a lot of going to and fro with coats and drinks and menus and it seemed a long time before he was sat opposite me and we could have a conversation.

"No cricket today then?" I started.

"Yes I did play today. I did rather well as it happens. I just knew I had to be away on time."

"Was that your local cricket team?"

"Yup. It's quite a pleasant set up. Nice guys. Some are getting on a bit. I won't be doing that when I'm getting on a bit."

"Why do you say that? It's probably a nice hobby? Keeps them fit?"

"Yes, but they can't play well and they let the team down."

"Is it that serious? Surely it's a team and everyone just does their best?"

"Yes – but, we do like to win! Someone needs to say 'Come on old boy, it's time to lay down the bat.' They go on forever. Difficult as no one wants to be the one to say it."

"So you're not over the hill yet? You don't think anyone is trying to say that to you!"

"I hope not, I got two sixes today, and bowled a man out. They would be lost without me!"

This is the thing about Internet Dating, as you're driving, you can't drink. So I had one gin and tonic and had to make it last a very long time.

I don't know what I thought about Patrick because as I've said before in this book, I'm not expecting to meet James Bond. And if someone has a great personality, and of course the requisite two eyes a nose and a mouth, they need to be given a chance. We had a history Patrick and I, of hundreds of hilarious emails. I knew a lot about him and he always made me laugh. That all had to count for something. But looking at this not very tall, skinny, bald man in a hideous purple flowery shirt, there was a problem. Try as I might I couldn't find him attractive. I tried to tell myself this would grow on me as we spent more time together.

We had a great evening, sharing dating stories and laughing. It was definitely a lot of fun, and as dates go it was right up there with the best of them. He seemed to trust me and quite sadly told me of the pain of his divorce and the loneliness afterwards. I felt very sorry for him.

His wife had decided she wanted to live in France, she was French after all, but his business is in the UK. He couldn't just relocate that to France. So she just went, took the boys with her, the youngest was only seven. One day he woke up, and they were gone. She sent the divorce papers a week later

He said he loved her, he had never been unfaithful to her, he would have given her anything to have her back, and he didn't care about the divorce settlement, he just gave her everything. He was too upset to care. He nearly lost his business too, as he had been working in a partnership, but this fell apart during the divorce. In the end he set up on his own and some of his loyal clients went with him. Now his business is established again and he can afford to pay the bills, but for a time, it was all very dicey.

Now she is remarried. They are friends and see each other at Christmas and kids' birthdays. He accepts it's over and the feelings are different. He just doesn't want to spend the rest of his life alone. Hence the dating.

At the end of the meal, we had coffee. When that was finished and I said I thought it was time to leave, I remember him saying

"Please, please just have one more coffee!" Later he told me he had had the best night of his life and he just didn't want it to end. I found that curiously surprising, as I had had a good time and a lot of fun, but I wouldn't have put it quite in that category!

Patrick walked me to my car. He asked me to wait a moment while he opened the boot of his car (it was dark and I didn't know which car was his!) and he then presented me with a bunch of flowers. I was very touched as he had thought about this in advance. However after this, things did not go so well. As he passed the flowers across to me, he tried to lunge at me and kiss me, on the lips. I wasn't ready for that and I stepped sideways in confusion and felt a bit embarrassed. But it just wasn't the right time, and besides, the flowers were squashed somewhere in the middle!

I felt a bit ungrateful. He was a really nice guy, BUT, I couldn't ignore it, the attraction just wasn't there. I couldn't summon it up, however hard I tried.

"Shall I follow you home?" he was saying, "Make sure you get home alright?"

"Patrick", I said, "it's two hours in the opposite direction to where you're going! I will be fine!"

"I'll phone you, it's midnight now so I'll phone you at 2am, OK?" (Remember, he doesn't have a mobile.)

"OK? If that's what you want, but there's no need honestly."

Driving home I felt a lot of things. It was flattering to think he found me so attractive. The fact he had enjoyed my company so much and that for him the evening had been such a success was all really positive. When you go through the pain of a divorce, your self-confidence hits rock bottom, so it's very encouraging to have someone do and say all the lovely things Patrick had done and said to me that night. I remembered all the funny emails and jokes, and Scooby Doo, and I thought how original and hilarious he was. And so romantic, not to want me to go into the pub alone, to bring me flowers and so on. He probably bought that shirt new for the evening and thought he looked nice in it!

Then I felt also very sad, because I didn't know if I could have those sorts of feelings for him. I couldn't help it. I know I like big tall heavy men and he was too sinewy and too lightweight and too bald. I like men to have some hair! I didn't like him putting his arms round me and I certainly did not want to kiss him. But he was clean and smart and maybe, just maybe the feelings would grow if we spent more time together. At my age and stage, I needed to give it time. He was honest, and hard-working and obviously capable of deep emotion. I decided by the time I drove into my driveway, I just needed to learn a lot more about cricket.

As I put the key in the lock the phone was ringing. It was Patrick.

"You didn't need to ring me, I'm fine, honestly" I said.

"Listen Daisy," he said all in a rush, "Tonight I had the best night of my life. You are totally amazing. And if I never see you again, you have given me one precious night! I won't be able to sleep, I can't stop thinking about you. And I will see you again won't I? And soon."

"Yes I loved it too" I said, embarrassed to voice any of my hesitations. "I loved my flowers. You shouldn't have!"

"I'll always buy you flowers" he said. "Always."

"I have to go sleep now, its two in the morning!" I said.

"Night, night, crazy Daisy!" he said. And off I went, to bed.

Pheromones, I concluded, there were just no pheromones.

And my poem slumbered on, hidden in the depths of my purse. Would I ever find someone to give it to?

Two questions:

How can you summon up an attraction for someone if you just don't feel it?

And if you do feel that attraction, how can you deny that either?

So to answer these questions, read my next chapter? It's all you ever wanted to know about pheromones, but were afraid to ask!

Read on and see. This book is brim-full of useful information!

What does Chris have to say tonight. He's at the piano again. Tonight he's singing *Yellow*.

It's a song about stars and devotion. Does he mean this is written in the stars. That somehow the attraction might develop if I give it time? Is he telling me to be patient?

Well, Patrick does seem to be devoted.

I'll sleep on it.

"Night, Chris."

"Night, night Daisy."

Then he said "I'll be here in the morning! Still hanging around on the wardrobe door, it's kind of cool."

How comforting was that!

Chapter Thirty-Two Dating Daisy's 'All About Pheromones': All you ever wanted to know but were afraid to ask

Ever wondered what it is that attracts you to that particular partner?

That moment when both your eyes meet across a crowded room? There may be dozens of hot hopefuls, but usually only one will capture your full attention. You seem to be drawn to them like a magnet.

How do we select who we become attracted to? What makes any one individual seem more appealing to us than others? It's a fact, that there may actually be more to this than merely admiration for this hot person's physical attributes. And sometimes, you seem drawn to someone who, when the chips are down, isn't even really that nice looking.

How can this be? Read on!

The answer?

Silently, and also completely invisible, there is a chemical transmission of magic particles – infinitesimally tiny atoms – actually taking place right in front of you!

I would call it – a Walt Disney moment! When that sparkly, magic, *Pixie Dust* really does – invisibly of course – create … a 'glass slipper' moment!

It does sound as if this is a fairy-tale occurrence. But let me assure you, it's very, very real.

Now, those star-studded, glittering but invisible magic dust particles, do have a highly scientific name. They are called 'pheromones' – pronounced 'fair-ra-moans'.

That's a pretty good name don't you think? And I'll tell you a bit about it.

Here's the thing.

- *The word pheromone, has a Greek origin. 'Phero' is an ancient Greek word meaning 'I carry'.*
- *The word 'hormone', derives from the Greek work 'hormon' meaning to set something in motion.*

Put these together and what have you got?

Pher-o-mone.

- *A chemical that conveys messages. Chemical messaging. (A bit like Internet Dating messages really.)*

Once two people have met, these unseen particles spread out into the atmosphere, and buzz across the room. They provide a unique and cleverly unseen means of intimate communication. And let's face it, this may well be the very first time these two people have ever met!

The pheromones travel as fast as a supernova, at 8 miles per second, across the space between you. You literally just need to put your head round the door and,

PIZAZZ! … ZING!,

It's happened in a flash. His pheromones ping to you, and yours ping immediately back. It's a two-way exchange.

You are just a sitting duck. Helpless to the onslaught.

Totally unaware.

Now, 'love atoms' are coursing through the bloodstream.

The game of love has officially started.

Now, once this magic hormonal fairy dust is released, and has been inhaled by the other party, a whole 'Wham, Bam, Thank you

Ma'am!' of thoughts and desires are unleashed!

So pheromones may play a large part in not just

- *internet 'dating'...*
- *... but internet – 'mating!'*

Read on and see.

Now I'm not suggesting that the pheromones travel down the fibre optic computer cables and barge on in to your desk top. Or that they float from him (or her) down the line and through the household atmosphere to the iPad.

Oh no! Pheromones can only perform their magic in the flesh. You do have to be in the same room!

Sorry about that!

There is a big difference between scanning the dating sites and looking at *the Muppets,* and *the no-hopamines,* and the *Crimewatch* suspects, in despair. (Will I ever get off this site?)

And then suddenly, you spot a nice face, OMG! That actually seems to appeal to you! Could there be one nice looking candidate out there after all?... is it at all possible, ever?

Click, click. You have a closer look. Two eyes a nose and a mouth. This is going well. However, I would call this a 'Michelangelo Phenomenon'. That face has been created to be physically beautiful by Mother Nature. This type of attraction is merely a visual thing, and cannot be anything to do with pheromones.

For pheromones to do their stuff, both sets of DNA, yours and theirs, have to be at the same geographical location!

You could go on to meet this beautiful person for a date, and sadly, not find there was a whiff of a pheromone anywhere!

For a successful relationship, physical attraction is not enough in itself. Of course this has to be there to pass 'GO', – and what have I concluded time and time again in this book about Internet Dating, about the absolute importance of the seeing the photograph early on!

But even if they look like Jamie Dornan (from *Fifty Shades of Grey*) – without the existence of those instantaneous magic pheromones, your relationship is doomed to failure, I'm afraid!

To be totally honest about this, the real facts about the role of pheromones in human attraction are still largely unknown. However there is some published, scientific evidence of their role in physical attraction and procreation. Let's see.

We 'Homo sapiens,' do have a special organ in the nose that very few people know we have. It's a very tiny thing, so don't go peering up your nostrils with a torch by the way, you won't spot it, but it does have a humongously long name.

It's called the vomeronasal organ, or VMO for short.

How's your VMO today?

Mine, as you know from this book, is working just fine!

Disappointing to know that in fact the size of the VMO is larger in a foetus than it is in an adult. It seems as we grow and age, the VMO is shrinking. Why would that be, if the VMO is so important for human reproduction?

Here's the thing. Nobody knows!

But, as far as producing pheromones is concerned:

(Sing-a-long!)

"Birds do it, bees do it

Even educated fleas do it

Let's do it, let's fall in love." (Cole Porter 1928!)

It's true! Honey bees give off different types of pheromones to defend their nests, to mark the eggs and to raise alarm if there is a need for defence.

- *Lady moths produce pheromones and even in tiny doses, such as billionth of a gram, can attract a mate from 300 feet away.*
- *Sea urchins and oysters produce pheromones which facilitate other sea urchins and other oysters to release their eggs and sperm at the same time. The more eggs and the more sperm, the more procreation there's likely to be. Isn't nature marvellous! Safety in numbers!*

So, what about pheromones and human beings? There are so many questions to ask.

Here's the thing. What do we know?

1. Can we control when and where we produce pheromones?
   - *No, it's involuntary. Pheromones are produced totally involuntarily from hair follicles, in sweat, in urine and from vaginal secretions.*
2. What evidence is there that pheromones have a role to play in human intimacy?
   - *Several studies have demonstrated that pheromones have a positive effect on emotion, mood and sexual attractiveness.*
   - *Here are three examples:*
     1) *In a 1998 study by Cutler, he randomly divided a group of 38 males into a pheromone group and a control group. The pheromone group applied pheromones, and the control group applied a similar substance but this was a placebo. The study subjects and the investigators were unaware whether they were using the pheromones or the placebo.*
   - *The results showed that over the next two weeks, the pheromone group exhibited significantly more sexual behaviours with their male partners, than the placebo group. These behaviours included more sexual intercourse, more sleeping in the same bed and more petting/kissing.*
     1) *This experiment was repeated by McCoy and Petino in 2002, but using female subjects. A similar affect was found to the Cutler study.*
     2) *In a well know experiment in 2003, Preti et al. collected the underarm secretions from a group of men and asked a group of women to smell them. They monitored women's reproductive hormone levels, and found that exposure to the pheromones in sweat, had a tendency for the women to become more relaxed, and to ovulate earlier in their menstrual cycle.*
3. If we are lacking pheromones, can we just borrow somebody else's?
   - *Good idea! But no! There are perfumes on the market that contain artificial pheromones, but these come from pigs, not humans! If you use them, beware on your next trip to the pig farm!*
4. What if our pheromones have got it wrong?

Tricky. We are who we are. It has been suggested that some men prefer the scent (pheromones) of other men, and some women the scent (pheromones) of other women. This is one theory about homosexuality.

But it's in our DNA. We can't change our pheromones, but we need to be aware of them if we want long term sexual relationships to be successful. That is my Daisy opinion anyway!

In Dating Daisy, I knew on every date, whether the pheromones were compatible. I could tell the instant I set eyes on my DDPs. Pheromones are not real smells, it's important to make that clear, although smells do feature as important in this book.

I do however think the smell of a prospective partner is extremely important, don't you?

Pheromones are actually nothing to do with aftershave or bad breath. This is the key point. The presence of pheromones is an almost supernatural event. They lurk in the air around the pair of you, ready to jump up and scare you. Ghostly apparitions. You can't summon them up. And if they choose to reveal themselves, there is nothing you can do about it. A pheromone, like a spirit from the underworld, can catch you unawares and freak you out, when you are least aware of it. You just have to read to the end of this book!

So there's a science to love and attraction that we just fail to appreciate.

When the pheromones are exploding from the loosened champagne cork, so are those other important love hormones are flooding through the brain and body.

Adrenaline: which causes your heart to race, to sweat and find your mouth is going dry.

Dopamine: the desire and reward hormone (which has been compared to taking cocaine!).

Oxytocin: the cuddle hormone, needs no further explanation.

Vasopressin: released after sex and important for the long-term commitment stage

Finding a partner is actually one long series of biochemical and hormonal events. No wonder it's not so simple as just logging on and clicking the cursor! Our bodies are actually in control and we are almost bystanders to a host of biological reactions!

So, if your date is a disaster, just remember – we can't control *the soup*! That's the chemical soup that's sloshing through our veins, uninvited, yet helping decide your future!

I have to say that despite all my disappointing dates, and all the pheromone let downs, my pheromones always… and I can say this as I know the end of the story

… get it right!

Read on and see?

Chapter Thirty-Three (In which Daisy updates the Amigos)

Sunday May 4th 2014

So it was time to visit the Amigos. I half ran down the path and jammed my finger on the doorbell. Malcolm opened the door surprised to see me as I hadn't let them know I was coming in advance. He was walking quite well as long as he wore his spinal brace. He said it wasn't too painful, as long as he kept up with the gin! Maggie appeared as if by magic, with the tea. We sat on the sofa, three ducks in a row. Life had returned fairly quickly to normal, except that for the time-being Malcolm wasn't allowed to drive.

"Come on, come on," they chorused, "We need to hear it all!"

"Ok, I'll tell you … give me a chance!" I replied. I was just as keen to share all that had happened as they were to hear it.

"Was it a wasted trip, just tell me that?" asks Malcolm.

"I don't know, I can't make my mind up. No not a wasted trip but just as usual, not what I expected."

Malcolm said, "Not good? Too fat, too thin, too tall too short, that kind of thing?"

"Did he have two eyes, a nose and a mouth?" asked Maggie/ Amigo Two.

"Was he dressed as Scooby Doo?!" asked Malcolm.

"No, no he wasn't. Nothing like that ... he was just ..." How could I describe it...? "Wearing a pretty hideous shirt with big purple flowers on it."

"Needs a woman's touch, that's all." said Maggie.

"And he had gangly arms. And he was sinewy thin, and bald, and no taller than me. But, he was great company, and very charming, and he looked after me, and he brought me flowers!"

"Flowers!" they both repeated at once.

"Yes, in the boot of his car! He gets brownie points for that as he had obviously thought of that in advance!"

"So, what was he like then? Did you have a lot to talk about? Did you get on well?" Malcolm was impatient to know the details. He had always had my best interests at heart.

"Yes, yes we did. He phoned me to say he had had the best evening of his life and if he never saw me again, he would never forget it!"

"Well how good is that?" said Malcolm.

" That's wonderful news!" echoed Maggie.

"But it isn't" I said dejectedly. "I can't help it. Yes he has got two eyes a nose and a mouth ... but ..."

"But?" enquired Malcolm.

It was a sad fact but I had to tell them. "I can't help it. Whatever the word is ... I just don't feel that way about him. I just don't."

"You just need to give it time," Maggie replied soothingly.

"I'm not sure that will make any difference. He's a really nice guy ... he's just not tall and heavy. He's the opposite. And try as I might, that's what I want. I guess it's because I'm not small, you see, and small men make me feel bigger, and big men make me feel small," I said.

"Well ... come on ... you said yourself that personality is the most important thing," challenged Malcolm.

"Yes, but there has to be some attraction. And you know what...

same old thing… he doesn't look anything like his photograph! I haven't quizzed him about it yet. But he just doesn't! Where is the debonair man I saw at the racecourse!"

"I do know what you mean actually. She can't force herself. If she isn't attracted to him, she isn't attracted to him. Full stop," said Maggie.

But Malcolm retorted, "Come on! This isn't *Romeo and Juliet*! It's real life. Think about all the fun they've had in the emails, and Scooby Doo!"

Then he said, "Now ask yourself why he did that."

"Why then?" asked Maggie.

"It's obvious. He knew he wasn't that attractive and he couldn't let her see him too early as he knew this would happen," replied Malcolm.

I was quick to interject "Oh come on. I'm not an oil painting either. We are as we are. It's lovely he was positive about me, but in his heart of hearts he probably wants a small skinny woman really. But he can't dial up one of those either. He probably thinks the same as me if he's honest."

"You can't say that! There are lots of couples where either the woman or the man is large and the other person is skinny. Some people like that! It turns them on!" argued Malcolm.

"Well I think you're asking too much. You can't expect to meet someone at any age really, but certainly not in mid-life, where there is an instant overwhelming attraction and the rest is history. I'm sorry but you can't! You need to give it time. This is real life not a romantic novel. You get on so well. You would be mad not to give it a chance," stated Malcolm.

I considered this. "So you think I should see him again then?"

"I do. And soon. And perhaps this time you will feel a little bit differently. You wait and see," said Malcolm, and Maggie was nodding sagely.

My Amigos are so wise. How could I carry on being Dating Daisy without them?

Chapter Thirty-Four (In which Daisy survives a ride in the lift with Patrick)

Sunday May 4th 2014

So I went home, and drank more tea, and did some normal things like washing and cooking and mused about things. Thankfully the plumbing was all working nicely, for once. (We were used to moving buckets in the study, to catch the drips from the ceiling. It was only a slow drip. One bucket could easily last a whole day.)

There was time for a swim before bedtime. Splosh, splosh I churned up the water thinking furiously.

Personality was everything. Look at Spacetime 3000 (why hadn't he messaged me?). But why was I still thinking about other internet hopefuls if Patrick was a serious option? I loved the Spacetime email. That was such a fantastic idea, to write such a piece on the internet. That was truly brilliant mind. Patrick had been inspirational but Spacetime 3000 might be something else completely. Or not? It's a lottery Internet Dating. You just don't know.

Patrick continued to email me, buoyed up but the success of the evening and desperate for good feedback. The thing is, I didn't want to say things that weren't true or give him false hope, so suddenly it all seemed a bit difficult.

"Daisy Daisy, give me you answer do ..." he emailed. "I'm half crazy, all for the love of you ..."

"What can I say?" I emailed back, "It won't be a stylish marriage. We can't afford a carriage, but you'll look sweet, upon the seat, with a cricket bat made for two!"

"We have to have another date," he wrote, "When, when when? I can't wait!"

So we agreed it. The following Sunday he would come to visit me in Brighton, and spend the day with me. A whole day. I was full of trepidation. How would it be, good or bad, enormous fun or agonising? Success? Or disaster? There was only one way to find out. It would be a long week of waiting and anticipation.

In the meantime, life went on.

In the meantime, I've been reflecting on my life in medicine. Whatever you say about a career in medicine, you do find yourself in some pretty incredible situations. So I thought I would share a story from my medical student days with you.

I was doing a stint in A&E as a final year medical student, many years ago now! It was pretty much like Casualty on TV, except without the BBC cameras, it was ten times as busy, and everyone was dead grumpy, or just dead or nearly dead. And grumpy. No one had time to teach me, and I was wandering around trying not to be a nuisance, wearing my medical student badge but still feeling a nuisance and in the way.

It's that age-old chestnut. To be useful, you need to have the experience, and you can't get the experience, unless you know how to do it.

How to break that cycle?

It's quite scary as a student – wondering if you really ever will be the person with the apron and the gloves on, resetting dislocated limbs, suturing major incisions, piercing the thorax with a chest drain, or perhaps **the** person in charge of the gruesome resuscitation process.

Me? – I always had this pressing need to find the nearest broom cupboard and climb in.

So I was loitering. Maybe Sister would ask me to make the tea. I've always been good at that. There was a nice little list on the wall by the kettle that says how everyone liked their tea. The list was pinned up next to an assortment of notices like 'How to test for MRSA', and 'How to avoid passing on Norovirus', and 'Which samples should be sent to the lab if a patient has intractable diarrhoea...' all those sorts of notices that you really needed to read while you were on your lunch break.

And the Registrar, a bearded chap from Azerbaijan, said to me

"You, you're a medical student?" he glanced at my badge. I felt so small I wanted to apologise for breathing. Someone had noticed me!

"Yes,"

"Do you want something to do? Clinical practice?"

"Yes please!" I sounded like I had just asked for a Mr Whippy with a flake on top!

"Well, go down to that end cubicle. There's a lady in there. I want you to examine the cardiovascular system, with particular reference to the apex beat."

"Yes, no problem" and off I scurried.

Behind the curtain is a large lady reminiscent of Hattie Jacques from the *Carry On* films. She had slid half down the bed, and lay like a beached whale, breathing rapidly into a plastic mask tied around her nose and mouth with a green tape. She seemed distressed and rather pathetic. The sheets and drapes were somehow swathed around her in a chaotic fashion.

"I'm a medical student," I said "Dr Dabou asked me to come and examine you. Would that be OK?"

"Yes" she nodded. "No problem."

"I just need to feel your pulse and listen to your heart," I explained.

She nodded. Speaking was hard work for her.

Tentatively I picked up her sweaty hand. The skin was crinkly but moist, crocodile skin I thought to myself. Having looked at the hands with some degree of scrutiny, as we are always taught as medical students, I progressed to feeling the pulse at the wrist. It was rapid.

One hundred and ten beats per minute, regular.

Well she's alive, I've established that.

I continued my examination as I had been taught, checking her blood pressure, and looking at the neck for the jugular venous pressure (veins in the neck). It was elevated, so this is likely to be heart failure.

"Are you in pain?" I asked her.

"No," she gasped, "I just can't breathe."

I continued my examination by lifting the nightie to look for the apex beat. You may know that this is usually located directly behind the left-sided fifth rib and by definition therefore, in women, lies underneath the left breast. For women who are well endowed, feeling for the apex beat means lifting the left breast and sliding your examining hand underneath it. This may be a hot sweaty, and probably rather unpleasant experience, for both the clinician and the patient.

So I did ask, "I need to feel for your heartbeat, so I just need to slide my hand under here, is that ok?"

"Ok," she replied.

I did the necessary. My fingers slid into the clammy recess under the gargantuan appendage that was the left breast.

But what was this? Something wet and spongey on my fingertips? Something that was not just the apex beat.

Frowning, I used my right hand to lift the breast and look into the cleft underneath it. I did a double take and looked again. Could this be? I was astounded!

There, in a triangular indentation under the breast, happily ensconced, was nothing other than a ham sandwich. Triangular, squashed and well past it's sell by date. But definitely, a ham sandwich.

I went back to Dr Dabou.

"Finished?" he asked.

Grinning, "Yes" I said.

"So what did you find on examining the apex beat?"

Without hesitation, I replied "A ham sandwich."

The rest of the team looked up in surprise.

"Good work," said Dr Dabou. "I think you'll go far in medicine!"

You know what? Imogen has been very secretive these past few days. She got a 'B' for her last essay, so she is pleased as punch about that. And this week she and I did a midnight run to Asda and came home and actually made fresh pasta ravioli – from scratch! It was pretty good if I say so myself. I had to watch a video on *YouTube* about how to do it. Amazing what you can find on the net. I think I could pass this course myself! But Imogen has been sitting in the lounge with her laptop and making strange faces at me, so there's something going on.

We haven't talked again about the sale of the house but the agent has given me a price, and the 'For Sale' boards go up next week; Imogen will just have to get on with it. Nothing I can do. It just has to happen.

So my second date with Patrick?

I had it all planned. There are eight miles of seafront in Brighton. Imogen could give us a lift to the Marina end of the seafront. We could walk the eight miles, from Brighton Marina to Southwick. This could easily take all day with a few coffee and picnic spots along the way. Then get an open top bus home. Perfect! We just needed the weather!

I don't know what Imogen thought as she opened the door to Patrick that morning. How embarrassing to be confronted with Mum's new boyfriend. (Boyfriend? Patrick? Really?)

"The traffic was dreadful," moaned Patrick as he stepped into our front porch. "It's took me nearly five hours to do the journey last night!" We had agreed he would come the night before but stay over in a Travelodge, as it was so far to come. I wasn't ready to ask him to stay.

We commiserated about Britain's traffic.

He was wearing a quilted jacket with padded oval shapes sewn onto the elbows. I didn't much like it. And an oatmeal baggy jumper.

I didn't much like that either. And Oh God, in his hand he carried … a pork pie hat! He looked very bald and beaky nosed standing there, and when I stood next to him in my stockinged feet, I realised something else. He was only about the same height as me!

As time was pressing and we had a full day, I suggested we set off immediately and have coffee in Jake's cafe at the far end of the Marina

As Patrick and I climbed into the back seat of Imogen's Renault Clio, I wondered if this was a good idea. Our thighs were jammed close together on the back seat. Patrick seemed to like this and clasped my hand. I wasn't so sure at all and suddenly wished I could call the whole thing off.

I remember it was a sunny bright day in May. The view of the seafront was panoramic. A little later, sipping hot coffee, and Patrick beaming at me across the coffee cups – there was a washing machine feeling somewhere around my solar plexus. We then walked along the promenade, heading west.

Patrick held my hand. Here's the thing, I adore holding hands, but only if it's with the right person. And this felt all wrong. His hand was marbley and boney. More's to the point I know people who live here and any moment someone could have spotted me holding hands with this Worzel Gummidge-type stranger. I don't like to say I felt embarrassed, but I did. I wriggled out of his grasp as soon as I could, I think to throw a stick for someone else's dog!, and dug my hands firmly into my pockets. I hope Patrick wasn't upset about that. But I just didn't want it. And as I contemplated this thought, I think I realised I just didn't want the whole thing. Here I was walking on the beach with some guy I met on the internet, in a pork pie hat.

My mind was speaking to me – as you know it does. *You got yourself into this! When all is said and done, it's a beautiful day to spend by the sea, which you wouldn't have done by yourself. And you're just getting to know a new friend, you don't have to fancy the pants off him. Why not just take the day for what it is? A nice day out, and don't think beyond that. Just be good company and ward off the amorous advances.*

What did we talk about that day? Patrick and I never had a problem talking. We talked all the time. That was the great thing. We talked about what we did in our spare time, his horse racing and cricket, my writing and swimming. I told him lots of Sexual Health stories. These are often so funny you just couldn't make them up. We talked about our failed marriages. He told me about the pain he still felt when his wife left him, a pain that is still there under the surface, but that he has learnt to live with. I'm a connoisseur of that type of pain. He said he was so distressed when she said she was going that he went to pieces and gave her everything. There was no argument, he just said she should have it all. To the point there was nothing in the bank and he could hardly pay his bills. His business collapsed and he was facing complete ruin. It was only the support of a few special colleagues that persuaded and encouraged him to set up independently and work for himself, that got him to where he is today. Now, about ten years on, he is solvent again and able to live a reasonable lifestyle. It is a time in his life he doesn't want to remember. He told me he visits his sons in France several times a year, and in the summer they come over for a month and he takes them on holiday somewhere in the UK. He looks forward to it all year.

Somewhere around early afternoon we went into the Brighton Fishing Museum on for lunch. It's an imposing old building with a bit of a leafy garden that looks out over the sea. They don't have much of interest in there, but it's a surprisingly genteel venue, considering it is what it is, a fishing museum, and the cafe is pretty good.

So I led the way to the lift as the cafe is on the top floor. Patrick stepped into the lift just ahead of me, and as I stepped in, I swivelled to press the button for the top floor. We were the only people in the lift, thankfully. For out of the blue I suddenly felt scratchy stubble crushing my face and a rubbery tongue like a little snake probing in and out of my mouth. Patrick, it seemed, was kissing me.

I didn't know whether to laugh or cry. I hadn't been kissed like that for as long as I could remember. And I did really like Patrick. But it was so unexpected and so awkward, and the feeling was sadly, shiveringly unpleasant, as his little tongue was reminiscent of some strange part that goes wrong with the hoover. He had thrown his arms around me too, but grappling me underneath my coat. I remembered how long and gangly his arms were when we had our first date, like Mr Tickle. If he was Mr Tickle, I was definitely Little Miss Not Impressed!

Daisy's Thoughts about Men and Kissing

Kisses are like fish . . .
The sea anemone kiss – all puckered up and sticks on you.
The dolphin kiss – darting in and out of the waves and flicking its tale.
The whale kiss – lumbering and uncertain, like waiting for Good.
The crab – not symmetrical, he's kissing my left nostril and seems to like it.
The salmon – always wading upstream, tickles the tonsils.

Patrick's kiss was ... I'm sorry to say it ... but the thought came to me afterwards ... a sea slug kiss.

Enough said ...

"Can we go in the lift more often?" he was murmuring. "I hope there are plenty more lifts on this walk."

I did a quick mental calculation that that wasn't the case. But I kept this information to myself.

The lift doors opened suddenly and we sprang apart and entered the restaurant nonchalantly, as people do when they've just been snogging in a lift. (Do all couples do that?) Patrick seemingly elated. Myself, just bemused.

Later, Imogen picked us up from the bus stop, as we had been waiting far too long for non-existent public transport, and it was time to go home and sit down. The surprise as we came through the door was that she and her friend Izzy, had cooked us a Greek meal. Knowing how much I love Greek food, (in particular my absolute favourite restaurant that I've already mentioned - in London, the Real Greek,) they had googled the menu and copied the recipes. I was amazed to see home-made Greek flatbreads, Tzatziki, hummus, stuffed vine leave, lamb kebabs and Greek salad. Imogen had even found baklava and pistachio ice-cream, my favourite, and a bottle of authentic Greek Retsina. I was so impressed with them. Really, my mouth opened and shut like a goldfish! (I think Miss Cunningham would have been most impressed!)

So we all sat at the table and ate this fabulous meal together. To be honest I was glad to be with a crowd as I was finding the constant one-on-one a bit of a strain. I was pleased to hear the girls talking to Patrick about cricket and sport, and concentrate myself on downing the wine. There was one hurdle to go. Patrick had driven here last night, and he did need to drive home. It was a long way to Tintagel, and I knew he would need to leave at a reasonable time. I was not going to encourage him to stay the night. I just had to pray he wasn't getting any ideas, as there was no clear plan how the evening would come to an end, and I was rather dreading it.

Eventually the meal came to an end. Imogen and Izzy made their excuses and left the table. I busied myself with plates and clearing up. I told Patrick just to relax in the lounge and watch some TV while I made us some coffee. Which he rather reluctantly went off to do. I must say I took as long over it as possible.

I felt very uncomfortable at that point. We had had such a great internet experience and had felt so happy to be meeting up. The saddest thing was that he had the hots for me, but it wasn't reciprocated. If we had both liked each other, or both not liked each other, it would have been different. But when one does and one doesn't, it's painful and I didn't know what to do. Should I just be honest, or should I go along with it? Was I just expecting to have feelings for him too early on. It was only a second date. Was I being unreasonable?

He called "Anything I can do?" from the lounge. My cue to go and join him.

"No, not all, I'll be there in a minute." I was assembling a coffee tray and made my way into the lounge.

Mr Tickle had arranged himself invitingly at one end of the sofa. There was nothing for it, I had to go and sit next to him.

I put down the tray, and walked round the coffee table to sit on the sofa. The sofa is positioned across the French windows, and as it was dark outside and the lights were on in the room, anyone outside in the road could see clearly into the lounge.

Patrick executed one of his usual crush and grab moments, precisely then.

He sort of jumped to his feet to do it, in the small space between the coffee table and the edge of the sofa. In a kamikaze moment I was tangled in gangly arms and the Dyson component was worming its way down my throat again. I sort of froze as it was so unprecedented. I was also knocked off balance and we both collapsed sideways onto the sofa in a heap of limbs. I also noticed his mouth was very dry. I had noticed that earlier but it hadn't registered. Lubricant is actually necessary for both ends of the body.

Here's the thing, it's impossible to disguise if you are turned on by somebody, but it's also impossible to disguise if you are not. So I think in that moment he just knew. While I was fighting for breath, and swaying over the sofa, worried about what my neighbours would think if they happened to walk past just now, with one eye open and anticipating the landing onto the cushions, I think he got the vibes. He pulled away a bit abruptly.

We sat, getting our breath, in front of the cafetiere and then we both started taking at once. I don't know what we said but the gist of it was, and this is how I dealt with it, and it is true, but I left out the just not into you bit.

"Let's not get too involved as we just can't do a long-distance relationship. It took you five hours one way for you to get here last night, how is that going to work?

You can't change your business, your clients are in Cornwall, you've already been through setting up again on your own and you can't do that again. I can't suddenly move to Cornwall for all the same reasons.

"I don't know what we were thinking of! I think we have to put this down as a great experience and so much fun, but I just don't think it can progress.

"I think you're amazing, funny, clever, smart, great company and so much going for you ... and I've had a whale of a time with the hilarious emails and everything. Totally fabulous. But I just don't think we can go forward from here. Do you?"

Then we had the where there's a will there's a way conversation. We started talking about getting the train at weekends to see each other, and sod the poor Sunday connections and the fact there's no direct route, maybe a coach would be better, maybe we could do this every other weekend, would it be enough. But I knew in my heart it wouldn't be enough. It just wouldn't.

I couldn't say it, BUT, it was simple really.

For me.

No pheromones.

As simple as that.

Chapter Thirty-Five (In which Dating Daisy sets out her Internet Dating lessons)

Dating Daisy's Internet Lessons

So, when I started writing this, all those months ago, I was a complete beginner. A novice.

- *A learner driver.*
- *'L' plates.*
- *Beep, Beep, Beep!*

What did I think would happen?

Did I think I would be swept off my feet by date number one?

Did I think I would get even one date?

Did I think I would meet the Belfast strangler?

Did I have rules, and stipulations? Six dates before you have sex, that kind of thing?

What have I learnt so far, albeit I am still a long way from knowing the end of my story?

So, my Internet Dating lessons start right here:

Dating Daisy's Internet Dating Lessons

Rule 1. Start this whole caboodle with a very deep breath. It will be a marathon and not a sprint.

Rule 2. My advice is to be totally honest. Don't lie about your age, or use someone else's photo. It will only end in tears at a later date.

Rule 3. Make an effort with your own profile. You can't blame the guy at the other end for having a blank page, if yours is pretty similar. Think about how you want to come across, mine was *dazzling, beautiful, smart and alluring.* I also wanted someone who was bright, who could tell stories and had a personality. So my profile had to reflect that I had those qualities.

Rule 4. Decide what is really important to you and stick to it. I started with the basic building blocks of mankind: two eyes, a nose and a mouth. But, then I whittled it down to **Looks, Personality, Education, Solvent and Local.** Don't forget that!

Rule 5. Which brings me to my next point. Long distance relationships just don't work. I would stick to a radius, of say 30 miles. Just far enough to get home safely after a night out, or to escape if things go pear-shaped. But these long-haul jaunts for example to Cornwall are soul destroying. At our age and stage, it's very difficult to relocate, so my advice is don't get started on that one. Look at Love Bug. Sad but sensible won the day.

Rule 6. (This is an extension of rule 2.) Don't believe everything they tell you.

Rule 7. The photograph, yes this is essential. No photograph no date. It has to be as simple as that. Get them to hold a bottle of champagne in one hand and take a selfie and whatsapp it to you there and then. That's the only way the photo is believable. (Read on, as the greatest example of a date with no photograph has yet to be revealed...)

Rule 8. There's a lot said about the need to meet in a public place etc. ... I would agree, but I would also say it's preferable to just meet for coffee or a drink the first time. That way you don't have to sit there for a couple of hours when you know instantly there's no hope, the minute you set eyes on them. (Case in point a date I left out of this book with a guy who turned out to be a Father Christmas look-alike with sheeps' teeth and a cardigan!)

Rule 9. You have to accept everyone on the site has baggage, emotional baggage. That's why they are there. Emotional pain is desperate. Ibuprofen doesn't help. You need empathy and patience. I have told myself firmly, that I can't do anything about the past.

Neither can my date. So we both have to live with that. But, here's the good bit, there's a lot we can do about the present. And what happens in the present then gradually builds into a future. So don't dwell on the past. It's the past and it needs to stay there. Just concentrate on making every day – and every date! – the best it can be!

Rule 10. Keep going. You don't know the end of my story yet. But it's enough to say that there is someone out there for everyone. Someone right now is hoovering their lounge, or sitting in a car wash, or polishing their golf clubs ... and they just don't know who is round the corner! ... You!

When I think about the Internet Dating rules, which rule did I break with Patrick?

Rule 4 and 5: He needs to be "local": why on earth did I ever think that 200 miles apart would ever be starter?

Rule 7: 'The photograph.' The photograph he showed me initially was obviously taken years ago, hence my shock when I saw the real Patrick, and the *Scooby Doo* episode. Trust your instincts. You may not need George Clooney but that element of attraction just has to be there.

So now I needed to follow Rule 10: Keep going. I felt deflated at the thought of having the build up all over again, perhaps for another let down. But ... I'm Dating Daisy! *Dazzling, beautiful, smart and alluring*! Onwards and upwards, and back to the boyfriend shop. Let's see who's in the *Muppet Show* today?

Chapter Thirty-Six (In which Daisy's "Boo" gets the desired attention.)

Monday May 5th 2014

So Patrick went home. We exchanged some sad emails over the next few days. I was tearful at times. I looked back at our imaginative emails and even now was amazed at the fun we had playing 20 questions and virtual cricket and re-enacting Cinderella. I tried to imagine myself getting over that just not into you feeling. But I knew I couldn't. The distance was also an insolvable problem and everything about that was exactly true. It wouldn't be helpful to have another date. So I tried to be friendly but not suggestive and let the situation cool down kindly. Meanwhile I looked again at the hopefuls.

Suddenly there was an email in my box from ChocolateLover. I had forgotten all about him.

Hi Crazy Daisy,
Boo again!!

Are you still out there? Can we speak as I'm not into great long emails. You never sent me your number? I'm in a hotel in Brighton this week on business and wondered if we could have a drink or a meal or something. It's a long week! I don't bite, honest!

If you send me your number I'll call you?

Jack

I looked again at his profile. It said he was 6ft tall. In his photo he had white blonde hair and large dark eyes. Perhaps that's why I had emailed 'Boo' to him as he looked vaguely spooky? It said all the right things. Likes sailing, cycling, walking, listening to music, cosy nights by a log fire etc. ... Occupation? 'Managerial.'

He had one son, aged 7, but didn't want more children. It was a bit of a sparse profile, but I decided he looked nice in his photo. He was local, at least for part of the week, and after all the emails with Patrick, do you know, I couldn't face another barrage of emails either. What the hell. I sent him my number.

So I must say it took about 30 seconds for my mobile to ring after I texted the number. I pressed SEND, and had hardly had time to browse anywhere before I heard my familiar ringtone. *Mission Impossible* by the way. Which this was turning out to be!

"Jack?"

"Daisy?"

"Well, you don't waste any time!"

"Ha! That's me. Once my mind's made up!"

"Well thanks. Good to speak to you. Where are you?"

I liked his voice. He was well spoken but he had a nervous little laugh that punctuated most sentences, and perhaps he was trying to sound cool, but the accent was vaguely American.

"I'm in this hotel. In Brighton. Near the seafront."

"How come? It must be for work?"

"Yes, I'm a director of a property company. Have to visit their sites in the South. So I travel a lot, and they book me into these places."

"It doesn't sound much fun really? You're obviously away from home a lot."

"Oh, I've got a house in Plymouth. I'm there at weekends, and I set off either Sunday evening or very early Monday mornings. I have a seven-year-old son and I'm very involved with looking after him."

"So, sorry to ask, but I guess your son has a mother?"

"Ah of course, yes, but we're separated. We are in the process of being divorced. But she's not very happy about it."

"Sounds difficult."

"Yes, it is. All very upsetting. But it's over. The marriage I mean. That's it. Finito. Anyway how about you?"

"I'm divorced now. After 26 years. I never wanted it to happen but it did – so – onwards and upwards."

"How long have you been Internet Dating?"

"Oh, only a couple of months. And you?"

"I don't know, a while. The thing is I'm never anywhere long enough to be able to plan, and at weekends I have to be in Plymouth. So it's very awkward. I probably shouldn't be ringing you. But you seemed so much fun and I thought I need to try and make an effort. Where there's a will there's a way. I won't be in this awful divorce situation for ever and when I'm out the other side I do want a better life!"

"It's important to focus on the positives. I agree. I've been there and I'm in the same boat!"

"Look, where do you live?"

"I'm in Brighton too." I didn't give my address.

"Well what do you know! Look can we meet for dinner? When are you free? How about tomorrow night?"

This was all going quite fast, but he sounded nice, and if we met in a public place what harm could there be. Before I knew it I heard myself agreeing, and the following night, me, Dating Daisy, had another date!

Chris gave me a quote at bedtime.

He just popped up and said

"Everything that's happening to you, is what's supposed to be happening to you,

so just relax!"

So that's what I have to do, relax.

"Night, Chris."

"Nighty, night Daisy"

And I slept. I really did.

Chapter Thirty-Seven (In which Daisy meets Robert Redford.)

Wednesday May 6th 2014

I recall I wore the little black dress for this date. I piled my hair up on my head and put on some Darcy Bussell dangly earrings. I tottered a bit on my heels as I wove through the tables in the *Inferno Pizza* Italian Restaurant. I was nervous as usual, but in truth I recall, there was now a small part of me that knew most of these dates were doomed, and was fatalistic. No doubt it would be another unmitigated disaster. Don't worry, I hadn't forgotten the poem!

Now I'm writing this dating account largely from memory, so you have to forgive me for the gaps. But here's the thing. It didn't turn out a disaster, it was actually quite the opposite.

Jack was very gentlemanly, and stood straight away to embrace me, help me with my coat and settle me at the table. I noted his thick white hair, snow white. And startling blue eyes, which very striking, but for some reason set in very shadowed tired-looking sockets. He looked pale, tired and like he was living through stress.

But you know what, he did look the guy in the photo I had seen on the internet. For once, I had known exactly who I was going to meet. How refreshing was that. It strikes of honesty straight away.

We stood about the same height, albeit I was in heels. If I had had any choice in the matter I would have dialled him up a couple of inches taller, but anyway, he wasn't shorter than me. He had quite a chiselled face that reminded me of Robert Redford. I noted his dark blue suit, with a crisp white shirt and slightly purplish tie, and was impressed.

From memory, we both had a Caesar salad. I had walked there, so was able to indulge in a couple of glasses of wine. He was driving, what I later discovered was a Union Jack, soft-top, Mini! Again, I thought this was very cute and funny. He took me home in it. (For anyone old enough to remember this was the car in the series *Butterflies,* which I absolutely loved, and never dreamed I'd actually have a ride in!)

We must have talked about all sorts. I think we talked about films, and his resemblance to Robert Redford! I think we talked about Internet Dating and how hard it is. And about our own marriages – or the state of them! – and the idiosyncrasies of life. He liked the idea of this book, *Dating Daisy,* and I told him to be careful as he just might be in it! He was working as a senior manager for a private housing corporation. He had done a degree in Estate Management, as a mature student, and transferred into this as a career as he hated his first job in the bank.

I don't recall a lot else, except that I did like him. When he dropped me home I let him peck me on the cheek, then I jumped out of the car. I was hoping this Robert Redford might be back in touch.

And he was!

Internet Dating lesson.

My first thoughts about this date, were that it had been a success. When I read through my dating rules on page page 285, I had just about followed my own advice! How incredible is that Daisy?

Looks, personality, education, solvent and local.

He ticked all the boxes, except a half tick in the local box, as he wasn't here at weekends. But that could be temporary.

The only other point, and this had not come up before surprisingly, was that he was still married. More about that to come.

Here's the thing, people who are still married, even if the marriage is over, are in a difficult place. The pressure of living with or without your other half, the bitterness, the arguments, the uncertainty, however calm you are, take their toll. And for the new relationship this is very hard to bear. It can work both ways and if both parties are going through separation and divorce at the same time, it's a recipe for a cataclysmic explosion. You can't help who you fall in love with, remember the pheromones, but try to focus your attentions on a date who is above all ... available.

I think I need to add this other word to my list – 'Available'.

Looks, personality, education, solvent, local and available.

Chapter Thirty-Eight (In which Daisy gets an intergalactic shock)

Saturday May 6th 2014

So here's the thing, one out, one in.

It's a game.

When one doesn't work out, you go back to the online boyfriend shop! It's a simple as that.

I did pine for Patrick and we exchanged a few sad emails. At one point we started again down the "Can't we do this at weekends on the train" conversation, but then between us we knocked that idea firmly into touch. It just couldn't be. I needed to concentrate on the here and now. I think that's an important message from this book if you are still reading. We can't change yesterday. All we can do is make the most of today – and tomorrow- will take care of itself.

So Jack was texting me all the time.

PING: Jack: Loved spending the evening with you! You looked lovely. And you are so funny! When can we do it again?

PING BACK: Daisy: I'm making a cake, I texted. **And I need two hands so you need to stop texting me!**

PING: Jack: But I'm at work too. And I can't stop thinking about you. What cake is it?

PING BACK: Daisy: It's a New Zealand Carrot Cake.

PING: Jack: Have you ever been to New Zealand?

PING BACK: Daisy: No, but I've had a lot of carrot cake.

PING: Jack: Why is it a New Zealand carrot cake?

PING BACK: Daisy: Because in New Zealand they grow a lot of carrots? I don't know!

PING: Jack: Well can you make one for me?

PING BACK: Daisy: I guess.

PING: Jack: Then I can come round and pick it up!

PING BACK: Daisy: Well you'll have to wait as I have to get the ingredients.

PING: Jack: Tell me what you need and I'll bring it round. You can show me how you do it!

PING BACK: Daisy: I can't do that now, it's late, and I've got work tomorrow.

PING: Jack: Well tomorrow evening then?

PING BACK: Daisy: It's Friday tomorrow and I thought you were going back to Plymouth after work? To your wife!

PING: Jack: You know my schedule better than I do!

PING BACK: Daisy: Well it does occur to me there's not much point striking up a relationship with someone I can never see at the weekend!

PING: Jack: Well it won't be like this for ever. And I can organise the odd weekend off, or a Friday night off, or a Sunday night off, with warning.

PING BACK: Daisy: Well we'll see. I think maybe we should just agree a date next week to look forward to?

PING: Jack: Sounds good to me?

PING BACK: Daisy: How about a walk on the beach next Wednesday evening? I'll meet you outside the restaurant we went to, and we can walk down to the prom. If we fancy it we can stop somewhere and have something to eat?

PING: Jack: Ok, you're on!

So I had to pass the weekend without a date.

Time to catch up with the rest of my life. It's very time consuming all this emailing and texting. One still has to shop and cook and wash and iron, and find time to internet date.

Somehow the dating seems to become all consuming. There's probably a Dating Daisy rule in there somewhere …

Internet Dating Rule: While Internet Dating, you absolutely must keep the rest of your life going. This Internet Dating malarkey, literally, could take – years – and you still need your friends, family and a way to pay the bills!

Imogen and I made a Black Forest gateau this weekend. We did the recipe three times, and the third time she did it all by herself. She piped the cream around the top very confidently I thought, and for once, she had something to take to college she could be proud of. If only she could put her mind so diligently to her essays!

That afternoon the phone rang. It was Dad.

"Darling! So good to hear you," he began.

"I'm fine Dad, honestly." (He seems to think that as I've been doing this terrible thing called Internet dating, I should have been raped, murdered, and/or been made financially destitute, by now.)

"I've got bad news I'm afraid," he said rather sadly.

I sat down. What could it be?

"It's Jeanie. I'm so sorry to tell you. She passed away."

"Oh Dad!"

"Yes, she was found dead in her bed this morning. Great way to go. Just faded away quietly in her own bed. And she was 97!"

"I'm so shocked. She's been phoning me. And been so full of life." I felt tearful.

"Tough old bird. Sure. It's being in the Military. Never leaves you."

"Well she did tell us she wanted to die. Over and over again." I reminded him

"She did," he agreed.

"But who's to know, if, when it came, she might have changed her mind," I said.

"Sure she didn't have any choice darling. When your times up, your time's up!"

"I guess."

"She had a good life. And a very privileged life. She was so fond of you," his voice cracked a little. "We had such a lot of good time together. Did you know she was the first person to know you were born? You Mum was so fond of her too. She would be so sad to know."

"I know. I was very fond of her too. Mum and Jeanie are in heaven together, Dad" I said. I like to think of heaven as a great big lounge with squashy sofas where you can sit until the end of time with free flowing gin and tonic, surrounded by all your friends and family of generations. Hopefully Mum and Jeanie were having their first G&T together up in the sky.

"She doesn't have any family," said Dad. "You know they never had any children. There won't be many of us at the funeral. I'm on the case, letting a few ex-Army people know. Guess I'll be next to go. Next in the pecking line."

"Dad, don't even talk like that!" I said. "Losing Jeannie is one thing, but I can't live without you."

"Well, I'm just being morose. Life in the old dog yet!" he said.

"I miss Mum," I said, the terrible flashbacks of her illness came flooding back into my memory. I had a deep breath. This is what I have learned, it's to take control and not let these negative emotions consume you. I have learn to live with them, not allow them to annihilate me.

But I felt deflated. Life is so unpredictable. But then some would say the death of a 97-year-old is not news. It's par for the course.

"Anyhow" continued Dad, "I knew you would want to know. The funeral date hasn't been confirmed yet, but I'll tell you in due course."

When Dad rang off, I felt consumed with sadness. Nothing in life ever stays the same. We have to be happy and in the moment. I thought about the day Jeannie gave me the bracelet, and what it had meant to her. I read somewhere that too often we only realise that – yesterday – we were happy. We fail to appreciate what's under our noses. A sobering thought. It's so important to get life by the horns, and shake it, very vigorously. That is what I am determined to do.

What can I do – to live?

I mean, what should I do – before I die?

I guess I'm asking *What's on my bucket list?*

I thought about that. Here's the thing, I know I need a companion. Think of the prairie vole. I need to find my other little prairie vole and everything stems from that. Some people are self-contained. They love their own company, enjoy solitude, enjoy having no one else to answer to. But not me. Sure, I want to do some things for myself, even by myself, but finding that special person IS all that's on my premium bucket list.

It's a short list.

Find my prairie vole.

FMPV.

Chapter Thirty-Nine (In which Daisy encounters the supernatural!)

Sunday May 7th

And suddenly, it happened.

There on my computer screen appeared an email. It read:

Do you ski off-piste?

And it was from, none other, than …

… the elusive Spacetime 3000!

As I read it, a chill swept through me.

This was the man with the mind.

And he was on the hook.

And do you know what? Immediately, all my dating rules flew straight out of the window.

Thinking back, I was mesmerised by him, from the first time I saw that profile. Even though, if you recall (see page 216) there was one **serious, monumental, exponentially catastrophic omission** from his dating site.

Can you recall what that was?...

... Answer...

There was no photograph on his dating site.

I repeat – no photograph on his dating site.

But, so carried away was I, with the wit of this Spacetime game, that I failed to let that thought even surface in my mind.

Anyone who could write like that, had to be, just had to be, a clone of Mr Big from *Sex in the City.* And that was just all there was to it.

Here's the thing, there is an etiquette to Internet Dating, and perhaps this is another Dating Daisy rule. It's always a good idea not to reply too quickly to any email, especially the first one, and to think carefully what you want to say.

If you reply too quickly it can look desperate, like *OMG let's get on with this quickly,* and they think it's in the bag. If you leave it too long, of course, some other predator may get in there before you, and pip you to the post! So you may never know what you are missing.

But ... so intrigued was I, that I forgot all that and fired my reply straight back.

I sent him my home email address. Yes ... I did!

Then I waited.

Now the thing is, it was about ten o'clock in the morning when this happened. A Sunday, I think. And I tried to keep busy, flitting around the web and clicking back and fro from the dating site to my email address. But frustratingly nothing happened. The screen stared defiantly back at me, dead as a dodo.

I had revealed myself probably as "too keen" with my immediate reply, and now I kicked myself. In fact, I ended up waiting about 72 hours for the response.

It seemed agonising. Should I send another email? What should I read into the delay? ...

Was he stringing me along with a dozen other hopeful Spacetimers?

Had he received my email ...?

Perhaps it had gone astray?

Had I misunderstood? (Perhaps he was inviting me skiing!)

I sat tight and did an uncommon Daisy casual nothing.

When eventually he did reply, this is what he wrote:

Daisy,

The fathomless details of your desires to accompany me on my extra-terrestrial mission are awe-inspiring. I am struck by your wild imagination. Suffice it to say, we would travel to the Diamond Planet and feast on space Rum and raspberries.

Now tell me what such a remarkable creature as yourself is doing on an Internet Dating site?

Is Daisy your real name by the way?

Cosmic Salutations,

Angus Robinson

What did I think?

Short. Eloquent. Giving nothing away. As clever as it was enticing. Angus? Scottish? Robinson? Like the orange squash. Or the song? Would I perhaps become THE Mrs Robinson!? I must stop this railroading of my mind. It's a marathon, not a sprint, and Angus Robinson is probably a lunatic.

Now most of the time, when there is an interesting email dialogue going on, there will be a few emails exchanged between a couple, in quite quick succession. For example, on a weekday evening, after supper, it's great entertainment to be having an email conversation with someone. The exchange can be quite witty, and there can be a real feeling of anticipation, waiting for the next reply.

But, with Angus Robinson this was not the case. I received one email a day, usually in the morning around ten o'clock, and after I had replied, I soon learned, I had to wait overnight for the next email reply. No matter how witty the email I sent, or how many questions I asked (by the way, he often deigned not to answer!) he was in complete control, and it was agonising, with only one daily email, and a British Rail style wait.

You have to remember that I didn't know who I was emailing. There was nothing on his dating site, about him at all, apart from the Spacetime journey. Oh and his age. It said he was 60.

Sixty? A bit older than I had thought, but 60? I am 53, so this doesn't seem too terrible.

When I replied, I wrote:

Angus,

Yes I was very impressed with your space mission idea. Unique and enthralling. Diamonds are indeed, a girl's best friend, and a whole planet of diamonds sounds like a dream come true. (Though somewhat uncomfortable to walk and sit on I would have thought, but there we are.)

I am on this site as I am divorced, I guess you read my profile, and like many others on the site, I would love to share my life with someone, if I can find that person. So far it's been a fairly miserable journey.

Can you tell me a little about yourself, as there is – as you know – nothing on your site apart from intergalactic – I hesitate to write this – trivia! (Don't take offence, it's a joke!)

Why are you on the site? What do you do? Where do you live? Oh and please may I have a photograph?

Of course Daisy is my real name. I take my name from a picture called a Breeze of Daisies. (This is true.)

And then I really didn't know how to sign off … so after some agonising … I just wrote:

Daisy

(It's quite hard sometimes to know how to end an email on a dating site. If it's a new person and you've never met, it doesn't seem right to put "Love Daisy." "Yours faithfully etc.," or "Kind regards" is too formal. I didn't feel I could copy the "Cosmic Salutations," – which was imaginative I thought. So in the end I just put "Daisy". Sometimes they say "less is more".

About 24 hours later this was his reply:

Daisy,

My reasons for being on a dating site are personal and complex. Suffice it say I am one of the growing cohort of the divorced masses. My ex-wife and I simply grew apart and our divorce was as unexciting as the final snuffing out of an exhausted candle.

If you were to drive north-west from your home – I believe you live in Brighton – you would find me. I don't have your postcode (yet) but the AA route-finder tells me you are 200 miles away. A bother of course, but a mere 200 miles you understand. It's hardly Honolulu. Or Mars for that matter.

I should like to hear all about you. And I mean ... ALL about you.

More salutations,

Angus

I grew increasingly frustrated waiting for replies from Angus. Did this increase or decrease the emotion? I can't decide, but I guess it helped build the intrigue. Every day I would log on before and after work to see if he had deigned to email me, usually that morning. There were long gaps of several days when there would be nothing.

And he revealed very little about himself. And. he never replied to my request for a photograph. He just ignored the question and I mean, totally ignored it!

Several days into this and I found myself quite besotted with it all. As I drove to the supermarket and to and from the swimming pool, ideas crept into my head for witticisms and possibilities. I had wanted so much to find a man who had a mind, who could write well, loved storytelling and was interested in my mind. Could I have found him?

Even with Patrick where our email exchange had been hilarious, I hadn't felt this intensity of emotion, this overwhelming desire to sit glued to the computer and such a thrill in opening his emails. (And he didn't have my postcode ... yet!)

And a little voice nagged inside my head.

There's no photograph.

Why isn't there a photograph?

Mr Big.

He just has to be Mr Big.

And the long waits for the emails were beginning to annoy me. It's difficult when you are Internet Dating as you may quite legitimately be emailing or even going on dates with more than one person at a time. This seems fair until you have made firm decision on a proper relationship. But you need the email exchanges to progress at a similar rate, or it doesn't help you make up your mind, if that makes sense. And I had Jack texting me and another date with him on the horizon. I needed to be fair and honest, and I had no idea how Angus – Mr Spacetime – would turn out? It was highly frustrating.

One morning an email appeared from Angus which said

Daisy,

I trust you slept well. I can imagine that pretty blonde head recumbent on the pillow.

I have been thinking about these emails. My own self is deep and curious. The relationship I seek is probably an impossible quest.

I need a totally complete union of mind, soul and body – in that order.

I need a perfect fusion with my other being, where two worlds connect in a utopian cataclysm.

I seek to share a depth of emotion and understanding that few could ever imagine.

And for me, there is no compromise. I cannot allow mediocrity.

Salutations and best intentions,

Angus

For some reason, I found this email very irritating. It came out of the blue. The questions in my last email had not been answered. The email revealed a slightly arrogant attitude, that he and only he, was capable of perfect deep emotion. And the relationship he was looking for was more than likely unattainable.

So, what did that say about me, who he knew very little about and hadn't met. How could he assume that I would not measure up to his supremely high standards?

Angus had this persona where he believed he was on a different plane to the rest of the world. How did he expect this ethereal relationship to begin, if he wouldn't even have a timely email conversation, or reveal anything significant about himself. I didn't know if he was tall or short, dark or grey, fat or thin, hairy or hairless, handsome or ugly, rich or poor, or just another muppet.

I got a bit angry and I wrote back, immediately:

Angus

You are like a ghost. Your emails just appear on my screen when they feel like it. You waft in and out completely as you see fit. You don't tell me anything about yourself. Like a ghost – a phantom.

Phantom of the Internet, actually.

From now on I'm going to call you

" IG ... Internet Ghost."

Are you really REAL?

Daisy

Writing this made me laugh out loud. You may recall my previous references to *Phantom of the Opera,* a long-time favourite of mine.

I was surprised then only a few minutes later to get an immediate reply. Not usually his style! This must be getting to him too!

Daisy,

I can assure you I am real. Very real.

If you are so clever, and I see you are a doctor so I know you are, you tell me. What does it mean to be really REAL?

Affectionately,

IG

So, this was like a red rag to a bull. I took up the challenge. Thinking about it, indeed, what does it mean to be real? How can you tell if someone, or something is real? Does it just mean it's not made of thin air? Or does it mean it has to have a beating heart? Does it mean it has to be alive to be real? Or can a dead thing still be real? Is something real if it's on the internet but you can't see it or touch it? I *really* had to answer the Internet Ghost's question.

And it had to be impressive.

It took about 24 hours to compose this, but this is what I sent:

Dear IG,

This is how you can tell if something is real:

"Real isn't how you are made,' said the Skin Horse. 'It's a thing that happens to you. When a child loves you for a long, long time, not just to play with, but REALLY loves you, then you become Real.'

'Does it hurt?' asked the Rabbit.

'Sometimes,' said the Skin Horse, for he was always truthful. 'When you are Real you don't mind being hurt.'

'Does it happen all at once, like being wound up,' he asked, 'or bit by bit?'

'It doesn't happen all at once,' said the Skin Horse. 'You become. It takes a long time. That's why it doesn't happen often to people who break easily, or have sharp edges, or who have to be carefully kept. Generally, by the time you are Real, most of your hair has been loved off, and your eyes drop out and you get loose in the joints and very shabby. But these things don't matter at all, because once you are Real you can't be ugly, except to people who don't understand."

Margery Williams, *The Velveteen Rabbit.*

So I guess what I am saying is, have you got any hair, do you wear glasses, and is there anything wrong with your tail?

If you are real, it seems you can't be ugly!

Yours informatively,

Daisy.

PS Where is your photo?

And I sent it.

I have to say that again on this occasion, I did not need to wait for a reply.

Daisy,

Touché! he wrote.

I am amazed you found that quote! Extremely impressed.

Not many women would have written such a witty and appropriate reply.

Let me see, I have plenty of hair.

I wear glasses for reading.

My tail is in good working order thank you.

Why the obsession with the photograph? To me, it's of no consequence.

Affectionately

IG

I exploded back I'm afraid.

IG, of course the photograph is of no concern to you, because you have seen mine, and you know who or what you are dealing with. I don't know if you are a toy rabbit or a toy horse! I am emailing an invisible ghost!

Let's get this right out in the open. I am realistic, we are in our 50s (or 60s?) and we can't expect to be Julia Roberts or George Clooney. I agree entirely that a relationship is more about two personalities, and that appearance to some extent, is not the most important thing. But the thing is, I've been doing this Internet Dating thing for about three months now, and I have learnt the hard way, that it is very important early on to know what the other person looks like. There has to be a degree of physical attraction. And if there isn't, there is no point exchanging hundreds of emails, or even meeting up. I have told

myself I won't email anyone, or meet anyone, unless I have seen the photo. So please just do it before we go any further. I love your mind. Let me know about the rest of you. Please!

Daisy

And I pressed SEND.

When I went upstairs to be that night, Imogen called me through her bedroom door, and I ventured in and sat on the bed. Very gingerly of curse. She was propped up with her laptop as usual.

"Just wondered how the Internet Dating is going?" she said.

She was so calm and polite about it. I sensed some sort of trap. But it never came. We actually had a civilised chat!

Chapter Forty (In which Imogen plans a surprise for Daisy)

Tuesday May 12th 2014

It's a work day. Clinic, clinic and more clinic. I do find my job very interesting of course, but I constantly marvel at human nature, and the way human beings live their lives. We can't choose the family we are born in to, or the way we are brought up.

We are victims of circumstance. How lucky was I to have parents who loved and nurtured me, and encouraged me to follow a sensible career pathway? My parents were firm educationalists, and strongly believed in the value of qualifications. For example, my mother had taught me to read, and I read very fluently before I ever started school. Not every child is so lucky.

Pinky and I went to a meeting this afternoon, to get a few educational points. One of the presentations was about new developments in contraception. Do you know they are developing a small sort of microchip that can be implanted under the skin and left in situ for 16 years! It has a low dose of hormone in it, which is released slowly to stop you ovulating. This is the funny bit – you can switch it on and off yourself with your mobile phone! How amazing! The only worry might be if somehow it reacted to a wrong number! It's not commercially available yet, but whatever will they think of next!

Here is a story about something that happened in clinic today.

One of our specialist nurses, Felicity, came to find me.

"Can you come and have a look at this?" she asked. "This young girl has a lump down below, she's with her mum, and they don't know what it is."

I stood up from my desk. We always help each other in clinics, no problem.

"She's on the couch" said Felicity. "I said you'd pop in and have a quick look."

"How old is she?" I asked as we walked down the corridor, towards their consulting room.

"Only 14," she said. "And she's never had sex."

"Oh," I said.

In the examination room, a middle-aged woman with a beehive hairdo and a fake leopard skin coat, sat holding the hand of her daughter. The girl, let's call her Rosie, lay with her feet in the stirrups, legs wide spread. Felicity had tactfully positioned a modesty drape. The way this room is arranged, you enter through the door and the patient is lying directly in front of you, so as you walk through the door, you are confronted with the feet end, or should we say – the vaginal end – and that's the way it is. So I met Rosie that first time, end on, legs akimbo and a white cover sheet draped over the lower half of her body.

"Hi Rosie, I'm the doctor. And hello, Mum, nice to meet you. What's your name?"

"Sue," she replied, chewing gum I noted.

"OK," I said, "so you've found a lump Rosie. When did you find it?"

"Yesterday," she said, propping herself up slightly on her elbows. I saw a bright-eyed teenager wearing braces on her teeth and with a shock of very curly dark hair.

"Does it give you any symptoms?" I asked. "Does it hurt, has it been bleeding?"

"No," she said "It's just – there – and it's really weird. Please can you just like – make it go away?"

I knew Felicity would have taken a full history, and she is a first-class colleague. She is always extremely thorough and very experienced. She said this girl had never had sex.

I washed my hand, put on my gloves, obtained consent and sat in front of the tail end of the couch, to do the examination.

I pulled back the modesty blanket and looked at the vulvo-vaginal area in front of me. Immediately I could see the lump. It was a genital wart, but on a bit of a pedicle, meaning it was sort of dangling on a thread of tissue from the vaginal opening. It was definitely a wart. And genital warts are sexually transmitted.

"This looks like a wart" I said looking up over Rosie's legs towards her end of the bed.

"A wart!" both she and her mother chorused. "How would she have got that?"

"Well," I said, "I'm not sure at this moment but I do need to ask you a few questions.

My colleague tells me you've never had sex Rosie, is that right?"

"Yes, I don't do that sort of thing."

"So, no boyfriends?"

"Not really."

"Well genital warts are sexually transmitted."

"Well they can't be because I've never had sex."

"I just need to ask you this. Would you like me to see you on your own Rosie? We could pop your mum in the waiting room for a while?"

"No! I want Mum to stay here!"

"Sure?"

"Yes, very sure."

"She's never had sex!" echoed her mother. "She wouldn't do that sort of thing. Do you think I don't know my own daughter?"

"Not at all. Well we'll have to have this conversation here then. So please Rosie, can you tell me when you last had a period?"

"I haven't had a period for six months."

"Six months?" Had I heard this correctly?

Her mother interjected "She had her appendix out six months ago, and our doctor said it's normal not to have periods for some time after you've had your appendix out."

I took this in, and didn't say anything, but for anyone reading this, that is, absolute nonsense.

"Have you had a pregnancy test?" I asked.

"A pregnancy test!" she repeated! But I can't be pregnant, I've never had sex."

"Well, call me stupid but I've been doing this job a long time and if any woman of reproductive age stops having periods, we do need a negative pregnancy test result in the notes. So, would it be ok please, for you to do me a urine specimen?"

"What? Now?"

"The doctor has been giving her a tablet, what's that tablet called Rosie, because you keep being sick? He said it's your stomach acids. Begins with an 'O'... something ... 'zole'. Is that it?"

My suspicions were definitely highly aroused by now.

Rosie sat up and went off to do her urine specimen. Felicity and I retired next door to the consulting room to write some notes. Between ourselves our eyebrows were very raised.

What a surprise a few minutes later, to discover Rosie's urine pregnancy test – was positive.

I went back into the examination room,

"I have some news for you that may not be good news I'm afraid," I said. "It's just one of those things. Rosie ... your pregnancy test is positive!"

"Oh God!" She burst into tears

"It can't be, it must be a wrong test, she's never had sex!"

"We've done more than one test," I said, "and I'm afraid the test is correct. We're going to have to talk about this Rosie and see what you want us to do to help you."

Rosie was crying loudly. "It can't be it can't be!"

I waited for her to compose herself.

"Rosie, it can't be an immaculate conception. That doesn't happen either! You must remember having sex with somebody? At some time? Maybe after a party, maybe you were drunk, were you raped or assaulted?"

"No!" she said, defiantly. "I've never had sex. I haven't."

"Well, we need to find out how pregnant you are," I said, "so I will need to examine you internally. Is that OK? Can you pop back up onto the couch please?"

Rosie stood up and began to undress and position herself on the couch. I had turned away to wash my hands and put on my gloves. When I turned round, I had another shock. Now I could see Rosie lying on the couch without the drape over her, there was large swelling in her lower abdomen. I didn't need to do a vaginal examination, this pregnancy was easy to feel, it stretched up as far as her umbilicus. She must be at least 20 weeks (5 months) pregnant.

I told this to Rosie and her mother, and they were aghast.

"How on earth ... who on earth could it be ...?" said her mother. The she said, "It must have been the surgeon who took her appendix out. He must have raped her on the operating table!"

Now I had heard it all!

In fact, she had scan that day and she was only a few days under 24 weeks pregnant, too late for an abortion even if she had wanted one.

The wonders of the human psyche never fail to surprise me, as she left hospital clutching a scan photo that day, knowing the baby was a boy and she was going to call him Alfie. Strangely both Rosie and her mother seemed excited to think there would be a new baby in the family by Christmas!

We did report this as a Child Protection case to Social Services, in case you are wondering, and I won't write any more about it. I saw Rosie several times to treat her warts in pregnancy, and also the subsequent positive chlamydia test. But the identity of Alfie's father has never been revealed

Meanwhile back at home, Imogen has been looking like the cat that got the cream.

She's completely smug and I don't know why. She did get an 'A' for her homemade ravioli. And I have been helping her with her current essay on 'The Fundamental Aspects of Successful Baking'.

"Mum," she says, "you have to be here on Saturday morning. At 10.30. OK? Oh, and you need to look really nice. Smart, Do your hair, that sort of thing."

I am curious of course. She has never done this to me before. Perhaps it's a hot date.

Maybe Jasmine's father has been unsuccessful so far on the Internet Dating front?

Please God it's nothing to do with Voldemort.

Could it be a friend, Pinky? Maggie and Malcolm? It isn't my birthday – we've had that.

Curiosity abounds. But she won't budge. I have to wait until Saturday.

Hang on, here's another dating possibility.

DDP 12?

Hephaestus
"Lesser known Greek God, seeks Goddess for modern mythology."
Newhaven
54, divorced,
86.3% match (apparently)
You have 12 things in common
Last login seven days ago

I read on. He's a captain on the Newhaven ferry ... career in the Navy and came out of the forces aged 50 ... divorced after a long marriage ... has two daughters who are both married, and three grandchildren. (Could I be dating a grandpa?)

6ft4! Yes – don't worry! – there is a photograph.

He has quite a long face with a longish chin. His hair is grey and has been Bryl- creamed back at the sides. He looks attractive. He has green eyes, two of them, a nose and a mouth. He is smiling and it's a warm smile. He's wearing a herring-bone jacket and a cream jumper underneath it. It looks smart. There is a little designer stubble. Scratchy – oh?

It says "... plays the guitar badly, plays football even worse I'm afraid ...

"... love fine wines, great country walks, *QI, Have I Got News For You,* any hilarious news related trivia..."

My ideal date?

... "Open to suggestion. I need a best friend, a soulmate and a lover. In that order. Oh, and if you like sailing so much the better. I have a little boat that's made for two."

I'm sending an email. Now. He needs to know of my existence.

Come on Daisy, does he tick the boxes? asks my brain.

Looks, Personality, Educated, Solvent, Local and Available?

I replied, *from what it says on this site it would appear so. That's the best I can say.*

What should I type in my first email? I think I'll do a bit of research into Greek mythology. I was quite shocked at what I found! Read on and see!

Dear Hephaestus

My knowledge of Greek mythology isn't great, but it looks like you are the only ugly god!! Why on earth did you choose that? If your photo does you justice you are being incredibly humble. I think you look pretty good! I would suggest you go for Adonis myself.

Which Greek Goddess could I be? Perhaps Peitho, who was a lesser known Goddess of persuasion and seduction?

Can I persuade you to have a look at my profile?

BW

Daisy

And I pressed SEND

By the time I had boiled the kettle, there was a charming reply:

Hi Daisy, or Peitho,

Yes I've read your profile and loved it. Thanks for contacting me. I am new to all this so forgive me as I find my way!

You could be: from your medical background Hygia the Goddess of health, or with your dance interest Terpsichore is Goddess of dance ... or perhaps ... and I am joking ... Mania, the Goddess of insanity! Ha Ha! Your profile made me laugh.

Let me know a few pitfalls about Internet Dating? How are you finding it? I'm shy myself and find it very hard.

Regards,

Alex Thompson

I typed back:

Alex,

Guess you could be Poseidon, with your love of the sea.

I am finding this Internet Dating ... varied ... interesting people ... funny things happen ... meeting a variety of different people. I don't know. I would just like to meet someone and get off this site forever! It can get a bit wearing.

Most of the men I have met have lied about all sorts of things and it's just such a letdown. So much I could tell you! But no, so far I haven't found what I was looking for.

Is that really you in the photo? When was it taken?

Have you lied about anything on your profile?

I want you to know I took my own picture the day I went on the site, and everything in my profile is true, including my age, height, weight, hair and eye colour etc. ... Believe me!!

Let me know if you want to chat more?

BW

Daisy

SEND

Hi Daisy,

I'm not at sea today, it's a rest day. So I am using my recreation time to chat to you, how's that?

Yes, my daughter took the picture of me a couple of weeks ago. It was her who persuaded me to try this Internet Dating thing. All her fault. She was here for Sunday lunch and I had to go outside and stand on the patio.

I haven't lied about anything. Everything I put is true and my life, my situation and my vital statistics! I am very tall, so I hope you are prepared for that.

Actually, looking at our profiles we do have quite a lot in common. I like the fact you like boats as it's always been such a passion of mine. I can't dance, but I've never tried and I would give it a go. I'm not medical, but my father was a GP and he worked from home, so I lived with the stress of being on call to your patients and have some idea of all that. Saw enough though not to want to do it myself!

I work shifts, so I am on for ten days, off for ten days, and that means it rather scuppers my social life. I'm just starting my ten days off, so it seems sensible to get on the scene so to speak, see who's out there!

Do you know what, this may be a bit forward, but shall we just get on and have a date? I feel I sort of know you already! Shall we just be brave and do it! I'm sure we can have a great date together, what do you think, or am I being too forward?

Regards,

Alex, (Adonis?)

PS Please tell me, is Daisy your real name?

Well I was enchanted. How nice did he sound! A beautifully written email. Apparently no lies on the internet, a super photo, and charm to boot! What was there to stop me meeting him? **Looks, Personality, Educated, Solvent, Local and Available.** Ticks in all boxes.

I did boil the kettle, again, and do some washing up, and sort out a bit of washing, before I replied. I didn't want to look too keen of course. I left it as long as I could stand it. The thing is, I just want to get on with my life. Patience is not one of my virtues. Plus, I am very decisive, and he looked just up my street. If I didn't act quickly maybe someone else would have him!

So I typed back:

Hi Alex,

Thank for your message. I agree we do seem to have quite a lot in common which is a great starting point. I do love boats, but you will have to be the skipper and myself the crew. (I have a lovely tee shirt for sailing which says on the front "Knackered sailor"!... so don't be too hard a task master or I'll have to wear it!)

I am believing you about the not lying, although maybe that's silly of me, as you never know what people will do or say on these sites, but anyway, you have a nice face and you seem honest. I'm delighted you would have a go at dancing. It's just so much fun!

I take your point that with your shift's – you want to make the most of your ten-day leave. So why not. Let's meet and see what happens? What did you have in mind?

I'm off to swim my lengths now. Hope we can chat more later? Oh and yes of course my name is Daisy. Fresh as a Daisy, Daisy!

BW

Daisy x

I did pop off and thrash out 40 lengths of crawl. It's a bit of a mindset to make myself do it. I have a Speedo swim suit, a hat and goggles, and today someone asked me if I was training for something! I must have looked the business! I've got a headache though. Real thumping in the temples. Internet Dating stress? What's the remedy, ibuprofen or a just agreeing a new date?

I'm thinking about what on earth Imogen could be up to. She seems very pleased with herself about something, and I've got all week to wait.

Back home, I had a shower, washed my hair, sorted myself out. Chris was watching me. It's a bit unnerving that my hero can see me naked. But heh ho. No secrets between friends.

So I can't resist logging back on, and Yes, there it is, an email from my Greek God.

Hi Fresh as a Daisy, Daisy,

Adonis here from Mount Olympus!

It just seems we should get on with it, to me! So, I've been thinking. How about a really great day out, perhaps in London. I'll book the day for us, and we can have a day to remember. How about this Sunday? I guess you are working in the week, let me know if not as I am free as a bird any day really?

I will meet you at Waterloo late morning and the rest is up to me?

Regards

Alex

PS. Thinking about it, I will run the itinerary past you to check these are things you like to do? Just in case …

Dear Adonis … oops… Alex,

What a lovely idea. How kind of you. I love a great day out in London. I've never lived in London, so I don't know it that well, and it's a complete excitement for me to go there for a day. Thank you.

Yes, I'm afraid I am at work the rest of the week, and Saturday I have something on with my daughter.

I'll wait to hear the details!!

BW

Daisy (aka the Goddess Mania?? Am I mad to agree to this when we've never even met?)

SEND

I was in truth just a little bit unsure about this date. So sudden, and let's face it. Likely to be very long!

What have I said before in my dating lessons? *Meet for a drink in case you don't like them, and then you can get away*. What if we met, there were just no pheromones, and I had to suffer the whole day with him? Well, to be taken out for the day in London by anyone is surely not be sneered at. When all was said and done, this was a great opportunity. So I thought I would go with the plan, and hope beyond hope, all was going to be good. *(Daisy, be careful,* said my brain. But rather stupidly as it turned out, I just told it to be quiet.)

The next email said this:

Hi Goddess Daisy! (Or? Terpsichore)

So glad you like my suggestion. So here's the plan, what do you think?

Adonis & Terpsichore have a dream day out in London

Day commences: Meet at Waterloo at 11 am in front of M&S.

11.45: Thames Rib Experience. It leaves right in front of the London Eye! This is an 80-minute ride of your life all down the Thames past the House of Parliament, to Greenwich, to the Thames Barrier and back. Amazing!

14.15: Lunch at the Slug & Lettuce. It's close by the London Eye, they actually do great lunches.

15.30: London Eye sky ride. I've never actually done it, have you?

17.00: Tea at the Ritz. This is amazing, white gloves, a pianist, cucumber sandwiches, champagne, scones and clotted cream, and then...

19.00: *The Mousetrap*, as it's London's longest running show and I've never seen it. You did tell me you love crime dramas!

22.00: Train home.

Wow, what do you think?

Regards as ever,

Alex x

Well, what did I think reading this? It looked on the face of it, totally amazing in every way. But, and there was a BUT, it seemed rather ambitious. There was a lot to fit into the day. The timings were pretty tight. What if the train was delayed, or the boat broke down, or there was security alert on the underground. There was no room for error in Alex's plan. And could we talk to each other, while zooming along in a rib on the Thames. Also – sorry Alex – but very bad for my hair! – but I wouldn't expect a man to think of that for a millisecond! I have always wanted to go on the London Eye and never been. And tea at the Ritz, well that sounded amazing. And yes, *The Mousetrap* was a good choice for me. I've never seen that either.

I did start to wonder about the cost of all this. In the end I did a bit of googling and worked out this itinerary would cost approximately £280 – each! Now I had not expected him necessarily to be treating me to all this, I do like to pay my way, especially on a first date. I've never been someone who doesn't immediately pay up. I hate that. (I had a life with Voldemort remember!) And I was quite embarrassed when I realised the cost. And I wondered what I could do about it. I didn't want him to think I assumed that he was paying. But, also it was rather expensive for me to just put £280 on the table, as it were. And I didn't want to dampen his enthusiasm. People can be funny about money. But some men are very chivalrous. I wasn't sure what to do or say at this stage.

So I decided for now just to be polite and enthusiastic. Here is man with ideas, creativity, who can organise things, who is not shy about coming forward with ideas of great things to do. And clearly not short of a bob or two!

Dear Alex,

I have to compliment you on putting together such a fabulous plan!

These are all things I would love to do, and you have put a lot of thought into it. I'm glad you have told me what we're doing so I can think about waterproof clothing!

Also I can book a return train ticket that's fine. I've never seen *The Mousetrap* and always wanted to! Very clever.

Ok, so Sunday is in the diary, and we'll meet at Waterloo outside M&S. And I'll bring some cash as I do want to make a

contribution to the cost OK. (I'll be the one in a pack-a-mac and red wellies!!)

See you Sunday!!

Exciting!

BW

Daisy

SEND

Suddenly I thought this dating business was going pretty well. I had managed to secure a fabulous day out for myself, with a handsome Greek God of a Sea Captain!

Chris winked tonight as I got into bed.

"Off to sea with the Old Sea Captain then!" he chuckled.

"It's not the sea, I said, "it's only a ride on the RiverThames!"

And I went to sleep, for once.

Chapter Forty-One (In which Daisy learns about mulberries)

Wednesday May 13th 2014

So Jack and I went down to the beach that Wednesday evening. I recall agonising over what to wear. It was towards the end of May, and unseasonably hot, so I wore the white jeans in the end, and summer sandals. I hoped I looked carefree, fresh and good enough to eat.

This was our second date. I wondered if he might try and kiss me. I wondered how I would react if he did. I wondered what he would say if he knew about Captain Adonis, or my phantom emails. But, at the moment, nothing was certain. As far as the phantom was concerned, I was only emailing a ghost.

Jack was quite talkative. He looked his handsome Robert Redford self, and again I noticed he had beautiful bright blue eyes. We met at the Pier and walked west, towards Hove, walking on past the basketball courts, through the small outdoor market and past the children's' playground. We passed the Peace Memorial, a statue of an angel with an orb, built in memory of Edward VII, who was known as Edward the Peacemaker. Very apt for what I'm trying to do I thought. Make peace in my life and for those around me. Eventually we found ourselves sat at a table at *Marrocco's* cafe. Jack ordered wine and pizza, and we sat looking out over the pebbles at the grey froth of the English channel.

Initially we talked about his work. He had gone into investment banking after completing his degree which had been in estate management. But he had never enjoyed working in a banking environment and had always really been interested in property. In the end he had taken a salaried position just six months ago, with a private housing company. It was a whole new way of working. He had responsibilities to ensure targets were met, local and national and his salary depended on it. He was travelling around inspecting building sites, meeting contractors, and customers and troubleshooting a wide range of issues. In the past his role had not included any of this. He was determined to do it and do it well. However as usual there were people in the company who had their own agenda.

We talked about my work too, and I entertained him with my repertoire of amusing sexual health stories. Some of these are just so funny, you couldn't make them up!

He had a good sense of humour and we laughed a lot.

In the restaurant I probed a little into his marriage issues.

"So come on then, fill me in on the marriage situation?"

"Oh you really don't want to hear about that?!" he shook his head disbelievingly.

"I do actually. If we have 3rd date, or even a 4th, it could be important!"

He sipped his wine.

"Yes I know, I s'pose we have to have this conversation."

"Well my bit is quite simple. My husband had an affair and made this woman pregnant. He kept it a secret from everybody, including his friends."

"My God," he looked very sympathetic.

"It's ok," I said "It happens. I'm certainly not the first person it's ever happened to and I won't be the last!

"Anyway, he's a pretty disgusting person. I'm so much better off without him. I'm as over it as anyone can be over it." I took a gulp of my wine. "Come on! Your turn!"

"Well," replied Jack. The pizzas had arrived by this time, and very delicious they looked indeed, so Jack was brandishing a pizza wheel.

"I can sum it up in one word."

"One word?"

"Yup!"

I looked at him expectantly.

"Handbags" he said. Then cut a large slice of pizza.

"Handbags?" I replied quizzically.

"Don't mention the word ever to me again! The thing is my wife, Christina, has an obsession with designer handbags. I think she had something like 133 at the last count."

I was stunned. I am not a handbag person, although you the reader may be.

"Vivienne Westwood, Michael Kors, Valentino, Saint Lauren, Ted Baker, Mulberry. I think the most expensive was £665."

(I have never spent more than £30 on a handbag in my life! I was flabbergasted!)

"Well how did she do that? I guess you have a joint account? Didn't you tell her to stop doing it?"

"Of course. We've had so many rows about it. She puts them all on the credit card and has them delivered. No matter what I say every month they come. Stockpiles of them."

"I'm speechless!"

"Well, I don't get it either, as she doesn't seem so bothered about clothes or shoes. It's just the bloody handbags."

"I've never understood women and handbags. On that you and I are well matched!" I said, feeling quite proud of my humble little white shoulder bag, which I acquired a few years ago in a charity shop.

"So last weekend, we had an almighty row, as I took her bank card and her credit cards off her. She doesn't have access now to our bank account. I am giving her cash once a week for food and for Tristan, and that's it. Anything extra will be by negotiation. I had to do it. It's ridiculous. We've got solicitors' bills to pay, we're trying to sell the house and then we need to pay for two lots of accommodation, I'm paying the school fees, it's expensive living away from home in the week. We just can't cope with hundreds of bloody designer hand bags!"

I was very sympathetic. I thought about Voldemort who wouldn't even buy me a cup of tea. If I had done that, he really might have killed me.

"It's awful, I can't pretend it isn't" he said. "She hates me being away, hates being left to cope with Tristan by herself. Sometimes she texts me on a Friday and says unless you get here in 20 minutes, I'm going out and he can be left alone until you get here. How am I supposed to get there at any reasonable time when I've worked a full day and its Friday rush hour traffic. As soon as I get there, she's out. I get threatening texts all weekend. If she does come home, we are in separate rooms. The atmosphere is hell."

"Can't you move out?"

"I'd love to, but the house is on the market. We've got a buyer actually. I didn't want to spend the money on another place and it would have been more difficult for Tris."

"So how's the sale going?"

"It's an old cottage. They knew that of course, but now they seem to be doing umpteen specialist surveys on the woodwork and the damp. I'm just bracing myself as I know they're going to lower their offer."

"It might be worth talking a hit on the price. Just so you can get on with your lives."

"Oh I agree. It's just that we have a big mortgage, and all our money is in the house. We haven't got much in the way of savings. And it's only been on the market about three months. So, I feel we need to stick it out for a bit."

I was reminded about the pain of marriage break ups from this conversation. So many repercussions. Hurt and angry people. Confused unhappy children. It's a miserable game.

Determined to be happy, I changed the subject and we left the restaurant in better spirits to walk back to the car. I enjoyed jumping into the Union Jack mini and Jack whizzing me home. Just like *Butterflies*!

But there was no goodnight kiss.

Just a wave and he was gone.

My poem again, stayed exactly where it was, asleep in the depths of my handbag!

Internet Dating lesson

Good. It was all good. Except …

Could I/should I believe what Jack was telling me? He could be just a married man who wants his cake and eat it! Maybe all the upset about the marriage was not true, although the handbag story sounded hard to dream up. But I had to keep a healthy degree of suspicion.

He was still married. So he was not ticking the "available" box.

Plus he had a seven-year-old son. Had I ever thought my successful date would make me a stepmother? How did I feel about that?

Nothing is going to be perfect. Life is full of compromises.

"Everything in my life was a fragile decision someone else made."

That's Chris who said that. A person who has achieved so much, yet humbly attributes his success to the choices of others.

But for myself ? I need to make the robust decisions. Just me, by myself. No-one can do this for me.

Chapter Forty-Two (In which there are IG revelations)

Wednesday May 13th 2014

So I put the key in the lock from my date with Jack, and felt that sinking elevator feeling in my stomach. I had given the Phantom a piece of my mind. I hadn't meant to, but that last email was very direct. What would he do? How would he react? Perhaps I would never hear from him again. Or perhaps he would take a long time to reply. He was always in control and seemed to enjoy making me wait.

I made tea and logged on.

But no, there it was. A phantom email! I took a deep breath and clicked.

Daisy My Dear,

You do amuse me. Is it George Clooney you are after? I wouldn't have thought Internet Dating was his style. As for Julia Roberts, stick thin with big teeth, it wouldn't do it for me.

You really do not need to see a photograph.

I can assure you I have all the right attributes, and you will not be disappointed.

We won't be speaking about it again.

I can tell you that I am divorced and have two daughters who are all grown up and don't live at home. My work is in the Stock Market and I work for myself.

I have a lot of interests, I read, enjoy theatre, love travelling, have four cars!, and adore good wine. My main interest is in people and in good conversation.

I have never found the type of relationship my heart desires, although I am always hopeful that it could exist. That nemesis of utter love and devotion, the union of minds and bodies, the joy that deep psychological understanding and closeness can bring to a physical relationship. Most people don't understand this at all. A quick moment of copulation is all that is required. Then they can return to watching *Eastenders*.

I am intrigued by your mind too. Your replies are witty and endearing. I need to know ALL about you. Only then can we pass to the realms of a deep emotional union that will satisfy us both.

Please write to me. Tell everything to me. Pour out your heart, I will mend it.

Yours optimistically,

IG

I read and reread this email. Was it creepy, or was it the first dating email I had had with any substance? The control was still there. But he had revealed some details about himself. There was humour in there. His hobbies were not dissimilar. I love people, and books, and theatre and good wine! He seemed to want to get to know me. The inner me. Could that type of love exist, Romeo and Juliet style? Could this happen to me?

But I still had no idea what he looked like. He assured me that he had all the right attributes. Perhaps he meant two eyes a nose and a mouth!

Anyhow it was late, and I had a lot to think about. I decided to go to bed, and face the Phantom in the morning. For once, it would be him, waiting for an email.

Chapter Forty-Three (In which Daisy experiences much emotional confusion)

Thursday May 14th 2014

I can't sleep. It's 4 am. This is bugging me. I just have to compose a reply to the phantom. Here's the thing. No one has ever said to me:

"Tell everything to me, pour out your heart to me and I will mend it."

I liked that. To really fall in love with someone you do need to understand them. It's by trust and confidence in the other person you can achieve this. I believe you have to love the other person more than you love yourself. And it starts by showing an interest in that person and standing in their shoes.

So I started writing, and it went like this:

Dear IG,

I have never before been asked to pour my heart out. I'm very aware that this anonymous internet medium is potentially dangerous. There is something enticing about letting go on a

blank piece of paper to an unknown destination. You could cover this page with anything. Anything at all.

And yet, if we were in the same room, it wouldn't be the same. When two people meet who don't know each other, they don't immediately voice their inner secrets. There are social taboos to go through. Niceties. Politesse. In this situation to tell you how I really feel would mean a large bottle of very good wine!

The funniest thing is, that from the moment I saw your Spacetime message, I was convinced you had the right mindset for me. Imagination, creativity, romance, sentiment, passion, and storytelling. What you put on your site was all of those things.

Paradoxically, sometimes I've heard it said that you can think you know someone very well, and then find out you don't really know them at all.

Take my ex-husband. He was six years older than me. He pursued me at university. He told me he wanted to marry me. "Marriage," he said, "or not at all." I obeyed him. Funny that word 'obey' but that's what I think I did.

We were married before either of us had graduated.

He worked me into the ground and bled me dry of my fun-loving, energetic, entrepreneurial self, and then, after 26 years, he was having an affair behind my back. He was lying and cheating. He didn't tell anyone about it. No one at all. And keeping the secret from his friends and family for a long time, possibly a couple of years, was so deceitful.

The thing is, the man I married would not have done that to me. Life exerted its toll on him and under the pressure he became a twisted form of his own self. He brought pain and shame to our family, and how he looks in the mirror every morning I have no idea.

But I know now, that it took me 26 years to get the measure of him. He comes across as a smiling out-going, amusing character, but underneath this charade he is calculating, obsessed with money and as mean as ninepence. This colours his whole life to the extent for example, that he won't pay anyone £2.50 for a cup of hot water and a tea bag! In 26 years, he never once took me out for a cup of tea! It's true, but enough said. Extrapolate that over the money matters of a lifetime.

The thing is, I don't dwell on the past. It's in the past and there's nothing that can be done about it.

The important thing is to make sure from now on I live my life my way, and I look after the present and the future will take care of itself.

I think for two people to meet in their teens or twenties and live together for 50 or 60 years is too much of a tall order. It's totally not going to happen. I guess at the turn of the century people didn't often live beyond 40 or 50 so everything was very different. But now, with the increase in life expectancy it just isn't very likely to happen. The divorce rate is about 60–70% I think! Who would ever marry anyone at all with those odds of failure!

Anyway, I count myself as lucky. I got away. I can make my own decisions. (Remind me to send you my chapter on why life is so much better without Voldemort.) It has been a difficult time. I had a year off work and a lot of counselling, when all that happened to me. But I feel so much stronger now. I'm back at work and enjoying my life, doing lots of different things. I swim, go spinning (that's cycling to music), see my friends, look after the house and my daughter who is 17 and lives with me, and write my book. (Did I tell you I am writing a book about Internet Dating? Watch out! You might be in it!!)

So I feel I have opened my heart to you, a little. You can see where I'm at. I don't need to be mended. I just need to be loved. And I hope when I finally get off these Internet Dating sites!, that may be the case!! Life is so much better sharing it with that special person.

So now, you need to open your heart to me IG!

What is it that has made you who you are today?

Do tell me!

Hope to hear from you soon,

Daisy x

(I couldn't help put the 'x')

SEND

When I sent that I immediately wondered if I should have sent it. It was still the early hours of the morning. I hadn't even really read it back and it seemed suddenly far too intimate. Anyone reading this, who has been through enormous emotional pain will understand.

You put the pain behind you because you have to. I still have the visual image in my mind of myself stuffing the pain in a box. It's a large packing crate. The pain is like a cloudy of sticky playdough. It's bright pink. I am gathering it by the armful and shoving it, cramming it down, down, down into the confines of the box. **Lock** it in a box, tie it shut, never open it.

When you have to open the box, which you do from time to time, the extortionate anguish is all too ready to leap at you and strangle you in its clutches all over again. So even writing about my past I find painful and I would rather not do it.

I have decided I will not let the last 26 years ruin the rest of my life. So I keep the box tightly shut. And plan to keep it that way. If you have had pain like me, try the *pink box trick*. It has worked for me.

Here's the thing, this dating thing gets into your system and you feel yourself drawn to the computer and almost unable to get on with real life. Everyone else on the sites also has emotional baggage, by definition, or they wouldn't be there. So as you become 'unlocked' in the email conversations, so do they.

You could say this is therapeutic. The problem is some people go over the top and you can see they are in such a mess inside they are not ready for a new relationship.

Finding out their "baggage" is part of the mechanism for internet success. I needed to find out the Phantom's baggage.

The surprising thing was that the Internet Phantom and I then went on to exchange a flurry of emails in quick succession.

He must have the insomnia bug too?...

Daisy,

I found your email exquisite. I feel you too have a way with words which has a profound effect on me.

The experiences in your marriage that you have eluded to are no doubt the tip of the iceberg in terms of heartbreak and cruelty. Reading between the lines it sounds like your ex-husband was controlling and emotionally abusive.

No one deserves to be treated like that in any relationship but a marriage is sacrosanct. That person should be so special to you they deserve the very best you can give. To be cherished and revered not humiliated and down trodden.

Even professional, successful people can have a psychologically disturbed personality trait, and carry out their abuse in clever ways, not visible to the general public, just under the radar, a grey area, that is inexplicably painful for the victim who doesn't even realise this is what is happening. You, I think, have been the victim of a clever, abusive fraudster and my heart goes out to you.

I married a woman I worked with, about 20 years ago. I married late, being the sort of man who found it hard to envisage one woman could ever fulfil me, and then I have to admit, feeling if I didn't make a decision I would be left on the shelf, and miss the opportunity to be a father etc. ... This seemed the best I had found so far. So I married, and we had two children.

But I knew it was a mistake very soon after the event. I had nothing in common with my wife who was ten years younger than myself, and actually preferred reading *Hello* magazine and watching *Eastenders* to spending and evening with me.

We just grew apart. We started accepting invitations by ourselves to things, and even going on holiday separately. I moved my business here about eight years ago, but she preferred to continue to work in London, so she has a flat there and we rarely see each other.

We divorced a few years back. It was easy as we both knew the marriage was over, wanted to draw a line under it, to be free. We are amicable, for example if the children have a birthday we can manage a family get together. But it is very strained.

So now, I feel I want to find a woman with whom I have something in common. All sort of things are on this list. Imagination, ideas and love of words is top of my list. But also shared hobbies and interests. I need someone who I can share my life with, not someone on a totally different wavelength. Someone too, who undoubtedly, I can enjoy a physical relationship with, and all the joy that that brings. It has to be said.

Yours truly, IG

By breakfast-time I had replied:

Dear IG,

Your email was very revealing and surprised me. To date you have been quite reserved and formal, but this email was personal and from the heart. Guess somehow you and I have crossed the line!

I had never thought of my ex-husband, who I call Voldemort by the way, was an abuser but actually you may be right. His new girlfriend is probably going through what I went through now and I actually feel sorry for her. I thank my lucky stars I got away.

I do think what doesn't kill you make you stronger.

I am definitely so much stronger in myself than I ever was before.

Funny story but Voldemort would only ever let me buy my clothes in Charity shops. So, after the split, I took ALL my clothes to the charity shop. ALL of them except what was standing up in. Then I took a large suitcase to John Lewis and bought myself a complete new wardrobe! I can't tell you what I spent but I didn't care. It's a new life and I can make my own decisions.

So, we agree we both like words. Let's do some Q&A?

What's your favourite novel and why?

Do you play Scrabble, and are you any good? Could you beat me – I doubt it!

Do you read the newspaper, which one and why?

Would you not speak to me if you thought I liked *Hello* magazine?

Do you like poetry, if so what do you like?

Do you like going to the theatre, what do you like to see? What was the best thing you saw in the past 12 months?

Thanks for cheering me up! It's good that someone seems to understand, and in fact even takes the trouble to try!

Daisy x

SEND

Still breakfast-time, he replied:

Daisy,

Another charming email from you. I must confess myself rushing to the screen the moment I get in to see if there's a message from you!

What a good idea ... Q&A ... I shall engage brain and do my best ...

Favourite novel? Well, the first one that springs to mind is *The Kite Runner* have you read it? It's a deeply moving tale of two boys who are friends, in Afghanistan, one from a wealthy background and one that is not. It is beautifully written and a joy to read, although incredibly sad. You begin to understand what life is like for people living in Afghanistan and it is just too wretched.

Yes, I play Scrabble. I have the book of two and three letter words, do you? I play with my daughter and I always win! Are you up for a challenge?

I read *Britain on Sunday* of course, why else would I be on this dating site?! I am not a politician in any shape or form and have to accept that the country will always be being run by least-worst or a terrible bunch.

Please don't read *Hello* magazine in my presence, that's all I ask.

Poems? Have you read "Love One Another" by Kahlil Gibran? It summarises exactly how I dream my new relationship will be.

I adore the theatre. I prefer plays to musicals. Funnily enough I went to see *The Curious Incident of the Dog in the Night-time* last month and it was wonderful. Very quirky and clever. The stage set is on a piece of squared paper! – as it's all about maths and numbers!!

I have to say I am enjoying this discourse with you tremendously.

Yours truly

IG

By coffee time I had replied:

Dear IG,

Oh my goodness it's so unreal because a lot of what you have written is exactly me!

I adored *The Kite Runner* and have read all Khaled Hosseini's other novels and loved them too. In fact, I think *A Thousand Splendid Suns* is actually even better! It's about the lot of women in Afghanistan and it's just unbelievably sad.

I will beat you hands down at Scrabble, it's my passion!

I'm sorry to tell you, that that poem by Khalil Gibran was the poem we had at our wedding! I don't mind you choosing it, because it is a beautiful poem, but it seems a strange coincidence that you chose it!

I like the theatre, but as a treat not every day. I loved the book of the *Curious Incident*, and I loved the play too. But it goes without saying that my absolute favourite is *Phantom of the Opera*. I do go about once a year, with a girlfriend, and I've seen it more than 20 times!!

And now I've met the real Internet Phantom! It seems too good to be true!

Isn't this amazing!

Affectionately,

Christine ... oops ... Daisy! x

PS I hate *Hello* magazine with a vengeance!

Then I had to drag myself away and do some normal life things, like food shopping.

So my phone was pinging all the time.

PING. Jack: I'm in the car, singing. Where are you?

Daisy: I'm in Asda. By the yoghurts if you must know.

PING. Jack: Shopping for more carrot cake?

Daisy: No. I'm not making carrot cake any more. Too many calories.

PING. Jack: You don't need to worry about that, you're gorgeous!

Daisy: Flattery will get you anywhere

PING. Jack: Anywhere?

Daisy: Well, within reason

PING. Jack: What's reason?

Daisy: Well ... Ok I'll write this ... you haven't even kissed me yet!

PING. Jack: Am I allowed?

Daisy: I should think so. We have had more than one date you know!

PING. Jack: So, if I pick you up on Wednesday, and we have dinner, can I expect an after dinner kiss then!

Daisy: Depends if it's a good dinner! The more expensive the bigger the kiss!

PING. Jack: Damn, I knew there would be a catch! I'd better check out the Michelin stars then!

Daisy: Now you're on the right track!

PING. Jack: I'm thinking about you. All the time actually.

Daisy: See you Wednesday. Oh and thinking about you too ...

So, what did I need anyway ... chicken, onions, leeks, broccoli ... Oh damn, I forgot the broccoli ... and why are there four tubs of natural yoghurt … I only ever buy two … better go and put two back …

Even the simplest tasks are testing my concentration.

When I get through the door like a magnet I am drawn to the computer. It now resembles a robot to me, a plastic companion with a keyboard, but heart and soul.

Yes. My phantom has emailed. He never disappoints me.

Daisy,

As you say these similarities are a welcome find! At least we seem to tick a lot of the same boxes. Here are some questions for you as you like this game...

Why did you want to be a doctor?

How did you become a Sexual Health Doctor?

What is your biggest achievement, explain?

What has been your greatest disappointment and why, apart from the obvious marriage breakup?

Tell me five things on your bucket list and why you chose them?

As for the Phantom, I am standing behind you, you just can't see me.

Wickedly!

IG

I dropped my shopping and sat down straight away, anxious to get finger to keyboard…

I did glance behind. Was he really there?!

I wanted to be a doctor because I never wanted to be anything else. We had to have an answer to this question when we went for interviews, and this was my answer. But it was true. Apart from wanting to be a vet when I was about four, then realising it was harder to be a vet than to be a doctor!

The truth is I had no idea what being a doctor meant. I had a glossy view of myself in a white coat diagnosing the measles and healing people who had been told they were going to die.

I hadn't really translated it into horrible things like bones and skin and blood vessels and hideous tumours and the fact ill people are usually miserable because they don't feel well, and because actually a lot of people can't actually be cured and your job is to cope with all of that. Not heal the sick, but look after the dying. (Did I write that?)

As for Sexual Health, I found female patients seek out female doctors to help them with female problems, so I thought I'd better be good at it. So I did a lot of extra training in women's health and that involved working in genito-urinary medicine, which of course includes the male patients. And that's kind of where I ended up.

My biggest achievement has been producing and bringing up my daughter. My ex-husband was never there as he was always at work. I had a series of au pairs to help me and juggled my career but I managed to keep all the balls in the air somehow; she is nearly all grown up and I'm very proud of her. She is a great young person.

My biggest disappointment has been the fact the realisation that medicine was probably the wrong career for me. The problem is that I'm not trained to do anything else.

It's not the subject i.e. the medicine, which is interesting.

And it's not the patients, who are generally extremely nice.

It's the NHS Management.

The way medical staff are treated by officious NHS managers. The working environment is poisonous. They add more and more patients to our clinic lists, so I have no admin time, and it's so stressful not being able to be on top of the admin. No one listens. They all want more for less – and it isn't humanly possible. They just want to flog staff into the ground to meet their targets and they don't care how they do it. Sorry I'm ranting but the fact is that the job is untenable.

OK so my bucket list:

1. **Stay in the Ice Hotel in Sweden. Looks such a great idea and so much fun.**
2. **Do a Vienese waltz in a Vienese ballroom. Do you dance by the way?**
3. **Flotilla sailing in the Med! Dream!**
4. **Do the Playtex Moonwalk! It looks such a laugh. If you haven't heard of it do Google it!**
5. **Visit the Galapagos Islands. I haven't got a great travel bug but the TV programmes make this look such an amazing destination to see the wild life.**

So, what's your bucket list Phantom?

Daisy x

PS If you are standing behind me please put your hand on my shoulder.

SEND

By the time I had put the shopping away, and made a cup of tea my phantom had emailed again. Before I could open it, my phone went PING.

PING: Jack: "I can't wait until Wednesday. What are you doing? Can I come round this evening?"

PING: Daisy: "Well." (I'm suddenly in a tizz, I need to shower, and what will I wear and I've got work tomorrow, I can't really drink much, does this matter ...) "I guess I'm not doing anything else."

PING: Jack: "See you at 7 pm. Great! It's a surprise! Xx"

So actually it occurred to me, rather surprisingly, that my date with Jack was going to get in the way of my emails to Phantom. Then I told myself firmly I hadn't even met the Phantom, in the flesh as it were, and who knows what I would think if I did. He could be a complete disappointment. Remember, and that little thought flashed through my mind, no photo, you haven't seen his photo. But the thought floated away into oblivion as quickly as it had floated in.

Daisy,

As a stockbroker I cannot imagine what it must be like to either want to be or to study to be a doctor. I admire your dedication and all the hard work you must have put in to pass all those exams.

I was sad to think you thought medicine had been a mistake. I doubt that is the case. If you are compassionate, which I think you are, I'm sure you have given an enormous amount to the profession. I do understand your frustrations with NHS management. I was in the same boat when I worked for a company, and I broke away to work for myself a long time ago.

Your daughter sounds as if she is doing well for herself. You must tell me more about her.

I loved the bucket list. In a way, you are a lot more adventurous than me. I do like holidays but I love my cars. I have several sports cars including a soft top Porsche and my ideal vacation is motoring through vineyards in Europe with the roof down. I don't dance I have to admit, as I have two left feet. For you, I would try it, but don't hold your pretty breath.

I looked up the Moonwalk and was bowled over. I think perhaps it's a good day – or night – to be in London to view the spectacle! What an idea. I wonder who thought that one up. I shall sponsor you handsomely.

Love the idea of the Ice Hotel and the Galapagos. Although I prefer warm to cold and may not survive a whole night in the ice bed.

Who knows where you and I might go one day.

I have thought I would like to have your mobile number. Please send it? We could speak ... or text? Let me know?

Admiringly

IG x

PS I am behind you. I have my right hand on your right shoulder.

I noticed ... He put a kiss.

So now Dating Daisy is in a state of utter confusion!

Jack or Phantom?

Phantom or Jack?

Jack is very nice and he is actually here.

And I've seen him.

And he is nice looking.

Phantom is a mystery to me. But he is pulling at my heart strings in a most peculiar way.

Some hours later and a frantic flurry through my wardrobe and I was ready and looking good enough to eat. I have a Hobbs dress in deep purple that is silky and clingy in all the right places. I've lost a bit of weight so it feels good. I've piled my hair up and gone for the dangly earrings. I have on shoes with a small heel as I don't want to tower over Jack. I'm ready for action, whatever that might be. Yes *Dazzling, Beautiful, Smart and Alluring.* That's me! And I will concentrate on jack tonight. Phantom won't get a ghostly look in.

But, I almost forgot to write this, I did do this before I went out:

IG
0778415625
Daisy
SEND

Chapter Forty-Four (In which Daisy makes a mistake)

Friday May 16th 2014

I will just have to write this the way it was. This is it. No holds barred. Be prepared.

The first part of the evening was predictable.

Jack arrived looking suave. He was very complimentary about me and we set off together in good spirits.

Actually, before we set off, we shared a bottle of champagne that I just happened to have in the fridge. And it went down very nicely. Luckily the place Jack had booked for us was only a short distance away, and it was a dry warm evening, so we walked. We were relaxed and happy together. I had laughingly chosen a very small unobtrusive handbag and hoped Jack had noticed!

The restaurant was a new one that had only just opened. It had an American theme so we ordered steaks and fries, Jack had a beer and I had some wine. Then he helped me finish the bottle. I recall him meeting my gaze over the table, and I felt something that I hadn't felt for years. I blushed as I realised what it was. Desire. Something that had been sadly lacking in my marriage for a very long time.

Funny really. Here's the thing. As I've written in this book before, when the kissing nonsense stops, love flies out of the window. Voldemort and I hadn't had any kissing nonsense for as long as I could remember. It is that physical intimacy that keep a couple together. I didn't know Jack that well, but I certainly wanted the kissing nonsense to start.

The evening was punctuated however by my phone going PING, PING, PING. And guess who was texting me? Yes, the Internet Phantom. This is what I saw when I looked at my phone in the Ladies:

I am standing beside you. Can I pour you another glass of wine? Surely I can tempt you to dessert? IG x

I ignored it as I was having a good time and tonight was for Jack.

Next I received:

I am tracing my finger along the neckline of your dress. Love the pearls by the way. Let's go for the Chocolate brownie and two spoons? X

How did he know I was in a restaurant, it was spooky.

After this I turned off my phone.

Phantoms! They get everywhere!

When we got home, it happened. Jack flung his arms round me and kissed me. He smelled like heaven and had a soft mouth a silky mesmerising tongue. We had the house to ourselves that night, so I had no qualms in leading him up to the bedroom. I put some soft music on, and we lay on the bed kissing and canoodling. I didn't consciously decide to have or not to have sex. I wondered what I should do, resist or nor resist. And as I lay there al whole kaleidoscope of emotions flowed through me.

I felt indignant as it wasn't me that caused the marriage let down. I'm not promiscuous. I've had two partners in 28 years (Voldemort and Jeremy). I felt sorry for myself as in fact Internet Dating is lonely and difficult and so often a disaster. What's wrong with being grown up and enjoying the moment, even if it was, just a moment? But I felt sure Jack was developing feelings for me, and vice versa. Why not kick start this relationship. It was a third date, not a first date, what was there to lose. He wasn't a mass murderer or a fraudster, I was sure of that.

So, I'm going to leave the next bit to your imagination. I can just say he stayed the night.

The End.

And let you guess what happened. But he had to go to work in the morning, and I had to see him out in my dressing gown. He was kissing me goodbye on the doorstep and telling me what a fabulous night it had been.

I closed the door, happy for once, and with a positive feeling I was on the start of something big. Would this, just would this, become a reason to part with my poem?

Only time would tell.

How wrong was I – as I just about never heard from him again?

Chapter Forty-Five (In which Imogen puts her secret plan into action)

Saturday May 17th 2014

It's Saturday and Imogen is smiling and smiling. She got me up early and brought me tea and toast in bed! An all-time first. It's the day she told me to keep free for her surprise, in case you had forgotten.

She asked me what I was wearing today. Wearing? Why? What's going on?

I did my best to look cool, not like a frumpy old mother.

I was downstairs, and was at the computer – as usual – when the doorbell rang.

"You answer it, you have to answer it," Imogen was giggling wildly.

I opened the door, rather nervously. Suddenly everything around me erupted into a blur of activity.

"Daisy? You are Daisy?" A middle-aged woman in a smart black suit and ten inches of foundation stood on the front porch, holding out a microphone towards me. A microphone? Yes! A microphone.

She looked vaguely familiar.

"Yes, that's me." I glanced back at Imogen.

"I don't know if you recognise me," the woman continued, "But I'm Clarissa Barton and we're from *Impressive Creations*, the TV show. Your daughter contacted us to say your house is in need of a bit of renovation? Yes? So we're here to make your dreams come true."

" What ... pardon ... I don't believe ..." Thinking that suddenly ten million viewers might be watching me, I was very unsure what to do or say. I was aware of the TV programme, who in the UK could not be, as it had occupied the prime TV slots for months. But privately I had always been sceptical about these renovations. They did them so quickly, could they really be being done properly. And what if you actually hated what they had done? I didn't really want half of the UK seeing the inside of my house. OMG there were cobwebs on the ceiling. I would have cleaned up a bit better if I'd had any inclination.

I felt myself being propelled into the lounge, and a stampede of followers with lights and cameras all charged in after me.

"Now we need to just get a feel for the problem," announced Clarissa, immaculately dressed, but with large gap between her front teeth. She had a Mancunian accent and bright pink lipstick. I felt ghostly pale and underdressed.

We were somehow now in the lounge, and I had sunk onto the large sofa.

"So Daisy," continued Clarissa, "Imogen, that's your daughter, she contacted us and basically, basically, unless you get some renovations done here you'll have to sell, is that right?"

"Shame, shame. Potentially this is a beautiful house, I'm sure we all agree –

"So what did you have in mind? I see, new kitchen, new bathrooms, new boiler, replace some windows, redecorate throughout, new hall and stairs carpet?... that sort of thing ... yup, yup. You've seen our programme before! We take ... what can often be described as ... old wrecks! Forgive me for saying that ha ha! – and we turn them into – houses of beauty!"

She turned to me again.

"I have to say this Daisy, what we want to do, absolutely, absolutely, is let you show us around and tell us what needs doing. We'll take some before shots of course. Then we'll get you to sit down with our property consultants and management team to agree what needs to be done, and the timescale. It has to be completed in under four weeks. Yup four weeks. Then, we come back in four weeks to see your reaction, and of course the after shots!! How cool is that! Daisy, a new home in four weeks. Just imagine!"

I didn't know what to say. Imogen, who clearly thought she was being so clever was smirking and smirking. She clearly thought she had saved us from having to move house. She obviously didn't understand that it was actually just as much a question of being unable to afford the ongoing costs, like a large mortgage and council tax on a six-bedroom house occupied by two people. I looked at her and I couldn't explain all that to her, at least not just now in front of ten million TV viewers. So I smiled and nodded and said all the right things. But inside I was very uncertain.

The camera never lies … does it … and the shots taken of our house were toe-curlingly awful.

What could I do? She hadn't taken her stiletto shoes off and she had trampled little spots of mud into the rug on the floor. What was her name again, Camilla? Cassandra, I couldn't remember. There was a balding man with an earring next to her with a clipboard, wearing a badge that said Mikey. There were seven of them I counted, all standing in my front lounge. Uninvited. To my horror all of a sudden I felt tearful. Deep breath Daisy.

But somewhere inside my sensible self was saying things to me like:

Don't look a gift horse in the mouth;

If they do up the house, they can do it up, you can still sell it after;

Any publicity is good publicity;

You can still be Dating Daisy, it doesn't affect that;

Imogen meant well, for once maybe this is a good idea, if you can get your head around the fact we're not really doing our dirty washing in public.

So, Miss pink lips was steering me back to the front door.

"Start with the entrance porch, always a good place to start! The way in!"

I really wasn't sure if this was being filmed live or not and in my indecision I decided to play safe and be cooperative. "Show us what needs doing here? Don't be shy Daisy, just tell it the way it is!" she had a quirky chuckle.

"Well, as you can see," I said "The roof over the porch is … er … leaking … you get wet drips down your back looking for the front door key in your handbag."

"Uh huh," the guy with the clipboard was scribbling.

"And the guttering up there" I pointed up over the front door to the front gables "that leaks too. It's far too high for me to get to it myself. These stone slabs weren't laid well down here, in front of the front door, it has no drainage and all the water puddles on top of it and then physically seeps under the front door."

"I see!"

"So the front door is warped. I think it's rotten in places. Probably needs replacing. And see this stained glass, in this little window bit up here, the black seals are damaged and the glass actually wobbles in the frame. Some of the little panes are fractured. But its antique glass, cost a fortune to have this renovated, so we've never been able to do it I'm afraid."

"Uh uh." The clipboard man was scribbling and someone was taking photographs.

I continued. Now I had an opportunity to really moan about the state of my house, they could have it. Both barrels! "This all means it's not good for security and the wind whistles through the leaky window into the house. I can feel the draft when I'm washing up at the sink in the kitchen! And look, this number 6 is at hanging at an angle, needs repositioning. The door needs painting, desperately, that goes without saying. And once you get inside, well, you might notice the house is cold. It's a twenty-year-old boiler.

"We haven't had it replaced because its right at the bottom of the airing cupboard and it's so difficult to get to the whole room would need to be knocked about to do it. A really expensive job. I can show you if you want to see it … you do?… Ok come this way."

Then I nearly died of embarrassment as the BBC camera man filmed the utility room complete with laundry baskets filled with mine and Imogen's smalls! Enough said.

So Clarissa – I got her name right in the end – and Mikey followed me round encouraging me to mention every last thing that was wrong with my house. In a way, it was therapeutic. In another way, it was humiliating.

They saw the damp patches in the bedrooms, the old wooden window frames that needed replacing, the terrible bathrooms with lime-scaled taps and filthy grouting. The stained worn out carpets and the old curtains and blinds that needed to be shredded. No holds barred. If they could help, I might as well take advantage of the opportunity.

The exciting part, as I decided eventually that I was rather enjoying it, was sitting down with Hector, the property manager and planning the refurbishment. Hector was short with round dark-rimmed spectacles and a cravat. He was breathless with enthusiasm.

"I see roses," he said, "growing round a new bright red front door.

"I see a warm house, new boiler, new window frames, new bathrooms, heated towel rails, underfloor heating. So warm and cosy! I see a new kitchen, top of the range. An Aga, perhaps an Aga in an old character house like this? I see an extension actually, a conservatory, wooden of course to fit the period. We need Simon our architect to get involved here I think, and Drew of course. He's our landscaper. We could do some wonders in your garden. Make all the difference. Can you leave the plans to me for now and I'll get back you? We're on a tight time schedule aren't we guys? How about I come back with the plans this time next week?"

And then Clarissa was saying, "That's all we've got time for this week. It's goodbye from me, and Mikey, and Hector, and of course Daisy and Imogen! Join us this time next Saturday for more – *Impressive Creations*!"

The funny thing was then, they just swept out, the way they had come, like an entourage. And Imogen and I were left standing in the hallway, wondering if what we had just experienced was real.

"Was I just live on the BBC?" I asked her incredulously.

"I think they edit it Mum, don't worry." Imogen had put an arm round my shoulders.

"So it isn't live."

"Sort of."

"Oh my God. Imogen! They saw my dirty knickers! And my pin up of Chris Martin. Why the hell didn't you tell me!"

"Mum! If I had told you, you would have gone mental! Now, we'll get a new house, thanks to the BBC, and we don't need to move...and ...it was my brilliant idea!

Oh God. I need a cup of tea. Or a gin and tonic. I need to think about this one.

In a way, it has to be too good to be true. There's always a catch, I keep thinking. What's the catch? The catch is the nation being inside my house! That's the catch.

OMG. I needed some time to think. I mustn't be angry with Imogen who clearly thought this was brilliant. Could I get out of it, refuse, what would happen then?

It looked like having being given this chance, if I refused it, my daughter would never forgive me. How could I explain to her it wasn't just the cost of the renovations, it was the cost of living there. Two little bunnies in an enormous rabbit warren.

Imogen went out shopping with her friend Izzy after that, and I was left alone, with all my frustrations, the teapot and the computer. I didn't want to be in this situation. All my friends, and my patients would see the shabby state we had been living in. I didn't want anyone's pity, I was just embarrassed. But also, I could see that if I had a magic wand that could put it all right, this was it. I probably just had to let it ride and see what happened. The house couldn't be any worse after the makeover surely, I comforted myself.

So I logged on. Actually I still had things to do, like decide what to wear for my date in London tomorrow with a Greek God! Oh and to buy my train ticket online.

I saw an email, it was from Alex, was he having second thoughts?

Hi Daisy,

How's your day? I was thinking about tomorrow. It's very exciting. And I'm really looking forward to meeting you. So please don't take this the wrong way. I hope you'll excuse me as it's very modern world we live in, but, it's going to cost about £300 each to do the proposed itinerary. Could I ask you perhaps to put a contribution into my bank account? Can you

send me your mobile number so I can text the bank details to you perhaps? Sorry to mention money. One of those things.

BW

Alex xx

Dear Alex,

Thanks for your message. I am looking forward to meeting you too. I just wanted to say that I always pay my way and was going to offer anyway when I saw you. I just want to say this and hope it doesn't cause offence. Surely the main idea about tomorrow is to get to know each other? Much as your plan looks great fun, we'll be rushing here and there, and shouting over the roar of the engine! Would it be an idea just to lighten the itinerary a little so we aren't under so much pressure? I'm happy with whatever you decide?

BW

Daisy

SEND

Dear Daisy,

I can see you have taken offence. Surely you didn't expect me to fork out over £600 on a first date! I only wanted to be sure you would turn up, if I'd booked everything in advance. I was waiting for you to offer about the payment, and you didn't, and we're going tomorrow, so I had to bring it up. Now I feel terrible. Have your other dates spent so much on you, at least the first time they met you? I bet they haven't. I don't want to fall out over this, but I really feel in this day and age it's not unreasonable to share the costs.

BW

Alex

Hi Alex,

Please don't get upset about this. It's fine. I never expected you to pay such a huge amount on a date with me. I was surprised and pleased by your suggestions, who wouldn't have been. You don't know me, but generosity is my middle name. There would be no problem as far as I am concerned. But now, I feel upset, it has to be said. One of the reasons my marriage failed was my ex-husband's attitude to money. I just can't have a relationship with anyone where money is an issue.

I think maybe a whole day in London when we had never met was going too far. Should we perhaps go back a step and just meet for coffee?

BW

Daisy

SEND

Hi Daisy,

I can assure you I do not have an attitude about money. I was merely suggesting we share the costs upfront. I didn't mean to start world war 3. I was happy with the plan, not sure what I could or would leave out of it. I must say I feel a little wounded that I went to so much trouble and you are throwing this back in my face! Most women would be thrilled to have such an offer. You are obviously one of those women I was told to look out for on the internet, who is out for what she can get. I was warned about women like you. Predatory women who just want sugar daddies to spoil them rotten.

I am sorry we've had this email exchange, but I guess better this way than finding this out in London.

I don't think there's any point us meeting for coffee. I am sorry for the upset.

Put your feet up tomorrow.

Alex.

Do you know what, I was incredulous. In the space of about seven days this apparently respectable, possible date had turned into a werewolf! I wanted to send him two words. Starting and ending in F. But instead I took some very deep breaths, and then deleted him from the site. I fiddled around a bit and worked out how to block any emails from him. Absolutely unbelievable.

So I spent Sunday, in my dressing-gown watching a box set of *Prime Suspect.* It was a pretty good way to switch off from my own dramas, by immersing myself in somebody else's.

Internet Dating Lesson

So which of my own dating lessons did I break this time? (See Chapter 35.)

Rule 8, and I quote "just meet for coffee ... so you can make a quick getaway of it doesn't work out."

And I/we went too fast. Slow down. It's a marathon not a sprint.

And what else did I write? Rule 10 ... keeeep going! There IS someone out there for everyone.

End of.

That night I heard Chris singing:

... Aw... he's trying to *fix* me!

I'm know I'm worth more than that Chris, don't worry!

Chapter Forty-Six (In which Daisy makes a sad decision)

Monday May 19th 2014

So it's Monday morning. I can't sleep. It's about 5.30 am and I'm at the computer. Again! And still not a word from Jack.

I texted him on Friday

PING: Daisy: Hope you are having a good day, but it can't be as good as the night before xx

By teatime there was no reply so I tried again.

PING: Daisy: Thank you for a lovely dinner. Let me know when we can meet up again. xx

By next morning, no reply.

On Saturday I was a bit bold, as he may have been with his wife and son, but I tried to ring him, twice, and it went to answer-phone.

By Sunday, today, I was fed up. For me, what happened on Thursday night was a big deal. I'm not in the habit of doing that sort of thing. It had been fantastic ... hadn't it? Or hadn't it? Maybe he hated it? Maybe I was a disappointment. I couldn't understand.

In the end, I emailed him. I was quite hurt and surprised by own feelings that alternated from blushing in shame, to thinking not to be so silly, there would be a rational explanation.

I thought about the whole situation.

How did I know what he said about his wife and son were true? And he lived in Plymouth, I wanted a boyfriend I could see especially at weekends. If he did get divorced it might be years away. My divorce took three years. And there was the Phantom pull as he was now texting me all the time and wanting us to meet. Jack seemed a very nice man, but he didn't have the imagination and wit of the Phantom. If I went for Jack and never met the Phantom how would I know what I might be missing?

Eventually these feelings turned to anger. I felt used and humiliated. I wouldn't be the first woman to have been used as a one night stand. But I had never thought it would happen to me. Well wake up, I told myself it just did. You are just one of the millions.

So I sent Jack an email just now and it said:

Hi Jack,

I can't understand why it's four days since we spent the night together and you haven't replied to any of my texts and phone calls. What happened may not have been a big thing for you but it was for me.

However this Internet Dating is an uncertain game. I can't imagine how you couldn't contact me at all for three days since it happened, even if you are with your wife and your son. It takes a moment to send a text from the bathroom!

The thing is, I really liked you. But I want someone I can trust, who puts me first and cares about me. This has shown me that I don't think you are going to do that.

Whether things would have developed I don't know, but I think I deserve more. So I hope you don't mind, but I have decided to move on and knock whatever is between you and I on the head. I am sad about it, but I gave you a big prize. I gave myself to you. And you haven't appreciated it. And I feel sad and let down.

So I am sorry that for whatever reason it didn't work out. And I hope you find happiness elsewhere.

And as I don't now feel I can trust you, should I have a chlamydia test?

With love,

Daisy x

SEND

I felt ashamed of myself as I sent it. What an idiot I had been. I should have listened to Jane and waited for the sixth date after all.

Anyhow, back to reality! Let's not forget the day job. I have a story to tell you of something that happened to me today!

Today I was fitting a contraceptive implant. This is a little rod, like a matchstick, that has to be inserted under the skin in the top of the arm. Don't try this at home! It has to be done by someone medically trained, and involves an injection of local anaesthetic.

So my patient was a very large girl called Stacey. She must have had a BMI of over 40. That is clinically obese. I feel sorry for the patients who are in this state, as I know how hard it is to lose weight, and many of them are overweight because they have been through some psychological trauma.

I sat next to her, in sterile gloves and apron, and got on with the procedure.

"Thanks for doing this, doctor," Stacey said, as I was washing her arm with antiseptic.

"The thing is, my boyfriend will be so relieved I've finally got some proper contraception."

"Definitely a good thing," I replied, marking the site for the insertion. "Little scratch," I said, as I inserted the needle under the skin.

"The thing is," she continued, "We've been together for two years, but we've never met."

"Never met?" this was very strange. Did she, or did she not need contraception? I hesitated to see what she would say next.

"The thing is," she carried on, "we met on this dating site. We were playing a game. All people from round the world. And he and I well we got on so well, we starting chatting off the site."

"Oh," I said.

"And the thing is, he lives in Canada. Neither of us can afford the plane ticket. We're saving up. So our whole relationship is over the internet."

"Um ... so you need contraception?" I asked

"Oh yes of course," she said. "It makes it more realistic! Don't you think?"

I was a bit perplexed, but I had to ask "So, are you – do you – have sex over the internet?"

"Of course," she replied "Wouldn't you?!"

I had some visions of dressing up and web cams and doing unspeakable things with hairbrushes and I didn't ask any more, I just fitted the implant. For all I knew there could also be another boyfriend right here in the UK.

But it did strike me as surprising the lengths people are prepared to go to have good internet sex!

The patients never fail to disappoint me!

Chapter Forty-Seven (In which Daisy experiences more than she bargained for)

Monday May 19th 2014

So I'm not going to brood on the Jack thing. It was a mistake. I am a novice at this and I got it wrong. I need to remain positive. Just learn from my mistakes. That's all.

Hmm...

I have a look around my four sites.

There's a few new faces. Hopeful faces. A chap from Chichester has been messaging me every day for a week or so. He has a nice profile but the more I look at his photograph the more I know I couldn't – and I'm really sorry about this – but I just couldn't, feel anything for someone who looks like that!

I have even been searching in London where there is vast array of characters. Someone who says he is an Airline Pilot is keen to meet me. There is a picture of him in his uniform with a peaked white cap. I've heard pilots and air stewardesses are notorious philanderers. Not for me.

So I give in and go back to my Phantom.

The last ghostly message, and text bore the words I was almost dreading:

When can we meet?

IG x

And it was up to me to set the date.

I had to do it, didn't I? How could I finish this book without finishing the story about the Internet Ghost?

So here goes …

We agreed to meet on a Bank Holiday Monday, in Tunbridge Wells which was about half way between our two homes. I suggested we meet at the pizzeria *Inferno*, so it was a very public place and I could get away quickly if he was a weirdo.

It was about a week to wait and I can't tell you the fevered anticipation.

One thing that was bugging me big time was that I had no idea what he looked like. No photo. I had no idea if he was tall or short, fat or thin, bald or hairy, or … I honestly didn't know. How would I recognise him? Would he recognise me?

I kept asking about this and he kept fobbing me off.

I did discuss it with my friends. Most of whom said I was mad to spend a Bank Holiday driving halfway across the country to meet someone who was definitely a weirdo.

I worried about that to wear, about my weight, about my hair. I changed and changed and changed again. I had a terrible week with poor sleep and trying not to be anxious about it, but trying to prepare myself for what was most likely going to be an enormous let down.

Meanwhile Phantom was having fun. He would text me when I was at work

PING: IG: Darling, can you get me another G&T, there's a love?

Then a few minutes later

PING: IG: Lime please!

Then after that

PING: IG: Oh yes, always with ice!

Then I would get:

PING: IG: What's for dinner sweetheart? Oh, steak again. Yes, yes, but can you do your special fried potatoes and I'll rub your back later, just the way you like it! xx

The morning of the date arrived and I woke to a text from him. It said, alarmingly:

PING: IG: Daisy, I can't wait to meet you. Today may be the first day of the rest of our lives. Drive carefully. I will be the one in the silver Mercedes. IG xx

PS. Don't forget to bring your passport.

Daisy! ... Passport!

I went for the yellow Daisy blouse and white trousers outfit. I had some heels on today and some black earrings. As usual my hair was washed and brushed to perfection. I have used the perfume Anais Anais since I was 16, so I sprayed myself vigorously, a worthy advertisement for Cacharel. I didn't forget that poem. The rather crumpled enveloped stared up at me from the depths of my handbag. Would I ever find anyone worthy of giving it to?

It was a good two-hour drive for me to get there. I know the way as it's the way I go to work, although Tunbridge Wells is much further on, and the journey seemed interminable.

I arrived and parked in the nearest car park to *Inferno.* This is a public car park behind the parade of shops. My red Kia was tucked in there nicely and there was a space left next to me. A space for a Phantom??

I was early as always. Anyone who knows me, knows I am always early. I hate the rush and stress of being late. Then I wondered if he had perhaps arrived early too. How would I know? I scanned the cars. I couldn't see anyone sitting alone obviously waiting. There were no silver Mercedes' in the car park – yet.

My heart was hammering. I don't know why I was quite so nervous but I was. This book is not 100% accurate as I am writing it from memory, but I think by this time we had exchanged over 100 emails. I knew a lot about this man, and he knew a lot about me. Moreover, he had got under my skin.

And yet I didn't even know what he looked like! I wouldn't recognise him if he walked past me in the street! I remember thinking that I was being stupid and I should just give up and go home. But somehow I couldn't. I just had to know the rest of the story.

We had agreed to meet at 1 pm, and in true Phantom fashion he was punctual to a T. At one minute to one, my mobile rang.

"Daisy," he said "Are you in the car park behind the restaurant? Good. I will see you in a couple of minutes."

I hung up, my heart beating and looked wildly round me and towards the car park entrance. I honestly wanted to turn on the ignition and drive away. But I couldn't.

Then, there it was. A silver Mercedes, driving through the car park entrance and up towards me. I realised he would have to reverse into the space, which meant I could only see the side and mostly his back profile.

First disappointment. It wasn't Mr Big. He had white grey hair.

I sat in my car head bowed, seemingly unable to move, until there was a tap on the window. Deep breath, I got out of the car. This was it. OMG.

There was a tall man, not ugly, with startling blue eyes. Clean shaven. Smiling. He looked a bit like my dad, in a blazer with a handkerchief in the top pocket and shiny lace-up shoes. He had an over-wide stripey tie. It was all a bit just out-of- the-bowls-club and a bit dated. But he had made an effort. At least there was no hint of Morris dancing. I must say though that that in that moment, although I didn't find him repulsive (then!) I thought he looked an old man, too old for me ...

There was sadly no spark of attraction. Not even a tiny one! He was just not my type. 100 emails ... but no sadly no pheromones. Not even a tiny whiff.

Simple as that.

If only I had stuck to my guns and insisted on the photo!

As I extended my hand to shake his, a bit formal perhaps but I didn't want to kiss him, he said his first word to me ... something like,

"Well, hello Daisy," ... and... .

I was bathed in halitosis!

This was something I had not bargained for.

If I haven't written this already a clean mouth and clean teeth are of monumental importance to me. Anyone with bad breath just would not pass Go! And yet here I was. With a man in need of Corsodyl. OMG.

I knew I had to go through with the lunch, even though I wanted to run away. One of my dating rules is always to meet for coffee or a drink so you can get away. Why don't I follow my own rules? Another one broken. I'm such an idiot.

He was beaming at me, seemingly very happy with what he could see before him. He was propelling me gently towards the restaurant and I was walking obediently in the right direction. I saw a couple of hours with this rather creepy, I decided, old man stretching before me and I wanted to make a run for it. But I didn't, I walked into the restaurant.

What can I write about that meal? We sat at a table by the window, and I liked that as it was a distraction to talk about the passersby. We ate pasta, and he didn't finish his. He seemed too busy concentrating on me. He stared at me intently for most of the meal. I got on with being me, explaining about my job, my life, my book. He smiled with a self-satisfied look like he had found a pot of gold at the end of the rainbow. If only I had felt the same.

I learnt a few interesting facts about his dating however. The Spacetime 3000 profile had got him over 1000 hits in the first month and more than 400 favourites, some of whom were in France, Germany and Spain. How embarrassing when you compare that to mine! The only other woman to rival me with her reply, was first in the queue purely as she lived geographically closer to him. But they had met, sadly not been attracted to each other, and so I was next on the list!

He talked about his son who was following him into the stockbroking industry, and his daughter who was madly into drama and wanting to go to drama school. He seemed to have a good relationship with his children, who live with his ex-wife, and he seemed very caring. I cannot abide men who father children and then don't have time for them, and this was not the case. So that was positive.

He did encourage me to talk about myself. I have no problem with that, in fact I welcome it, as I have so many stories to tell and explanations to give, I am unstoppable. And he just sat there smiling and nodding at me like a cat that had got the cream.

I recall two scary moments in that lunch. At one moment, he leant forward and said to me that he would have no problem relocating his business to Brighton! This was going a bit fast for me. Moving in together when we were on our first date! I was shocked and it seemed very inappropriate.

Later I told him the story about how my lovely Saab convertible blew up, literally, and I had to ditch it and get a reliable car, a Kia, instead. He sat forward, grabbed my hand and told me he would like to buy me a new Saab. "How much are they?" he said. "Thirty grand... no problem. When we are together you can pick any one you like."

The thing is, he went on, "I want to take care of you, so your ex never gets near you again, and I can support you and your children, if you'll let me."

"I know you," he said, through and through, "and I know how to look after you. Trust me."

Trust an internet Phantom! I don't think so. This was the icing on the cake. I knew I couldn't do this, I had to go. When I got back from the Ladies, he had paid the bill.

As we waited for his card to be returned, he put an arm round my waist and drew me to him in a sort of embrace. I bristled. I think he felt it and released me quite quickly.

When we walked back to the cars, it had started to rain. I was thankful as there was every reason to hop into the car and not to linger as I had a terrible feeling he was going to try and kiss me. I drove away, with such a feeling I had made a great escape. I wished I had never done all this, as I now had a two-hour drive home. My overriding thoughts were that this had all been a terrible mistake.

And what's more, my poem again lay dishevelled in the depths of my hand bag. Despair! Would I ever find anyone to receive my Shakespearean poetry?

Within moments of setting off, my phone went PEEP, PEEP. When I looked at the message later it said:

PING: IG: If I could I would give you my last Rolo! Miss you already! IG x

I actually slept like a log that night, the mystery over. It was a disappointing end to a whirlwind romance online but that's the nature of the Internet Dating game. It's just usually a round of disappointments. Although quite often as you have seen in this book, disappointments that can sometimes be quite amusing. Who would have thought that I, a time-honoured fan of *Phantom of the Opera,* would actually meet my own internet Phantom! No mask unfortunately, although his face had been invisible to me for a long time. No disfigurement, when I did get to see him, but no Mr Big either.

In the morning, there of course was the Phantom's email.

G, he wrote,

From now on I shall call you G, for gorgeous, as that's what you are. Totally gorgeous. I have set up a special email address only for you and me called justforus@hotmail.com. Let's use that in future just for us. All my hopes and desires were achieved when I saw you get out of your car. I so enjoyed our lunch didn't you.

That's what I need. Charm, wit, beauty, enthusiasm about life. You have it all. I thought about you all the way home.

I wasn't joking about relocating my business. I want to be with you, urgently, now I've seen you. Please can we have another date and soon.

Yours feverishly,

IG xx

Justforus@hotmail.com! I felt a stab of panic! No one has ever set up a private email address for me before!

Do you know what? I ignored the email. I knew he was desperate for some feedback, and wanted some positive encouragement, but I just didn't know what to say.

How could I let him down after all this and not hurt his feelings? He had put a lot into the emails and tried to build up a relationship with me, and it had been very intense. How could I tell him he looked like had just left the bowls club and he just didn't do it for me!

I felt completely like a rabbit in the headlights. I didn't know what to do.

So – I did nothing. To Phantom's extreme irritation. Silence. For once! I needed to think.

As the day progressed something else happened. I was still smarting over the one night stand with Jack. Having dealt with it the way I did, I was proud of myself. But I was still bewildered, as we **had** had a great night together and it can't just have been me that felt that. But men are strange creatures, and as soon as they think they might have to commit to a relationship, a lot of them run in the opposite direction. He probably isn't really at the stage of his divorce to commit to anybody and I should have seen that straight away.

Internet Dating tip! Don't go for the ones who are still married. Only go for those who have come through the divorce process and come out the other side! That really is good advice, take it from me.

But out of the blue a message appeared on my screen that day. It said

Dear Daisy,

I was shocked and sad to get your email. I wanted to contact you but I couldn't. The day after our night together

I had terrible food poisoning. Stomach pains and diarrhoea. Terrible.

I had to drive home to Plymouth (don't ask me the details of the journey) and see the doctor and I was in bed over the weekend. Perhaps it was something I ate in the restaurant. I wondered if you were alright? In the meantime I've had mobile phone failure. I did tell you my phone, which is paid for by the company, was complete crap, when I saw you. Well it stopped working altogether and I couldn't get anything done about it over the weekend and because I couldn't leave the house.

For the record, I did want to contact you. I think you are amazing. I did value our night together. I was developing feelings for you and for your information, I think I could have stayed with you for a lifetime.

However, I am not divorced yet, my life is all over the place and I think we should accept that if that's your view and I am where I am, we draw a line under it as you suggested.

Please don't think badly of me. I did love our time together, and whoever ends up with you will be extremely lucky.

Jack xx

I sat staring at the screen drumming my fingers on the desk. Could I believe this? Was it real or a complete fabrication? He didn't strike me as a liar. However, I started to think, we had been emailing. Just because his phone was out of action and he had an upset stomach, he must have a laptop or a desktop and could have sent an email. No, I decided. If I had meant anything to him he would have made sure he contacted me soon after the night before, and if he didn't for whatever reason, he's not going to be the man for me. I liked the phrase "for the record, I could have stayed with you for a lifetime"...

... that ... was strangely comforting.

But now I had to decide what to do about the Phantom.

He of course was very persistent.

By my very silence, he knew something was up. He bombarded me with texts and emails, all very flattering.

I started to question all of this. Here was a man with an incredible mind, ostensibly wealthy, with a flourishing business, a host of cars, devoted to me, wanting to come into my life and have a serious relationship with me, look after me and take an interest in my children, oh and buy me a new Saab convertible. He was tall, reasonable looking. Ok so he has bad breath, isn't it easier to say OK to him and just buy him a new toothbrush?!

There's a lot on offer here. Perhaps I'm just being picky. Lots of women marry men for their money. (Not me!) But I don't want to be alone, and I don't want to be poor. Look at that amazing piece on his dating site and the 1000 replies, of which mine was at the top. Am I completely stupid to reject him? Perhaps this is what's meant to be and I have to get real.

And just buy him some mouthwash.

Isn't that a whole lot simpler?

But I couldn't do it. After 72 hours of pings and buzzes, I eventually sat at the computer, and this is what I wrote.

Dear IG,

I know you are waiting for some reaction from me and hoping it will be a positive one. There is no easy way to say this so I just have to say it. I'm sorry but I don't think you and I are whatever you want to say – compatible.

A lot of things became apparent when we met. I saw a tall distinguished man, nicely dressed who was very pleasant company for our lunch date. You didn't do or say anything wrong. But, there are lot so differences between us.

You are a stockbroker and I am doctor. Once we've got the sex out of the way, what on earth will we talk about? I love popular music and you like classical. You love cars and motoring, and an afternoon driving along in the sunshine. I want to get out of the car as soon as possible and actually prefer to fly.

I love sailing, boats and water. You told me you can't swim. I love crime novels, you love historical fiction. I love Wave 105 and you want Radio 4. I prefer white wine, you love red.

You are nearing retirement and I have ten years left to work. Apart from Scrabble, what on earth is there we can share and enjoy?

I've loved the emails and the texts and it e been a lot of fun. But there are 998 other women out there who loved your profile, so hopefully one of them will be the one you are looking for. I'm so sorry but it isn't me.

Bye Bye Phantom,

Regretfully,

Daisy (aka Christine)

And I sent it to skyfullofmagic.com and not to justforus@hotmail.com.

There wasn't any "us". At least not as far as I was concerned.

I did have the grace to feel sorry for him opening this email, as I knew he would be disappointed. I wondered if it would have been a kindness to mention the toothbrush and the mouthwash, but I decided against it.

So now, I was wary, waiting to see what the controlling Phantom would do next. And the funny thing is, there was nothing at all from him for three days. I was beginning to think I had shaken him off and how easy was that, however, when an email arrived in my box.

It said:

Daisy,

I can't open your email. I just can't.

IG

OMG! What should I do?

I typed back:

Read the email. Just read the email.

Daisy x

SEND

Daisy, I can't. I think I know what's in it.
IG

IG,

Well if you know what's in it, it won't be a surprise will it! Just open it.

Daisy

SEND

Daisy,

I opened it. I am heartbroken and will be replying tonight. Don't go away.

Your IG x

I waited, and later that evening this is what he sent:

My Dear Daisy,

This is probably one of the hardest things I have had to write. Even the Spacetime profle did not take as much energy as this.

When I set about looking for a lifetime partner, I wanted a woman who was attractive, bright, had a creative mind, who was organised, amusing, generous, fun to be with, let's face it sexy and downright perfect for me. When I met you, you firmly ticked every box. If I could dream up a perfect partner, it would be you.

We have exchanged so many emails, and you have opened your heart to me. The point it that I understand you. I know the hurt and the heartache you have suffered. I want to be

with you to heal that pain for ever and to make sure you never, ever have to feel that way again.

I think you can see I have taken great trouble to learn about the details of your life and what matters to you. What matters to you, matters to me, and I will ensure that you have a happy, stress free life and want for nothing.

My business is sound. I make money, so what? I can run my business from anywhere. It would be simple for me to move to Brighton and let our amazing life together begin. I don't want to scare you but I promise you great things. Health and happiness foremost, but someone who will love you more than life itself.

I don't agree with your list of differences between us. We are both professional people. If we were peas in a pods life would be tedious. We will much to talk about and to share. I am quite happy to travel by plane and share a bottle of white wine. I took my daughter to an Oasis concert a few years ago and loved it. You can have the TV remote. I don't care. I think we have a lot of similarities that matter, and that is what we need to capitalise on, not make problems.

I just need to see you again. Please don't say you won't see me. I feel I want you and need you in my life. It's such an exciting prospect. Don't you feel it too? Please reread what I have written, sleep on it and reply tomorrow.

Sleep tight my Christine,

With my love,

IG xx

There was only one thing for it.

Tea with the Amigos.

So, I flew down the hill and rang the doorbell. Malcolm, Amigo one answered the door, adjusting his hearing aids. Maggie, Amigo two made the tea. We all three sat on the sofa, like ducks in a row. I loved being with my Amigos, I couldn't have done this Internet Dating without them.

Malcolm was keen to get started, "Come on then, let's hear it!" he said, excitedly.

"Yes, come on, we want all the gossip!" said Maggie.

I sipped my tea. "Not gossip – I hope." I said, "You're not telling anyone about this are you?"

"Of course not, just a turn of phrase," replied Malcolm, Amigo 1. "Has he got 'pixie ears?!'" (This is Malcolm's way of asking if he was well endowed by the way!)

"I don't know! We didn't get anywhere near any of that! – But, well, listen this is it," and I was off. I love telling stories!

And I told them all about my scary trip to Tunbridge Wells, the punctual arrival of the silver Mercedes, the grey-haired man who was not Mr Big in the from-the-bowls-club shiny shoes outfit, the awkwardness of the lunchtime encounter ... and the halitosis.

I told the story word for word, including the phantom's offer to relocate and to buy me a brand-new Saab!

They listened agog. Whatever you say about the Amigos, they are good listeners, that's for sure. I finished my story by saying

"And so, he wrote me this email," and I handed them a printed copy. "Just read it, to yourselves, not out loud. What do you think?"

I waited. It seemed a long time.

"Well, I would say he seems to have taken a lot of trouble to get the measure of you," said Malcolm in a considered fashion.

"He put a huge amount of thought into that," agreed Maggie.

"He's really been standing in your shoes. He's very taken with you."

"Look what he's promising. Sounds amazing!"

I was quick on the uptake, ""But you haven't met him, honestly... "

"But you have, you must know!" said Maggie.

"I met him and I didn't like him. Everything was wrong!" I said, dejectedly.

"Such as?" asked Amigo Malcolm.

"I told you! The clothes, the manner, the breath ... everything. I just didn't feel any ... pheromones. If only he had sent me the photo early on, I wouldn't be in this situation," I retorted.

It was Malcolm who replied first "Look, you said yourself that the person was more important than the looks. You told us time and time again you knew at this age you had to be realistic."

"Yes, but … "

"No yes buts!" interjected Maggie.

"Yes, yes. If he had two eyes, a nose and a mouth. He's an option for you. Come on! And you said he was tall, and you like tall men, and not skinny," that was Malcolm again.

I managed to get in one "Yes but …"

"I said no Yes buts! He is an option," said Maggie.

I couldn't help the 'buts'. "But … but … he had terrible breath. I told you."

"Come on! You get to know him … you jokingly buy him his own head for your shared electric toothbrush! That's easily solved."

"But, I can't explain it. I think he's controlling. He hasn't been completely open with me about his job, his address, his family," I heard myself say.

"What do you mean?" asked Malcolm.

"Well is he a stockbroker maybe he's a fraud? And I don't even know if he really lives as that address, or if it's a mansion or a council house!"

"Well let's look him up!" suggested Malcolm.

So I sat there while they got the iPad out, and googled my Phantom. Mr Angus Robinson.

Yes he had a registered business address. We couldn't find any reviews, sadly. But next we Google mapped his home address. It was hard from the road to be sure, but it looked like it was a large house set back from the road. If he actually lived there. And if he really owned it. All these thoughts flashed through my mind. And yet with Patrick, I never questioned what he told me for a minute. Was there something wrong, or wasn't there?

"I think you are just scared because you've actually found someone who might be right for you, and you are frightened to take the plunge," said Maggie.

"Do you?" I wasn't sure of that at all.

"Well after what happened to you, you're always going to find it hard to trust anyone," said Malcolm.

"True," I replied.

"I think this guy is slightly older than you, not a bad thing, with a good career, plenty of money, a creative mind and he wants a serious relationship with you. He's prepared to move here for God's sake and he's only met you once!" said Malcolm, with a bit of a flourish.

"Isn't that odd?" I asked.

"No, he knows what he wants and he sees you and he knows he's hit the jackpot!" replied Amigo Malcolm.

"You wouldn't need to go to work, he wants to look after you!" said Amigo Maggie.

"I want to go to work. I don't want anybody for their money. I don't know. I just got out of the car and I didn't like him. I can't put my finger on it. Whether it was the clothes or the haircut or the tie or the shoes or the bad breath. There was just nothing … but a feeling I had to get away."

"You know what this means?" concluded Amigo Malcolm.

"What? What does it mean?" I asked, apprehensively.

"You could lose so much if you don't take this seriously … and he swung round to face me…

… You need another date!"

Chapter Forty-Eight (In which Daisy makes another brave decision.)

Tuesday May 19th 2014

Here's the thing. I value my Amigos who have seen me through thick and thin. Their opinion counts. It's already a few days since the ominous date and perhaps I have jumbled it all up in my head. Maybe my recollections are inaccurate. Perhaps I have embroidered all of this into some form of ridiculous negativity. Maybe I am damaged goods and can never commit to anybody. Maybe I am being too fussy, ridiculous even. On the face of it this man is offering everything, why do I hesitate?

Looks, Personality, Educated Solvent, Available.

Apart from a creative mind, does this count as **Personality**? I'm still not entirely sure he ticks any of these boxes. Only I can make that decision.

So, deep breath, I sit at the computer …

IG, I wrote,

This is your lucky day. I have thought carefully about what's

happened and where we are at. I agree we have shared so much, and there is potential, it just needs to be unlocked.

So, here is what we need to do to.

We can have one more date.

You say you want to love and protect me, to take care of me, to spoil me even. This is your chance to prove it.

I would like you to take me to see *Phantom of the Opera,* next Saturday if you can get the tickets. I will meet you at Waterloo station at 12 o'clock. It's up to you to plan the date and look after me.

Don't blow it!

Affectionately,

Daisy x

SEND

So ... now, I think I have a date to see Phantom of the Opera, my favourite ever musical,

WITH,

- *the real Internet Phantom!*

How good is that?!

It's going to be a long week!

Now the sad thing is this afternoon I went to Jeannie's funeral.

Here's the thing, apart from Dad, myself, her friend Marion and the Matron of the Nursing Home, who was called Brenda, there was nobody there. I found it very disturbing.

We stood in the crematorium, the four of us, and made an effort to sing 'Praise My Soul the King of Heaven', and 'Morning Has Broken'. I just can't get those high notes these days and it was a pathetic caterwauling. Really.

I didn't look at the coffin, I just couldn't. In my mind I remembered Jeanie with her smart white bun, and her beautiful face, hardly wrinkled for 97. How she had surprised and touched me with her gift of the special watch. Her phone calls. It occurred to me that Jeannie had been *dazzling, beautiful, smart and alluring.* She had.

Effortlessly, and at 97.

If she could do it, so could I.

Later Dad gave me a letter Jeanie had left for me. It read:

My Dear Daisy,

It's been such a pleasure to get to know you, something that developed between us in the latter years of my life, and after the terribly sad passing of your mother, who was such a best friend to me.

I want to die, so don't feel sorry for me. I have Lionel waiting up there for me, and I am impatient to feel his arms around me again.

I have had a wonderful life and now I must move over for somebody else to have their turn.

I have loved hearing about your Internet Dating Daisy, dear, and I feel sure you will meet someone, as you are too special to live on this earth by yourself. It will happen. Trust your instincts.

Wear the watch, it may bring you good fortune!

I will be watching you from heaven and giving you my best love and luck of course.

I love your father so much too. Look after him for me.

I haven't got much to leave anyone as I've had to pay so much for the Nursing Home and I had no idea I would live this long! But my dear, I am leaving you £500 to give to a charity of your choice. I know you will choose wisely.

I wish we could all live forever. But of course we can't and I miss Lionel and your mother so much, I know they will be waiting for me in heaven.

Think of me when you wear the watch, as you have been so special to me.

With all my love,

Jeanie xx

I need some time to reflect on this.

What a fabulous lady.

Chapter Forty-Nine (In which Daisy has her date with the Internet Phantom)

Saturday May 24th 2014

I was in a tizz, that was official. It was Saturday morning and my bed was littered with discarded dresses. As usual I hadn't slept even a tiddly wink. I didn't know which shoes to wear as I couldn't totter around London all day in heels, but I needed to look my best.

Dazzling, Beautiful, Smart, Alluring.

That's what I had promised myself.

My dresses were all too frumpy. Or too tarty.

It was impossible.

And I had to wear *The Watch*!

In the end I was on the train to Waterloo in a red mini-dress fit for a Phantom! I had always had good legs. I'd lost weight and I felt good in my dress. It may have been a bit bold for middle aged me, but this was new me. A me who was set to kill. And my poem sat deep in my handbag.

I was nervous, nervous as hell. Two voices in my head, one saying this man has all the hallmarks of success. Wouldn't it be great to get off the internet once and for all? Your journey over. The future cast.

The other saying, he's a creep. He's a bit fishy. Trust your instincts. What are you doing with a man like that?

But I have always adored the *Phantom of the Opera,* my favourite and I couldn't miss a free opportunity to see it could I! When all was said and done, it was a free trip to my favourite musical. Probably dinner, then home.

I could hack that.

I could.

Even accompanied by possible Quasimodo! Remember this was his opportunity to impress me. I would be there. But the rest of the organisation was up to him. He promised he would take care of me? Well here was a test. Just how would he measure up?

So, I was at Waterloo at about ten minutes to twelve. If I haven't said this already I am always early never late. And I hate people being late.

It's now twelve.

Actually ... ten past twelve.

In fact ... twenty past twelve.

... ? Something's up. Am I being stood up?

My phone rang. It was him.

"Daisy."

"Angus" (I couldn't call him a Phantom to his face, but I almost forgot his real name!)

"Listen, are you there?"

"Of course. I'm waiting for you." I sound irritated. I was.

"I decided to bring my Porsche, as I want to drive you home afterwards."

"To Brighton!" OMG I've broken out in a sweat. I didn't want him taking me home late at night to Brighton!

"Yes, to Brighton."

"But it's miles out of your way." I said desperately.

"Never mind that, and anyhow, I'm stuck in London traffic. I'll be at least another half an hour."

"What time is the show?" I asked.

"2.30"

"Oh, so we have time?"

"I think so."

"I tell you what I'll walk in the direction of the theatre."

"OK, I need to park the car."

"Well shall we meet in half an hour? Say at the London Eye?" I'm not good at the geography of London but I did know the way there.

"Fine."

"OK I'll walk down there and see you there in half an hour."

"Great, good idea ... I'm looking forward to seeing you."

"See you soon." I felt alarmed. This could just be the date from hell.

"Bye."

I was perturbed as I walked. Should I get into his car? What would I do in Brighton. I would be obliged to ask him to stay the night. I didn't want that. Wasn't ready for that. What could I say? I was determined I would be going back on the train!

I wasn't impressed either. If you have to be at Waterloo at 12 o'clock and you live a long way away, and money is not a problem, you would come the night before. This was a let-down.

I tried not to let it bother me as I walked on down to the Embankment and stood, trying unsuccessfully I'm sure, to look inconspicuous in my red mini-dress amongst the tourists, in front of the London Eye.

So, here was the thing. The world and his wife walked by.

But no Phantom.

After half an hour, I was very fed up.

I had chosen some heels and my feet were killing me.

My phone rang.

"Daisy."

"Angus." This time I did remember his name.

"I'm still in traffic."

"Still in traffic!"

"I'm so sorry, you know what it's like in London."

"Well you'd better hurry or we'll miss the show."

"Look, you go on towards the theatre."

"It's still an hour and a half before the show. I'll find a Costa near the theatre and text you address. Meet you there?"

"Ok, see you soon." He rang off.

I was irritable then. Boy was I irritable, but I tried to control it. I couldn't help thinking that this date, his one chance to impress me, was failing miserably minute by minute.

Nothing for it ... I set off for Covent Garden. I got myself there, followed Google maps to Her Majesty's Theatre, and plonked myself down in a Costa directly opposite. Very well situated in fact!

I remember there was a queue in Costa and I wondered if I should get Phantom a coffee while I was being served, otherwise he wouldn't have time to queue up etc. etc. ... but inevitably if I did that he wouldn't show up for ages and the coffee would be wasted ... so I didn't. I sipped mine slowly, watching the minute hand on my watch crawl towards 2 pm, then past it, and still no word from Phantom.

I absolutely hate being late and in a rush. And this is exactly what he was doing to me. I wondered if he was in London at all or just leading me a merry dance. I phoned him. Now ten minutes to curtain up.

"I'm on my way," he said. **"Don't panic, I'll meet you in the foyer."**

So I flew over the road and stood amongst the last few stragglers who were scurrying towards their seats before curtain up. I tried to hide my annoyance but I was very fed up.

I'm not joking when I say that about one minute before curtain up, I recognised a grey head bobbing towards me on the pavement. He had just got out of a taxi. As my eyes focussed and I realised it was actually him, I felt my heart sink into my boots. If I wasn't sure about him last time, one quick look today and I was in no doubt. This person, this man, was NOT for me.

I've written a lot in this book about pheromones and I really believe in them. They are invisible magic rays that none of us can do a thing about. But if they don't appear, they don't appear and there's nothing you can do about it. I wonder if there are anti-pheromones, because in that moment I felt what probably actually amounted to disgust. I wanted to turn on my heel and leave, but how could I?

It was a hot day in May and I remember thinking how crazy he was as he hurried towards me, sweating profusely, to be wearing a woollen polar neck jumper. He had beads of perspiration running down his neck and forehead, and in fact not only was the usual halitosis to deal with, there was now an insidious body odour.

My nostrils probably flared quite involuntarily.

He grabbed my hand and we flew up the stairs to find our seats in the Circle. Later I discovered he had a friend who ran a ticket agency who was able at short notice to get us such good seats. But all I recall was squeezing along the row in my mini-dress, and sitting down, with him clutching my hand in his sweaty one. His hand felt strange, podgy, wet, like holding a warm cucumber that has started to decay in the fridge. And as we sat the salty, seaweed aroma of his perspirations wafted over me in waves, accompanied by a shock draft of bad breath as he whispered comments about the show to me in my right ear. It was … disgusting. I felt embarrassed. The people sitting around me assumed we were a couple, and I suddenly knew I very much didn't want to be. This was all wrong. Terribly wrong. I fingered Jeanie's watch. No good luck watch on this occasion sadly!

I sat there watching my favourite show with the Internet Ghost himself. Remember, in the story, it is Raoul who gets the girl. My story would be no different. Escape the Phantom and find Raoul.

Who would be my Raoul? Not Patrick, not Jack?

Not any of the idiots I had met on Britainonsunday.com, buzz.

com, skyfullofstars.com or coulditbemagic.co.uk. On my four sites, so far no successful suitors. It didn't seem funny anymore, it suddenly seemed hard work.

I'm just going to say what followed next is the truth. After the show we walked to the river and had dinner in a restaurant on the South Bank. I tried to be good company and to be polite, but I couldn't wait for it to be over. He seemed happy, smiling and pouring the wine, but I was dreading what had to come next.

I just did not want to get into his car. Porsche or no Porsche. I was trying hard to think of an excuse as to why this was impossible. But I couldn't. I considered telling him the truth, but I couldn't. The only salvation was, he didn't have my home address. So one way or the other I would be safe once I got away.

So ... this is what I did. I thought about Daisy's Internet dating lessons, and all the dating experiences in this book. (Thanks David!) And it didn't take long!

It was time to go to the Ladies!

So I told him that's where I was going ... I said something like, there's always a queue in the Ladies, I'll try not to be too long!

... disappeared in the direction of the toilets ... and legged it!

I took off my heels and ran all along the Embankment, in bare feet, as fast as I could in the opposite direction. At Waterloo I jumped on the next train to Brighton. I sat gasping in my seat, and deleted his number from my phone. That I told myself, was that.

No more Phantom. Not ever.

Internet Dating Lesson

I think here I need to put. Trust your instincts.

You can tell almost instantaneously if you are likely to be able to develop a relationship with someone. I knew the first time I saw Phantom he was not for me. Not one pheromone atom revealed itself at our first meeting. And I knew that, I just let my Amigos persuade me to give it another go. They were doing their best. I should have listened to my Daisy heart and stood my ground. So my advice is, choosing a mate is a guttural experience and when you meet the right person, like a buffalo charging along on an African plain, you will be in no doubt about it. That feeling will hurl itself towards you and you will just have to reach up and catch it. Catch it and hold it gently, in the palm of your hand.

The funniest thing was, that when I got up to my bedroom that night Chris was waiting for me as usual.

"You're late tonight," he said. "I was worried about you."

"Aw ... "I replied, "It's just a ghost story, but then you know all about those!"

"You bet," he replied. "As you well know, *Ghost Stories* is the name of my new album!"

I switched on the CD player and he *ghosted* me off to sleep.

"Night, night, Chris."

"Nighty night," he said.

Chapter Fifty (In which Daisy reflects)

Sunday May 25th 2014

Yes of course I was bombarded with phone calls, texts and emails which I ignored. In fact, I blocked him from my sites. I didn't want to have to explain it, but I felt stupid. Humiliating to be drawn into that intimate world of anonymous texting and emailing when you really don't know who is on the end of it all.

The photo! I can't underestimate it.

You must see the photo and early on.

If I had seen it, I would never have let things get this far and saved us both a lot of disappointment and heartache.

If Phantom is reading this, and he may be, I'm sorry this is on paper and so personal. But this is about Internet Dating lessons. And my readers can learn a lot from this episode. About how not to let get things out of control. And what's important in the early stages of getting to know someone on line. I got sucked into it all and did it all wrong, as you can see.

I was actually very upset. Goodness knows I want to find someone and get off these sites. Amusing as it may be, it's emotionally exhausting. And you have to be suspicious, watch your back, remain slow to trust anyone, look after your pride and your dignity. It's actually a very difficult process that usually, as you can see from this book, ends up in disaster. When, if ever will anything go right?

So it's the funniest thing. I started this dating fiasco 46 days ago. Wow, that's less than two months, but it seems a lifetime. four dating sites, more than 1000 emails, 13 DDP's, all a disaster. What a track record! And still no perfect match.

Here's the thing. Look at the positives. I have proved a lot of things to myself. I can be independent, make decisions, make things happen. I can control my future, at least to some extent. I have been *dazzling, beautiful, smart, and alluring.* I have discovered men do find me attractive, even though I am over 50.

I've found that everyone on these sites has baggage. Painful divorces, miserable ex-wives, even widowhood. I came to this process with my own pain. But in truth, something about this experience, and writing about it, has helped me come to terms with my own issues, and put them firmly in the past. Its' been therapeutic. Maybe by reading this, I will help someone else deal with their pain.

I've been swimming. I've lost weight. I have a new wardrobe. I've written a whole book! I've proved to myself I can be me, outside of a miserable marriage and all by myself.

Who needs Internet Dating? The secret has to be -and here's the thing – to be happy being you. Once you are happy being you, you can take the knock backs and laugh. There is always something great around the corner. And it doesn't have to involve men and sex!

So I'm thinking. I have a lot of things in my life.

My daughter who has stood very loyally beside me. My lovely father who would be relieved to hear I had given the whole Internet Dating thing up! My lovely Amigos who make the tea and sit on the sofa and try to help me the best they can. A good job, an interesting job it has to be said. And enough money in the bank to enjoy my leisure time.

I want to dance again. I used to dance with my teacher for a partner, Why not?

I want to travel, go to Australia, New Zealand.

Go on a cruise.

I want to sail, maybe Club Med.

I want to do more exercise. I want to do the Playtex Moonwalk! Who wouldn't want to walk around London at night in their bra! Why not!

I want to drink nice champagne and sit in hot bubbles and dream.

No one can take my imagination away.

I want to sleep. Throughout this whole book, I haven't slept. Perhaps I can sleep now.

It's time to give the dating a rest ...

And funnily enough, that night, I did actually sleep. Unbelievably.

In the morning, as I woke up, I saw a piece of paper had been slipped under my bedroom door. Curious, I slipped out from under the duvet.

It was from Imogen.

She had written me – a recipe? It went like this:

Recipe for Love

Feeds 2

Preparation: One lifetime

Skill required: Experienced chef's only

Nutritional value: Inestimable

Cooking time: ?You can tell me

by Imogen

Ingredients

- *One mother: Daisy*
- *One central processing microchip: her computer*
- *Thoughts and memories, finely chopped*
- *A jar of hearts' desires, roasted*
- *Four quirky dating sites: you know the titles*
- *Infinitesimal neuronal connections: his nervous system and yours*
- *Sky full of stars (all lucky of course): it's Chris Martin – again!*
- *One male human species: chromosomes XY*
- *Pheromones – one bucketful: see Chapter 32*

Method

Take the Daisy out of the refrigerator and begin at room temperature. This is very important as the recipe will not work in the presence of ice crystals.

Set up the food 'love' processor. Choose a setting designed to create the perfect blend.

Finely chop the thoughts and memories. Use a sharp knife. These must be carefully fragmented almost to a pulp.

Separate the heart's desires, the despair from the hope. Add the hope immediately to the blender. The despair can be beaten firmly until it stands up in stiff peaks.

Roll out the four dating sites separately, quite thinly, and lay on a sheet of baking parchment. They will only truly crisp up, if you have used the correct technique.

The neuronal connections should be only coarsely grated. For perfect results, this love dish needs to retain its texture.

Melt the sky full of stars over a pan of hot water. For passionate love, blood must pump through the veins like molten lava.

Assemble the dish, and at the last minute, pour in the X&Y chromosomes.

Stand back – and flambé!

Serve, red hot, scattered with a fistful of pheromomes.

I was amazed. Did she really write that? Never underestimate a young imagination. My daughter had sensed my sadness and in her own way was willing me not to give up.

Chapter Fifty-One (In which Daisy takes another look ...)

Sunday May 30th 2014

So, it's a whole week since I last logged on. It's nearly midnight. I've had a couple of large G&Ts.

I was at the dentist this week, and I read the local paper in the waiting room. I rarely do this. I opened up the paper and guess who's face was staring back at me? It was Captain Adonis himself Alex, under a big heading that read Newhaven Sea Captain Guilty of Fraud. He was wearing the same herringbone jacket! Curious I read on.

James Arrowsmith of 46, The Laurels, Newhaven, was found guilty yesterday on several accounts of fraud and attempts to obtain money with menaces. 69-year-old Mr Arrowsmith, was reported by several women who had met him on the popular dating site skyfullofstars.com. After a rapid courtship and seduction, Mr Arrowsmith would request loans of up to £3000 at a time from his victims. From one victim, over a period of three years, he obtained £22,000. A spokesman for skyfullofstars.com said, "Women need to be very careful when they start Internet Dating. Although it's very popular and can be successful, it is a breeding ground for meeting fraudsters and the sex criminal underworld. We recommend women take advice before they start Internet Dating, on basic rules of how to stay safe."

James Arrowsmith – so that was his real name!

My Goodness, I thought. I had a narrow escape!

But guess what! skyfullofstars.com is recommending women take advice on Internet Dating. Skyfullofstars.com seems to be recommending my book!

But … I digress.

It's a Bank Holiday Weekend, and there's nothing in my diary. I don't care.

Do I?

Maybe it's the gin. Maybe it's just me, or human nature, or prairie voles, or something…

Dad phoned.

"Hello darling," he said. "I just wanted to have a word with you."

"Great," I replied. "How are you?"

"You know, so, so, but …"

"But? …" I asked, wondering where this was heading.

"Well, this Internet Dating business …?"

"Yes, what about it?"

"Umm, how's it going?"

"Well Dad, it's a bit all-consuming really. And I've met so many people, and had so many dates, and I'm still here. Not dead! But not hitched either! But I know what you're going to tell me, so please don't start …"

"No, No, I wasn't going to say any of that. Actually, it's the opposite. You see my friend Bernie Laverstock, well he's my age, 82! And he's just got married to this woman he met, on your site I think ... is it called *skyfullofstars?* Anyhow, you could have knocked me down with a feather. He's such a smart chappie, and she's a real smasher. I knew you were doing it too. He said to me to get on, he said I should try. He said it's not over 'til it's over, and there's life in the old dog yet and I got to thinking that your mother wouldn't want me to be lonely, and I thought perhaps it's time I did something a bit revolutionary. I've always thought of myself as a bit revolutionary, you know."

"Dad!"

"Well, I'm not getting any younger."

"OMG! Dad – you want me to help you start Internet Dating?!" I was absolutely incredulous.

"I suppose that's what I'm saying."

"Dad! This is great. There is someone out there for everyone! – Why don't you come and stay with me next weekend and we'll set you up with a profile?"

"Oh that would be smashing, I don't know what that is, but could you?"

Even Dad, has some prairie vole in his DNA!

But I must just look at the internet one last time. Foolish I know.

Here's the thing, on coulditbemagic.co.uk, they send you four hopeful suitors every day, that they at 'Royal coulditbemagic.co.uk HQ' have matched to your personality profile. They are the only site that does this by the way. I have to say I scoffed at it as I don't believe people even answer their silly enrolment questionnaires with any degree of seriousness or accuracy, but any way, that's what they do. I think they try to match likes and dislikes, occupations, views on nuclear bombs, that kind of thing.

And now, at nearly midnight, I have finally relented and I'm back on the internet – call me a hypocrite – and I've have had a look at todays' options. Now I have to say I usually just DELETE, DELETE, DELETE, as they are always hideous men for whom I just know I would have the rotted whale meat reaction.

And also, for the record, remember Frankie 10. I'm not sporty, not really, so generally any man that flashes up in front of me in sports gear I would delete, just because if sport is that important to him, I probably won't be the right person.

But that night, I thought to myself, if I'm too restrictive, I'll never click on anybody. And I thought plenty of men probably photograph themselves in sports kit to look hot, but they may never actually do the sport! And for some reason I thought I needed to be more open minded. Perhaps the sporty types needed some consideration after all.

So ... I noticed one of these four hopefuls, had a nice face. That's what I first thought. Honestly. He was tall, standing in front of his garage and propping up a bike. A road bike or a mountain bike I don't know, but a bicycle. He looks like he is a cyclist. He has on a proper cycling top, white and bottle green. He is smiling. I can't see because the photo is too far away, any details. I can't see the colour of his eyes for example. But he has a nice gaze at the camera and a warm smile. I wonder who took the photograph?

I looked at the photo for a few moments, my finger as ever hovering over the DELETE button. I was tempted to press it. My common-sense self said that serious cyclists are not really on my radar.

But then I looked again. Was he really that keen a cyclist? It has to be said he had a rather wide girth. How can I put that nicely, a little spare around the midriff? In fact, thinking about it, he simply looked like a nice middle-aged man, trying to get fit!

Now I saw him in a different light!

I opened the profile.

Edward, it said, (No crazy internet name – just Edward – and that's my father's middle name)

Professional and Solvent.

Aged 57.

Divorced.

And I read on, and I liked what I read.

This was all I needed! What had I decided?

Looks, Personality, Educated, Solvent and Local.

This met my requirements to perfection. Bingo!

So, with a brave flourish, as I really thought my Internet Dating had come to an end, at least for now,

I sent him a **smile.** ☺ You can do this you see, if I haven't mentioned this before. Send a smile as a sort of "*I like the look of you.*' Instead of a proper message. Or a wink. It depends on the site.

(I don't think I had ever been brave enough to send anyone a smile during this whole story!)

I would have sent him *a Daisy* if I could.

But there is no internet option for that one!

Chapter Fifty-Two (In which Impressive Creations start work.)

Tuesday 1st June 2014

Imogen and I have been told to find alternative accommodation for two weeks. *Impressive Creations* arrived today to get started, and we have to be completely out of the picture until the refurb is complete in two weeks' time. So we're staying at the Amigos, where else. The thing is, they only live round the corner a few doors away, so as I drive in and out I can see lorries, and workmens' vans going in and out of our garden gates. I have no idea if I should be letting them do this to our home. I can hear the drilling and hammering from the Amigo's front garden. It's most disconcerting.

Imogen is on the last leg of her cookery course. She has her exams next week. Maggie who is a brilliant cook has been helping her practice. She has to cook and serve a professional roast dinner in an hour and a half. Needless to say, we have had a roast every night so far. Roast beef, rare in the middle, gargantuan Yorkshire puddings, crispy potatoes and parsnips, perfectly chopped carrot batons, rich syrupy gravy. She needs to pass, and pass well. (I can't risk getting any fatter!)

Everyone is driving me crazy, Wendy, Pinky, Dad, Malcolm, Maggie, even Imogen. They ask me all the time how the dating is going. As if it's simple to pull a Mr Right out of a hat. I'm having a rest, it's official I told them. That's just how it has to be.

I drive to work to and fro and wonder about life. How did I ever get into medicine, and genito-urinary medicine at that. As I near the end of this book, it's actually power for the course to think back to the beginning. The beginning of my medical career.

I was thinking back to my days as a medical student, which I never realised would be quite so formative. We were thrown together, around on hundred supposedly bright young people, and for five years we sat in lectures and suffered humiliating ward rounds.

We had some amazing experiences. The very first night in my hall of residence, and of course was the night before my very first day at medical school, a note was pushed under my door. It said to turn up at lecture theatre two, wearing a dressing gown and carrying a urine sample. It seemed realistic enough, and I was wondering if my dressing gown was clean enough, and if I should do the sample over there, or when woke up and take it with me etc. ... Luckily, I popped up the corridor for a cup of tea with some other prospective medics, only to find this was a great big joke! Thank goodness I didn't actually do it!

We did have a chap who sat at the front of the lecture theatre, in a suit, with a waist coat, a pocket watch and monocle. He held a large box on his lap with a T-shaped handle, so it resembled an archetypal portable bomb! And over his head there was a large sign that read "Make it interesting or I'll detonate!" Guess he wouldn't be allowed into the lecture theatre these days!

We all did anatomy. I loathed my trips to the anatomy room. Why would anyone give their body to medical science? It was about the foulest thing you can ever imagine. For example, when we studied the gastrointestinal system, they made a cruciate incision on the cadaver's abdomen. You were supposed to lay your hand on the outside, i.e. on top of the flesh, and try and imagine what was inside, then lift the skin flap and actually put your hand inside the corpse to see if you were right. My reason for remembering this now however, was just because after one anatomy session we were all called to a meeting. Something serious had happened. A hand had gone missing. Would whoever had taken it please return it.

OMG, who would want to take a real, live, but actually really dead, human hand home to keep in the bedroom! I never heard if it was returned. But as far as I know, no other body parts went missing.

The other funny memory was the picnic on the roundabout. We all walked along to this medium-sized roundabout, not far from the medical school, that sat in the middle of the dual carriageway. We walked in a crocodile, with wicker baskets and tartan rugs, and proceeded to have our picnic there. As the bemused traffic rattled on past. we munched on our cucumber sandwiches. In the end a young policeman was sent to move us on our way. It's illegal to picnic on a roundabout apparently, and we were disturbing the peace!

We also had hilarious ward rounds. One of the Consultants used to open the window, and we were on one of the third floor of the hospital, and sit on the window ledge with his feet dangling outside. Then he would ask us all questions on the proviso, 'if you get it wrong, I WILL – jump!' He never did! But it sharpened the memory!

I recall this amusing story about medical student ward rounds, that is a dinner party favourite, and I thought I'd write it down before I get to the end of writing this book.

In a busy London teaching hospital, a group of medical students stood round the examination couch. A patient lay there, on his left side, knees to his chin, under a sterile drape. He had had previous bowel cancer and had had previous surgery necessitating a colostomy bag. This was his annual check-up. An eminent consultant was performing a colonoscopy. This a flexible telescope inserted up the back passage to investigate if there are any diseases lurking in the bowel. It's a thin tube, incredibly mobile and easy to squeeze round the bends, as it were, but still quite unpleasant both patient and endoscopist.

"Come on, come on," said the consultant impatiently to the group of students. "Surely one of you can step forward and take a look." He proffered the eyepiece at the end of the scope in the direction of the group. These students were either stupid, or incredibly timid, or both.

There was a large polyp there just waiting for action. A very good example. Great teaching opportunity. He wriggled the scope a little more to get a better look, lost the damn thing, wriggled the scope a bit more.

"You," he exclaimed eventually, "please, step forward and take a look."

The student, who had been dreading this, stepped forward.

It was agonising having to wash his hands, gown up in a sterile robe, and wriggle his hands into those sterile gloves. Red-faced, he was finally ready to take hold of the scope. He could feel the curious stare of rest of the group, as he tentatively pressed one eye against the eye piece and tried to manipulate the hand control. By wiggling the hand section, where there were various knobs and buttons, you could make the far distant end of the scope, now somewhere deep inside the patient's bowel, turn through 360 degrees, and move forwards and backwards. What was he looking at? It looked – quite frankly – just like a lot of red mush. How could anyone really know what was going on in there?

"Come on, come on," said consultant with great annoyance. These medical students were really hopeless. "What can you see?"

"Umm," stammered the medical student, trying desperately to get the controller to focus, "I'm doing my best, sir."

"Well hurry up about it!" retorted the consultant. "For goodness sake, surely you can see something! You've got a bird's-eye view!"

"Yes, yes I can, sir," he replied. "Something's coming into view now, sir."

"Well what the hell is it! We're all waiting?!" the consultant exclaimed with raised eyebrows/

"Well, sir," said the student. "You know what? – It's a red London bus."

There was a titter from the assembled group.

"I beg your pardon?!"

"Yes Sir, I can see a red London bus."

"Let me have a look at that!" the consultant pushed him roughly out of the way and adjusted his eye to the eye piece.

After a brief moment "By God, you're right," he exclaimed, looking at the group, and feeling somewhat perplexed.

The endoscope had wriggled itself out through the patient's colostomy stoma, and was facing out of the window!

I used to love all these medical stories. Dinner party stories!

Now I've written them down, they can't be forgotten!

Chapter Fifty-Three ('The Victorian Dilapidation')

Saturday June 12th 2014

So it's here. The day I am permitted to re-enter my own home. Whatever's left of it!

At the Amigo's, Cassandra Barton, world famous TV presenter rings their doorbell. The Amigos love the chance to be on the telly! We're actually featuring on *Impressive Creations*! OMG!

The crew are busy, camera, lights, action, and I being swept up the road in the middle of the entourage, to see what they have done to my poor old house.

As I rounded the corner and stood by the front gate, I looked down the driveway at my house, and the house looked back. It seems a little sheepish in its new glory. Now of course, incredibly beautiful and transformed beyond imagination.

They had stripped off all the Virginia creeper, and repainted the outside of the house, re-gravelled the driveway, planted out the flower beds, mowed and trimmed the lawn. I scrunched down the gravel to my new front porch, bespoke restoration complete, stained glass just so, the door newly painted brilliant red. Inside the house, we moved from room to room and I was literally open-mouthed.

Imogen and I gasped as we set foot in the new country kitchen, complete with Aga. A large, new state of the art square conservatory led off the dining end of the kitchen, opening onto a large decking area of patio. There was a new boiler and utility room. A totally new boiler! New bathrooms with under floor heating and heated towel rails. The window frames had been replaced. The interior designer had pushed the boat out, with bold furnishing colours and heavy, plush fabrics. Everywhere I looked was majestic, freshly painted and papered, a house now clearly fit for a king. – Or a queen and a princess! Myself and Imogen!

I watched the TV programme myself later, despite loathing seeing myself on camera.

The episode has been given the title, 'The Victorian Dilapidation'. How demoralising is that?! However, the transformation that their team made, in two weeks was completely astounding. How lucky was I they chose my house for their makeover. Imogen had really had a great idea here and I hadn't appreciated it fully. Did any of my dates see me on TV? I cringe at the thought of it. (It was David who was so into property.) I just really hope not. But the whole nation is watching. Thank goodness Clarissa didn't ask me anything on screen about Dating Daisy!

Here's the thing. Just so there are no misunderstandings here, what they have done for my house, hasn't cost me a penny! Although they obviously have the legal rights to the TV episode. How much easier would the house be to sell now! And the profit is all mine! Sorry Voldemort! Who's got the last laugh now?!

I loved seeing the before and after shots. Rags to riches. And funnily enough, designer residence they may have made it, but it still felt like my home. That was the most important thing. I can still close the front door, and put my feet up in front of the TV, just as I always could, but now, a thousand times more comfortable thanks to the new, top class, luxury sofas. And the enormous flat screen TV mounted on the wall. I can sink into a cloud of bubbles in my new Jacuzzi bath, wrap myself in heated towels, and sink onto my ostentatious new bed.

It's having a house to be proud of, and not ashamed of, that makes such a difference. I can invite friends – or dates! – here without fear of embarrassment.

I need to do the maths now. Can we really afford to stay here? Just the two of us in our six-bedroom perfect home?

So that night, when the TV crew were long gone, and Imogen had gone out with that boy Luke for a drink, I felt myself drawn again to the internet.

I started to think how much nicer it would be to share my new home with a special person. I had to be positive. I had made good progress on the internet. Learnt a lot. Met some nice men really, just men who lacked pheromones, and not a thing could they do about it.

Come on Daisy, said my indefatigable brain. *Open some wine tonight. Sit at your new computer desk. Just have a little look.*

A lot of voices in my head were saying:

It's a waste of time.

There are no really nice guys on there, just a load of muppets.

Why don't you just give up now, and save a lot heartache?

But …

… I can list a whole of women who found the going tough, but never gave up … Marilyn Munroe, Oprah Winfrey, Vera Wang, Carey Mulligan, JK Rowling …

… need I continue?

If they can do it. I can do it. I'm a prairie vole. It's in my genes.

So I pressed the button and fired up the computer.

What was happening on my dating sites tonight? It was a full two weeks since I had last logged on, so I just hoped there might be something.

…. and there was.

Remember I had just sent Edward a smile?

He had sent me an email!

An email!

So that smile was the beginning of the end.

… Or the end of the beginning

… Because

We did meet very soon actually.

… I wore Jeanie's watch.

And … He was ***The One!***

Yes – I did give ***him*** my poem! - He was totally amazed by it – and that I had chosen to give it to ***him!***

And three years later, and it's nearly May 30th 2017.

We are living together happily!

And Dating Daisy really has come off the internet …

FOREVER!

Chapter Fifty-Four (In which Dating Daisy has the biggest surprise of all)

Sunday 13th June 2017

But that's not quite the end of the book!

Here's the thing. I can't just leave you the reader in limbo! You will be dying to know what happened! The romantic details, the full Monty!

I can only tell you, that he fell in love with me the first time we met, the moment he saw me get out of my car!

It was mutual.

There were pheromones ***everywhere****!*

That day, we walked up to the bar in the pub where I had booked the table for us to have dinner.

"I booked a table," I said to the lady behind the bar.

"What's the name?" she said.

And I said my name.

It just popped out – my REAL name! …

Edward said immediately, with such a look of disappointment on his face. "But I thought your name was Daisy!"

"That's my Internet Dating name." I replied. "Haven't I told you?"

The bar lady looked on in amusement.

"But I love 'Daisy'," he said, with a tone of disappointment in his voice!

Then he said, "Can't we keep it?"

(And when he said "Can't we keep it?" I knew that within the 60 seconds it taken for us to walk in from the car, we were onto something big!)

So, we kept the name Daisy, and now I have a whole new life, with a whole new name to match!

We do ballroom dancing together, and he is the best dance partner I could ever have. His mother was a ballet dancer, and he plays the piano, so he has rhythm and talent in bucketfuls. Our favourites are Quickstep and Foxtrot.

He sails, so we go on flotilla holidays to distant islands and frolic on deserted sun-drenched beaches.

We went to Vienna, and we did a Viennese waltz in a Viennese ballroom!

And we survived a night in the ice bed at the Ice Hotel.

And we live in a beautiful home with a hot tub, where we drink far too much champagne and look at the stars.

I am the luckiest person who ever dared to try dating on the internet.

We agree, he and I, we are never Internet Dating again!

Oh yes, and Edward became, the 4th Amigo!

In the meantime, I have attached two more chapters to this book for your amusement.

The thing is, I had emailed Edward "Dating Daisy's Kissing Tips," before he ever kissed me! So, he had a very hard act to follow!

In the weeks that went by I was amused, and I went on to write dating "Dating Daisy's Advanced Kissing Tips."

Edward was very embarrassed to tell me that he snored. And in the beginning he was full of apologies about it. I tried to tell him his snoring was nothing to worry about! (Not when I had to sleep next to Voldemort for 26 years and it was like lying next to an Intercity Express Train!)

Anyhow, Edward, apologetically, decided to go and see and orthodontist.

He had a very curious little contraption made, called the 'Snore Guard'!

And I couldn't resist writing about it as it was so funny. So please carry on and read Dating Daisy's Anti-snoring Tips. It's highly amusing!

Well forgive me, but this book is nearly over.

After all, I have created a Dating Manual – of sorts!

Here's the thing, Internet Dating can work.

It did it for me.

Daisy xxx

PS: And ... I have £500 for the Playtex Moonwalk!

PPS: And ... Don't forget to read to the **very last page of the book**!

Chris of course found this highly amusing.

"I wrote a song about this," he reminded me. It was about finding someone in a sky full of stars.

And he did – Edward chose me - from a skyfullofstars.com! – to be precise!

"Sorry Chris," I said, as I unpinned his poster from my wardrobe door.

"I have a new life now. I'll just be watching you on TV! But thanks for your friendship."

"No worries!" said Chris. "I loved it. Keep in touch!"

Dating Daisy's Advanced Kissing Tips

Section one of my kissing tips covered the basic essentials. The sort of when, what, why and who of kissing and dating, or maybe the reverse order, of dating and kissing. This section assumes kissing skill and experience, so please don't read it unless you have read and practised section one.

It's like your piano practice, 'A Tune a Day'. Unless you do you do your repetitions, fair weather or foul, happy or sad, drunk or sober, you will not be able to become a master kisser. The test of the kiss after all is the relationship. And as my counsellor used to say – the relationship is in the cupboard. If you want it to come alive and reveal itself, not to mention last a lifetime, then the kissing is the holy grail. Without kissing the jar is empty. The cupboard drawers are firmly shut.

Remember – "When the kissing nonsense stopped, love flew out of the window."

So if you are up to it, read on, if you dare.

Daisy always tells it as it is ... and not a wet fish, flat fish in sight.

***Tip 1**: Surprise. Be unpredictable. Everyone loves to be taken by surprise. If you think about it, that's the very opposite of being taken for granted. Kiss her anywhere and everywhere and to hell with the consequences. This is love in glorious Technicolor.*

Tip 2: Soup. All the right ingredients must be there, soft lips, tantalising smell, clean breath, warm breath, wet tongue, gentle breathing, eyes shut, and holding her tight. But now, the difference is the rhythm. Luxurious soft and gentle kisses that are slow, reach into the soul, are full of longing, then build to a climax and result in you both reaching for the naughty bits. If you are doing it right, you will both feel the soup in the abdomen. If you get the soup, you are heading firmly in the right direction.

Tip 3: Geography. Don't just kiss the mouth. There are so many other pseudo-erogenous zones. The inside of the wrists, the ear lobes, the little hollow just beside the pelvic bone. Do I need to go on?

Tip 4: Time out. Concentrate on giving the other person pleasure. The best kissing is about feeling the response of the partner. If you kiss and kiss and she just wants to clear her throat and come up for air, something is wrong. Kiss and feel the response, the tremor, the sigh, the gentle moans that escape because she can't help herself – you will get pleasure from her pleasure – funnily enough probably much more than from the pleasure she is trying to give you. You can test this out, by one at a time, each of you stopping kissing back and just allowing yourself to be kissed. This means you can lose yourself in the sensation of the moment. Try it, and you will see what I mean.

Tip 5: Exotic locations. There are erotic places to kiss. My favourite is in the hot tub. The water is frothing around me and I am enveloped in clouds of steam. He pushes my head back gently against the cushion in the corner. It's the buoyancy, and the bubbling, it pushes him unwittingly towards me and I can feel the hardness of his chest on top of mine. My arms are round his neck. It's easy to hold the back of his head and steady him just on top of me. I can control the pressure of his soft mouth and tongue on mine. I feel his fingers playing with the edge of my bathing costume and as he does this I shiver, despite the heat. I must be in heaven or close to it. My eyes are shut, I am drowning in love and lust. Sorry to mention it but yes lust.

Tip 6: Erogenous zones. The Full Monty. You may kiss anywhere including the parts some beers don't reach. Be adventurous. Licking and biting are good, so long as they are playful and gentle. Oh, and love bites are definitely out. Sorry. But they are just not acceptable for grown up love, ok?

Tip 7: Mind and body. The way to make love to a woman is to start with her mind. Now for black-and-white thinking men, who just want to get their leg over, this may seem an absolute impossibility. But in all seriousness, the way to do this is incredibly simple. Be complimentary. Tell her she looks lovely tonight. Tell her she makes the best lasagne this side of Watford. Tell her that green eyes are your absolute favourite (not if hers are blue of course). Tell her she smells divine. Tell her that her kisses fill you with soup. And tell her, repeatedly, that you love her. Women need to be loved. It's a biological requirement, like needing air to breathe. And it needs to be repeated. The fact you said it in 1986, after the wedding reception, just isn't enough ok! Tell her you are going to tell her, tell her and tell her what you just told her. And then, if you want a seriously exciting orgasm, do it all again! Just do!

Tip 8: Silence. Do you know that song "You say it best, when you say nothing at all?" Well it's a good song. Sometimes words can't express what you are feeling, or what she is feeling. It's bigger than both of you. It's the feeling you want to want to jump inside her skin. It's a difficult emotion as it's hard to know what to do with it. Romeo had it and killed himself. I wouldn't suggest that of course. But if you have that overwhelming feeling of total unison, acknowledge it and revel in it. You have a rare utopia that not many couples ever find.

Tip 9. Kissing takes time. Did you know it takes a minimum of 20 minutes' stimulation for a woman to have an orgasm? So, no wonder a few pecks on the lips, lifting the skirt and *wham bam, thank you mam,* is so unsatisfactory. Like anything in life, the more you invest in it, the better the returns. Set aside enough time, to make this time, and every time, as special as the last. What else in life, in all honesty, is as pleasurable as a perfect love making experience? We all desire it, wish for it, hope for it, search for it, but how many of us actually find it? Maybe more people need to read Dating Daisy's advice?

Tip 10. Making Love. So, this is it. Yes, you can. And if you have followed the rules it will be mind-blowing and meaningful. There's no humour here, because there is a serious side to this book. It's about the end of the journey. Finding the person who makes love to you like no one ever has before. Someone you can cherish and love in return. A someone so on your wave length, it's actually quite scary. Someone you can't live without. Someone who makes you heart go pitter-pat when you hear their voice, whose smile lights up the room. When you meet this person, you will fall in love like quicksand.

I know, because it happened to me.

Dating Daisy's Anti-snoring Tips

Ok, Ok. So it's not romantic. End of.

He snores in a curiously enchanting way. Not a peep as he breathes in, but a cataclysmic earth shift as he tries to breathe out. It's like the air trying to rush out of a leather balloon under pressure, a sort of suffocated pneumatic drill. Having said that, it pales to insignificance when you think about Voldemort, and Stuart too, and I actually don't dislike it. But he is worried about it, and too true, if it's damaging his health, he needs to deal with it. So, I did my bit. Gave it my full attention.

I sat up and filled in the partner's section on the snoring questionnaire. I couldn't have tried harder. Where it said "partner's name" I wrote *Dai*sy, and it looked good, seeing my name on the paper next to his. Even if it was just a snoring questionnaire.

Now here apparently is the orthodontic solution – the Snore Guard. And it looks like it's here to stay. Not 'Marley and Me' but 'The Snore Guard and Me', and I guess I just have to get used to it. (My sceptical self says the orthodontist has been watching too many horror movies, and has his heart set on a new Maserati, but heh ho! Who am I to cast aspersions?)

So, in all seriousness, if it stops the insidious sleep apnoea *and* the incipient heart failure *and* the probable premature death, not to mention it saves this relationship ... its fine by me. Really. Let's just get our heads around it ...'er, quite literally! ...

So – The Snore Guard. It's a Hannibal Lecter anti-snoring contraption. None other. Designed to frighten off the nastiest of witches and vampires.

So what does Dating Daisy have to say about snoring and anti-snoring and the Hannibal Lecter head-piece?

Tip 1: Do all the kissing before applying the Snore Guard. This may stand to reason, but it needs to be said. Perhaps this is a call for an early night.

Tip 2: Make sure you have also finished all the romantic chitter chatter before applying the Snore Guard. Repeatedly taking it off and reapplying it just to say I love you is plain irritating, let's be honest.

Tip 3: The most important thing to realise about the Snore Guard, is that when it's in place you can basically kiss anywhere, *except* on the mouth, ok? – and maybe the nostrils. This calls for imagination. I like to start with the big toe, do you?

Tip 4: Whatever happens, try not to look at him in the Snore Guard. This always results in helpless giggles and is not an aphrodisiac. Try to imagine him as he used to be B.S (Before Snoring) young, handsome, fit and oblivious to the word snoring. Snoring is after all a word that belies middle-age sadly!

Tip 5: You could make him feel at home by coming out in sympathy. I find sleeping in a ski helmet is helpful. It's like 'standing in each other shoes' if you get my meaning, but quite literally, the other way up! And at least you are protected from any accidental damage during the night.

Tip 6: When he's got it on, don't ask him if he's set the alarm clock! Just don't ok. From experience, he usually goes bonkers. I know ... I know ... but he just does!

Tip 7: This may be the moment to re-read the section about 20 reasons why life is better without Voldemort. Remember about his snoring, OMG, and my brilliant survival tactic? So, swivel round, and put your head by his feet, albeit his feet are under the duvet. This however comes with the sick satisfaction that while he sleeps, he is gently inhaling your feet, all very innocent you see. (Tee-hee, and my feet these days are always spotlessly clean!)

Tip 8: If you feel up for it in the night, don't snuggle up to the Snore Guard – you may get a black eye. Just run downstairs for a tin opener and a bottle of Viagra, that should do the trick, but not necessarily in that order!

Tip 9: Whatever you do, do not snore yourself. This will result in interminable conversations about whose turn for the Snore Guard tonight. Believe me, once the ski helmet is in place, he won't hear you. It **will** be ok.

Ps! PTO...and this is what my best date EVER, wrote for me!

Picking Daisy, by Edward

It's a good name,
Daisy.
The smell of coconut hair and summer sunshine
Laughter and cuddles
Giggling behind the beach huts
Love.
It's a good day,
Daisy.
A walk in the gardens hand in hand
A fountain of kisses
Gin and tonic
Love.
Its' a good night,
Daisy.
Gentle kisses
Caresses and pleasure
Warmth.
Love. Actually.

Daisy & Edward's Quickstep.

References

Daisy Icon made by *http://www.flaticon.com/*
http://www.flaticon.com/free-icon/daisy_185801#term=daisy&page=1&position=1

Lexicon definition

Wikipedia: *Lexicon,* formally, in *linguistics,* a **lexicon** is a language's inventory of *lexemes.* The word "lexicon" derives from the *Greek* λεξικόν (*lexicon*), neuter of λεξικός (*lexikos*) meaning "of or for words.

The Daisy
"There is a flower, a little flower. With silver crest and golden eye. That welcomes every changing hour. And weathers every sky."
James Montgomery
Quotes. Source A Field Flower
www.worldofquotes.com
Daisy Flowers

photo of dance feet
https://www.google.co.uk/search?q=free+photograph+icon&espv=2&biw=1920&bih=925&source=lnms&tbm=isch&sa=X&ved=0ahUKEwj8x72rqf7RAhVHDsAKHYp4BbsQ_AUIBigB#imgdii=1wdhG82fsoTIBM:&imgrc=nNdh-0CFHR6htM:

http://www.freepik.com/free-icon/message-typing_696304.htm

https://www.google.co.uk/search?q=free+photograph+icon&espv=2&biw=1920&bih=925&source=lnms&tbm=isch&sa=X&ved=0ahUKEwj8x72rqf7RAhVHDsAKHYp4BbsQ_AUIBigB#imgdii=1wdhG82fsoTIBM:&imgrc=nNdh-0CFHR6htM:

http://www.freeiconspng.com/free-images/work-icon-4445

http://www.freeiconspng.com/free-images/case-icon-png-2676

http://www.free-icons-download.net/texting-on-phones-icon-92597/

http://all-free-download.com/free-vector/poetry.html

http://www.freeiconspng.com/free-images/sleep-icon-15519

http://www.freeiconspng.com/free-images/email-attachment-icon-11166

http://www.iconarchive.com/show/windows-8-icons-by-icons8/Food-Teapot-icon.html

http://www.freeiconspng.com/free-images/teachers-icon-18091

http://www.freeiconspng.com/free-images/christmas-star-png-33896

http://www.iconarchive.com/show/windows-8-icons-by-icons8/Music-Harp-icon.html

Margery Williams, "The Velveteen Rabbit."

http://www.clipartpanda.com/clipart_images/downloads-1970635

http://www.freepik.com/free-icon/shopping-checklist_723197.htm

http://simpleicon.com/wp-content/uploads/sun.png

http://www.flaticon.com/free-icon/happy_187130#term=smiley&page=1&position=1

Let's Do It Lyrics Cole Porter 1928
*https://www.google.co.uk/search?q=lets+do+it%2C+lets+fall+in+love&oq=lets+do+it%2C+lets+fall+in++love&aqs=chrome..69i57j0l5.7215j0j8&sourceid=chrome&ie=UTF-8#q=lets+do+it,+lets+fall+in+love+lyrics&**

Lightning Source UK Ltd.
Milton Keynes UK
UKOW04f0648071117
312328UK00002B/436/P

9 781911 525752